Kiku's Prayer

WEATHERHEAD BOOKS ON ASIA

WEATHERHEAD EAST ASIAN INSTITUTE, COLUMBIA UNIVERSITY

WEATHERHEAD BOOKS ON ASIA

Weatherhead East Asian Institute, Columbia University

LITERATURE

David Der-wei Wang, Editor

Ye Zhaoyan, *Nanjing 1937: A Love Story*, translated by Michael Berry (2003)

Oda Makoto, *The Breaking Jewel*, translated by Donald Keene (2003)

Han Shaogong, *A Dictionary of Maqiao*, translated by Julia Lovell (2003)

Takahashi Takako, *Lonely Woman*, translated by Maryellen Toman Mori (2004)

Chen Ran, *A Private Life*, translated by John Howard-Gibbon (2004)

Eileen Chang, *Written on Water*, translated by Andrew F. Jones (2004)

Writing Women in Modern China: The Revolutionary Years, 1936–1976, edited by Amy D. Dooling (2005)

Han Bangqing, *The Sing-song Girls of Shanghai*, first translated by Eileen Chang, revised and edited by Eva Hung (2005)

Loud Sparrows: Contemporary Chinese Short-Shorts, translated and edited by Aili Mu, Julie Chiu, and Howard Goldblatt (2006)

Hiratsuka Raichō, *In the Beginning, Woman Was the Sun*, translated by Teruko Craig (2006)

Zhu Wen, *I Love Dollars and Other Stories of China*, translated by Julia Lovell (2007)

Kim Sowŏl, *Azaleas: A Book of Poems*, translated by David McCann (2007)

Wang Anyi, *The Song of Everlasting Sorrow: A Novel of Shanghai*, translated by Michael Berry with Susan Chan Egan (2008)

Ch'oe Yun, *There a Petal Silently Falls: Three Stories by Ch'oe Yun*, translated by Bruce and Ju-Chan Fulton (2008)

Inoue Yasushi, *The Blue Wolf: A Novel of the Life of Chinggis Khan*, translated by Joshua A. Fogel (2009)

Anonymous, *Courtesans and Opium: Romantic Illusions of the Fool of Yangzhou*, translated by Patrick Hanan (2009)

Cao Naiqian, *There's Nothing I Can Do When I Think of You Late at Night*, translated by John Balcom (2009)

Park Wan-suh, *Who Ate Up All the Shinga? An Autobiographical Novel*, translated by Yu Young-nan and Stephen J. Epstein (2009)

Yi T'aejun, *Eastern Sentiments*, translated by Janet Poole (2009)

Hwang Sunwŏn, *Lost Souls: Stories*, translated by Bruce and Ju-Chan Fulton (2009)

Kim Sŏk-pŏm, *The Curious Tale of Mandogi's Ghost*, translated by Cindy Textor (2010)

Xiaomei Chen, editor, *The Columbia Anthology of Modern Chinese Drama* (2011)

Qian Zhongshu, *Humans, Beasts, and Ghosts: Stories and Essays*, edited by Christopher G. Rea, translated by Dennis T. Hu, Nathan K. Mao, Yiran Mao, Christopher G. Rea, and Philip F. Williams (2011)

Dung Kai-cheung, *Atlas: The Archaeology of an Imaginary City*, translated by Dung Kai-cheung, Anders Hansson, and Bonnie S. McDougall (2012)

O Chŏnghŭi, *River of Fire and Other Stories*, translated by Bruce Fulton and Ju-Chan Fulton (2012)

HISTORY, SOCIETY, AND CULTURE

Carol Gluck, Editor

Takeuchi Yoshimi, *What Is Modernity? Writings of Takeuchi Yoshimi*, edited and translated, with an introduction, by Richard F. Calichman (2005)

Contemporary Japanese Thought, edited and translated by Richard F. Calichman (2005)

Overcoming Modernity, edited and translated by Richard F. Calichman (2008)

Natsume Sōseki, *Theory of Literature and Other Critical Writings*, edited and translated by Michael Bourdaghs, Atsuko Ueda, and Joseph A. Murphy (2009)

Kojin Karatani, *History and Repetition*, edited by Seiji M. Lippit (2012)

TRANSLATED BY VAN C. GESSEL

A NOVEL

ENDŌ SHŪSAKU

Kiku's Prayer

COLUMBIA UNIVERSITY PRESS

NEW YORK

This publication has been supported by the Richard W. Weatherhead
Publication Fund of the Weatherhead East Asian Institute,
Columbia University.

The translator and Columbia University Press wish to express their
appreciation for the generous grant given by the College of Humanities
at Brigham Young University toward the cost of publishing this book.

Columbia University Press
Publishers Since 1893
New York   Chichester, West Sussex
cup.columbia.edu

Library of Congress Cataloging-in-Publication Data
Endō, Shūsaku, 1923–1996.
Kiku's prayer : a novel / Endō Shūsaku ; translated by Van C. Gessel.
p. cm. — (Weatherhead books on Asia)
"This translation is dedicated to the memory of Hondō Shun (1936–1997)
a kind and gentle man who was nothing like his namesake in this novel."
ISBN 978-0-231-16282-1 (cloth : alk. paper)
ISBN 978-0-231-53083-5 (e-book)
1. Young women—Fiction. 2. Christianity—Fiction. 3. Persecution—Japan—
History—19th century—Fiction. 4. Nagasaki-shi (Japan)—Fiction. I. Title.

PL849.N4K435   2012
895.6'35—dc23   2012021712

Columbia University Press books are printed on permanent and durable acid-free paper.
This book is printed on paper with recycled content.
Printed in the United States of America
c 10 9 8 7 6 5 4 3 2 1

COVER DESIGN: Julia Kushnirsky

This translation is dedicated to the memory of
Hondō Shun (1936–1997)

a kind and gentle man who was nothing like his namesake in this novel

CONTENTS

ACKNOWLEDGMENTS

The translator would like to express his sincere gratitude to the College of Humanities at Brigham Young University and Dean John R. Rosenberg for granting a sabbatical to complete this work; to the author's widow and son, Endō Junko and Endō Ryūnosuke, for permission to do the translation; to the pair of very careful anonymous readers for Columbia University Press who helped me improve the accuracy of the translation; to Marcia Robertson Hippen for being an astute, invaluable reader and critic; to my superb editor, Margaret B. Yamashita; and to Jennifer Crewe at Columbia University Press for unstinting support over the years.

Kiku's Prayer

MITSU AND KIKU

AT THE OUTSET, I must introduce two girls who are characters in this novel.

Their names are Mitsu and Kiku. They are cousins only one year apart in age.

They have no last names, having been born toward the end of the Tokugawa period into farming families in the Magome District of Urakami Village, which borders Nagasaki.

Consequently, the government officials in Nagasaki and the Buddhist prelates at Shōtokuji Temple recorded in their registries: "Mitsu, daughter of Mohei of Magome District, and Kiku, daughter of Shinkichi from same district." Shōtokuji was the ancestral temple for this region.

Were you to drive in Nagasaki toward the epicenter where the A-bomb was dropped, on the right side of the highway you would see a temple with a sign reading "Shōtokuji Preschool." That area used to be known as Magome District.

These days there is nothing to see there but a drab national highway with cars and trucks weaving in and out, but around the time Mitsu and Kiku were born, this area was right next to the ocean.[1] The Shōtokuji was perched on a hill at the edge of the water.

Mountains pressed up against the shore, leaving little land that could be cultivated. So the farmers in Magome, just like the peasants in the neighboring Satogō, Nakano, Motohara, and Ieno Districts, used the slopes of the hills and made their living by planting rice crops in the valleys between. The

1. Land reclamation projects from the 1850s onward have significantly changed the proximity to the ocean of many Nagasaki neighborhoods.

population of all these villages combined could not have exceeded nine hundred households.

Nothing remains of those days, with Magome now buried under modern housing developments. But each time I visit Nagasaki, I always pause there and close my eyes, imagining what it must have looked like when Mitsu and Kiku were still alive.

Mountains covered with groves of camphor and alder trees. Farmhouses dotting the slopes. From the tops of the hills one can look straight down into Nagasaki harbor with its new rice lands reclaimed from the sea.

Several years after the two girls were born—in 1885, to be exact—the French writer Pierre Loti, author of the famed *Madame Chrysanthème*, sang the praises of the verdant trees hovering over Nagasaki harbor. It was this same inlet, glimmering in the sun and lush with greenery, that Mitsu and Kiku saw every day.

The little community of Magome, too, was blessed with sunlight and greenery and yet was so astonishingly quiet. Little birds chirped in the camphor trees. At midday, as those voices tapered off, somewhere a rooster crowed.

The adults all are out working in the fields, and the children are at play. So many ways to amuse themselves. I can almost make out the small figures of Mitsu and Kiku among the children racing up and down the slopes.

It was the grandmother of Mitsu and Kiku who said it: "Mitsu is a spoiled little girl, and Kiku is a tomboy!"

Her Granny may have called her "a spoiled little girl," but Mitsu wasn't the sort to cling like a puppy dog to her mother or her older brother.

What was unique about Mitsu's personality is that she would accept unquestioningly anything said by an older person. She believed everything she heard so implicitly that some people were left to wonder whether she was mentally deficient.

For instance, when Mitsu was five, her older brother Ichijirō gave her some flower seeds.

"Hey, see these? They're morning glory seeds!" Ichijirō dropped the gray seeds—one, two, three—into Mitsu's tiny hand. "Now, Mitsu, if you plant these and water them every single day, some cute little sprouts'll come up!"

"OK." With a nod, Mitsu set out running. Across the way, her cousin Kiku was playing jump rope with some other children. Mitsu gleefully showed her morning glory seeds to Kiku, and then with a refined gesture, like a high-class lady dropping her valuable jewels one by one into a box, she planted the gray seeds in the ground.

Seated by the hearth that evening, Ichijirō, who was ten years older than Mitsu, asked her, "Mitsu, did you plant your seeds?"

"Yup," Mitsu nodded.

"Great. Now remember—you have to water them every day. Every single day!"

"OK." It was in these moments that the look in Mitsu's eyes suggested that she had total trust in everything an older person said to her. She never lost that guileless look, even after she grew up.

Seeing his innocent little sister crouching down and staring tirelessly at the ground each day thereafter, Ichijirō laughed, "The sprouts'll come up when they're ready, there's no point trying to rush them!"

Eventually the pretty morning glory sprouts broke through and peeked up out of the ground. They looked just like a baby's hand. Mitsu never failed to water them, just as her brother had told her to do.

One rainy day, Mitsu held an umbrella over her own little morning glory garden as she sprinkled water on them. Ichijirō, headed out to work in the fields, realized with a start what she was doing.

"Mitsu, what in the world—?!"

"I'm watering my morning glories."

"Moron! You don't have to water them when it rains. Rain's the same as water!"

Mitsu stared wordlessly into her brother's face, and several seconds passed before she cried out, "I get it! They don't need water on days when it rains!"

Right then, Ichijirō seriously began to worry that his sister might be a little slow in the head.

Compared with simple Mitsu, who throughout her childhood was considered a bit learning disabled, her cousin Kiku, who was separated in age from Mitsu by only a year, appeared to be a lively, loquacious, clever girl, and it was no accident that she was labeled a tomboy by her grandmother.

The differences in personality between the two girls were immediately evident when they played together. Partly because she was older, it was invariably Kiku who gave commands to Mitsu, no matter what they were doing. If they were going to sing a song, Kiku would first hum it and then order Mitsu, "Now you try to sing it." Mitsu would cheerfully comply.

Sooo cold, it's sooo very cold!
They've set fires on Mount Atago
Hurry and come!

If you come, you'll be cold!
If you don't come, you'll be hot!

In her childhood, Mitsu always walked behind her cousin Kiku, played the way Kiku played, and did everything Kiku told her to do. For her part, Kiku took on the role of Mitsu's protector and always shielded her younger cousin from rough hooligans and wild dogs.

Speaking of hooligans, there was a boy who lived not far from Kiku and Mitsu who always had two rivulets of green snot coursing down from his nose.

Since it was a bother to blow his nose on leaves, he always wiped it with the sleeve of his kimono. As a result, his sleeves always glistened, as though slugs had left slithering trails on them. Every time Kiku and Mitsu played jump rope with some other girls in the neighborhood, he would stare at them from a distance and then eventually race over to pester them.

This hooligan had an accomplice whom everyone called Crybaby. He was a weakling who would burst into tears if he were alone when Kiku scolded him, but he'd start to swagger when Snotnose was with him.

Snotnose and Crybaby—these two were the enemies of all the girls in the neighborhood. Even when she was up against one of the boys, though, Kiku would tear into him and never back off.

"You're a good-for-nothing!" she'd taunt him, and Snotnose would respond, "You're an idiot, and Mitsu's a moron!" Then Crybaby would repeat exactly what he had said.

"Thug! Clown!" Kiku would snap right back at them.

This exchange of insults would continue for a while, with Snotnose jeering, "Mitsu's a bed wetter! I'll bet you peed in your bed last night!"

"And you're a wet noodle!"

"Wet noodle? What does that mean?!" ·

"You don't even know what a wet noodle is? It's long, but it's not good for anything. That's you—a wet noodle!"

"You turd!"

"Snotty pug-nose!!"

Kiku's string of machine gun–like insults left both Snotnose and Crybaby speechless.

One day that spring—

Kiku and Mitsu and some of their girlfriends were picking the lotus flowers that covered the paths between the rice paddies.

The large evening sun, orange as an apricot, had begun to set, and Kiku propped a crown of lotus blossoms on her head and asked Mitsu, "What do you think? Aren't I beautiful?" Though still a child, Kiku very much wanted to be a beautiful woman. "Well!?"

"Yeah. You're beautiful." As always, Mitsu said whatever Kiku wanted to hear. Or perhaps she just innocently believed anything Kiku said.

Kiku haughtily spun her body in a circle and gazed around her. She hoped that some adult working in the fields would notice how smart she looked.

Just then she spotted two boys next to a shed, brandishing a pole as they seemed to be beating something. It was Snotnose and Crybaby.

No doubt they were torturing some poor creature. Probably a kitten or puppy they'd stumbled across.

"What are you guys doing?" Kiku shouted as she raced toward them. Mitsu and the other girls scurried along behind her.

Just as Kiku had imagined, the boys were jabbing at the haunches of a mud-spattered kitten and beating it with the pole.

"Why are you being mean to that cat?" Kiku, ever the champion of the oppressed, could not bear to see any weak creature abused. She was always on the spot to protect a younger girl who was being harassed by a boy.

"Stop it! Give the cat to me."

"Why would we give it to you?" Snotnose staggered back a step and glared at Kiku.

"Why would we give it to you?!" True to form, Crybaby mimicked Snotnose's words.

Snotnose remembered losing a recent squabble, and stung by his defeat he retorted, "I found it. It's my cat!"

"Well then, how about if you give it to me, and I'll let you have these flowers."

"Flowers?! " Snotnose sneered. "There's more lotus flowers over there than there is dog shit."

"So you're not gonna let me have it no matter what?" Kiku took a step forward.

Snotnose, under the glare of her narrowed eyes, retreated a bit and spat out, "If you climb to the top of that tree, I'll give you the cat."

The tree was a large camphor laurel, and though it was impossible to guess its age, it stood straight and tall, like a giant reaching both its arms into the sky. Camphor laurel trees of this size were by no means rare in Magome. Many varieties of birds sang from these enormous trees early each morning, and their branches provided the villagers with shade through the hot summers.

"You can't do it, can you?" Snotnose peered at Kiku, who had hesitated for a moment, and he snorted up a green rivulet of snot.

"There's nothing to it," Kiku replied, placing her hands on the trunk. But when she wavered, Snotnose taunted her:

"There's no way you can climb a tree that tall!" Crybaby, of course, echoed the identical words. An indignant Kiku grabbed a branch. The hem of her kimono was turned up, and her white legs peeked out.

"Kiku!" A girl cried out almost in tears. "Don't do it! You could get hurt! Let's go back home!" But Kiku had already wrapped her pale legs around the branch.

"Wow!" Crybaby exclaimed in admiration, dazzled by the sight of Kiku's bare legs.

Kiku was not the sort of girl who could scamper up a tree like a monkey. Clinging frantically to one branch, she clutched desperately at the next, stretching her leg up onto that branch and making her way inch by inch up the tree, her face flushing a bright red. With each upward move she made, some object or another—a clump of dried leaves, or the debris from an abandoned bird's nest—dropped down onto the heads of the children who were watching her. Meanwhile, the kitten responsible for this display staggered over to a puddle of water, thrust in its head, and began noisily lapping away.

One girl began to weep. She was terrified, certain that Kiku was going to injure herself.

"Kiku's gonna fall!" The girls pointed their fingers at Snotnose. "If she falls, it's all your fault!"

Startled by the accusation, Snotnose stammered, "It's not my fault! She's the one who decided to climb it!"

"You told her to!"

Snotnose glanced around him. Then with no warning, he spun around and sprinted away, shouting "Not my fault!!" Seeing that, Crybaby also took his heels.

"Kiku—hurry and come down!" The girls cried out in one voice as they gazed upward.

Just then, the branch Kiku was standing on broke with a dull snap. Kiku dangled in midair like a tangled kite.

Suspended from the branch that she clutched with both hands, as though she were doing a chin-up, Kiku frantically struggled to find a foothold. With each twist of her body, her white thighs and abdomen were on full display, but she had no time to worry about such things.

"Kiku!"

"Kiku!!"

Every one of the girls, Mitsu included, had burst into tears. The adults were too far away to summon, and there was no doubt that if they tried to go for help, Kiku would run out of strength and plummet to the ground like a stone.

"Somebody—help!!" Mitsu yelled with her hands up to her mouth. The other girls joined in; "Help!!" they shouted.

A young man, perhaps having heard their cries, came racing along the footpath through the fields. He wasn't from Magome. They had never seen him before.

"Help me!" Dangling in the air, it was Kiku's turn to cry out.

"Hang on! I'll help you!" The young man ran, breathless, to the tree. "Don't let go! I'll climb up to you!"

He threw his arms around the trunk and nimbly raised a foot onto a limb. He straddled the next branch up, placing his body directly below Kiku's legs. He patted his neck with one hand and called, "Step down onto my shoulders."

She was young, but she was still a girl, and for an instant Kiku blushed with embarrassment.

"Hurry! There's nothing to be shy about!" He seemed more mature than his years. His face wore the promise of good judgment. Hugging the trunk of the tree with one arm, he wrapped the other arm around Kiku's waist and lifted himself up to catch her on his shoulders.

Riding on his shoulders and now with both arms encircling the gigantic tree trunk, Kiku realized that she had been saved, and she began to sob loudly.

"You're OK now. You don't need to cry." The young man looked up in surprise at Kiku's face. Supporting the sobbing girl's body and helping her along, he descended the tree slowly. Kiku's wails grew even louder once her feet touched the ground.

Just then there was a shout from behind them. Mitsu's older brother, Ichijirō, had appeared out of nowhere. Misunderstanding what had happened, he grabbed the young man by the collar and snarled, "Why'd you make her cry? Just who the hell are you?!"

"I—" Taking two, then three blows from Ichijirō's flat palm, the young man fell to the ground and protested, "I—didn't make her cry."

"If you weren't doing anything to her, then why is she crying?" Raising his fists, Ichijirō glanced back at Kiku. "What did this bastard do to you?"

"He didn't do anything bad," Kiku explained to her cousin through her sobs. "I climbed up the tree and couldn't get back down. . . . He came to help me."

"What's that?!" With a sheepish look, Ichijirō lowered his fists. "Really?"

"Really."

"Why didn't you say so sooner? You there—where are you from? Nagasaki?"

Timidly the young man replied, "Nakano."

"What? Nakano?" A look of displeasure clouded Ichijirō's face. "What's somebody from Nakano doing loitering around here in Magome?"

"I've been to the farmers' market in Nagasaki," he said, blinking his eyes.

"Farmers' market? Don't lie to me. You're not even carrying anything!"

"My dad went ahead and took all the stuff."

Ichijirō continued to eye the young man suspiciously from head to toe. "We don't want any of you Nakano types hanging around with no reason to be here. I hate you *Kuros*!" He ordered the young man to leave with a jerk of his chin.

The young man slipped his feet into his sandals and hurried away, looking back over his shoulder regretfully. His figure grew smaller and then disappeared into the copse of trees that marked the end of the path through the rice fields.

"Are you hurt?" Ichijirō asked as he pulled a leaf from Kiku's shoulder. "What's a girl doing climbing trees anyway? That's why you get called a tomboy."

"What are '*Kuros*'?" Back on her feet, Kiku remembered that Ichijirō had said "I hate you *Kuros*!" to the young man.

"*Kuros*?" With a rather grim look, Ichijirō replied, "Never mind about that. Don't you remember that we're always telling you not to go near kids from Motohara and Nakano and Ieno?"

"I know, I know."

"So, if you run into that guy again, you're not to speak to him."

"What's wrong with speaking to him?" she asked, wide-eyed.

"That's nothing a child needs to know." Ichijirō responded with a disgusted look. He would tell her nothing further or even say another word on the subject. But he strictly enjoined his young sister and niece against having any association with youth from Nakano or Motohara.

"Why can't we play with them?"

"Because . . . Nakano and Motohara are different from us here in Magome. It's because they're *Kuros*."

"What does that mean?"

"Nothing for a child to know." The look on Ichijirō's face was withering, so even Kiku asked nothing further. But a serious doubt was planted in her heart.

Just what is a *Kuro*? Even in her youthful mind, the word *Kuro* conjured up images of a somehow ominous, dark place. But Kiku couldn't imagine—it seemed flat-out contradictory that such a kind young man could live in such a scary, dark place.

The youth's face was still vividly etched into her eyes. He wasn't anything like Snotnose or Crybaby—he was a trustworthy, gentle young man. She still clearly remembered his voice, as calming as that of an older brother, when he circled her legs with his arms, lowering her onto his shoulders and climbing down from the tree, and then he had said, "You're OK. Don't cry."

She couldn't imagine why the simple fact that such a remarkable young man lived in Nakano would upset Ichijirō so much.

"Granny?" The next day, she went to talk to her grandmother, who was relaxing in the sun. "Nakano and Motohara are *Kuros*, huh?"

"*Kuros*, you say?"

"What does *Kuros* mean?"

Her grandmother stared fixedly at Kiku, "Where'd you hear that word?"

"From Ichijirō. He said to stay away from Nakano and Motohara."

"Ah, yes. You mustn't go over there to play." Just like Ichijirō, she gave her granddaughter a stern gaze. "You'll be cursed if you go there."

"Cursed?!"

"That's right. Something bad'll happen to you for sure. That's why you mustn't go there."

Her grandmother's words filled Kiku with an inexpressible anxiety and fear. Something terrible would happen to her if she set foot in Nakano or Motohara. But why . . . ?

A slender stream formed the border separating their community from Nakano and Motohara. One of the branches of the Urakami River flowed through the area. To Kiku, the stream seemed like the boundary between a place of safety and a place of terror. On this side of the stream was an area where the adults said it was OK to play; on the opposing side was a frightening space she must never set foot into. But that kind young man who had saved her lived on the other side of the stream. . . .

Not long thereafter, Kiku had a dream.

In her dream, Kiku was playing with Mitsu and some of the other girls. It was a spring afternoon, and just as before, lotuses and violets and white dandelions bloomed all around them.

As the girls romped along, picking the flowers, someone called out from behind them. When they stood up and looked in the direction of the voice, that same young man stood in the sunlight, looking their way and smiling.

"If you want to pick flowers, I can show you a place over here where there's a lot more of them. Come this way!" He innocently motioned for them to follow him.

Guileless Mitsu cried out "Let's go" and was about to dart off when Kiku stopped her.

"We can't!" She had remembered the stern injunction from Ichijirō and her grandmother. A stream they must not cross flowed between them and the spot where the young man stood.

"We can't go!" Kiku was almost to the point of spreading her arms wide to stop the other girls from advancing. "We can't come over there!" she called out to the young man.

"Why not?"

"We've been told we mustn't go to Nakano or Motohara. Something bad will happen to us if we do."

At Kiku's words, a look of inexpressible sorrow flashed across the young man's face. He nodded, his look filled with resignation, and he pivoted and walked away, just as he had on that earlier occasion. From behind, he looked incredibly forlorn.

At that point, Kiku awoke from her dream.

But the memory of the dream remained powerfully in her head even after she woke up. For some reason, as she recalled the lonely retreating figure of the young man, she felt that it was all her fault. It was as though he had looked so sad because she had treated him maliciously.

It wouldn't be wrong to see him again, she muttered from her bed. *He saved me, after all.*

A certain resolution settled into her mind. She leaped from her bed, nearly kicking it away from her. That afternoon, she furtively confessed her resolution to Mitsu and the other girls.

"We're going to go over to Nakano."

"What?!" The girls' eyes widened. Mitsu warned, "Kiku, don't you remember that Ichijirō said we couldn't ever go there?"

"I know that. But I hear that all kinds of flowers are in bloom over there."

"You're gonna have to go by yourself. We'll stay here." That was the consensus of all the girls except for Mitsu, who did not respond.

Kiku set out by herself along the brightly sunlit path. Purposely disobeying her elders filled Kiku with fear and guilt, but a part of her wanted to stand up to the adults.

"Kiku! Don't do it!!" Her friends cried out in chorus from behind her. But the unyielding girl didn't even look back at them.

She had only gone about three-quarters of a mile when Mitsu came running after her, shouting her name.

Kiku bristled. "What are you doing here? You need to stay with the others," she growled. But Mitsu said nothing and continued walking behind her until Kiku brightened and said, "You mustn't tell Granny or Ichijirō about this."

Weaving through the terraced fields that had been cultivated halfway up the hillside, the two girls reached the edge of Magome District. The sun was brilliant, and black-eared kites twittered faintly overhead. A flying insect, drawn by the smell of sweat on the faces of the two girls, began to flit tenaciously around them.

A small stream trickled past. This was the branch of the Urakami River and the end of Magome District.

Dipping her bare feet into the stream, Kiku called out with deliberate cheer, "Mitsu, come try this. It feels wonderful!" Inwardly, though, she knew that once she crossed this stream, she would be entering a place where Granny had told her something bad would happen to her, and she felt a slight stab of pain in her chest.

Ever compliant, Mitsu immersed her feet in the stream and giggled unaffectedly, "Wow, it tickles!"

"Let's go!" In an attempt to dispel her gloomy thoughts, Kiku quickly leaped to the opposite bank, with Mitsu hurrying along behind her.

A copse of trees rose up before them. It was only a grove of trees, but Kiku's chest was pounding, as though the moment she stepped into its precincts, she would be sampling a forbidden fruit, and she licked her lips in trepidation.

Once they made their way through the trees, cultivated fields stretched in all directions. The sun glittered on the fields, and a waterwheel spun with a recurring slap. A cow was munching on grass just to their side. It stared at the girls with misty eyes, gave a languid "Moo!" and resumed its chewing.

Two thatched-roof houses stood in the distance. The sky was blue, and one cirrus cloud hovered in the sky.

How could anything bad happen in a place like this? It wasn't the slightest bit different from their own community in Magome. So why did the villagers have only dreadful things to say about Nakano and Motohara? It made even less sense to Kiku now.

"Mitsu, let's pick some flowers!" The two girls crouched down and began gathering the flowers at their feet. Though doubts persisted in their minds. . . .

THE SEARCHER

AROUND 3:00 IN the afternoon—

The French warship *Carcassonne* finally sailed into the rain-swept bay. As the wind sliced the milky clouds into tatters, the hills on either side of the bay bit by bit came into view. The hills were so intensely green that the man standing on the deck didn't feel so much that the boat was steaming into a bay as advancing slowly through a sea of trees.

From the surrounding hills, he could hear the unbelievably irritating screeches of cicadas. It seemed as though the hills were infested with vast swarms of the insects.

"*Mon Père*, this is Nagasaki." A passing sailor carrying a bucket called out to the man leaning against the deck railing.

"Ah! We've finally arrived." He smiled and nodded.

"So, Father," the sailor inquired, "will you be searching for those folks . . . ?"

"Of course. That's one of my reasons for coming to Nagasaki."

"It would be wonderful if you found them."

"Oh, I'll find them, all right."

Once the sailor and his bucket had departed, the priest turned his eyes once again to the hills blanketed with drifting rainclouds.

There was a chance that dwelling somewhere within this intense greenness, somewhere amid the annoying screeches of the cicadas, were the people he was searching for. But how oppressively muggy the heat in Japan was! It had been so much better last year when he lived in Naha in the Ryūkyū Islands: even though the temperature was the same as that in Nagasaki, the humidity had been much lower.

Through the rain he noticed a Japanese ship with a white sail hoisted. Somehow, each time he saw a Japanese ship with its sails spread, he was reminded of white-feathered birds.

Eventually he caught a glimpse of the distant shoreline. The huts of the fishermen, topped with gray tiles or shingles, clustered together in claustrophobic heaps. Three or four wooden houses built in Western style were conspicuous among them.

As the ship reduced speed midway out into the harbor, several small boats set out together from the shore and rowed toward the ship. They looked like a colony of ants swarming toward their prey.

Each of the tiny boats carried a Japanese peddler. The peddlers reached into the baskets or boxes tied to their backs and pulled from them lanterns, vases, teacups, and saucers. Grinning and bobbing their heads toward the French sailors who peered down at them from the deck, they began hawking their wares, loudly crying, "How'd you like some of these?" "Take a look here! Really cheap!!"

The warship cast its anchor. As he listened to the grating of the anchor, the priest wondered whether some of those he was seeking were among these peddlers.

"All men going ashore assemble on deck!" After the officer had given these orders, he said to the priest, "Father, please board the junk with me."

4:30 in the afternoon—

Joining a group of sailors including Ensign Guirand, who had invited him onto the junk, the priest transferred to a skiff that a Japanese man was rowing.

"How about some of these?" Even then, the boats crowded around the skiff and peddlers called out from both sides. They grinned affably and repeatedly bobbed their heads in deference.

"You there!" The priest abruptly passed a coin to one of the peddlers and whispered, "Do you know where I can find any Christians?"

The pleasant grin that had seemed plastered on the peddler's face vanished, replaced by a look of fear. He shifted his eyes and turned his back to the priest, as though he had gotten too close to something taboo.

"Father, what did you ask that man?" Ensign Guirand, who spoke no Japanese, inquired.

"I asked him whether any of his fellows were Christians."

"So that's why he looked so edgy." The ensign nodded his head. "If you're a Christian in this country, you get the death sentence, you know."

"I know that. But that wasn't the case until 260 years ago. Back in those days there were more than 400,000 believers on these islands of the Far East. Here in Nagasaki, several beautiful churches had been built, and even little children sang hymns as they played together."

"As many as 400,000?"

"Or possibly even more. But then the rulers of Japan developed a hatred for Christianity, and not only did they ban any missionaries from coming here, but they slammed shut the doors to the country itself. As you know, they allowed only a few Dutch traders to live in Nagasaki." As he gave this explanation, the priest once again shifted his eyes toward the surrounding hills. The rain clouds were finally clearing away, and white billows of steam began to swirl skyward from the valleys between the hills. Still the hordes of cicadas continued their monotonous, melancholy droning. As though it were some sort of heretical hymn. . . .

"Yes, but . . . But I . . ."

"But what, Father?"

"Of course, this is just a selfish dream of mine, but I intend to find out whether any of the descendants of those early believers still follow our religion."

"I shall pray for your success, Father." He spoke encouragement with his lips, but it appeared that Ensign Guirand had little interest in this topic. Instead, his head was filled with thoughts of the "geisha" in Nagasaki, whom he had heard about from a fellow officer who had visited Japan last year. They were supposedly as tiny as dolls, and as compliant. . . .

"Father, your welcoming party is waiting on the shore." The ensign pointed to the makeshift wharf, piled high with stones. Another priest dressed in white stood as a tiny figure in the distance.

The wharf was populated with not only those who had come to welcome the arrivals but also forty or fifty Japanese who had come to see the foreign warship. The priest had experienced the same phenomenon at Yokohama: the Japanese people, most likely because they had been isolated from the outside world for so long, displayed an inordinate curiosity about foreign things.

Dark-skinned men wearing dismal kimonos with dismal expressions on their faces. And women with their teeth painted black. Swarms of naked children capering about. These were the Japanese. No wonder that Father Furet[1] stood out in his white summer habit.

When the skiff reached shore, Father Furet approached with both arms outstretched and a beaming smile on his face.

---

1. Louis-Théodore Furet (1816–1900), a French priest of the Société des Missions-Étrangères de Paris (M.E.P.), arrived in Nagasaki in May 1856 after spending nearly a year in Naha awaiting the chance to travel to the Japanese mainland. Furet was instrumental in the planning and early construction stages of the original Ōura Church in Nagasaki, erected in a spot overlooking the execution ground where twenty-six Christians had been martyred in 1597. Furet was replaced by Bernard Petitjean and Joseph Laucaigne in 1864.

"You're here, Bernard!" The new arrival[2] moved into those outstretched arms, and they gave each other a tight embrace. Two years earlier, they had been comrades studying Japanese as they waited in Naha for the day when they could begin to spread the Gospel in Japan.

"I'll wait here. Leave your trunk there. I'll have someone deliver it. You'll need to go see the Japanese authorities to take care of the procedures for disembarkation and to obtain a residence permit. They're difficult, I assure you."

"I'm well aware."

The sailors who had reached shore ahead of the priest had already formed two lines and were being questioned by the authorities. The man doing the interpreting appeared to be Dutch.

The authorities were, indeed, difficult. They took special pains with the priest to drive home the fact that he must not give any books relating to Christianity or any holy implements such as crucifixes to the Japanese and made him swear an oath to that effect. By the time all the bureaucratic formalities were completed, the sun had already set, and the hills surrounding the harbor were turning a dark purple.

"Stay well, Father." After exchanging a firm handshake with Ensign Guirand, the priest returned to the spot where Father Furet was waiting for him.

"Phew! That was exhausting," he grumbled to Father Furet.

"Yes . . . But I'm sure you're aware of how strictly the Japanese have proscribed Christianity for more than two hundred years."

The two remained silent as they climbed a sloping path. Giant camphor trees with spreading branches edged the path that traced its way beside a long fence. Evening cicadas shrieked mournfully from the trees.

"What is this area called?"

"Ōura."

He repeated the strange name over and over in his mind. It was the name of the place where he might live out the rest of his life.

"Let me ask you," he finally broached the question that had been on his mind, "Have you found among the Japanese you've met any who are secret believers in Christianity?"

2. This is Bernard-Thadée Petitjean (1828–1884), one of the key figures in the reintroduction of Catholicism to Japan in the latter part of the nineteenth century. Petitjean, like Furet a member of M.E.P., arrived in Nagasaki in August 1863. The following year, he began teaching French at a Japanese government school. He was consecrated as bishop of Japan in 1866 and labored in Nagasaki as well as Yokohama and Osaka. He died in Nagasaki.

"Not one," Father Furet shook his head. Father Furet had come to Nagasaki six months ago. Just four years earlier, in 1858, Japan had finally allowed the doors of seclusion to be opened a crack. They had signed treaties limited to commerce.

As a result, trade representatives from the treaty nations of the United States, Great Britain, and France had taken up residence in Nagasaki along with their families.

These people naturally needed a church. They needed the church that the Japanese had reviled for so many long years.

Faced with demands from the trade treaty nations, the Tokugawa shogunate with great reluctance gave permission both for the building of churches that only foreign citizens would be allowed to enter and for the presence of missionaries. However, this was on the condition that they must not seek to spread Christianity among the Japanese.

Consequently, Father Furet had come in January in order to build a church here in Nagasaki.

"How is the construction coming?"

Father Furet responded jovially, "It's going very smoothly, Bernard. In fact, when it comes to working with their hands, these Japanese are the most skillful in the world. Despite the fact they've never seen a Western church, these carpenters have already completed more than half a chapel that combines Gothic and Baroque styles, basing their work solely on the diagrams and pictures and explanations I've given them." He pointed toward the summit of the hill. "You'll see it as soon as we reach the top of this hill. The view of the bay from the church is extraordinary! I don't think there's a bay this beautiful in all the south of France."

Petitjean responded with a thin smile while wordlessly bristling at the shrieking of the cicadas. But Father Furet went on animatedly describing the process of erecting the church.

This is where this good priest and I differ in our views, he thought to himself. He had not come to Nagasaki for the benefit of the various foreign representatives who would live here temporarily with their families. He had received permission from his superiors to come to Nagasaki to seek for . . . *them*.

Them . . .

Four years ago, he had endured a protracted ocean journey from France to come here to the Far East so that he could preach the Gospel in Japan. Two years ago, when at last he had settled in Naha to learn Japanese, he and Father Furet, along with others of their company, heard a remarkable story.

The story was related to them by a Chinese sailor. The man told them he had been to Nagasaki four or five times. He was missing one ear, and at midday he was already drunk on Naha's strong liquor.

"So listen to this. There's still some fellers in Japan who are hidden followers of Christianity. There was a fisherman from near Nagasaki who drifted here in a storm . . . and he would cross himself just like you men do."

Father Furet and his comrades laughed off the story as the drunken delusions of a Chinese sailor. Such a story simply could not be true.

But one priest received a powerful shock from the story, so severe he could not sleep that night.

While he was still living in Paris he learned that more than two hundred years earlier, nearly 400,000 Christians converts had been won in Japan. The Société des Missions-Étrangères de Paris had been organized to bring together priests who had decided to labor in foreign lands. The society's headquarters building had on display relics of their predecessors who had proselytized in various Asian lands, along with items that memorialized their sufferings. The building also had a library of books dealing with Asia.

In that library, Petitjean read the diary and letters of Saint Francis Xavier. Xavier, of course, was the first father to preach Christianity in Japan. It was he who had written, "The Japanese are the finest, wisest people we have yet encountered in Asia."

In addition to Xavier's writings, the library holdings included books containing the blood- and sweat-bathed reports of priests who came later to Japan from such distant lands as Spain, Portugal, and Italy.

From these books, the priest learned that Japan, where Christianity had flourished for a time, had abruptly slammed its doors shut, isolating itself from the rest of the world, and had also relentlessly banned the practice of Christianity and worked all manner of tortures on the believers.

He learned that when the 400,000 Christians were compelled to decide whether to die for their faith or to abandon it, more than half of them apostatized against their wills.

Not one Christian is left in Japan. That was the conventional wisdom in the Parisian missionary society. That had also been his conclusion.

All the more reason why the drunken Chinese sailor's story came as such a shock to him.

It might just be true. Perhaps the descendants of the original Christians in Japan continue to secretly preserve their faith.

Unable to sleep, he arose from his crude bed and set a match to a dish filled with lamp oil. Outside it was raining, and he could hear the raindrops slapping the leaves of the hardy banana trees in the garden. Nights in Naha were muggy. Geckos clung to his ceiling.

If it's true, I must find them.

He obtained permission from his superiors to spend a half year required to travel from France to India, from India to Indochina, and then on to Japan. He now had been living for several months in Naha, along with companions who shared his determination. He had achieved the first of his goals.

Because the Japanese government still strictly prohibited its people from believing in Christianity, he was able to enter Japan only under the severe limitations that the shogunate had placed on priests, who were allowed to minister only to the foreign populations in Yokohama and Nagasaki.

But if there were a group of believers among the Japanese, despite the proscription on their faith . . .

I shall seek them out.

From that day forward, this became his solitary quest.

As they approached the crest of the hill, they saw a small light moving ahead.

"Ah, it's Okane-san and her husband." Father Furet raised a hand and waved to them. "This couple are Japanese who take care of our cooking and laundry. They aren't Christians, of course. In fact, they're fervent followers of the Oinari faith."

"Oinari?"

"It's a Japanese religion that worships foxes. In this country they believe that foxes have been given special powers by the gods. . . ."

The light drew near. It was a short Japanese couple carrying a lantern.

"Okane-san, Mosaku-san—this is Father Bernard Petitjean." Father Furet patted his shoulder as he introduced him to the couple.

"Yes. My name is Petitjean. Very pleased to meet you." He gave the sort of Japanese greeting that had appeared in his language textbook.

The couple bowed humbly, their backs bent so politely that it almost seemed too polite. This was how the Japanese always behaved.

"Has his trunk arrived?"

"It has," the husband answered. "A carrier just brought it a few minutes ago from the wharf, along with some other packages."

The scene was just as Father Furet had described it. Atop the hill was a wooden building designed somewhat in the Western style. It was still only a frame, but a tiny, bluish-purple Gothic-style steeple soared overhead.

"Bernard, this is the first house of God to be built in Japan. The very first church!" Father Furet's voice brimmed with emotion. "You could see it more clearly if it weren't nighttime. But tomorrow you'll be able to savor the beauty of the harbor view from up here."

There was certainly a commanding view of the harbor from where they stood. But the harbor was now shrouded in the dark of night, and the green vegetation was only faintly visible because of the moonlight, not because of lights from the houses.

"It's still primitive here compared with Yokohama. They have no gas or electric lights. They make paper lanterns. They set a flame to vegetable oil and use that as a light in the darkness. When I first got here, they didn't have any candles, and it was quite perturbing."

"How is the food?"

"We get only Japanese food. That's all Okane-san knows how to make. But now that you're here, perhaps we can begin to teach her how to prepare something we'll find edible."

"Have you made any Japanese friends?"

"Friends? Well, if you're talking about detectives from the magistrate's office, I've gotten to know a number of them. But they're wary of me. Because I'm a Kirishitan.[3] The officers here detest Kirishitans even more than do their counterparts in Yokohama."

A thatched farmhouse beside the partly built church was quarters for Father Furet and Petitjean.

As the days passed, Petitjean recognized that Okane-san and her husband were certainly faithful servants, but with his halting command of Japanese he often couldn't understand the Nagasaki dialect they spoke.

The lively noise of construction filled the air each day. Generally when Father Furet had finished saying Mass and had had his breakfast, he would head for the building site to discuss various aspects of the construction with the carpentry foreman. From time to time the foreman would cock his head, scribble a diagram on the ground, and then stare at it in deep thought. In a way, the look on his face reminded Father Petitjean of an image of some Asian philosopher.

But the Japanese were certainly fond of their tobacco! When their labors for the day were finished, everyone from the foreman down to the carpenters would pull a slender bamboo pipe from a pouch hung round his waist and pop it into his mouth. He was even more surprised to see even Okane-san smoking through her blackened teeth.

As the construction progressed, spectators began to gather. Nursemaids carrying infants on their backs, children, and even some adults went out of their way to climb the hill and assemble near the construction site, gaping at the partially completed structure.

"Please come closer. It's OK to come have a look." Even though Father Furet extended the invitation in their peculiar Nagasaki dialect, not one person made a move. They would never come even a single step closer. They knew that police from the magistrate's office could show up at any time.

---

3. Endō here uses the common term applied to Japanese Christians of this era; it is distinct from *Kirisutokyō*, which is elsewhere translated as "Christianity."

And from time to time, a detective with several companions would arrive from the magistrate's office.

"Go home! Go home!" they would brusquely order the spectators. "This isn't a carnival show. And you know you can't have anything to do with the Kirishitans."

At that the crowd would scatter like baby spiders, but the next day, a new flock of spectators would materialize.

One day, after making sure no detectives were around, Petitjean quietly approached the group.

"What do you call those?" he asked purposefully, pointing toward the cicadas emitting their stifling cries from the gigantic trees. He hoped, of course, to create a friendly camaraderie with the Japanese. The adults said nothing for a moment, so a child responded, as though speaking to a dimwit, "It's called a *semi.*"

Petitjean, hoping to elicit a laugh, mimicked the shrill cry of the cicadas. "Many *semi*. Jii! Jii! Jii!" It was true that swarms of cicadas here in Nagasaki screeched throughout the day.

The children snorted at his silly imitation.

Then he pointed to his head and quietly said, "I am Kirishitan. Do you know any Kirishitan people?"

At this point, the spectators clammed up, with the same frightened look on their faces he had seen just days before among the peddlers on the tiny boats.

But obviously these Japanese were filled with the same curiosity, industry, and intelligence that had impressed Saint Francis Xavier more than three hundred years earlier. That was evident from watching how the carpenters worked. The workers here could finish in only three days tasks that would take carpenters in Petitjean's homeland of France a week to complete. They worked assiduously, the only exceptions being during lunchtime and their midday break.

And how deft they were with their hands! Petitjean could watch them move their hands every day without tiring of it.

"What is this?" He would point one after another at the tools the Japanese carpenters used and be impressed by their replies.

The spectators who hovered around the construction site similarly eyed him with curiosity, but keeping an almost self-conscious distance from him, in subdued voices they discussed his pocket watch or the shoes on his feet.

The Japanese were amiable toward him so long as he did not ask that one certain question. But should he venture to bring it up, their countenances would change, just as though a clear sky had suddenly clouded over, and they would lapse into an ill-humored silence.

The question was the short, casual inquiry, "Do you know any Kirishitans?"

When he described this standoff to Father Furet, the priest responded, "Well, what did you expect? For a very long while they've been ordered to report to the police any friends or neighbors who are secretly practicing Christianity. A man will be punished if he's even aware of the existence of a Christian believer and doesn't report it, so these people certainly consider it an insult that you're even asking that question."

"Then there's no way to locate the descendants of the first Christians in this land," Petitjean said with a defeated look.

"Now, don't give up. I'm putting all my energies into the construction of the church, so why don't we make it a competition to see who achieves his goal first?" Father Furet grinned like a boy trying to encourage a younger brother who was stuck on a baffling homework problem.

But when he learned that Petitjean continued to badger the spectators with his questions, Father Furet had to say something to his colleague, and with some degree of awkwardness he reported, "Actually, I hadn't wanted to tell you this, but I've received a complaint from Itō Seizaemon, one of the magistrate's officers. He wants to know why you're asking that particular question of the Japanese, and he suspects you're harboring a secret desire to spread the Gospel among them."

"I see." Petitjean stared at the ground. "I hope I haven't caused any problems for you."

Father Furet lowered his voice. "I think it would be best if you didn't go around quizzing them so openly. If you keep this up, I fear they might call a halt to the building of our church."

Petitjean recognized how conflicted Father Furet felt. For the present, the chief task here in Nagasaki was to get a church constructed, in the expectation that it would form the foundation for spreading the word of God. He must refrain from doing anything that might endanger that plan in any way.

And so Petitjean changed his tactics.

Whenever he had a free moment, he would go out of his way to stroll around the streets of Nagasaki. That would make people aware of his presence. Everyone would know who he was. And perhaps he could begin to form friendships with some of the Japanese in this city.

If that were to happen, someone might just volunteer the information he was seeking. Perhaps someone would cautiously share a secret that only the two of them could know. A secret that "there are still some Kirishitans among the Japanese."

After hitting on this strategy, he began to stroll around the streets of Nagasaki for two, sometimes even three hours. The "stroll," of course, was merely a pretext for his real purpose.

But how remarkable to discover that Nagasaki was a city filled with hills and temples and trees! Three hundred years ago the Portuguese had built this city on a narrow strip of land facing the inlet, and now you could barely take a step in it without bumping into a hill. Or you'd run into a temple encircled by a long wall. Giant trees grew along those stretches of wall, and in those trees a seemingly infinite number of cicadas cried out as though in their death throes.

His usual practice was to walk down the hill from the house where he lived, passing through the Chinese *quartier*. The temples in this Chinese neighborhood were painted vermilion, and often a Chinese with his hair in a braid would appear from the shadows of one of their thick doors.

As he passed through the Chinese district, he came upon a fan-shaped, man-made island called Dejima. The Japanese had allowed only Dutch merchants to live on this island, which was surrounded by a black moat, during the centuries of seclusion. It was a truly minuscule point of contact, no wider than a cat's forehead, between Japan and foreign lands.

The slope rising from Dejima into the hills behind was jammed with black-tiled roofs. That is the city of Nagasaki. Private homes, the steeples of temples, more private homes, more temples. With scores of hills in between them. Trees grew in thick profusion, and cicadas screeched everywhere.

As Petitjean walked along, Japanese would move to the edge of the road and let him walk past. Young girls would flee fearfully into their homes, and young boys with fingers stuck in their mouths would stare at his every movement.

"Hey, it's a barbarian from the south![4] Come look at him! His nose is *huge*! And his face is bright red!" Those were the kinds of comments shouted as he walked by.

From inside some of the houses, he could hear the languid, monotonous sound of a stringed instrument being strummed. It was a samisen, a musical instrument often played by Japanese women.

Each time he heard those listless, monotonous tones, Petitjean felt an indescribable sorrow and emptiness. The never-ending repetition of the same notes. The relentless reiteration of that tedious cadence!

"This is the 'nothingness' that Buddhism teaches about," the Christian missionary thought. He had the feeling that a listlessness resembling the sound of the samisen permeated every part of Nagasaki.

4. *Nambanjin*, the term applied to the first group of Europeans who went to Japan in the mid-sixteenth century, literally means "Southern Barbarian," a reference to the fact that Saint Francis Xavier and other missionaries and traders traveled to Japan by way of India, Southeast Asia, and Macao en route to southern Kyushu.

A listless, tedious cadence.

The European Petitjean experienced that nothingness not just in the samisen but in every part of the city as he strolled about. Squat, black two-story houses stretched as far as his eye could see. As he walked down the narrow roads, he wondered what sorts of lives the Japanese eked out in these tiny, dark houses. Pondering the question, he could imagine the ineffably languid rhythm of the lives of these Japanese, and the thought gripped his heart like a vise.

Occasionally there would be a break in the rows of tiny houses, and he would encounter a long wall. Whenever he came across such a wall, he knew the odds were high that he would soon come up to a Buddhist temple.

Not a narrow-minded man, Petitjean did not reject outright the sacred places of the heathens. He looked with admiration at the large wooden buildings that were so different from those in his native land. He was particularly fond of the line of the heavy roofs and the shimmer of the black tiles that he saw through the gates of the compound. When he ventured inside the gates, the sutra chanting which he took to be the prayers of the heathens, coming from somewhere inside the main temple building, sounded to him like the indolent, droning rhythm of the samisen—evoking the same feelings of emptiness that pervaded Nagasaki.

The samisen, the sutra chanting, the screams of numberless cicadas coming from every corner of this city. He could even detect the odor of nothingness in the voices of these insects that shrieked the same shrieks from morning till night.

This is what Japan is like, Petitjean thought. *Japan has remained exactly this way for two hundred years. Isolated from the rest of the world....*

But now Japan, undisturbed for so many years, was in the process of change, minor though it might be. He had come to Japan right at that turning point of change. Perhaps he himself might even have some impact on the changes coming to Japan.

He had returned from one of his walks and sat down to eat the dinner prepared by Okane when Father Furet came back from the construction site and asked with a touch of sympathy, "Well, have you found them yet?" Father Furet was mindful that even as his own project was progressing smoothly, that of his brother was meeting with no success whatsoever.

"Nothing again today."

"It would seem, then, that there really are no Japanese left who are secretly practicing Christianity. Perhaps that Chinaman was simply lying."

"I haven't abandoned hope yet," Petitjean said, forcing down the still peculiar Japanese food. "If the people can just get a little more comfortable with me . . . they may tell me where to find the Christians. Or maybe some of them will identify themselves to me."

"Yes, but . . ." Father Furet's face clouded over. "The Japanese here in Naga-saki . . . no, not just here; all the Japanese are kind on the surface, but they'll never reveal to a foreigner what's really in their hearts. They won't let their guard down with us. They believe they are fundamentally different from us."

"I think that's to be expected," Petitjean replied. "It's our fault that the Japa-nese are wary of us foreigners. We Europeans started invading the nations of Asia more than three centuries ago. The Japanese are well aware of that fact. That's precisely why they can't yet open up to foreigners. It's why they're mis-trustful of us."

"You certainly have taken their side," Father Furet teased, seeing how seri-ously Petitjean had responded.

"Yes, I have taken their side. Japan will be a second home to me. I want to feel love toward this country where my bones will be interred," Petitjean responded, his eyes glistening. "The truly sad thing is that Christianity in the past collabo-rated in those invasions. That makes it completely reasonable for the Japanese to reject Christianity. We have to do something to dispel their misapprehension of us. We must acknowledge our mistakes as mistakes."

"My friend, it's fine for you to say such a thing to me, but you really mustn't repeat it to our superiors back in Paris." Father Furet prized Petitjean's genuine-ness but worried that this quality might put their obdurate superiors in a foul mood.

"I realize that."

After dinner they took candlesticks and went into a tiny room they had labeled their "chapel." With the flames from their candles flickering like the wings of moths, the two joined their voices in prayer.

When the Liturgy of the Hours concluded, Petitjean whispered his own prayer to God:

"Where can they be? I am resigned if they no longer exist. But if any are still alive somewhere here in Nagasaki, please show me where they are. Please help them to know that I have crossed the distant seas and come here to Japan to find them."

After their prayers, the priests withdrew to their separate bedrooms.

A night in Nagasaki was the very essence of stillness. Okane had strung up mosquito nets in both of their rooms, but it was hot inside those nets even with the windows thrown open. Insects came flying in from every tree if he lit a candlestick for even a moment—including those loathsome cicadas. . . .

Half a month passed since his arrival in Nagasaki. During those two weeks, he had descended and ascended the hills of the city every single day, whether in blistering heat or in drenching rain. He had made his way along narrow paths, hearing the strumming of samisens, and he had quietly made his way alongside the long walled temple compounds.

"They're gigantic, these Southern Barbarians!"

"I can't believe how huge their noses are!"

He had heard these whispered comments many times over. Each time he heard them, he turned and smiled at the speaker, whether a child or an adult. With those smiles, he hoped he might create an opportunity for conversation that would lead to friendship, until ultimately he would be able to hear one of them say "I know where the Christians are."

But it was all futile.

NAGASAKI

TEN YEARS HAD passed since the tree-climbing incident. Mitsu was now fifteen, and Kiku was sixteen.

The two girls had naturally forgotten all about that young man. Or it might be better to say that the shyness of young girls in those days compelled them even more than it would today to remain unaware of young men.

Compared with the tranquil Mitsu, Kiku was as spunky as ever. Her almond-shaped eyes flashed even more brightly when her grandmother would say something such as, "You know, Kiku, when you grow up you're going to be a real beauty." Kiku herself became aware of her own beauty around the age of ten, and more than once she quietly asked, "Mitsu, do you think I'm pretty?"

To which Mitsu would always nod unaffectedly and compliment her cousin, "Yes. You're prettier than any of the girls in Nagasaki." Nagasaki was the city of dreams for the young girls of Magome District, and the combs or wooden clogs that their fathers or Ichijirō would bring them once or twice a year from Nagasaki became jewel-like treasures to them. They envied and resented the girls of Nagasaki, who freely wore such treasures around town.

While girlishly hoping to become as beautiful as those city girls, Kiku turned her nose up at the young men of her village. She blissfully ignored them.

"She's a stuck-up girl, that Kiku." Snotnose and Crybaby, now fifteen and sixteen years old and no longer either snotty or weepy, roomed together at a youth dormitory in the village, where from time to time they would plan out naughty nocturnal raids. Whenever Kiku became the topic of their conversations, they reviled her, calling her a snob because she darted looks of scorn at them whenever they crossed paths.

"We oughta raid her place and leave her bawling!" They bravely discussed various insolent plans, but neither of them had the courage to actually carry them out. They were constantly aware of the disquieting face of Ichijirō lurking behind both Mitsu and Kiku.

The only opportunities for the young men and women of Magome to meet in public came on the night of the Obon Festival and in the first month of the year, when all the villagers were compelled to trample on the *fumie*, images of Christ or Santa Maria. On the eve of the Obon Festival, the young men and women who had felt a spark of attraction for each other would arrange quiet rendezvous, the same as the youth in every Japanese village did. But the *fumie* ritual at the beginning of each year was performed with particular severity in and around Nagasaki, where in the distant past the Kirishitan population had grown to vast numbers.

When Kiku was a young girl, on every fourth day of the first month in Naga-saki, neighborhood councilmen and those responsible for the conduct of each local citizens' association dressed up in their finest clothes and made the rounds of every home, where they required each family member to trample on a brass image of Christ or the Virgin.

The trampling ritual was carried out every year on the twelfth day of the first month in Magome, at the home of the village headsman, Mr. Takaya. On that day, all the young men and women of Magome queued up in front of the headsman's house.

Stepping on the *fumie*, of course, served as a witness to the officials that an individual was not secretly practicing the illicit religion of Christianity. Each person ground his bare foot into the plaque etched with the face of either Christ or Mary, thereby affirming beyond question that he did not believe in the "heretical faith of the Southern Barbarians."

Both old and young gathered at the headsman's home on the twelfth day. They lined up outside and then filed in one by one, where they stood in the dirt floor entrance of the house. A *fumie* on loan from the magistrate's office greeted them as they stepped up onto the blackly glistening wood floor. Seated in front of them were the sullen-faced headsman, Mr. Takaya, and a priest from the Shōtokuji, the local Buddhist temple where each family had its name registered.

Under the watchful gaze of these two men, the villagers stepped up one at a time onto the wooden floor, paused before the *fumie*, and then trampled on it.

Ichijirō inevitably grumbled each time this day arrived. "They should know by now that none of us are Kirishitans without making us do that." The hard-working young man maintained that he could have produced several pairs of straw sandals in the time it took him to go the headsman's house and come back.

Once when Mitsu was young, she stood before the *fumie* and turned back to ask her brother, "Who are these people?"

"The ones on the plaque?" Ichijirō replied loudly enough for the headsman and the priest to hear. "It's an evil man and his mom. He did terrible things. That's why he got punished in that way."

Innocent Mitsu believed without question what her older brother told her. And following her brother's instructions, she placed her tiny foot on the *fumie*.

The *fumie* on which her tiny foot rested was engraved with an image of the mournful Santa Maria, both her arms cradling the body of Jesus that had been taken down from the cross. Jesus's face was filled with grief, and Mary's was wet with tears.

Unlike Mitsu, each time Kiku stepped on the image, she felt vague misgivings. She had once asked Ichijirō, "What kind of awful things did this man do?"

"He told a lot of lies to deceive people. Anyway, it's a story that belongs to the Southern Barbarians." Since he knew no details, Ichijirō was not confident in the response he gave to his young cousin's question.

"What are you grumbling about there?" The Shōtokuji priest scolded Kiku. "When someone older tells you to step on it, you'd better hurry and step on it. Your problem is that unlike Mitsu, you're always pressing your luck."

Kiku was frightened of the priest. At this rebuke, even the feisty Kiku dejectedly stomped on the *fumie* with all her might.

One day, the priest of the Shōtokuji brought news to Mitsu and Kiku of an opportunity to work as domestic help. The employer was a mercantile house by the name of Gotōya in Nagasaki.

"No matter how you look at it, Kiku is an insufferable tomboy. And Mitsu is a pampered child. That's why I think that going to Nagasaki and working for about a year would prepare them to be good brides," was the assessment of the chief priest.

Shōtokuji was the temple among the many in the region where the citizens of Magome were required to register their religious affiliation and where all their weddings and funerals were conducted. Every birth and death had to be reported to this temple. That made the chief priest of the temple a counselor to all the adults of Magome and a teacher to all the children. Parents of the village gave diffident ear to everything he said.

His current proposition was not out of the ordinary. Many young women of Magome had gone to work as servants at merchant houses in Nagasaki at the urging of this chief priest. When they were given leave to return home for Obon and the New Year festivities, the girls who still lived in the village were eager to hear their stories. Their curiosity sprang from the fact that unlike the boys of the village, the girls were virtually never allowed to visit Nagasaki, even though it was not far away. Relatives who had gone to the farmers' market told them that there were Chinese (called *Acha* by the locals) and Dutch people in

Nagasaki, but the girls' curiosity to see them was tempered by a fear that they might be roughed up by those foreigners, who thus far existed only in their imaginations. Still, each time they heard about the Nagasaki Kunchi Festival[1] or the bustling activity around Shian Bridge, their hearts began to pound.

And that is why, when her parents and grandmother hesitated to answer, muttering something like "Mitsu and Kiku are still a little young to be maidservants," Kiku jumped right in and said, "Reverend, I'll go!"

"So you'll go, will you, Kiku?" This put the priest in good spirits, but he made sure to emphasize for her: "But Kiku, working as a servant isn't like going on picnics or a flower-viewing excursion. You can't be unruly the way you are here at home. You have to accept the fact that there will be difficult times as well. . . . And what about you, Mitsu?"

"If Kiku's going, so am I," she answered without hesitation, as if it were only natural. Since their childhood, she'd formed the habit of following after Kiku in everything.

"Well now, well now . . ." Their parents delayed giving a final answer, and after the priest had left, they discussed with Kiku the trials of working in a stranger's home.

"But if I work there, it will help out our family, too."

They had no answer to that. It was true that having Kiku and Mitsu working at a merchant house in Nagasaki could certainly bolster the household finances a bit.

"Mitsu." When the two of them were alone, Kiku gave her gentle cousin some encouragement, "There's nothing to worry about. We'll learn so much more in a place like Nagasaki than here in this village that always stinks of manure."

"I'm not worried. I'll be with you," Mitsu said with a grin.

It was around the end of the Spring Festival[2] that the priest of Shōtokuji made the final arrangement for Kiku's and Mitsu's employment. During the Spring Festival the children of Magome fashioned a white rat out of *daikon*

---

1. The Kunchi Festival in Nagasaki, held at the Suwa Shinto Shrine over a three-day period each autumn, "was first celebrated in 1634. . . . [It] was originally a part of the [shogunate] policy to forge a Yamato spirit for Nagasaki, which up to 1614 had been Japan's only Christian town. In other words, the Kunchi festival started out as an anti-Christian festival" (Reinier Hesselink, "The Dutch and the Kunchi Festival of Nagasaki in the Seventeenth Century" [manuscript]).

Containing elements of both Dutch and Chinese culture, the popular festival includes snake dances, Chinese dragons, and the parading of large wooden boats.

2. Setsubun is a celebration held on the eve of the vernal equinox. Part of the traditional festivities includes tossing roasted soybeans while shouting "Out go the demons! In comes good fortune!"

radishes, which they placed on a tray and brought out in the morning, racing from house to house and shouting, "The White Rat's here!!" This was seemingly in imitation of what the children in Nagasaki did, but Kiku and Mitsu and her friends had been doing this since they were young.

Granny sang an auspicious "bean throwing" song for the benefit of her two granddaughters, who hereafter would be living in a stranger's home. It was a song from Sotome Village where Granny grew up.

Ebisu, the god of plenty,
Has come into our home
Scattering oh so many beans!
Just as Watanabe no Raikō,
Governor of Settsu Province,
Exterminated the saké-drinking demon
Of Mount Ōe in Tamba Province
(It's OK to say it,
It's OK not to say it),
Cast the evil spirits out,
Bring good fortune in!
Evil spirits out,
Good fortune in!
That's the way, that's the way!
Bring in lots of money!!

Kiku and Mitsu collapsed in laughter as they watched their Granny's toothless mouth spout out these words, but the realization that they would be leaving this home tomorrow made them somber. And they worried that they might make stupid mistakes in that unknown household or become a laughingstock. It was discouraging that nobody knew anything about the master of the house or any of its occupants.

"Ichijirō, you be sure and come visit us after you go to the farmers' market," they kept reminding him, and each time Ichijirō smiled and nodded, "Sure, I will."

The skies were clear the following morning. The two girls, escorted by Ichijirō and the priest, headed toward Nagasaki. When they left the house, their parents spoke not a word, and Granny wept. Neighborhood children gathered to watch in wonderment.

To their right, the ocean glittered brightly all the way to the horizon, and one large sailing ship floated atop it. This was the first foreign vessel that Mitsu or Kiku had ever seen. Neither the priest nor Ichijirō had any idea what country it belonged to, but the priest remarked, "The attitude of the magistrate's office has changed of late. Many ships of the Southern Barbarians come to Nagasaki now." He went on to mutter with some disgruntlement that the barbarians were now proudly walking the streets of Nagasaki. To his mind, America and Great Britain and Holland were all Southern Barbarian nations, and the barbarians themselves were believers in a profane religion.

"Of course, sir." Ichijirō, who had no idea what any of this was about, bowed his head apologetically, as though the priest's irritation was his own fault.

A black kite soared across the brilliant sky. They had walked for a long while, and the road along the beach became an incline. This hill was called Nishizaka, where in the past an execution ground had been located. Dozens of the heretical Christians so hated by the chief priest of Shōtokuji had been executed here.

Once they climbed the hill and began their descent, the city of Nagasaki lay before them.

Unlike Magome, where every home was a thatched-roof farmhouse, here the streets were jammed with black-tiled residences. They could also see the steeples of churches. They noticed a red Chinese-style building.

"Well now, this is Nagasaki!" Ichijirō poked his sister's shoulder.

It was so unlike their village of Magome, which was dotted with farmhouses built between rice paddies and fields and groves of trees. The two girls were utterly overwhelmed, and all they could do was walk forlornly beside the priest and Ichijirō, making sure not to get separated from them.

"Oh, look!" Mitsu came to a dead stop, her eyes wide in astonishment as she spotted some Chinese walking along, their braided hair sweeping down over the shoulders of their mandarin garb. They climbed the stone stairs directly beside where the Japanese stood and disappeared through the vermilion gates of a Chinese temple.

As the group from Magome continued on, the priest stopped and pointed to a stone bridge crossing a river. "This is Meganebashi—Spectacle Bridge. See, it looks just like eyeglasses, doesn't it?" The supports of the bridge reflected on the surface of the water in such a way that the shape really did look like a pair of glasses.

Houses, then more houses. A long wall surrounding a temple, followed by a gigantic roof. They climbed one hill, turned to the right, then ascended yet another hill.

"We're almost there."

Soon they were standing in front of a large dry-goods store. Apprentices and customers of the shop scurried in and out through the dyed curtain at the doorway. The name "Gotōya" was written boldly across the curtain.

"Wait here." Leaving the other three standing next to the shop, the Shōtokuji priest nimbly disappeared through the curtain.

They waited a long while.

"What do you think's going on?" Mitsu tugged nervously at Kiku's sleeve. Ichijirō, who had been carrying the girls' two wicker trunks, finally lowered them to the ground and sat on one. Then suddenly he got to his feet and whispered to his sister, "Mitsu! There's a Southern Barbarian heading this way!"

A tall man who appeared to be totally encased in white robes was coming toward them.

His nose truly was enormous. His hair was as golden as corn silk. And his skin was pinkish.

"Oh, my!" Even more astonished than when she saw the Chinese men, Mitsu swallowed hard and gripped Kiku's hand. Their hands tightly joined, the two girls watched apprehensively as the foreigner passed by them.

"G'morning!" As he walked by, the barbarian suddenly smiled and greeted them in an oddly accented voice, but the two stood frozen and said nothing.

Finally Mitsu exhaled something that was either a sigh or a moan and said, "That was scary!"

"What was scary about it? The Southern Barbarians aren't devils, you know," Kiku chided her.

Eventually the priest reemerged from the shop. "The Mistress says she will meet you. But you three can't come in this way. Employees have to enter through the service door." He pointed to a narrow doorway at the side of the shop.

What transpired thereafter neither Mitsu nor Kiku remembered very well, having been so stressed as it was happening. The Mistress of the Gotōya came out holding a toothache plaster against her jaw and examined the two girls from head to toe.

"You girls simply must work in good harmony with all the others," she announced, summoning the oldest servant, Oyone, who apparently held a position something like head servant, and after instructing Ichijirō to take the girls' trunks to a room on the second floor, Oyone introduced the girls to Tome, who worked in the kitchen.

"Tome came to us from the Gotō Islands. Many of the men serving here at our shop come from Gotō, just as the shop name says. I myself was born in Ōmura," Oyone smiled, showing her gums.

Tome was the same age as Kiku. Tome gave a brief nod and went back to work, watching from a distance as the two new girls were taught many things about the shop.

"So there's five shopboys. Making breakfast for them will be enough to make your head spin. There'll be no sleeping in for you." Then Oyone lowered her voice and said, "The Mistress here is pretty rough on her employees." Again she smiled a gummy smile.

"Ichijirō, it's OK for you to go now," Kiku called out to her cousin who waited quietly and anxiously in a corner of the entryway. "If you don't go now, you won't make it back to Magome before the sun goes down."

"Yeah." Ichijirō nodded, but he cast a worried look at the two girls and said, "You two give it your all now." He nodded to Oyone and went out onto the road, where the sun still shone brightly.

When Ichijirō had passed from view, Mitsu felt as though she had been abandoned. Now her cousin Kiku was the only person she had to rely on.

Oyone, after ordering the two girls to help Tome clean the kitchen and the earthen floor of the entryway, disappeared inside.

As Kiku wrung out her cleaning rag, she asked Tome, "Is the Mistress really so strict?"

Tome nodded. "Yeah, she is. It's like the missus in 'Three Years at Hard Labor.'"

"Three years at—?"

"You don't know that? On Gotō in the old days, if a family couldn't pay their land taxes, their daughters were forced into three years of hard labor for the ruler." In a soft voice, Tome sang a folk song from the Gotō Islands:

When you're shipped out for three years at hard labor,
Your mistress will be strict. . . .
In the morning, she sends you to the fields;
At noon, she sends you to the mountains;
At night, you work till eight.
No doubt the mistress will have no worries in the future,
While we'll end up cripples.

That was the start of Mitsu's and Kiku's lives in Nagasaki.

"You can't be pampered children anymore," the priest of the Shōtokuji had repeatedly cautioned them as they were leaving the village. And he was right: Starting the day after their arrival, their lives became incredibly demanding, even for girls who were accustomed to the challenging daily routine at a farmhouse.

For starters, they had to wake up at the first cock's crow. The maidservants had the responsibility of preparing breakfast and cleaning up after the servants and the family who operated the Gotōya. Their first task was to light the fire, boil the water, and draw drinking water.

When the sky began to grow light, the girls raised in the backwater of Magome had the unusual experience of hearing the voices of door-to-door tradesmen making their rounds.

"What are those voices?" they asked Tome, who explained to them what the men were shouting.

Shibayashi bai!
Hana ya hanai, hanainai!
Ko-ko! Kyu!

They gathered that the fellow calling out "*Hana ya hanai, hanainai!*" was strolling around selling flowers, but it was news to them that the man shouting "*Shibayashi bai!*" was talking about the evergreen branches that people placed on the tiny Shinto altars in their homes, and that "*Ko-ko! Kyu!*" came from a man hawking the radishes and other pickled vegetables that they served with breakfast.

They had no problem lighting fires or boiling water, since these were things they had done back in Magome, but they were left breathless when it came to racing back and forth over and over between the well and the kitchen in order to scoop water with little pails and pour it into a huge kettle. When the Mistress of the house finally got up and saw Kiku and Mitsu working at that together, she scolded them:

"Mitsu should be able to do that by herself. Kiku, you go sweep in front of the shop."

The Mistress was just as tough on her staff as Tome had warned, and she found no shortage of faults to pick at.

"Mitsu, why are you so out of breath?"

"Tome, this rice is as hard as rocks. It's inedible!"

About the time they completed their chores, the apprentices had gotten out of bed, and the girls began to wipe down the floors inside the shop. They crawled around on their hands and knees, polishing the floors until they glistened.

When the shop master awakened, he gathered all the clerks and apprentices and his wife to offer up prayers before both the Shinto and Buddhist altars. Then breakfast would begin. The maidservants were allowed to eat at seats on a lower level, but they had little time to savor the taste of their food, since they had to be constantly scurrying around refilling the men's soup and rice bowls.

Both Kiku and Mitsu lost themselves in their work for the first five or six days. They didn't even have time to think "I hate this," or "I'm so sad," or "I want to go back to Magome!"

"Mitsu, those cracks must hurt!"

Blood was seeping out of cracks in Mitsu's hands from having to scoop out water almost ceaselessly. Kiku winced as she looked at Mitsu's hands and mumbled encouragingly, "My hands really itch where they got chilblains."

Still, Kiku's determined self-respect would not allow her to utter a word of complaint, since this work was something she had volunteered to do.

And then something unexpected happened.

Some six months since they'd come to work at the shop, they awoke to a cold morning, even though the spring equinox had passed.

The servants had to get up extra early that day, since the master was taking his head clerks on the "Seven High Mountains" pilgrimage. This was an event in which the participants visited seven of the hills around Nagasaki and made votive offerings at each mountaintop temple. Many of the shop owners participated in this ritual.

Puffing on her hands that were numb with cold, Kiku swept the road in front of the shop with a broom. Mitsu endured the pain in her chapped hands as she scooped up water.

"*Mozukuhyai, O-sahyai!*" The cries of the morning tradesmen echoed from down the road. Both *mozuku* and *o-sa* were kinds of seaweed sold in early spring in Nagasaki.

One young tradesman, only slightly older than Kiku, drew closer to her as she swept and asked, "Need any *mozuku?*"

"Nope," she answered curtly. But then she took a quick glance at the man's face and gulped hard. Even though ten years had passed, she still remembered the young man's face.

She couldn't forget it.

It was the young man who had saved her when she had tried to climb the huge camphor tree on a dare from Snotnose and Crybaby.

"Ummm—" Kiku hurriedly called to him as he started to move on. "Ummm—" Nothing else would come out of her mouth.

"Yes?" The youth smiled, showing healthy teeth. "The miss would like to buy some *mozuku?*"

"Aren't you from Nakano in Urakami, sir?" Her manner of speech became a bit more polite.

The young man gazed curiously at this girl who knew what village he was from. "How do you know that? Are you from Urakami, miss?"

"Yes," Kiku nodded. "I know you."

"You know me?" He eyed her suspiciously.

"I do. When I was little, you saved me when I climbed up a tree and couldn't get down."

"Saved you?" He crunched his eyes into an even narrower stare, trying to summon up an old memory as he looked into Kiku's face. "Ah! I remember when that happened. . . . Well, you've certainly become a fine young lady."

Kiku blushed and averted her eyes. "Another girl from back home works here, too. She's over there." She pointed toward Mitsu, who was dipping up water.

Mitsu was pouring water from the well bucket into several smaller pails she had arranged in a row. The well water was still as cold as ice.

"Mitsu!" She turned around at Kiku's voice. "Hey, take a good look. You remember this fellow, don't you?"

A young peddler wearing a familiar smile stood next to Kiku.

"You've forgotten, haven't you? Remember when I climbed that tree and got stuck, and there was a young man who saved me? That was this gentleman!"

Mitsu's jaw dropped open vacantly as she stood with empty buckets in each hand.

Kiku said proudly, "He was passing by here on his morning sales route. He sure took me by surprise!"

The young man looked piteously at Mitsu's bare wet feet and chapped hands and said to Kiku, "I guess being a maid is rough, eh?"

"But I'm not by myself. Mitsu and I work here together. It's not at all lonely."

The young man nodded but said nothing and began pouring water into a bucket that Mitsu had set down. "I'll dip out the water for you. You just carry in the pails."

Mitsu nodded and set out for the kitchen with a full pail.

"My name's Kiku." Kiku announced her name loudly, as though she were disgruntled that the young man had focused his kindness on Mitsu.

"I'm Seikichi," he answered as he worked.

"So you come to Nagasaki every morning to do your sales?"

Seikichi smiled and nodded in response.

"Then I guess you go by here every morning . . ."

"Not every morning. Depending on the day, I sometimes go by way of Teramachi."

Knowing none of the directions in Nagasaki, Kiku had no idea where Teramachi might be.

"Why don't you come this way?"

Her disappointed look caught him off guard. "Well . . . I don't really care which way I go, so long as there's somebody willing to buy *mozuku*."

"Ummm . . ." Kiku paused a moment, then swallowed hard. "Please come by here every morning. That way we can talk." After she said it, she blushed.

Seikichi flinched at Kiku's boldness, but soon he was grinning. Just the way an older brother smiles wryly at a willful younger sister.

"Fine, fine. I'll come by here as often as I can."

"Really?" Kiku beamed as she clutched her broom. "You're telling the truth, right?"

Oyone called loudly to Kiku from the kitchen. "Kiku, don't be dawdling out there. Hurry in here and light the stove!"

Kiku clacked her tongue. "Horrible woman!" But after cursing her boss, she said, "I'll see you again. For sure, yes?" and ran toward the kitchen, carrying her broom.

For the rest of the day she was in a daze and was frequently scolded by Oyone and corrected by Tome. In actuality she spent the day staring blankly, wandering off from her chores, and gawking at an empty spot in space.

"Kiku!" Even docile little Mitsu couldn't stand it anymore and asked, "Is something wrong with you? You stand there looking so clueless!"

"Mitsu, what do you think of Seikichi?"

Her question caught Mitsu off guard. "What do I—?" Stuck for a reply, she said, "I think he's a good person."

"I really like him." *Like*: it wasn't customary for sixteen-year-old girls to come right out with no embarrassment and announce that they liked a young man.

"Kiku!" Mitsu was awestruck and virtually shouted, "What in the world has happened to you? You've lost your mind!"

But with calm composure Kiku proclaimed, "Mitsu, you can't tell anybody, but I'm going to marry Seikichi." Her words were also intended to put Mitsu on notice that she mustn't fall for Seikichi herself, even if by accident.

Mitsu gaped wide-eyed at her cousin. Since their childhood together she had known Kiku to be assertive and unequivocal and frank, but she had never imagined that she would blurt out something so discomfiting.

"Well, OK, but Seikichi . . ." Mitsu hesitated a moment. "He's from Nakano, you know. Your family would never permit it."

"And what's wrong with Nakano? Everybody there's the same as folks in Magome!" Kiku responded as though she herself were the one being vilified.

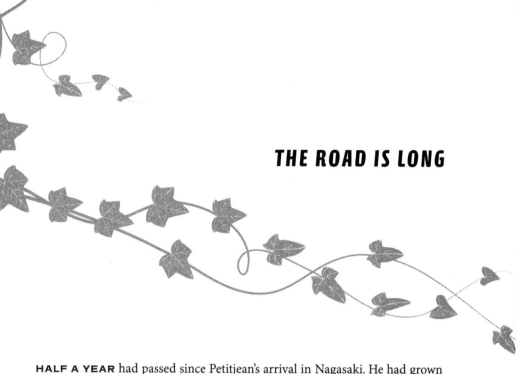

THE ROAD IS LONG

HALF A YEAR had passed since Petitjean's arrival in Nagasaki. He had grown quite comfortable with life here.

What left him most nonplussed was not the sweltering heat of the summer or even the strange flavors of the Japanese food that Okane cooked for him. As a priest who had come to Japan to preach the Gospel and who was determined to have his bones interred here, he was not bothered by such trivial things as the topography or the climate or the food.

What plagued him most was the fact that even with the Japanese language ability he had acquired in Naha and improved on with further study in Yoko-hama, he still could not understand much of what was being said in the Naga-saki dialect.

For instance, on one occasion Okane's husband, Mosaku, abruptly asked him, "*Bapo-san, oro-no?*" And he had no idea what the man was talking about. Only later did he learn that "*Bapo-san*" was their way of saying "the Master," with the master of the church here being Father Furet, and so the question meant "Is Father Furet here?"

Out of necessity he began studying the Nagasaki dialect each morning, with Mosaku as his study partner.

"*Donku*. What does that mean?"

"That there's a frog."

"I don't get *yosowashika*."

"It means 'filthy.'"

As he took his customary afternoon strolls through the streets of Nagasaki, whenever he heard a word he didn't understand, he quickly noted it down and asked Mosaku about it.

Just yesterday some women saw him and whispered among themselves, "*Yō chōmawari ba sareru to ne.*" He knew that *yō* meant "a lot," but no matter how hard he thought about it, he couldn't figure out what *chomawari* meant.

"*Chomawari?*" Okane's husband cocked his head, stumped by Petitjean's peculiar pronunciation, so he repeated it to himself several times until he said, "Oh, I think you mean *chōmawari.* If that's what it was, it means to walk around the city a lot."

Every day he was out *chōmawari*-ing. He set out every afternoon, come rain or wind. It was almost to the point that there was hardly anyone left in Nagasaki who had not seen him out walking in his cassock.

The people of Nagasaki were very kind. They always smiled and were gracious to him. If he asked for directions, they would explain politely until he understood, and sometimes when he took refuge from the heat in the shade of a tree, they brought him some cold well water to drink.

"Please come to my place and have a look around," he would invite them. "We have many unusual things for you to see."

Sometimes he took candy from the pocket of his cassock and offered it to children who were playing nearby, or he showed people his watch and his glasses, and he would point to his own nose and say "I am Petitjean," making every effort to help people feel comfortable around him. His objective, of course, was more complicated.

His strategy began to bear fruit. Before long everyone in Nagasaki had heard the name of Petitjean, who was living at the Nambanji, the Temple of the Southern Barbarians,[1] which was under construction. Once his name had spread abroad, some of the people he passed on the street began to acknowledge him with a smile.

The first to grow close to him were the children. Petitjean's stumbling attempts to use the Nagasaki dialect had melted away any trepidation the children might have felt toward him. Before long, children would bring him fruit when he paused in his incessant walking and rested beside the long wall surrounding a Buddhist temple.

"Mom said to give you this." Apparently this was an expression of gratitude for the candy he had previously given the children. But the parents of these children would not approach Petitjean themselves, instead having their children give him the fruit. He wasn't sure whether the parents were too embarrassed or still too guarded toward him.

---

1. The Nambanji (formally known among the Catholic population as the "Church of the Twenty-six Japanese Martyrs," in everyday parlance called the "Ōura Church") was completed in 1864.

One day, however, he quietly asked a group of children, "Do any of you know where I could find any Kirishitans?" At a loss, the children just shook their heads.

And for some reason, starting the next day they stopped flocking around Petitjean.

He tried gesturing to them to approach, saying, "Come here, don't you want any candy?"

But the response was, "No. My mom'll get mad."

"Why would she get mad at you?"

"She said I couldn't talk to you."

Petitjean was made aware that simply by asking, "Do you know where I could find any Kirishitans?" he had made the parents of these children exceedingly wary of him. He lamented his own rashness.

"It looks like it's going to take quite some time to win over these Japanese," he confided to Father Furet, who nodded in agreement.

"Even among themselves the Japanese regard someone as a foreigner if he lives just over the mountain or the other side of the river. How can we expect them to open their hearts to us foreigners in a mere six months or a year?"

"Is that because their country has been closed to foreign interaction for such a long time?"

"It's not just that. After all, the Japanese are surrounded on all four sides by oceans, so they've hardly ever met any foreigners before."

Petitjean, who had started out so optimistic about his mission, gradually grew perplexed as he sensed a thick wall separating himself from the Japanese people. Having experienced only courtesy and smiling faces—on the surface at least—among the people of Nagasaki, he never would have imagined that such a stubborn wall existed.

He began to lose hope. Perhaps the ramblings of that drunken Chinaman in the Ryūkyūs were all lies after all. If there really were any Christians hiding out here in Nagasaki, they should have come to him by now.

They probably just don't exist. In an effort to avoid total despair, Petitjean tried to persuade himself gradually.

But then one day something happened. It occurred while Petitjean was taking his customary stroll through the streets of Nagasaki.

He had passed through the residential district of the Chinese, whom the Japanese called Acha, and, as always, had emerged near Shianbashi. Just to the side of the bridge was the sort of pleasure quarter that would cause a missionary like him to knit his brows in disapproval, and the name of the bridge, Shian, meant "to ponder," because men who were about to yield to the temptation to visit the quarter would stand here and ponder whether they should enter.

He happened upon a crowd of people at the base of the bridge. There appeared to be some sort of fight going on.

Because he was so tall in stature, Petitjean merely had to stand behind the short Japanese in the crowd to have a clear view of what they were looking at.

Two tough-looking men were beating and kicking another man, who wasn't so innocent looking himself. The man being attacked appeared to have been drinking a great deal since morning, and he was unable either to stand and fight or to run away. He was left to the devices of the other two.

"This good-for-nothing—" Cursing as they indiscriminately kicked the man's head and face, the two men paused when they saw a Southern Barbarian in a white cassock suddenly standing before them.

"You mustn't do this! Stop it!" Petitjean shouted.

"What the—?" The two toughs, realizing it was a foreigner interrupting them, had the wind taken from their sails and grunted, "What do you want?"

"Stop it!" Petitjean shook his head. "Let him go."

"Let him go?" One of the toughs sneered and mocked Petitjean's words. "Well, since you put it that way, I totally surrender." He lowered his fist that was raised in the air. "This is the first time I've ever had a fight broken up by a Southern Barbarian. Wait till the guys hear about this!"

The two thugs laughed and walked away, but the onlookers continued to stare at Petitjean and the cudgeled man.

"Are you wounded?" Petitjean took a handkerchief from his pocket and wiped away the blood that was streaming down the man's cheek. "This must be painful."

"Yeah." The man's bobbed his head up and down in grateful humiliation.

"Where do you live? Would you like me to take you home?"

"No, I don't need you to do that." The man staggered to his feet and again gave a bow. The crowd began to disperse.

Seeing that the fellow could manage to walk, Petitjean gave a shallow bow and turned to leave. But the man called out to him, "Sir?"

Petitjean turned back. "What is it?"

The man flashed him an obsequious smile. "Mr. Foreigner, tell me something I can do for you." He bowed again.

"Something you can do?"

"To thank you for saving me. I'll run errands or do anything. I can take you to see a nice young lady."

The fellow had no idea that Petitjean was a priest. He likely wouldn't know what a priest was even if he heard the title.

"No thank you." Petitjean looked a bit angry. He had often watched with disgust as sailors from foreign warships that had docked in Nagasaki harbor came ashore looking for Japanese whores.

He took five or six steps away but then abruptly changed his mind. When he turned back around, the man peered at him with a somewhat surprised look.

He didn't seem able to grasp why his offer to provide a "nice young lady" had been refused.

"Will you really do anything I ask of you?" Petitjean peered unwaveringly at the man, then reached into his pocket and took out a one-franc silver coin that he had brought with him from France. "Take a look at this. I assume you know what silver is."

Petitjean saw greed flash across the man's eyes as he gazed at the foreign silver coin and continued, "If you do what I ask, I'll give you this."

"You'll give to me?"

"That's right."

The man displayed his yellowed teeth in a smile.

"What do you want me to do?"

"Do you know any Kirishitans?"

"Kirishitans?"

"Yes."

The man cocked his head and mumbled, "Kirishitans," but his face evinced none of the fear or hesitation that other Japanese had shown in response to this question.

Just maybe . . .

Petitjean felt a faint hope stir in his heart for the first time. Perhaps this man would give him the information he sought. If that were to happen, he would not begrudge a single franc coin: he would gladly give away all his means.

"Do you know any?"

"You have some business with Kirishitans, do you?"

"Yes."

"It'll be difficult," the man sighed deeply. "The Kirishitan faith is banned, you know. B-a-n-n-e-d."

"So you don't know any Kirishitans." Petitjean deliberately twirled the silver coin between his fingers. "Then you won't be getting this." He thrust the coin back into his pocket.

The man swallowed audibly. The foul sound was like a bald display of the man's lust for the silver foreign coin.

"All right," he muttered with a sigh. "I'll take you to them. But who knows what kind of punishment I'll get from the magistrate if I get found out. This is a dangerous bridge to cross, Mr. Foreigner."

Then the man thrust three fingers into Petitjean's face. He was giving clear notice that he would not take on this task for a single coin but that he required three.

The man had obviously read Petitjean's heart. He seemed quite aware of how keenly this Southern Barbarian wanted to find out where the Kirishitans were hiding.

Petitjean stared at the man's three extended fingers, then looked at the cunning face, and for a time he said nothing.

He had a powerful impression that he could not trust this Japanese fellow. But he would be left without any way to locate the people he was seeking if he didn't make a decisive wager on this man.

"Fine." Petitjean nodded, keeping his eyes riveted on the man's face. "But you're being truthful with me, aren't you?" He searched his pocket, pulled out one silver coin, and handed it to the man. "Once you actually take me to the Kirishitans, I'll give you the other two."

A filthy hand with grime under its fingernails shot out and grabbed the coin and jammed it into the man's pocket. For some reason Petitjean pictured Judas betraying Lord Jesus.

"Are we going right now?"

"Now?" Surprised, the man shook his head. "We can't go till after dark. We'd best meet up here again at Shianbashi after it gets dark."

Petitjean had the feeling the man would not show up. But he could not argue with the man and was left with no choice but to agree with his plan.

When he returned to Ōura, Father Furet was standing in his customary spot at the work site, observing the progress of the construction. When Petitjean told him what had just occurred, Father Furet laughed heartily.

"You're so gullible. You've just tossed your money into a swamp."

"So you think he was lying?"

"Of course he was! You've been taken in, my friend."

Petitjean went to his room, opened the window, and gazed out at the bay of Nagasaki as the sun set, all the while keeping in check his mounting anger.

Even so, he finished his dinner quickly, slipped out without Father Furet noticing, and hurried down the hill. Someone was flying a kite above the slope that was surrounded by farmland.

The area was bustling with people as he approached Shianbashi. They all were on their way to the pleasure quarter, known as Maruyama. Petitjean stopped at the foot of the bridge and searched for the man. He was there . . . !

Reflecting back later on how he had felt when he spotted the man, Petitjean remembered that an overpowering joy had suffused his heart. An elation that the man had kept his promise. But his joy was overshadowed for a brief moment by the humiliation he felt for having doubted the man.

Petitjean tapped the man's bony shoulder. "I'm sorry, friend. Have I kept you waiting?"

"Ah, Mr. Foreigner." The man flashed the few remaining yellowed teeth he had. And the smell of liquor issued from his mouth. Evidently he had traded away the silver coin he got from Petitjean and had spent every subsequent minute drinking in some bar.

"You've had quite a bit of liquor, haven't you?"

"I haven't been drinking. No, sir, I haven't been drinking, Mr. Foreigner." The man waved his hand in denial, but he couldn't conceal the unsteady gait that was the result of his drunkenness.

"Well, Mr. Foreigner," the man scanned their surroundings. "So you're looking for *Kuros*?"

"*Kuros*?"

"Don't say *Kuro* so loud, Mr. Foreigner! If the police hear it, you won't be the only one they'll take off in ropes." With one hand the man wiped the saliva from his mouth and then mumbled a number of words Petitjean couldn't understand.

Exasperated, Petitjean said curtly, "Please take me to them right now."

"I will, I will!" The man set off falteringly, clinging to the bridge railing to steady himself.

Mount Kazagashira soared blackly against the darkened sky. From Shianbashi, the man started up a road in the direction of Mount Kazagashira, in the opposite direction from Dejima and the Ōhato.[2] The road climbed a steep slope that passed over the mountains and then descended to Mogi Bay.

"Wait just a minute." The man stopped along the slope, and as he relieved himself he said, "The *Kuros* don't like being found out, so we've gotta keep that in mind."

The zigzagging slope was edged on either side by fields and rice paddies. Arable land was so scarce in Nagasaki that plots were cultivated up onto the hills and even up the mountain slopes.

They spotted a large thatched farmhouse surrounded by fields.

"That's it." The man stopped and lowered his voice. "That's a house where some *Kuros* live."

Petitjean took a deep breath and peered at the gray, melancholy house. His heart began to pound like a drum as he realized that he might have finally located what he had been looking for from the day he met that Chinese man in Naha.

"Kirishitans are in there?" He asked in halting Japanese, his voice quivering. He continued forward along the path between the fields and approached the farmhouse.

He could hear the faint voices of a large number of people inside. A large group of men had assembled in the house and were talking about something in low voices.

"What are they doing?"

"Dunno." The man shrugged. "I don't know much about what the Kirishitans do. Maybe they're having some kind of chat."

2. Ōhato is a post station on the harbor, located just across the canal from Dejima.

"A chat?"

"Look, Mr. Foreigner, I kept my promise. Can you just give me the money?" The man thrust out his hand and gave another avaricious grin, displaying his few remaining teeth.

"No, no." Petitjean shook his head. "I'll give that to you later."

"What do you mean, 'later'?"

"You'll get it once I find out whether this is really them."

Petitjean listened intently through the paper sliding doors. A bright candle glimmered within, and the men inside the room occasionally sighed or stirred. Among them, one high voice was giving some sort of instructions to the others.

Are they praying? He wondered as he listened to their voices. There was a certain rhythm to the voice giving direction, like the leader of a choir. Then it sounded like pages were being turned and some object being tossed about.

He looked behind him and saw the man who had brought him here peering anxiously toward him from some distance away.

"Come over here."

"No! I'm no Kirishitan. Just hurry and give me what you promised."

When Petitjean tossed a single coin, the man clambered like a dog and scooped it up, then fled like a dog. No doubt he feared being associated with the Kirishitans.

Petitjean stood in place until the voices stopped. If he were suddenly to show himself in his priestly garb, he wondered how these Kirishitans would respond. Would they be happy to see him?

The voices broke off. He could almost sense the flickering of the heavy candle's flame.

"Who's there?"

Had they seen his shadow against the paper doors?

"Do you think it's the boss from the Fukuda Shop?"

"He wouldn't be coming tonight."

After this exchange, the paper door was jerked open.

"Ah!" A tattooed man with a band of white cotton cloth wrapped around his abdomen cried out in surprise. The priest saw all the men sitting in the room hurriedly conceal wooden talismans that were set in front of them.

"Wait, you're—" He recognized the face of one of the men who leaped to his feet. It was one of the two toughs who had been beating the man at Shianbashi earlier today.

"Hey, it's a Southern Barbarian! Why would one of them be coming here?" one man cried hysterically.

"A Southern Barbarian?" A rough-looking fellow emerged from the back of the group. "Say, this is the foreigner we ran into at Shianbashi today, isn't it?"

Then someone said, "So you know him, Tatsu?"

"Naw, he's no friend of mine. Around noon today, there was a guy who was trying to sell stuff at Maruyama without a license, and we were smacking him around at Shianbashi when this foreigner here got in the middle of it. That's all I know about him."

Then this fellow called Tatsu said to Petitjean, "Mr. Foreigner, what brings you to our little gambling den? You a dice player?" The man coiled his fingers and pretended to be shaking dice. The men in the room burst out laughing.

Petitjean wasn't sure what the man was saying, but he opened his eyes wide and asked, "Then you men aren't Kirishitans?"

"Kirishitans? You trying to pick a fight with us, Mr. Foreigner?"

Seeing the outraged faces of the men, Petitjean realized that he had been hoodwinked by the man who had brought him to a place totally unrelated to his search.

"You're not going to find any Kirishitans in Nagasaki, no matter where you look," Tatsu asserted. "We Japanese have been warned in no uncertain terms that we can't believe in that sect. You'd better leave, Mr. Foreigner." Then he looked around at his colleagues. "Damned intruder! It's a bad omen." With one hand he slammed the paper door shut with a bang.

Left standing outside alone, Petitjean turned around, but the man who led him here had disappeared into the night. Simply put, Petitjean had been conned out of his money.

That night he returned to Ōura with bloody feet—he had stumbled across stones on his return up the slope—only to run into Father Furet, who in his concern over Petitjean's whereabouts had set out with Okane's husband to find him.

"Bernard." Father Furet placed a sympathetic hand on his brother's shoulder and tried to console him. "I know just how you feel. But this senseless obstinacy isn't healthy for you. Let me just come right out and say it: There's not a single Christian left here in Japan. It's been more than two hundred years since the ban was imposed. They all either died or succumbed to the beastly persecution. How could they possibly have passed on their faith to their descendants? You must give this up."

The words "give up" sank bitterly and despondently into Petitjean's heart. But he was, in fact, utterly weary of the quest. Father Furet was right. It was hopeless to try to find any Christian believers here in Japan . . .

Winter gradually made its way toward spring. The hue of the clouds floating above Mount Inasa softened and took on a pinkish tint. The clouds reminded Petitjean of the flocks of sheep that were raised in the countryside of his faraway homeland.

Though spring was at hand, Petitjean's heart was weighed down in gloom. The young priest was deeply discouraged by the realization that the people he had been searching for in Japan did not exist.

In contrast to the despondent Petitjean, Father Furet was in fine spirits. Thanks to the diligent labors of the workmen, construction on the church was progressing remarkably well.

The building was neither strictly Gothic nor completely Rococo but, rather, a mix of the two styles, and naturally it showed every sign of becoming the most unusual and modern building not only in Nagasaki but in all of Japan. The foreign residents in Nagasaki were of one voice in acclaiming it a "charming little church." Apparently to these Europeans, who were accustomed to seeing majestic cathedrals all around them, the church seemed tiny and enchanting, as attractive as the young ladies of Nagasaki. But the Japanese in Nagasaki surely regarded it as a magnificent structure, on the scale of a grand palace.

Spectators thronged nonstop around the building. Some, hearing rumors about the church, had reportedly come from as far as Sotome to see it.[3]

"This church," Father Furet triumphantly informed the Japanese, "is not a person's house. It is the house of God."

He was amused that whenever he said this, the Japanese spectators, whose mouths had dropped open, retreated back a few steps and with worried looks muttered, "Really?"

Of course, because they were prohibited from having any association with Christianity, none of these Japanese spectators would make even the slightest move to go inside the nearly completed building.

Father Furet lamented that fact. He wished he could show these Japanese the statues of Jesus and the Blessed Mother inside and explain to them just what manner of house of God was here. Were he to give even the slightest indication of doing so, however, the eyes of the officers from the magistrate's office would flash with anger. No doubt he would receive complaints from an official named Itō Seizaemon, who came to the site every other day, claiming it was just his "normal rounds."

While Father Furet was absorbed in the completion of the chapel, Petitjean continued his afternoon strolls of Nagasaki. He no longer had any expectation of encountering hidden Christians, but he was convinced that having the people on the street remember his face would serve him in good stead when the time came that he was allowed to proselytize.

---

3. Sotome, a tiny fishing village that has recently been incorporated into Nagasaki City, is both the model for Tomogi Village in Endō's famed novel *Silence* and the location of the Endō Shūsaku Literary Museum. It is approximately a forty-minute drive from downtown Nagasaki.

One day he came upon something truly unusual. Some boys had set up two poles, and they were gluing tiny shards of glass to a string stretched between them.

"What are you doing?" he asked.

One boy jabbered, "Making *ikanoyoma!*" animatedly.

Petitjean had made it a practice whenever he didn't understand something in the Nagasaki dialect to ask what it meant, even if it came from the mouth of a child.

"*Ika*? What's that?"

The boy gaped at him as though he were an idiot and said, "*Ika* is an *ika*, of course. It means 'squid,' but it's a kite! When you stick a paper tail on it, it looks like a squid, you know?" Kites in Nagasaki at this time were called either *ika*, squid, or *hata*, flags.

"And what is a *yoma*?"

"It's this string." It gradually dawned on him: these children were busily gluing a mixture of glass shavings and rice kernels to the string of a kite.

"Ah, yes!" Petitjean remembered that Okane's husband had told him that Nagasaki was famous for kite flying. Each spring the citizens held a heathen festival honoring Kompira, the guardian god of seafaring. It was a highly animated celebration, with pilgrims gathering from near and far, jostling like waves on the ocean, and each local participated in what they called the Clash of the Kites.

The Clash of the Kites was a competition in which participants attempted to get the string of their kite tangled with the string of an opponent's kite and cut the enemy's string. Both adults and children took this contest seriously. Undoubtedly these boys were gluing glass shards to their kite strings in preparation for the Clash.

"Is it OK if I watch you for a while?" Petitjean always had ready some candy made from potatoes for just such an occasion. The potato candies, called *tankiri*, were a gift to help him make friends with the children.

Thanks to the *tankiri* that Petitjean gave them, the boys were more than happy to let this Southern Barbarian watch as they industriously glued the glass shavings to the string that they had wound around the poles, which were held up by a horizontal bar.

Soon, however, a man appeared from an alley and eyed Petitjean suspiciously.

"Mr. Foreigner, would you like to buy one of these *ika*?" he inquired.

"Are you selling them?"

"Oh, yes. We make 'em so we can sell 'em. This one here is called an *agoika*—she'll cut a lot better than your regular kite." He proudly pointed out to Petitjean a kite with a scarlet triangle drawn on it. "What do you say, Mr. Foreigner? Why don't you try competing with one of these kites?"

Petitjean smiled. "What, me? I don't think I could."

"It's not that hard, Mr. Foreigner. . . . I'll teach you." He explained that Chinese from Dōza[4] and Dutch from Dejima participated in the Clash of the Kites. People flocked to the festival this one day from as far away as Shimabara and Isahaya.

Aha. So I could use this to make my presence known not just in Nagasaki but in some of the surrounding villages as well. There's a chance I might find "them" among those who gather here.

The dream that he had abandoned was revived.

"All right, I'll join the fray!"

That evening when he described the events of the day to Father Furet, his comrade looked uncommonly sullen.

"Bernard, you can't go on forever chasing dreams like a little child. There is much important work awaiting you at this Ōura Church that's about to be completed. In place of me . . ." He paused. "Actually, a letter came today from our Society in Paris. I . . . I have to go back to France for a time."

"Can that be true?"

"Why would I lie to you? And so you simply must abandon your dream of finding the descendants of Christians here in Nagasaki."

"But you will be returning to Nagasaki, yes?"

"Of course I will. I can't just forsake this church I've built."

Despite the scolding he received from Father Furet, Petitjean's objectives remained unchanged. In such matters he was as stubborn as a mule.

The following day, he began learning from the kite man, whose name was Sakichi, how to get a kite up into the sky, how to maneuver it in close to the enemy's kite, and how to cut their strings.

"Now, watch closely."

Open fields were numerous in Nagasaki. Sakichi took Petitjean to one of these fields, had him take hold of the kite, and then put his own grimy hand on top of the priest's and began his instruction.

"OK. First I've got to teach you how to get the kite up in the air." As Sakichi nimbly played out or pulled in the string, the kite floated like a living creature into the sky and finally began to circle slowly overhead.

The fingers that worked the string seemed like those of an artist deftly strumming a musical instrument. Petitjean for a time lost himself in his enjoyment of the duet between Sakichi and his kite.

"See, Mr. Foreigner? The kite's a living thing. If you work in harmony with her, you can move her around freely. If you wind the string on top of your finger like this, you can bring 'er right up next to your enemy's kite."

4. Until it was closed in the mid-eighteenth century, a mint where copper coins were cast was located in the Dōza (copper guild) District of Nagasaki.

Once you're lined up with the enemy, you don't challenge them right away. You have to watch for the right opportunity and then "go in for the kill," Sakichi taught him. In the language of Nagasaki, "going in for the kill" meant to intertwine your kite with your opponent's.

This was not the time to yank on your string. Instead, you let it out. In the local parlance, you "give her string." If the enemy is a worthy opponent, he will let out his string, too. It's in that moment that the contest begins.

That afternoon, like a laborer being taught skills by his boss, Petitjean was corrected and admonished by Sakichi and coached how to take in and let out his string.

It was a while before he noticed that a group of about ten adults and children had gathered in the open field and were grinning as they watched Petitjean's clumsy handling of the kite.

"OK, that's enough," Sakichi nodded, wiping away the sweat. "Mr. Foreigner, we'll have another practice here tomorrow. At this next Kompira Festival, you've got to beat out that hairy barbarian from Dejima."

Petitjean was stumped by this strange comment, so Sakichi explained. Every year on the tenth day of the third month, in every corner of town kite-flying competitions are held in conjunction with the Kompira Festival. The locations are not limited to Mount Kompira. Any open field will do. There were even some who climbed up on the roof of their own house, sent up their kites, and did battle with their neighbors.

But three years ago, a young Dutchman challenged the Japanese of Nagasaki to a battle of the kites from the roof of a Dutch trading house in Dejima.

"He's just a silly Dutchman!" Men from surrounding roofs who were seeking out opponents laughed scornfully at him and took him up on his challenge, but he was unexpectedly skillful.

Every single Japanese contender was vanquished, and their kites with severed strings plummeted helplessly into the bay or onto the streets of the town.

The following year on the day of the Clash, the young, blue-eyed man again climbed up onto the roof of the Dutch trading house. With great show he set his kite, emblazoned with foreign writing, high into the sky. The kite danced haughtily overhead, as though mocking the people of Nagasaki. Again that year, no kite could best his. All were trounced the following year as well.

"So, Mr. Foreigner, you've got to slaughter that Dutchman!" Sakichi grinned, hoping to incite Petitjean to action. He seemed to enjoy the thought that he and the other Japanese could watch these foreigners battle one another.

"I doubt I have any chance," Petitjean protested, but inwardly he wondered whether this contest might not be a good thing. The Japanese used different labels for the Dutch and the French, though both groups were foreigners. The Dutch were called Northern Barbarians, and the French were Southern Barbarians.

Petitjean was well aware that over the long years of national isolation in Japan, the Protestant Dutch had incessantly filled the ears of Japan's rulers with slander against the Catholic nations.

Now he would have the chance to fight a decisive battle with his kite against the Dutch. He supposed that when Father Furet heard the news he would become seriously angry, but young Petitjean, spurred on by Sakichi's encouragement, wanted to try his hand at the contest.

"So, do you think people would talk if I were to engage the Dutchman?"

"Mr. Foreigner, it would be the chief topic of conversation for everyone in Nagasaki!" Sakichi nodded, his excitement evident on his face.

"And people would come from nearby villages to watch?"

"You bet they would!"

Then perhaps some of them *would come to watch as well. They would discover that the foreigner flying that kite was none other than a Kirishitan padre. And were that to happen . . .*

"I'll do it!" Petitjean grinned at Sakichi.

THE TEMPLE OF THE
SOUTHERN BARBARIANS

TSUCHIFURU—

Tsuchifuru are the yellow dust storms that blow in from the Chinese continent. The storms sweep over Nagasaki shortly before the arrival of spring. The sky becomes an amber cloud, and those who venture out of doors are shrouded in specks of wind-borne dust that cover their faces and necks.

As soon as the storm ends, spring comes.

"I've been looking forward to this," Mitsu snuffled and whispered to Kiku from her chilly futon. Beside them, Oyone snored soundly and Tome slept curled up like a cat.

Both Mitsu and Kiku had been eagerly awaiting the arrival of spring. The third day of the third month was the Spring Festival. On that day, the girls at the Gotōya, with the exception of Oyone, were to be given the special dispensation of a one-day holiday from work. But they had to be back that night to sleep at the shop.

They arranged for Ichijirō to come and meet them on the morning of the third. Mitsu wanted to go back to Magome for the day, but Kiku had her own ideas.

"Even if we leave early in the morning, it'll be past noon before we reach Magome. We won't have any time to relax. I think it'd be better to go have a look around Nagasaki. . . . Listen, we could walk around and look at hairpins and tortoiseshell jewelry."

The rows of shop fronts in Nagasaki shone lustrously with beautiful hairpins and tortoiseshell jewelry designed to delight young women. Kiku wanted to hold one of them in her own hands and see how it looked in her hair.

"Ichijirō's not gonna go for that." Mitsu looked a bit worried. "He won't want to go to shops for girls. The only thing he can think about right now is the kite-flying contest."

That was true. Although it was an annual event, each new spring the young men of Magome were bursting with excitement to see the Clash of the Kites that would soon be held in Nagasaki.

Abruptly Kiku stopped the washing she was doing and asked, "Mitsu, why don't we go see the Temple of the Southern Barbarians?"

"The *what* temple?"

"The Nambanji—the Temple of the Southern Barbarians. It's a temple for foreigners that they've just about finished building in Ōura. I hear that instead of paper doors or lattices to let the light in, they've put in colored windows." Kiku narrowed her eyes and seemed to be imagining what Western colored glass might look like, since she had never seen it. "They say that when the sun shines through, they just sparkle. . . . It must be so pretty!"

"Who told you all that?"

"Doesn't matter who."

"I bet it was Seikichi."

Mitsu's jab made Kiku blush. But she hadn't heard about the Nambanji from Seikichi. She had overheard customers who came to the shop gossiping about the Southern Barbarian temple with the Master or the clerks.

"Seikichi doesn't come by lately. I wonder what's happened to him."

"He's taken a job in Isahaya. They're working on some roads over there, and he said the pay is good," Kiku answered confidently, full of pride that she knew all about Seikichi's activities.

It grew warmer. Tinges of green began to burst out on the willows planted along the river. The yellow blossoms of the weeping forsythia started to bloom through fences around the town, and the sounds of people practicing the samisen echoed from inside some of the houses. The coming of spring to Nagasaki was leisurely, even drowsy . . .

Finally, the spring Peach Festival, which Mitsu and Kiku had so been looking forward to, arrived on the third day of the third month.

"He's still not here! What in the world is he doing?!" Starting at dawn, the two girls dashed out to the front of the shop every time they had a break from their chores, eager for Ichijirō to come for them.

He finally appeared, having left Magome in the middle of the night in order to accommodate these two.

Once they had voiced their gratitude to the Mistress for the holiday and said good-bye to Oyone, and with Tome joining them as they left the Gotōya, they felt an indescribable, almost tangible, feeling of liberation and elation. Though they'd been working at the shop for only a month, this was the first time they'd been able to take off an entire day to have fun.

"Isn't this wonderful, Tome?"

"Yeah!"

"Do you eat *futsu* dumplings for the festival on Gotō Island, too? Back home in Magome we go around and give *futsu* dumplings to all our relatives."

In Nagasaki, mugwort dumplings were called *futsu* dumplings. Ichijirō grinned as he listened to the girls' animated conversation.

Crowds of people were walking in the warm sunlight. Buddhist priests. Chinese people. The daughters of merchant houses showed up in their finery, accompanied by their mothers and their aged maids. Each was on a pilgrimage to a Buddhist temple or a Shinto shrine.

From time to time one of the three girls would stop and stare at the kimonos or hairpins of the young women their age who were walking by. Tome and Mitsu gaped with envy, but Kiku looked openly belligerent.

If I put on makeup, I'd look just as good as they do! Inwardly she was full of self-assurance.

The three continued walking, then jerked to a halt when they finally reached the shops displaying tortoiseshell jewelry, combs, and hairpins; the blood rushed to their faces, and they swept their eyes intently across each of the items. Ichijirō, left to fend for himself, sat down at the base of a willow beside the shop and absently gazed at the passersby.

From time to time he would grumble, "That's long enough. Let's get going," but the response was always "Ichijirō, please wait just a little longer." And so he would wait patiently, thinking, *This was a big mistake.*

Eventually the girls had had their fill, and when the four left the shopping area, they decided to head for the celebrated Nambanji.

"I understand we can't go inside," Tome commented, and Kiku, exasperated that the girl knew so little, explained, "The Nambanji is a temple for the Kirishitans. It's being built for the foreigners, so of course Japanese can't go in!"

Today Ōura looks nothing like it did when Kiku and Mitsu first visited there.

If you walk around the neighborhood of the Ōura Catholic church today, you will occasionally spot one of the old wooden structures built in the Western style back in those days, looking now very much like abandoned houses. All of them were, of course, constructed after the Meiji Restoration of 1868, but in Kiku and Mitsu's time, several temples, a few houses, and the steeple and chapel of the nearly completed Nambanji peeked out from among the terraced fields, but except for those few structures, the rest of the landscape was unspoiled hills.

That afternoon when Kiku and her companions went to see the Nambanji, some twenty or thirty curious spectators were standing in front of the church, gaping up at the almost completed building and the terraced fields rising behind it.

The church, with two small towers on each side and a steeple in front capped with a crucifix, was the very first Christian church that the Japanese had seen since the country had adopted its isolation policy in the 1630s. The Japanese carpenters, who knew essentially nothing about the Western world, had built the church by carefully following the instructions they received from Father Furet.

"Oh, wow!" As they climbed the slope, Mitsu, Tome, and Kiku all dropped their jaws and looked up at the exotic building.

"It's a weird place!" By weird the girls didn't mean "amusing." To them, anything they had not seen before puzzled them and got slapped with the label "Weird!"

"What's that thing up on top?" Mitsu asked her brother, pointing to the crucifix atop the steeple.

"Dunno," Ichijirō shrugged. A young man next to them who was also examining the building said self-importantly, "It's a symbol of the Kirishitans."

Standing behind the throng of spectators, the four gazed up at the facade of the Nambanji. There were three doorways; above the largest door in the center there was a large window shaped something like a chrysanthemum, and its deep blue glass brilliantly reflected the sunlight.

"Wow!" Kiku blurted out. "Mitsu, it's so beautiful!" When she realized how loudly she had shouted, Kiku blushed a bright red, hunched her shoulders, and furtively looked around her.

But none of the spectators had turned to see where the shout had come from. Every man and woman was staring with wonderment at the unusual building and its stained glass. And there among those faces was . . .

Kiku caught her breath. Her eyes widened as she peered from a distance at the face of one young man.

That must be Seikichi. What's he doing here? He said he was off working in Isahaya.

The profile was most certainly Seikichi's. There could be no doubt. He was gazing up at the cross atop the church, not with astonishment like the other spectators, but with intense concentration.

"Mitsu!" Kiku tugged at Mitsu's sleeve and whispered, "Don't you think that's Seikichi?"

"Huh?" Mitsu looked surprised. "I thought he told you he'd gone to Isahaya." She had a gift for asking the obvious.

"I'm sure that's what he said."

"Why do you think he lied to you?"

An inexplicable disappointment gripped Kiku. She felt all the more betrayed because Seikichi was someone she had respected and trusted until now.

"I have no idea," she said angrily, quickly turning her face away. But before long she stole another glance at Seikichi.

Just then a Southern Barbarian wearing a long white robe emerged from one of the side doors of the Nambanji, accompanied by a man who appeared to be one of the magistrate's officers.

"I completely understand, Lord Itō," the foreigner said in surprisingly fluent Japanese.

"I just ask for your cooperation, Father Furet." In one hand the officer named Itō carried a bottle of foreign wine, apparently a gift from the priest, and he nodded with exaggerated affability, as though he were conscious of the presence of spectators.

The Southern Barbarian gave one more polite bow and disappeared back through the door. When Itō came down the stone steps, the observers instinctively retreated a step or two.

"Now, now . . . it's fine for you to look at this place, but you must never go inside. Only foreigners are allowed into this Nambanji. It remains strictly off-limits to Japanese." He looked condescendingly at the group and then started down the slope with tottering steps. Apparently he had been served some wine while he was inside the Nambanji.

The main door of the church opened.

This time a different young foreigner emerged, cradling something in his arms.

One woman in the crowd whispered to a friend, "That foreigner is the one who takes long walks around Nagasaki."

Her friend boasted, "I know. He once asked for some water from the well next to our place. His name is Petitjean, and evidently he's practicing to compete in the kite contest."

As the foreigner called Petitjean climbed down the stone steps, he suddenly displayed the object he was carrying, as though by accident.

It was a crucifix, the symbol of the Kirishitans, just like the one that decorated the steeple of the church. The gold cross caught the rays of the sun and shone brilliantly in Petitjean's hands.

At that moment—

Kiku realized that Seikichi and a couple of other men and women standing beside him were making some strange sort of gesture. They first placed the thumb of their right hands on their foreheads, then touched their chests, their left shoulders, and finally their right shoulders.

It happened so quickly that no one but Kiku noticed. Only she had seen their peculiar movements.

As soon as they finished their strange gestures, Seikichi gave a signal to his comrades. They nodded to one another, swiveled away from Kiku, and quickly separated themselves from the crowd of spectators.

Kiku's eyes followed them closely as they disappeared down the sloping path that knit its way between the terraced fields.

"Miss Kiku, what are you gawking at?" Tome asked. "Do you have a headache? You look pale."

"It's nothing," Kiku shook her head.

Seikichi's lie to her had wounded Kiku's pride. Even more painful for her, today Seikichi seemed like a totally different person, one she couldn't connect with. He seemed to Kiku like someone who harbored a secret in which she had no part.

I'm not having anything more to do with the likes of him. She scowled as if to dispel the image of his face that was still vividly imprinted onto her eyelids.

Then suddenly she remembered something from her girlhood. It was the scornful manner in which Ichijirō and Granny had talked about the people of Nakano where Seikichi lived. They had spat out the words, "They're *Kuros*, you know." But neither of them had explained what a *Kuro* was.

She went over to Ichijirō and asked, "Say, what's a *Kuro*?"

"*Kuro*."

"Yeah."

"A *Kuro* is . . . well, I'm not really sure. But from what I hear, they're creepy."

"So why do they call people from Nakano *Kuros*? I don't think there's anything creepy about them."

"Listen." Ichijirō suddenly grew suspicious of the reasons for his cousin's question and said, "The folks in Nakano . . . they're just different from us. . . . People say they do strange things there."

"What do you mean by 'strange'?"

"Well, for instance, so a baby's born. I hear they do some kind of secret thing to the baby, and when they do, they absolutely won't allow anybody from a different village to be there. And they totally refuse to marry someone from another village. And there's other things, too."

"They won't marry a person from outside their village?" Kiku's voice rose in volume again.

"That's what I hear."

"Why not?"

"'Cause they're *Kuros*. That's what it means to be a *Kuro*."

Kiku bit her lips and said nothing. Ichijirō's words had struck her another blow.

So does that mean Seikichi won't marry anybody except a girl from Nakano? She wondered to herself. It was a question she couldn't bring herself to ask Ichijirō.

Midday was approaching.

The four sat with their legs stretched out on the shore where the Ōura River flowed into the bay and ate the lunches Ichijirō had brought from Magome.

Each bento box contained only black rice balls and some pickled vegetables, but since Granny had made it, as they ate they could almost smell their home back in Magome.

"Kiku." As Ichijirō sucked up a rice kernel that had stuck to his finger, he asked with concern, "Why are you so quiet?"

"No reason." With her palm she scooped up some sand from the shore and shifted her gaze toward the spring ocean. The waves that softly drifted in, then softly broke against the shore with a melancholy sound, were the color of mother-of-pearl. Kiku's heart, too, felt melancholy. It was a feeling she had hardly ever experienced before today.

Does every girl feel this miserable when she starts to care about a boy? She asked herself as she played with a pink seashell. Suddenly Mitsu and Tome, who had always seemed so much like her, looked more like younger children to her.

"Miss Kiku, let's go find some pretty shells!" Mitsu and Tome stood up and ran barefoot to the edge of the waves. Ichijirō was lying on his back stretched out on the sand, enjoying an after-lunch nap. Mount Inasa was visible through the spring haze, and white sea birds flitted over the surface of the water.

Oh dear, Kiku sighed. *Someone like Mitsu isn't going to be able to understand how I feel. She's still so young.*

Being as strong willed as she was, Kiku realized that the next time she saw Seikichi, she was going to have to interrogate him about today's events. She knew she wouldn't feel satisfied unless she did.

For the remainder of the day they paid their respects at the Suwa Shrine,[1] had a look at the Sōfukuji Temple built by the Chinese,[2] and then Ichijirō escorted the young women back to the Gotōya before the sun set. That concluded their Doll Festival[3] activities, a day that was enjoyable for Mitsu and depressing for Kiku. Tomorrow they would resume their busy work schedule.

That night after they crawled into their futons, Kiku told Mitsu in a whispered voice about the strange gestures she had seen Seikichi make that day.

"He put his fingers like this up on his head, and then on his chest, and then on both shoulders."

"What in the world could that be?" Mitsu looked puzzled.

But then Tome, who they thought was asleep beside them, suddenly interjected, "I've seen some fishermen secretly doing that on the Gotō Islands. When

---

1. Suwa is a Shinto shrine originally built in the mid-sixteenth century. During the Christian era when Nagasaki was gifted to the Jesuits, the shrine was destroyed, but it was rebuilt under shogunal orders in 1625.

2. Sōfukuji, the oldest Buddhist temple in Japan built in the Chinese style, dates to 1629.

3. Also known as Girls' Day, the Doll Festival is held every year on March 3.

I asked them what they were doing, they laughed and said it was some kind of spell to keep the seas calm."

"So it's a spell, is it?"

"Seems to be."

Kiku was all the more eager to see Seikichi again so she could ask him what kind of spell it was.

No sooner had the Doll Festival passed than the Kompira Festival was upon them, on the tenth day of the third month. It was the day for the kite competition. Nagasaki is, after all, a city of many amusements and many celebrations.

Beneath the spring-like sun, men swaggered around Shianbashi with rakish looks on their faces. Their swaggering postures were reminiscent of earlier days in Nagasaki when the "Strolling Song" was popular.

> Above the bridge at Kōyamachi,
> Bands of boys scuffle over the banners
> Flying above their bamboo boats.
> Though five or six men come to quiet them down,
> It may take four or five days.
> Strolling, strolling
> Strolling around Nagasaki.

But the realities of life in Japan were not that carefree. By 1864, the collapse of the shogunate was imminent, and the vast changes of the age were pressing like waves on Nagasaki. The common people basking under this spring sun appeared utterly unconcerned about such matters. The "Strolling Song" was still sung to a samisen accompaniment in the pleasure quarters of Maruyama.

> In the seventh year of the Kaei era,
> The year of the tiger, the cycle of the tortoise,
> Russian sailors go sightseeing
> At the harbor battery on Shirō Island.
> Strolling, strolling
> Strolling around Nagasaki.

Kiku herself was feeling as unsettled as the times. Every day as she swept the storefront at the Gotōya, she fretted that she had still not seen Seikichi go by. Two entire days had passed, and though she heard the calls of other street peddlers, there was no sign of Seikichi.

"I wonder if he's still working on the roads at Isahaya?" Gripping the handle of her bamboo broom, she stared incessantly down the long stretch of road.

Eventually she was brought to her senses by the scolding cries of either the Mistress or Oyone, "Why are you loitering around? Hurry and start dusting!"

Another two, then three days passed with no sign of him, and Kiku said to herself in a huff, "I'm having nothing more to do with him. Even if I do see him, I'm saying nothing. I'll just ignore him." But she knew when push came to shove she couldn't ignore him.

And she was right. . . .

On the morning of the fourth day, the angry girl heard the voice of a tradesman calling out from the distance, "Taro! Bean sprouts! Daikon!" It was the familiar voice of Seikichi.

Tightly clutching the handle of her bamboo broom, Kiku narrowed her almond-shaped eyes and glared in the direction from which the voice came. The expression on her face made the still adolescent woman appear startlingly beautiful.

Seikichi appeared. He recognized Kiku in the morning light and smiled broadly, but Kiku did not so much as grin back at him. She struck a standoffish pose.

Seikichi took the scale that carried taro and bean sprouts from his shoulder and with a grin spoke to Kiku, "It's gotten warmer. I'll bet you've been working hard, haven't you?"

She was still aloof and coldly responded, "Yes." She resumed her sweeping and said nothing further.

At a loss, Seikichi asked, "Need any taro?"

"Nope."

"Well, then." Seikichi hoisted the scale back onto his shoulder and started to leave, but Kiku called out his name and then blurted out, "Seikichi, did you really go to Isahaya to work?"

"Yes, I did."

"Even on the third? The day of the Doll Festival?"

Seikichi looked at her apprehensively, so she pressed him, "Are you sure you weren't having a look at the Nambanji that day?"

A look of surprise brushed across Seikichi's face, "How did you know that?"

"I was there looking at it, too."

"Oh? I didn't know that. Why didn't you say hello?"

Kiku was annoyed by the calmness in his voice. Recalling how depressed she had felt that day, and feeling bitter that Seikichi was so clueless about the feelings of the woman he had lied to, she said, "Even if I'd wanted to say hello to you, Seikichi, you left in such a hurry."

"Yeah, I wanted to get back to Nakano."

"When you were there you made some strange gesture. . . . What was that?"

"Strange gesture?"

Kiku kept her eyes fixed on him as she took her finger and touched her forehead, chest, and both shoulders. It was exactly what Seikichi had done when the foreigner came out of the Nambanji. "That's what you did, isn't it?"

The blood rushed out of Seikichi's face, and he turned pale. "I don't know what you're talking about. I never did that," he disavowed feebly.

"Liar! I saw you with my own eyes!"

"It wasn't anything in particular. Probably my head just itched."

It was obvious to Kiku that Seikichi was lying. Why did he have to be so dishonest?

"Liar! That wasn't what you'd do if your head itched. It looked like some kind of spell to me." Triumphantly Kiku took a step toward him and, though he was older than she, boldly taunted him, "Seikichi. What's a *Kuro*?"

Seikichi scowled at Kiku but said nothing. It seemed as though the single word had deeply wounded him.

Kiku hesitated for a moment, but then, as if explaining to herself, "Well, you're from Nakano, right? In Magome they call people from Nakano *Kuros*."

Seikichi hoisted the scale back onto his shoulder, sighed, "You're mean," and began to walk away. There was a loneliness in his retreating figure. Kiku bit her lip and watched intently until that solitary figure had disappeared into the distance.

She had never imagined this would happen. All she had done was to get angry at Seikichi for telling her that he'd gone to Isahaya to build roads but then come to Nagasaki without even telling her, and she'd merely voiced her indignation to him. If Seikichi had just apologized for irritating her like an older brother would, then she would have calmed down.

But in a burst of anger she had said the word *Kuro* to Seikichi and dealt him an utterly unexpected blow.

"You're mean," Seikichi had said bitterly, and then he had walked away.

Remorse welled up in Kiku's heart. She had no idea why that word had made Seikichi look so sad. But there was no doubt that she had tactlessly hurt him.

Seikichi's angry with me. Now he's never going to like me. Kiku realized for the first time that her actions had produced the opposite effect to what she had anticipated. She forgot all about her cleaning chores and stood in a daze.

Gloomy days followed, one after another.

"Kiku, what's wrong with you?" Mitsu worriedly asked Kiku, who had fallen into a terrible slump.

"I . . . did something so stupid!" Kiku explained every detail of what had happened to Mitsu, but as she confessed the events of that morning it all came back vividly to Kiku's mind and stabbed at her heart.

The spring Kompira Festival arrived amid those dismal days, on the tenth day of the third month.

Management of the Kompira Festival rotated each year among the seven chief neighborhoods in Nagasaki. Though it has declined in popularity today, in Mitsu and Kiku's day it was one of the liveliest of all the festivals in Nagasaki, whether Shinto or Buddhist.

On the eve of the festival the shrine precincts were already jammed with pilgrims. Food stalls and booths were crammed together on the grounds and along both sides of the road to the shrine.

"Let there be good weather tomorrow!" Children and youths pressed their palms together and petitioned Kompira, the great avatar of the sea. Especially since the customary kite competition couldn't be held if the weather was inclement.

Thankfully, on the day of the festival the skies were clear and there was a light breeze. It was an ideal day for kite flying.

On this day, the men who worked at the Gotōya were given permission to go with the Master to Mount Kompira where the Clash of the Kites was held. Some of the larger mercantile houses prepared food and drink and invited their best customers to watch the kite flying to the accompaniment of samisen and drums.

Because Kiku and Mitsu, along with Tome and other girls, had been allowed to leave the shop for the recent Doll Festival, this time they had to stay at work. Still, if they climbed up onto the wooden racks where clothes were hung out to dry, they were able to see swarms of kites dancing in the sky like flocks of birds.

"Kiku, come on!" Making sure the Mistress didn't overhear, Mitsu came to summon Kiku. She was certain that they would earn another tongue-lashing if the Mistress found out they were watching the kite clash on the pretext of hanging clothes out to dry.

But perhaps the Mistress was willing to wink at what they were doing today because even though Tome and even Oyone had congregated on the drying racks, she wasn't uttering a word of complaint.

"Look! There's a helmeted Brahman!" Oyone, who had lived in Nagasaki for a long while, proudly pointed out one kite swirling in the wind.

Though they all were called "kites," those that were entered in the Clash of the Kites were of many different varieties. Each of the kites, with their colorful designs and shapes, had their own names, like "Bald-Headed Priest," "Footman," "Bat," "Paper Door," "Tiny," "Flying Fish," and so on.

As these various kites now creaked and swooped through the sky, they closed quarters with each other, tangled, stormed at one another, and soared upward or plummeted downward.

"What do you think? Will that Dutch House at Dejima send up that wicked foreigner's kite again?" Oyone asked, shifting her body and looking toward Dejima. She told the other girls that for the past two years, a young foreigner had flown a flying-fish kite from the roof of the Dutch trading company and challenged the Japanese kite flyers.

"It was so humiliating. Not a single kite could beat it."

"The foreigner was that good? Where do you suppose he learned how to fly a kite?" Mitsu asked, wide-eyed.

"Which one of those kites belongs to the foreigner?"

"He hasn't sent it up yet. I wonder if he's not participating this year?" Oyone marveled, but almost immediately she cried, "Oh! He's up there on the roof!"

Mitsu and Tome and Kiku turned as one in that direction, forming a row like a flock of society finches.

Just as Oyone had described it, they could see two Dutchmen sitting on the roof of the Dutch trading company in Dejima, laughing and watching the competition. And they weren't mere spectators—it was clear from the flying-fish kite they had prepared next to them that they planned to join in the contest.

Before long the two Dutchmen checked the direction of the wind and began to fly their kite.

This year it was a pitch-black kite. It was slathered with black ink and bore no other color or decoration. The sinister-colored kite bobbed up and down for a few moments, but it soon caught a current of wind blowing in from the bay.

The black kite—

It sailed indolently overhead, as though glaring down at the spectacle below. Its movements seemed to be challenging the other kites in its vicinity, as though it were saying, "Well? Think you can win, do you?"

The surrounding kites began darting in response to the black kite's taunts.

Kiku and the other girls on the drying rack were not the only ones watching this sparring. People walking along the street and those crossing the bridge all stopped in their tracks and lifted their heads to gaze into the sky. Some raised their arms and pointed to the Dutchmen's kite. It felt as though virtually the entire population of the town had been anticipating this battle.

For two years now the Japanese residents of Nagasaki had been participating in this contest and had been consistently beaten by the Dutchmen's kite. They could not imagine where these foreigners had learned their skill or whether they had applied some unusual substance to their kite string, but the fact remained that they were a truly formidable antagonist. Above all else, they were powerful.

Everyone knew that.

"This is deplorable."

The residents of Nagasaki, unlike other regions of Japan, had, over the course of time, learned to treat foreigners with great respect. They had lived in harmony with both the Dutch in Dejima and the Chinese who had lived here for many years.

But when it came to these out-and-out competitions, for a fleeting moment they all became patriots. Even the women ground their teeth and grumbled, "Isn't there anybody who can smash their kite? The men of Nagasaki really are cowards!"

A kite decorated with two colorful broad stripes surged toward the black kite. Then, like two prizefighters who exchange jabs as they try to assess their opponent's strengths and likely moves, they gently poked at each other, then pulled back, pulled away then poked again, each competitor watching for the moment of opportunity.

That opportunity, that skill. Those are what make the difference between victory and loss.

"NOW!" A man standing on the street suddenly clenched his fists and cried out.

The two kites coiled and intertwined with each other.

The man below shouted, "BRAVO!!"

The kites disengaged and pulled away from each other. The victor had been decided.

The double-striped kite had been cut loose from its string and was plummeting to the ground. It had lost.

"Damn!" a group of children barked and then raced off with poles on their shoulders to snag the vanquished kite.

"Oh no! Oh no!" Oyone groaned.

Kiku, a sore loser herself, pounded her fists on one of the supports holding up the drying rack.

A DAY OF HOPE

PETITJEAN ALSO WAS watching the kite contest. To his side stood Sakichi, his arms folded in evident frustration.

Sakichi clacked his tongue in disdain and sputtered, "If that's the way they go in for the attack, it's no wonder they got their string cut!"

After the first kite suffered a tragic defeat, another flying-fish kite that had been waiting its turn slid up to the Dutch house's black kite, seeming to boast, "My turn now!"

It drew near. It pulled back. It attacked. It looked like a battle to the death between two cuttlefish in the depths of the sea. The colored square kite even resembled the shape of a cuttlefish.

From time to time Sakichi forgot himself and shouted out, "Hurray!" Despite his cheers, however, one after another the Japanese kites spiraled headlong into the ocean.

"Mr. Foreigner, what are we going to do?" Sakichi looked nervously at Petitjean. He was hoping to gain some fame for his kite as one foreigner competed against another, but he seemed to be losing confidence. In all honesty, from the time the black kite first climbed into the sky, Petitjean too had concluded he had no chance of winning.

He had never told Father Furet that he had made a kite at Sakichi's request or that he had thrown himself into training with it. Were he to be found out, he had no doubt that the priest would be genuinely outraged, as Father Furet was busy preparing to return to France by way of the Ryūkyū Islands.

"It doesn't really matter if I win. You made this kite for me, Sakichi. I'd just like to see it fly." Petitjean pointed to the kite that Sakichi was holding. A

Christian cross had been painted on the kite so that onlookers would immediately recognize that its operator was a priest.

"And you've worked really hard to learn how to fly it, Mr. Foreigner," Sakichi nodded, handing the stick wrapped with kite string to Petitjean. "The wind's coming in from the ocean. Keep a close eye on shifts in the wind." Sakichi had repeatedly emphasized to him that he must not rely solely on the strength of the kite to win the battle. If he took advantage of the power of the wind, the potency of the glass-encrusted string would double.

Slowly, slowly the string Petitjean held in his hands was dragged into the sky. He felt the resistance in his hands as the kite rose above the rooftops and soared upward as though sucked up into the spring sky.

A kite plainly emblazoned with a scarlet cross. It should be visible from every direction in Nagasaki. If there were in fact any descendants of the Kirishitans in this city, they would surely see this kite painted with a cross. Therein lay Petitjean's aim.

The black kite glided languidly above. Like a bald eagle riding the wind currents, his wings spread wide, he ruled the skies over Nagasaki. Compared with him, all the other kites were no better than second-rate birds. And now the flying-fish kite with the scarlet cross was closing in on the eagle.

"Who's flying that kite?" Pedestrians below stopped, gazing up at this reckless melee.

"I hear it belongs to one of the foreigners at the Nambanji. That makes this a battle between foreigners from two different countries. Very interesting!"

"Really? Foreigner against foreigner?"

Just as Sakichi had anticipated, at every street corner and along every road, spectators had gathered into small groups and were staring up into the sky. It was a foregone conclusion that the black kite would emerge victorious, but with its drawing so many people's attention, Sakichi planned to make the rounds afterward and announce, "I made that kite!"

The kite string transmitted the kite's groan to Petitjean's fingers. It seemed almost to be trembling in anticipation of the battle. "Don't move in yet!" Sakichi, the military strategist, cautioned Petitjean as he checked the strength and direction of the wind. "Not yet! Not yet!!"

Though it closed in on the black kite, the crucifix kite did not attempt to interlace its strings just yet. Petitjean smoothly let out his string, like a knight desperately restraining a horse that snorts and strains to break into a mad dash.

It was a battle of patience. The black kite advanced, as though out of patience, but Sakichi calculated the strength of the wind and cried, "Not yet! Not yet!!" He also gauged the direction of the wind. And in a moment he shouted, "Now! *NOW, Mr. Foreigner!!*"

With a whoosh the string jerked tight against Petitjean's index finger. The pain was so intense he wondered whether his finger had been severed.

"*BRAVO!!*" Sakichi yelled out. The two tangled kites moved apart at that instant.

The black kite was wobbling. The kite bearing the scarlet crucifix pulled away from it.

The spectators at the crossroads cried out in one voice, "The black kite has lost!!"

But that wasn't the case. It was the kite with the scarlet crucifix that plummeted to the ground. It was Petitjean's kite. . . .

Petitjean offered some words of encouragement to a downcast Sakichi, but he himself was satisfied with the outcome. He cared nothing about victory. His purpose had been to get a kite with a crucifix floating in the skies over Nagasaki. If any of *them* had seen it, it must have given them a great deal of courage. That was sufficient.

However, someone told Father Furet about the day's events, and that evening Petitjean was roundly censured. "Have you completely forgotten that Christianity is banned in this country? And still, like some foolish child, you go fly a kite with a cross on it. Tomorrow, no doubt, Itō Seizaemon will come here in a rage. There are limits to what we are allowed to do, for heaven's sake . . . ! You'll never stop chasing your delusions, will you? There is absolutely no possibility, no matter where you search in this land, that there are any descendants of the first Christians. I've told you this time and again. If there were, they would have contacted us in some form by now."

Petitjean hung his head and listened to this violent rebuke from his superior.

"Evidently someone as pigheaded as you has to be shown instead of just told things. Tomorrow you're coming with me."

"Where are we going?"

"Where, indeed! There's a place I absolutely must show my pigheaded friend. It may turn into a two-day journey, so make the proper preparations. For tonight, go straight to bed."

Father Furet said nothing further about where they were going or what he wanted to show his fellow priest. Petitjean overheard the father instructing Okane to prepare a day's worth of food to take with them.

Early the next morning, after finishing their Masses, Father Furet had Mosaku prepare horses for them. "All right. Get your things together and get on your horse."

The priest helped Petitjean, who looked as though his nose had been tweaked by a forest sprite, onto his horse, then mounted his own horse and said to their guide, "To Mogi."

Mogi was a fishing village on the other side of the hills behind Nagasaki. It had a tranquil bay similar to Nagasaki's, though not nearly as large.

They arrived in Mogi near midday and from there took a boat.

"You'll see what this is about when we get there." Father Furet, smirking, said nothing further. That evening, the boat proceeded along the Shimabara peninsula. At twilight the ocean had a rosy tint, and the Japanese fishing boats had set their nets. In the distance, the islands of Amakusa rose like shadows.

Eventually they sighted a white castle at the lip of the land. It was Shimabara Castle.[1] At the boat landing below the castle a number of spectators, who seemed to have gotten word of their imminent arrival, had gathered to look at the strange Nambanjin.

"Lord Okugawa!" When Father Furet disembarked, he raised one hand and called out to an official who looked as annoyed as Itō Seizaemon generally did. "Do you remember me? We met here once before." He bowed his head politely. "Today I've come with a friend to hike up to Unzen."

The official named Okugawa broke into a smile when he saw the bottle of wine that Father Furet held out to him as a gift. Suddenly he became very solicitous. "So you're climbing Unzen, are you? That will be exhausting! Have you made arrangements for lodgings?"

They stayed the night in Shimabara, but the two priests couldn't get to sleep until very late because the curious spectators had assembled close to their inn, and Okugawa showed up with a colleague to pay his respects.

Even after they crawled into bed, they could hear the sound of water flowing somewhere in the distance.

Petitjean knew that Unzen was a tall mountain, but why was Father Furet bringing him to such a place?

Early the next morning, they climbed onto two horses provided by Okugawa, and led by two guides, they ascended Unzen.

At the base of the mountain spring, flowers had begun to bloom, but as they climbed, a magnificent landscape, still evincing signs of winter in its withered trees and valleys, opened up before the four men. Though they had heard the call of nightingales only a few minutes earlier, at this elevation the cries of shrikes echoed piercingly from between the trees that shimmered silver in the sun.

Gray clouds lowered overhead, lending the enormous mountain an air of solitude, even ferocity.

---

1. Built between 1618 and 1624, Shimabara Castle stood until the early Meiji period, when most of it was torn down to make way for a school and farmland. Restoration of the keep and towers of the historic castle began in the 1960s.

"Well, then." It was almost midday. Father Furet, who had been watching the movements of the clouds, said, "Do you have any idea why I brought you up to this mountain?"

"I've wanted to ask you," Petitjean replied, "but I decided to say nothing until you volunteered the information."

"Then I'll tell you. This mountain path we're climbing right now—more than 210 years ago, they too were forced to climb it. . . ."

"'They'?"

"Yes, the Japanese Christians."

"For what purpose?"

"To be tortured." Father Furet blinked his eyes, as though the light hurt them. A shrike screeched in the woods.

"Tortured? Why would they be tortured in these mountains . . . ?"

"You'll understand soon enough."

Their conversation broke off, and their horses set out once again behind their two guides.

Just about the time the sunlight began to wane, they spotted beneath them a valley thick with white smoke. At first Petitjean mistook it for the white smoke of a volcano, but then he realized that it was not smoke but steam that reeked of sulfur.

When the horses caught the smell, they stamped their hooves in fear and refused to move any further.

"Fine. We'll walk." Father Furet dismounted and the other three followed suit.

They could hear murmuring like that of a mountain stream. No doubt it was a mountain stream. But it was a stream of boiling water, of water at a blistering temperature. And the foul-smelling vapor from the stream blew like smoke on the wind.

"I suspect the fires of Gehenna mentioned in the Bible were like this," Father Furet muttered as he covered his mouth with a handkerchief. "Watch your step. If you fall in, that water, which must be several hundred degrees hot, will melt your legs off. And—" He paused for just a moment and then in one breath said, "The Japanese Kirishitans who would not abandon their faith . . . were thrown into this boiling water. The flesh on their legs melted off in an instant, and when they were pulled out again, nothing but their bones remained. Do you understand, Bernard? Nothing was left of their legs but white bones. . . ."

Though spring had begun, evenings in Unzen were still bitter cold. But they were able to endure the cold because of the warmth of the steam spurting from this boiling mountain stream.

"Bernard, this is the kind of tortures the Christians of Nagasaki had to suffer. They were burned alive, subjected to water torture, and plunged into the boiling water here at Unzen. . . . Come, open your eyes and look down there!" Father

Furet pointed at their feet, almost angrily. With an eerie popping sound bubbles from the boiling water rose to the surface and burst.

"Bernard?"

"Yes."

"If you were made to stand here, and you were told that if you did not deny God and Christ you would slowly be lowered into these ghastly waters . . . would you stand your ground?"

Petitjean lifted his head in surprise at Father Furet's unexpected query. But the look on his superior's face was solemn.

"Well? Could you endure it?"

"I—" Petitjean stammered painfully. "I—I don't know. What about you?"

"Me? To be honest, I don't know if I could bear it or not. I know I would pray to the Lord. . . . Bernard, that's why, even if the Japanese believers who were subjected to this kind of torture ultimately abandoned their faith . . . we have no right to condemn them."

"I agree."

"And another thing. With this degree of persecution and torture going on for so many long years, it's no surprise that not a single Christian remains in Japan. It's to be expected."

Petitjean finally understood why Father Furet had brought him all the way to Unzen. The priest was trying to turn Petitjean from his dreams back to reality— something he had not been able to persuade him to do in words—by bringing him to the spot where some of the horrifying tortures had taken place.

"Bernard. I'll be leaving Nagasaki in four days."

"In just four days?"

"Yes, that's when a ship is leaving for the Ryūkyūs. My departure has been moved up. You're going to have to care in my stead for our newly completed church at Ōura."

As Petitjean nodded apprehensively, Father Furet slapped him on the shoulder and said, "Don't worry. You're not going to be alone. Father Laucaigne[2] is coming to Nagasaki to replace me. That's why I need you to snap out of your reveries and your childish imaginings that there are still descendants of the first Japanese Christians who secretly maintain their faith. . . ."

With a flushed face Petitjean listened intently to Father Furet's admonition.

"Let's be rid of the past, shan't we, Bernard?"

Petitjean nodded feebly.

---

2. Joseph-Marie Laucaigne (1838–1885) was ordained a priest of the Société des Missions-Étrangères de Paris in 1862 and became auxiliary bishop of Japan in 1873. After nursing Bishop Petitjean through his final days, Laucaigne himself succumbed to a fatal illness.

Father Furet left Nagasaki on the third day after their return from Unzen. Petitjean, Okane, and Mosaku saw him off at the Ōhato boat landing and kept waving their hands as he set off on a tiny skiff toward the ship that would take him to the Ryūkyūs.

In the absence of Father Furet, the Ōura Church seemed hollow and deserted. Petitjean's heart swelled with alternating feelings of loneliness and responsibility. More than ever before he was acutely aware of the weighty presence that Father Furet had been. Petitjean anxiously looked forward to the arrival of Father Laucaigne, Furet's successor.

He now had a clearer understanding of the horrors of the persecutions that were heaped on the Japanese Kirishitans at the hell of boiling water he had seen at Unzen. Father Furet's counsel to abandon his childish fantasies stung him just as a pungent antiseptic causes the teeth to tingle.

"I'm responsible for taking care of the Ōura Church," Petitjean repeated to himself. He made up his mind that in order to fulfill that responsibility, he would study Father Furet's ledger books, keep the church's journals, compose letters to France, and send the weekly report to his superiors in Yokohama. And he put an immediate stop to the "long walks" that had previously been part of his daily routine.

Two days later, the day Father Laucaigne was scheduled to arrive in Nagasaki, the skies were clear. It was a day no different from any other. Petitjean instructed Okane, "Please ask your husband to sweep the garden." After he finished his lunch, he took a dry cloth and went inside the new chapel. Standing in front of the altar, his eyes took in every corner of the sanctuary that the Japanese carpenters had so industriously fashioned under Father Furet's direction.

It's beautiful, he thought. It was not a grand, lavishly ornamented Catholic church like those back home in Chartres, Paris, and Reims, but to him it was as pristine, as fragrant with the scent of wood, and as immaculate as any of the graceful Buddhist temples of Japan. He was grateful that this lovely church had been entrusted to him.

With his cloth he dusted the altar, then the statues that were placed on either side of the altar—one of Jesus, the other of the Blessed Mother cradling the infant Jesus. Then he arranged the candles and counted the cruets of wine used in the Mass.

Today as every day he could see through the partially opened door the crowd of spectators who were peering curiously toward him.

Because of the prohibition by the magistrate, the Japanese would not take one further step toward the church. He had no sense how long the proscription on Christianity would be continued.

When he finished with his cleaning, he knelt down in front of the altar and clasped his hands together. Easter was approaching.

Sunlight poured through the stained-glass windows. The time was just barely past 12:30.

He heard a faint sound behind him as he prayed. Thinking it must be Okane's husband, he turned around. And there Petitjean saw four or five Japanese quietly staring at him. . . .

They wore shabby clothing and their faces had been baked brown in the sun. They gazed at him timidly, their eyes like those of mice that scrutinize their surroundings from the shadows, but when Petitjean turned his head in their direction, they quickly retreated. No doubt they had come through the forbidden doorway out of curiosity and were sneaking a quick look at the inside of the chapel.

With a strained smile he again clasped his hands and made to resume his prayer.

Again he heard a faint noise. This time he remained in his kneeling position and paid them no attention. He calculated that this would give the Japanese a little more leisure to examine the altar and the statues of Jesus and Mary.

Just as he anticipated, they seemed to have taken a bit of courage: behind him he heard footsteps moving two, then three paces forward. There they stopped, and Petitjean could sense that they were gazing at the altar with the intense curiosity so common among the Japanese.

Ah, they've become a bit brazen! The Japanese seemed to be coming even closer. Were they trying to move up close and get a clear view of the altar, the gold cross atop the altar, and the candlesticks? And were they then going to boast of what they had learned to their comrades who waited nervously outside?

"These strange things lined up here . . . Do you know what they're called?" They were so close Petitjean could overhear their conversation.

Then a woman's voice spoke. "Sir . . . Our hearts are all the same as yours."

It was the voice of a middle-aged woman. She stood directly behind him, whispering softly as though she were divulging an important secret. "Sir . . . Our hearts are all the same as yours."

Petitjean was jerked back into reality, as though startled from a dream, and with wide eyes he turned to look behind him.

The woman must have been about forty, perhaps a little older. It was difficult for a Frenchman to guess the age of a Japanese woman. She was so nervous that she was on the verge of tears.

"Our hearts are all the same as yours."

He was so dumbfounded he didn't immediately grasp the meaning of her words. The instant her meaning became clear to him, he felt as though he had been struck with a large club.

It was *them*! *They* had finally appeared!

The woman asked, "Sir . . . Where is the statue of Santa Maria?"

Petitjean tried to stand up, but he couldn't get to his feet. The intensity of his emotions made it impossible for him to move.

"The statue . . . of Santa Maria," he whispered. "Come with me."

Petitjean led the woman to the base of the statue of the Blessed Mother on the right of the altar. The young Immaculata stood smiling, a crown on her head and the infant Jesus cradled in her arms.[3]

The woman, along with the other men and women in the group, lifted their eyes to look where Petitjean was pointing. They were silent for a time, until the woman muttered, as either a sigh or a moan, "So precious!" The others sighed as well.

Petitjean's voice was hoarse when he asked, "Are you Kirishitan . . . ?" His throat was parched.

"Yes," a young man at the front of the group nodded as spokesman for them all.

"I—" Petitjean wanted to tell them that he was a priest. But there was not yet a word in Japanese for "priest." "Petitjean. Petitjean." He pointed to his nose and repeated his name. "Where have you come from?"

"Urakami."

"Urakami?"

"On the other side of Mount Kompira." Unsure where that would be, Petitjean said nothing. The silence was prolonged.

"Sir," the young man struggled to use an unfamiliar level of politeness in his speech, "are you truly a padre?"

"Padre." It meant "father" or "priest" in Portuguese. Petitjean didn't know Portuguese, but he understood the meaning from the Latin and nodded his head. "Yes, a padre."

But the young man still seemed skeptical. "Then you're familiar with the day when Lord Zeusu was born, and His days of sorrow?"

Petitjean knew that "Zeusu" was their name for Jesus, but he couldn't immediately grasp what was meant by "days of sorrow." He assumed, however, that it probably referred to the week before Easter.

"I am. We are in the 'days of sorrow' right now." When he gave that response, every member of the group smiled at him as would a mother pleased with her clever child.

"Are there many Kirishitans in Urakami?" It was his turn to ask a question.

"The people in the Magome District of Urakami are Buddhists," someone answered.

---

3. The statue is still on display in the Ōura Church in Nagasaki.

Just then, a voice called from the entrance, "Hurry! An officer is coming!" Those in the chapel swiftly turned away from Petitjean and disappeared like smoke through the exit.

Petitjean stood motionless in the empty chapel. Wave after wave of inexpressible emotions came crashing against his heart. He felt like shouting. He wanted to shout to Father Furet: *You see! They are here in Nagasaki! They really do exist! What a splendid city this is!*

Through two hundred years of ruthless persecution and fierce oppression, the Japanese Christians had endured like a single tree in a downpour, and some of them still remained. What the drunken Chinese in the Ryūkyūs had told him was no lie. Petitjean was overcome with a dizzying excitement as he realized that he was the one who had first met up with the Japanese Christians who had hidden themselves underground.

"O Lord, I thank Thee. I . . . I thank Thee!" He knelt and folded his fingers in prayer as a flood of tears poured from his eyes. Through the tears that veiled his eyes he saw the lovely statue of the Blessed Mother. "So precious!" The woman's words still echoed vividly in his ears.

I'm sure they'll come here again. Surely they will. Petitjean could not believe that the people who had just vanished like smoke would now sever all contact with him.

I must be prudent. If I'm careless and someone like Itō Seizaemon from the magistrate's office finds us out, all will be lost.

He realized that he must labor to display a face that revealed nothing to the spectators outside. With a posture of utter indifference he went out of the church and gave Okane an errand to run.

The next day it rained. His heart pounding, he waited for them.

As he anticipated, that day a larger crowd of spectators than usual stood in front of the church. Petitjean deliberately swung open the door to the church to make it clear to them that it was not locked.

Before long, a handful of people crept silently in. They stopped before the statue of the Blessed Mother, whispered in soft voices, then quickly departed. A few minutes later, another four or five slipped in.

They each wore crude clothing. Their rustic faces and sunken eyes were evidence that these were peasants who had endured long years of hard labor.

Toward evening, a rather unhappy-looking Itō Seizaemon made an appearance.

"Lord Petitjean," he said, gazing suspiciously around the chapel, "I'm sure Father Furet told you this, but . . . you need to understand that Japanese people are forbidden from coming in here."

"Why can't they come inside?" Petitjean feigned ignorance. "This is the first I've heard of such an agreement. I know that I am not allowed to teach the

Kirishitan faith to the Japanese, but no one told me that I had to stop them from looking at the church."

Seizaemon looked bewildered. Surprised at how stubbornly defiant Petitjean was, Itō left, evidently uncertain how to handle this situation. But the following day, he and some of his subordinates set up headquarters at a Buddhist temple close to the church. From there they sent lookouts every half hour to monitor any contact between the spectators and Petitjean.

"Padre, you must be careful," the young man he had met the previous day sneaked into the church, avoiding the eyes of the officers, and whispered to him. "They suspect that something is going on. Some of the officers have removed their swords so they can blend in with the other spectators, and they're keeping a close eye on us."

Petitjean nodded. He, too, had noticed this.

"When we see you from a distance, Padre, we'll put our left hands like this on our hearts. That'll mean it's someone from Nakano Village."

Somebody coughed from the shadow of the doorway. It was a signal that an officer was approaching.

"I want to talk with you somewhere. Let me know where we can meet," Petitjean hurriedly called after the young man who was hurrying out.

"Tomorrow in the early afternoon, we'll wait for you at the entrance to the Suwa Shrine at the base of Mount Kompira." He quickly went outside.

When the officer appeared, Petitjean was nonchalantly tidying up the altar. There was no sign of any other person in the sanctuary. His contact with the Kirishitans had been handled prudently, and the spectators simply pretended to be observing the church from afar.

He could hardly wait for the next day. It took a disquietingly long time for the sun to set that evening.

Petitjean wrote a letter to his superiors in Yokohama, reporting the miraculous discovery of some Japanese believers. His hand occasionally paused at the joy of his news, leaving an ink smudge on the paper.

The next day Petitjean lied to Okane and her husband to keep them off-guard. "I'm off on one of my long walks."

"Long walk? You haven't taken one of those for a long time!" Mosaku laughed.

Petitjean planned to stroll down the hill as he always did, passing between fields and coming out on the road near the ocean. When he stepped out of the church, the startled spectators bowed their heads to him, and Itō Seizaemon, who was standing in front of the church, blinked his eyes with curiosity and asked, "Lord Petitjean, where are you off to?"

"I'm going to learn more about kite flying." With a lighthearted look on his face, he mimed the pulling of a kite string with his right hand.

"Excellent." Seizaemon nodded, appearing quite relieved. He knew that Petitjean had engaged in the kite battle with the Dutchman.

Petitjean came out onto the coastal road that was separated from Dejima by a canal, then strolled leisurely in the direction of Mount Kompira—just as he always had on his long walks. So seemingly carefree . . .

His diversionary tactics were supremely successful. Because everyone knew about Petitjean's "long walks," not a soul was even the least bit suspicious seeing him unhurriedly climbing the slope leading to the Suwa Shrine.

The spring sun illuminated the stone steps of the shrine. A young man was sitting on the sunny steps, a scale set down next to him. It was the young man who had promised at the Ōura church to meet him here today.

The young man was equally cautious. Even though the only people in the vicinity were two children kicking rocks, he gave no sign of recognition when he saw Petitjean, but merely stood up, hoisted the scale onto his shoulder, and began walking. Petitjean realized at once that he was meant to follow along.

The young man walked along beside the shrine and headed toward the mountain. The mountain was Kompira, famous for kite flying. On the other side of this mountain were the villages that made up the Urakami District, including Nakano and Magome.

The cherry trees were in bloom. Somewhere on the mountain a bush warbler squawked. These two peculiar men acted like total strangers to each other and maintained a gap between themselves as they climbed the mountain path. They saw blossoms along the path and heard birds crying overhead.

Eventually the young man stopped and turned around, appearing to think they were now in a safe location.

"We're OK here." He invited Petitjean to sit on a rock alongside the path, and he took a bamboo flask out of the basket he had carried on his shoulder. "Your throat's probably dry."

Petitjean greedily gulped down water from the bamboo flask. When he had finished drinking, he handed the flask back to the young man and asked, "What's your name?"

"Seikichi."

"I've been searching every single day for Kirishitans. I've taken long walks, I've quizzed the children . . . but all to no avail. Did you know I even went kite flying?" Petitjean muttered with some resentment.

"Yes, I knew."

"Then why didn't you identify yourself to me sooner?"

"Padre. It's dangerous." Seikichi shook his head in consternation. "The magistrate's office is keeping such close watch . . ."

"Seikichi, please tell me," Petitjean almost choked on the words. "Are there Kirishitans in places besides your village?"

"Not so many. Besides Nakano, a lot of the people in Ieno and Motohara are Kirishitans. And I've heard there are Kirishitans in Sotome and Hirado, and on Ikitsuki Island and the Gotō Islands."

Petitjean had no idea where Sotome or Hirado, Ikitsuki or Gotō might be located. But it moved him to the point of breathlessness to learn that in each of those places, followers of Christ had lived in silent fear for more than two hundred years.

"*Miracle! C'est miracle!*" Petitjean unexpectedly cried out in French. But how had these Japanese Christians maintained their faith undetected by others?

According to the piecemeal information he gathered from Seikichi—

With no priests to teach them and no church to provide them a spiritual foundation, the people of Nakano and Ieno and Motohara Villages had no recourse but to transmit the teachings of their parents orally to their children and grandchildren.

But everything had to be done in secret. They must not ever let people from any other village know that they were Kirishitan.

Under orders from the magistrate, every household became Buddhist. Once each year the *fumie* was set out, and they each had to trample on the face of Christ or the Blessed Mother.

However, they covertly continued to have their infants baptized as Christians, celebrated Christmas and Easter, and offered up their daily prayers.

Naturally, since they had no priest to perform their baptisms or offer their Masses, they chose from among their group those who would perform those various roles.

The person who calculated the dates for Christmas and Easter each year and communicated them to the others was known as the *Chōkata*, the "Register Official."[4]

The one who performed baptisms as soon as an infant was born was called the *Mizukata*, the "Water Official," because he sprinkled water on the infant's forehead at the time of baptism.

The individual who formed the line of communication between the Mizukata and the Chōkata was known as the *Kikiyaku*, the "Listener."

Yet even though they had created these clandestine roles and maintained a strict sense of group solidarity, there was always the possibility that they might sometime be detected by the magistrate's office.

---

4. I have adopted the translations of these roles from Stephen Turnbull, *The Kakure Kirishitan of Japan: A Study of Their Development, Beliefs, and Rituals to the Present Day* (Richmond, Eng.: Japan Library, 1998).

There had, in fact, been several crackdowns on Urakami by the magistrate's office—twice in the Kan'ei period (1624–1644) and once in the Tempō period (1830–1844). Urakami was a problematic, untrustworthy village in the eyes of the magistrate of Nagasaki.

"But they haven't brought us down!" Seikichi smiled with the pride of youth. "We're being very obedient right now, so the magistrate can't clamp down on us. For one thing, they'd run into trouble with the higher-ups if they created a big incident right now, so they pretend not to see anything we do."

"Seikichi." With a sparkle in his eyes, Petitjean unexpectedly asked, "Will you take me to Nakano? I want to meet your people. Meet them and administer *bautismo* to their infants. I want to celebrate Mass for you."

With the cries of the bush warblers echoing over their heads, the two men parted by separate paths. Seikichi went over the mountain and returned to Nakano, and Petitjean went back to his church at Ōura, a look of sheer innocence on his face.

But Petitjean had not realized or been aware when he headed toward the Suwa Shrine, pretending that he was taking one of his "long walks," that a man was stealthily trailing behind him.

The magistrate of Nagasaki was not such a pathetic fool after all. . . .

SPIES

AFTER WATCHING PETITJEAN disappear into the church, the man who had been following him returned to the Buddhist temple just down the slope from the church. The temple, which was serving as the locus of operations for the detectives, was called the Nikkanji and still exists today.

"Ah, you're back." An anxious Itō Seizaemon greeted the man. "So, where did the foreigner go?"

"He took a leisurely walk as far as the entrance to the Suwa Shrine. But I felt like there was something suspicious about the way he was behaving, and sure enough, a young man carrying a scale was waiting at the entrance. . . ."

"Hmm."

"The two of them climbed up Mount Kompira. While I was watching them through the trees, they carried on some secretive conversation. I think the peddler was a young man from Urakami."

"So I was right. That foreigner says all the right things, but he's quite the charlatan." Seizaemon nodded and nervously batted his eyelids.

"What are we going to do?" the man asked. "Would you like me to rake the young fellow over the coals?"

"Hold on now! If things get more serious, we can always resort to that. This involves a foreigner. If we take matters into our own hands and try to deal with him, it could end up in a quarrel between countries. We'd better consult with Lord Hondō."

It was not so much discretion that Itō was displaying as a fear that all responsibility might fall on his shoulders, so that afternoon when he returned to the magistrate's office he gave a report to the interpreter Hondō Shuntarō and then sought his advice.

Hondō Shuntarō had come to Nagasaki from Edo in order to learn Dutch, but he was also under orders to work as an interpreter at the Nagasaki magistrate's office. He was given the nickname "Stone Mortar" later in life, not primarily because his body was as massive as a mortar, but because in all situations he was scrupulous and never made a careless move.

"Lord Itō, you did well to be patient. Rather than making the situation worse through a hasty decision, I think it's best to watch and wait for a time. If this becomes known publicly, the Nagasaki magistrate might well be accused by the shogunal authorities of turning a blind eye to the outlawed Kirishitans. . . . That would be awkward."

Hondō deliberately repeated the word "awkward" in a low voice while pretending to slit his own throat with his hand. "I think the best plan would be to pretend for a time that you're not aware of what is going on."

"But won't the Kirishitan peasants and the foreigner end up going too far and make a fool of the magistrate?"

"No, when I said 'pretend that you're not aware,' I wasn't saying you shouldn't be watching them. In fact, you must keep a close eye on the Ieno, Kano, and Motohara Districts in Urakami. You should hire on a trustworthy peasant to be your spy."

"Hire a peasant?"

"That's right. Even if you send in an unarmed officer from the magistrate, they're eventually going to sniff him out. Meanwhile . . . I will keep an eye on the foreigner's movements." Hondō spoke confidently, though Itō did not know what he had in mind.

Unlike the other officials at the magistrate's office, Hondō Shuntarō had his own concerns about the future of Japan because of his study of Dutch and his interactions with the Dutch at Dejima. The others in the magistrate's office were so caught up in issues concerning their own stipends and status that they accepted without question the shogunate's conservative closed-country policy, but Hondō was a proponent of opening the country, believing that at some point Japan would have to throw open its heavy doors and interact with the other nations of the world. But he was sufficiently shrewd to know he could not openly advocate such a position so long as he worked at the magistrate's office.

However—

Though he favored opening the country, he found it hard to forgive the foreigner Petitjean for breaking his firm promise to the magistrate and covertly scheming to spread the Kirishitan teachings.

A promise is a promise. The magistrate gave him a house in Ōura and allowed him to build the Nambanji on the condition that he would not advocate the

Kirishitan teachings. But the foreigner has treated that exceptional magnanimity with contempt and seeks to violate his promise even more blatantly.

It seemed to Hondō that the foreigner considered the Japanese as fools.

But it would be a mistake to take the man into custody too quickly. In negotiations with foreigners, logic was more important than feelings. One must assemble evidence to support one's logic. This he had been made fully aware of through his interactions with the Dutch.

Consequently—

He had given orders to Itō Seizaemon to remain watchful while he himself would make a casual call on Petitjean.

As for the purpose for his visit, he had thought it through and decided to tell the foreigner that as an interpreter of Dutch, he also wished to learn French. That would leave no margin for suspicion.

"From me?"

Two days after his secret meeting with Seikichi, an unsuspecting Petitjean received a visit from a plump young samurai, but surprise filled his eyes when he heard the samurai's reason for coming.

"You say you work as a Dutch interpreter at the magistrate's office?"

"I do."

As his visitor nodded, Petitjean did a quick mental calculation, as he always did in such situations. *This fellow seems fairly bright. He might be useful to me in following the magistrate's movements.* He was convinced that as he taught the man French, he could elicit from him just how much the magistrate's office knew of his activities.

"All right. I'll teach you." Petitjean smiled as he nodded his head.

Beginning the next day, before lunch, this peculiar tutorial began. Although it was a teacher–pupil relationship, the real focus of study for both of them lay in probing each other.

"*C'est une table*," Petitjean would recite, and Shuntarō would respond, "*C'est une table*," though their motives were unrelated to these drills.

Because he already knew Dutch, Shuntarō made far more rapid progress than he had anticipated in his study of French—which had started with the *ABC*s.

Three hundred years earlier, Saint Francis Xavier, the first man to come to Japan to preach Christianity, had been astonished at the quick minds of the Japanese, and Petitjean, too, could not help but be impressed with the intellect of this young man from the magistrate's office.

During breaks in the lessons, Petitjean would summon Okane to bring out the coffee she had prepared, and as he offered it to Shuntarō, he made casual conversation. It was in casual conversation that he hoped to achieve his true goal.

"Is it bitter?" Petitjean laughed as Shuntarō screwed up his face at the taste of the coffee.

"No. I want to experience everything from your country." The young Japanese man's face flushed as he tried to swallow the liquid.

"You want to experience *everything* from my country?" Petitjean pressed the question.

"Yes," Shuntarō nodded, but he appeared to have understood Petitjean's true intention, because he corrected himself by adding, "Of course, only those things that wouldn't poison us Japanese . . ."

Petitjean immediately went on the counterattack. "Poison? What is there from France that could be poisonous to the Japanese?"

Shuntarō did not respond. Instead he sat holding his coffee cup in one hand and staring intently at the missionary.

Under that unwavering gaze, Petitjean understood precisely what this young Japanese from the magistrate's office was saying. In a voice laced with a trace of anger, he asked, "So do you think that the Kirishitan teachings are poisonous to the Japanese?"

"I don't know . . . whether they are a poison or a palliative. But for a long while we Japanese have avoided the Kirishitan teachings as a kind of toxin. You mustn't forget that."

"I am well aware of the fact, Lord Hondō."

"Then allow me to ask you a question. . . . In the Kirishitan teachings, is the breaking of a promise considered righteous behavior or an evil act? Which is it?"

"It is, of course, evil."

"Then . . ." Shuntarō set his coffee cup on the table and quietly replied, "I would appreciate it if you kept your promises."

"My promises?"

"Yes. The magistrate gave you permission to build a Kirishitan temple here in Ōura . . . but only for foreigners, not for Japanese. You need to keep that promise with exactness." His voice was soft, but there was force in it. Petitjean was flustered and blushed.

"Now, then," Shuntarō said, as if nothing at all had transpired, "shall we resume our lessons?" He adjusted himself in his chair.

Ichijirō had been planning in the near future to run some errands to Nagasaki and to check up on his sister Mitsu and cousin Kiku.

He wanted to praise them for enduring the harsh winter and carrying out their first employment responsibilities without incident. He also needed to pick up some medicine for Granny, whose cough had worsened.

He kept putting off his departure, thinking, "I'll go tomorrow," "I'll go tomorrow," until one day an acolyte from the Shōtokuji Temple came to summon him as he worked in the fields.

"His Eminence . . . wants to see me urgently, you say? What could it be about?" he mused, but the acolyte pleaded ignorance and hastened back along the road that had brought him here.

Ichijirō set down his hoe and headed straight for the Shōtokuji.

The chief priest of the temple was seated in a parlor adjoining the main hall, conversing with a samurai, but when he noticed Ichijirō come through the garden and kneel outside the doorway, he called out, "Ah, you're here," and turned to say to the samurai, "This is the Ichijirō from Magome I was telling you about. His younger sister works at a commercial house in Nagasaki."

Then to Ichijirō he said, "This is Lord Itō Seizaemon from the magistrate's office. I asked you to come here because I have received orders from the magistrate to send them a young man who could be useful to them, and after mulling it over, I thought you would do well." He gave an artificial smile.

Ichijirō could not imagine what this might be about, and it worried him that they might force him into doing some backbreaking labor, but he kept his head bowed.

"Ichijirō," Itō Seizaemon spoke between sips of tea, "it's just as His Eminence has said. Will you lend a hand to the magistrate?" He spoke as if it were a trifling thing.

"Yes, sir."

"It's not a particularly difficult task," the priest inserted himself in the conversation. "But it appears that some of the people in Nakano and Motohara are behaving suspiciously of late. As you know, for many long years now we've been discovering Kirishitans, or *Kuros*, as we call them, in those villages. After numerous interrogations we thought that we were rid of them, but lately the foreigner at the Nambanji in Nagasaki has been secretly visiting there. We'd like you to keep an eye on them."

"That's correct," Itō Seizaemon nodded at the priest's side. "If we sent someone from the magistrate's office, they'd be wary of him. But if we send a farmer from the same area, they're likely to open up to you and perhaps even expose their secrets. Will you do this? We'll reward you, of course."

It was a request Ichijirō could never have anticipated. His eyes widened in astonishment.

Ichijirō was, by nature, an honest man with a strong sense of justice, and he despised those who divulged the secrets of others or informed on someone else. Whether these people were *Kuros* or Kirishitans or whatever, so long as they weren't causing him any harm, he didn't like the idea of spying on them.

"Sir." He curled up his lips and grudgingly gave a vague response.

"You'll do it, then." The chief priest of the Shōtokuji stood up, as though it were a foregone conclusion that Ichijirō would agree to the request. "Lord Itō, that's all we need to talk about here. But it's been a long time since we've played . . ." He held up his fingers as though he were grasping a *go* checker piece.

"It has." Itō Seizaemon also stood up, and the two men disappeared into a different room.

That night Ichijirō's father, who was pounding straw to soften it, noticed that his son seemed disheartened, so he asked, "Has something happened? You don't look well."

When Ichijirō explained what had transpired that day, his father was silent for a time, but then with some bitterness he muttered, "Can't be helped." "Can't be helped"—the words of resignation a peasant utters when he is left with no choice. Ichijirō's own feelings were that it "can't be helped."

He was in no hurry to visit Nakano or Motohara Villages. A feeling of guilt and a heaviness of heart were weighty shackles on his feet.

But ultimately one must do what one has been ordered to do. To a peasant such as Ichijirō, an order from the magistrate was absolute.

One evening he finished his labors in the fields early, and telling only his father where he was going, he crossed over the Urakami River that formed the border between Magome and Nakano.

The scene at twilight was nothing out of the ordinary. Backed by groves of trees, fields, and hills, the squashed-looking thatched roof houses huddled together in small clusters here and there.

He walked into a thicket of trees, trying to avoid being seen. With the coming of spring and the eruption of new buds, the grove smelled verdant. He plucked one of the buds and put it into his mouth.

For a time he leaned against the trunk of a tree, staring at the houses and following the movements of a child leading a cow, but soon he wearied of that. Ichijirō had never had the desire or the curiosity to be a spy.

There's nothing here. It's no different from Magome. He thought that's what he would report to the chief priest at the Shōtokuji. Then he could quickly be relieved of this vexing assignment.

But just then—

He realized that an adult was walking by, concealed by the cow that the child was leading along. It was a tall adult.

This was no peasant. But the man didn't appear to be a samurai or a merchant, either. It was a foreigner dressed up as a farmer. The foreigner was wearing the work clothes of a peasant.

Suddenly he gasped. He had seen this foreigner somewhere before. He felt he had met him. He tilted his head and thought, and then suddenly the memory revived. *At Ōura . . . at the Nambanji.* When he had taken his sister and Kiku to see the renowned Nambanji at Ōura, this young foreigner had appeared through the doorway. *So it's him. I guess they were right . . .*

Apparently the suspicions of the officials at the magistrate's office were not unfounded. Otherwise, there would be no reason why the foreigner from the Nambanji would come all the way out here to Nakano Village, even going to the trouble of dressing in work clothes and hiding himself behind a cow.

The foreigner, the child, and the cow all came to a stop in front of one house, then studied their surroundings. The door of the house swung open, and someone swiftly poked his head out. The foreigner swept through the door as though it had swallowed him up, and the cow and the child began walking again as though nothing had occurred.

This is serious!

He didn't know just what was serious, but Ichijirō felt the words "This is serious!" swirling like a whirlpool inside his head.

He clung to the tree he'd been resting against, concealing himself behind it, and squinted his eyes to see.

There was nothing else unusual at the house the foreigner had entered. But before long, two peasants came walking nonchalantly past before vanishing into the house.

They were followed by three women who came from a different direction, and they, too, went inside the same house. Subsequently a number of other men and women evaporated into the house.

"Hmmm." It was now perfectly clear to Ichijirō. The residents of Nakano were in that house having some sort of criminal conversation with the foreigner.

What could they be talking about?

He thought of moving closer and trying to listen in on them. But he concluded that all his efforts would be for naught if he approached the house and were discovered, so he decided that for today he would go back to his village.

When he returned to Magome, stars were already glistening in the sky, but he shouted through the doorway to his house that he was going to the Shōtokuji and scurried over to the temple.

"Indeed? I thought they were up to something, but . . . so that's what it is." The chief priest set down his chopsticks and pondered.

"Is that all you need from me?" Ichijirō was hoping that his work as a spy would be terminated here, but instead the priest upbraided him. "All we need? You've got to keep a sharp eye now and find out what those people are up to."

"If they're such a concern, why haven't you already arrested the people in Nakano?"

"We have orders to let them be for now. To let them be and watch what they do. We have to have them do something they can't excuse away. In any case, the foreigner has joined them now, so the magistrate has ordered us to proceed with caution."

It wasn't a work to his liking, but Ichijirō subsequently paid three or four additional visits to investigate the activities in Nakano.

The foreigner appeared perhaps once in every five days, and when he went into that house, one by one the people of Nakano, from old men to youngsters, gathered there. Sometimes even a mother or sister carrying a baby on her back would attend the gathering.

He had no idea what went on inside the house. He tried to find out, but he realized they had someone on watch, so he would hurriedly find a place to hide.

It was clear that the people of Nakano were up to something, doing something that involved the foreigner as the key player.

Still, Ichijirō couldn't help but feel that what he was doing was shady. No matter how hard he tried, he couldn't begin to regard it as a good thing.

Ichijirō's purpose in going to Nagasaki after such a long absence was to go to market to sell the straw sandals and baskets that the family had woven over the winter. But he was also eager to see his relatives there and to try to forget his feelings of self-loathing for spying on these people. He was certain that his spirits would rise if he could just get a glimpse of Mitsu's honest face.

As always, he left the house at daybreak, and pulling a cart laden with sandals and baskets, he crossed the Nishizaka mountain pass. When he arrived at Nagasaki, he unloaded his cargo at a shop that would accept the items for sale, and once he had finished his work, he hurried directly to the Gotōya shop.

Since it wasn't proper to walk right in and ask to see one of the shop's employees, he waited around at the back entrance for a while until someone came out.

Nearly an hour later, a maid about the same age as Mitsu and Kiku stepped outside.

"Otome-san!" He recognized her as the girl who had accompanied them when he took Kiku and Mitsu on a tour of the city on the day of the Doll Festival, so he called to her from the shadows.

"Oh goodness!" For some reason this girl from the Gotō Islands covered her face with hands swollen from chilblains and scrambled back into the shop.

Before long, Mitsu gleefully poked her head out the rear entrance. "Ichijirō!"

"Ah, Mitsu! Have you been working hard?"

"I certainly have!" She grinned pertly. His younger sister would always be a child in Ichijirō's eyes.

"Dad and Mom are doing fine. Granny's all right. And how's Kiku?"

"Kiku is . . ." Mitsu hesitated for a moment. She stared at the ground as she muttered, "She's not doing so well."

Taken aback, Ichijirō asked, "Is she sick?"

"No, she's not sick. It's just that . . ." Mitsu let her words trail off.

Ichijirō pressured his sister. "Tell me what's going on. What's happened to Kiku?"

Mitsu looked up at her brother with resignation. "You can't tell Dad or Mom. Promise you won't."

"I won't."

"Kiku's miserable 'cause she hasn't seen Seikichi."

"Seikichi? Who's he?"

"He comes by here selling things in the morning. I think you'd remember him . . ."

After Mitsu reminded him that Seikichi was the young man who had saved Kiku years earlier when she couldn't get down from the tree but ended up being scolded for it, Ichijirō recalled the clever-looking face.

"She's a little too forward for her age." Ichijiro gave a wry smile as he thought of how precocious Kiku was compared with the late-blooming Mitsu. Then abruptly he asked, "Say—wasn't he from Nakano?"

"Yes."

"Absolutely not!" There was a fierceness in his voice that startled and frightened Mitsu. "This can't be. She can't be allowed even to think about someone like him." Some of the rage in his voice came from his own guilt over spying on the young man's village. "You've got to be very clear with Kiku about this. A girl from Magome absolutely must not fall in love with someone from Nakano, no matter what!"

"Ichijirō, what are you so angry about? And why can't a girl from Magome love a man from Nakano?"

"They're *Kuros*, that's why! I've told you this a hundred times. They secretly worship that forbidden Kirishitan nonsense. What's to become of her if she gives her heart to a man who's going to end up arrested before long and dragged off to the magistrate's office? She can't do it!" No sooner had the words escaped from Ichijiro's mouth than he regretted saying it. The only people who knew for sure that Nakano Village was made up of Kirishitans were himself, the chief priest of the Shōtokuji, and the magistrate, and he had been warned to say absolutely nothing about it to anyone.

Flustered, he tried to seal his sister's lips. "Mitsu. You mustn't say what I just told you to anybody."

"Not even to Kiku?"

"To Kiku . . . ? No, not even to Kiku. Just tell her that your brother says he won't allow her to fall for a man from Nakano. Give her that message." When he finished with that admonishment, he realized he had frightened her. "I'll be back again soon. Next time I come, I'll bring you some boiled taro, OK?" With those strained words of consolation, he hurried away.

When Kiku found out from her cousin that Ichijirō had come for a visit, she railed, "And why would he leave without seeing me?!"

Helplessly, Mitsu told her everything.

Seikichi's a . . . a Kirishitan . . . Dazed, she mused over what her cousin had said. *Seikichi is a Kirishitan. . . .*

To a girl from Magome, being a Kirishitan more than anything meant death. She pictured a menacing prisoner who has been condemned to die. Until now she'd simply believed that a Kirishitan was a criminal who broke the law by believing in something that was forbidden.

When she learned that Seikichi was one of those Kirishitans, she felt as she would have had she just been stirred from an unattainable daydream.

It just can't be! She muttered lifelessly.

But—

It wasn't as though nothing had happened to make her suspect Seikichi. Those kinds of memories came flooding back into her mind.

The rumors that everyone spread about Nakano. Seikichi's peculiar gestures at the Nambanji. Each memory served as evidence that what Ichijirō said was true.

"Then . . . ," she asked Mitsu in a frail voice, "do you think Seikichi will be arrested by the magistrate soon?"

Mitsu was dumbstruck and lowered her eyes. It was as though she, too, could picture Seikichi with both hands tied behind him, hoisted onto a bareback horse and paraded through the streets of the town.

Why did he become a Kirishitan . . . ? Kiku couldn't begin to understand it. It made no sense at all for Seikichi to join a heretical sect that the authorities had strictly banned, a religion so despised that every citizen was forced to trample on the *fumie* at the beginning of every year.

"Ichijirō said that the magistrate knows everything?"

"Uh-huh."

"Then I've got to warn Seikichi right away . . ."

Mitsu's eyes showed genuine fear at Kiku's declaration. "My brother will really light into me if you do that. . . ."

"Fine. It's all my fault. You don't have to say anything."

For the rest of that day, whether she was doing the cleaning or helping Oyone in the kitchen, Kiku was mute and lost in thought. Mitsu glanced nervously over at her cousin's face as Kiku stared at some point in the void, and she feared for what might happen. Ever since their childhood together, she knew that Kiku was the sort of girl who would never waver once she had announced her intentions. Over the years she had grown accustomed to the fact that once Kiku had made a decision, she would invariably follow through on it.

That night, after they had gone to bed and the rest of the house had quieted down, Mitsu tried to talk to Kiku in the hope that she might change her mind, but Kiku ignored her and pretended to be asleep.

It was raining the following morning. Mitsu noticed that Kiku, who had been at work just moments before, had suddenly disappeared. She had fled the store without permission.

With no umbrella to protect her from the drizzle, Kiku had broken into a trot as she headed toward the Nambanji in Ōura.

If there was anywhere Seikichi might happen to show up, the Nambanji was the place. That's what Kiku had concluded after thinking it through.

Tucking up her damp skirts and baring her white legs, she ran at nearly a gallop along the ocean road. That road no longer exists. Even that part of the ocean was later filled in through land reclamation.

The rain-swept ocean washed the shore with melancholy laps of its waves. Four or five fishing boats were still out in the dark sea. The gray roadway dotted with puddles wound its way between the sloping houses of the fishermen and continued as far as Ōura.

With heaving shoulders, a breathless Kiku began the climb up the hill to the Nambanji. There were no spectators today, perhaps due to the rain. She could not even see any officers standing watch.

Her clothing and face sopping wet and her hair splayed across her forehead, Kiku stood at the entrance to the Nambanji and looked around her. The pace of the rain had intensified, and the ocean and beach were swathed in haze.

She stepped beyond the boundary set by the officials and passed through the gate. Softly she opened the door at the entrance to escape the rain.

The thick door yielded with a dull creak, and she had a clear view of the tall ceiling, the black pillars, and the altar at the innermost part of the sanctuary. Gingerly she went inside, feeling a mixture of fear and curiosity.

To the right of the altar was a statue of a woman arrayed in foreign attire. The woman in the statue was cradling an infant, and she wore a crown on her head.

Taking a deep breath, Kiku stared at the woman. Never before today had she seen the face of a woman so pure, so clear. The woman in turn looked down at Kiku from her platform. It seemed as though the face looking down at her wore a gentle smile.

Ah . . . it's you, isn't it?

Kiku took a step backward, just a little afraid of the strange female image. She stood there frozen, not moving a muscle.

The sound of the rain outside faded. She heard the call of a sparrow that must have been hiding somewhere until this moment.

Just then the door at the entrance rasped. A man drenched by the rain stepped in noiselessly. Unaware that Kiku was watching him, he walked ahead, bent forward in front of the statue of the woman, knelt down, clasped his hands and bowed his head. . . .

It was Seikichi.

On those mornings when he came by the shop, carrying his wares on a pole over his shoulder, Kiku could never have imagined Seikichi in such a pose. She had never pictured such a look on his face. It was a look of rapture that was beyond her comprehension.

An inexpressible anger welled up inside her. Her rival was nothing more than an idol, but it made her unbearably jealous that Seikichi could look at another woman in such a way.

"Seikichi!" Her voice from behind him was piercing. "What do you think you're doing?!"

BATTLES IN THE DARK

FEAR, WORRY, THEN confusion. The three emotions swirled like a revolving lantern across Seikichi's face. He couldn't understand what Kiku was doing here, and he was embarrassed that she had seen him in the attitude of prayer. To disguise his feelings, he asked, "And what are *you* doing here?" It was almost an angry cry, and he hurriedly rose to his feet.

"Me?" Kiku did her best to remain composed. "I was just trying to get out of the rain. And you . . . ?"

He said nothing.

"I saw, you know. I saw what you were doing just now." Kiku's triumphant announcement left Seikichi even more bewildered.

"You saw what? What was I . . . ? I wasn't doing anything."

"You don't have to hide it. I know everything. I know that you and the people in Nakano are Kirishitans."

"Who . . . who's telling lies like that?"

"Lies? Seikichi. You're the one lying to me."

Seikichi's face contorted with indescribable pain.

"Seikichi!" Kiku cried. "Why are you a Kirishitan? You've got to leave them! The priest at Shōtokuji says it's a dangerous heresy."

Again Seikichi had nothing to say in response.

"They only teach you evil things, those Kirishitans. That's why the magistrate has banned it. So why can't you give it up?"

"The Kirishitan faith . . . is not a heresy!" Seikichi spoke resolutely, his fists clenched. "It's not a heresy. How can you just say such things when you don't know anything about it?"

"But it's what everybody says. They say that everything the *Kuros* do is strange."

"What kinds of strange things? Let's hear one."

Kiku was stumped for a reply. She really knew nothing about the Kirishitan faith. "Well, why is the magistrate ready to arrest everybody in Nakano?" With reluctance she played the trump card she held.

"The magistrate? Who told you that?" He grabbed her arms and held them tightly.

"Doesn't matter who. That hurts! Let go of me!"

Seikichi scowled but did not release her. "It does matter who it was! Tell me who!"

"I won't tell you. But it's not a lie. Seikichi, that's why you've got to give up this Kirishitan silliness!"

It was then that Seikichi sensed that something lay behind Kiku's desperate voice and desperate expression.

Until that moment, Kiku to him had been a willful, impertinent girl who got peevish and livid over the tiniest things. But now he understood why this brazen girl was quick to sulk and bluster.

Abruptly he let go of her arms. His face flushed in embarrassment. In the Kiku he had always thought of as a young girl, he now could sense a woman.

"Seikichi, won't you give up these Kirishitan beliefs?"

"I can't . . . I can't do it."

"Why not?"

"It's the faith my dad and mom and all my ancestors have believed in for generations. The faith that all the people of Nakano have defended. How can I be the only one to give it up?"

"But Seikichi, if you don't abandon it, you'll be punished by the magistrate. Is that . . . OK with you?" As she said the words, tears filled her lovely almond eyes.

"I can't do anything about it." As he spoke, Seikichi realized that he had to find out how this girl had learned about the intentions of the magistrate. And he must swiftly report all this to Nakano Village and to Petitjean. "I can't help it. Even if I am punished."

"I can't bear that! I can't!" Kiku covered her face with her hands, shaking her head.

It was her first declaration of love. This first love had not brought her happiness, only pain and sorrow.

"I'm sorry this is so hard for you, but . . ."

"Isn't there anything you can do?"

"Kiku. You really don't want me to be punished, do you?"

"Of course not."

"Then why won't you tell me? Tell me who you heard this from. That the magistrate will be raiding Nakano soon."

After some hesitation, Kiku finally admitted that it was her cousin Ichijirō.

"Ichijirō?" Seikichi pondered. What Kiku said was surely not a lie. "Listen, Kiku. I have got to get word of this to the people in Nakano. If I don't notify them, we'll all be bound up and carried off by the magistrate."

Kiku realized how the words she had carelessly spoken had set a vortex in motion. She was guilty of betraying and selling out not just the magistrate but Ichijirō as well.

"Don't worry." Had Seikichi sensed the workings of her mind? He shook his head. "I won't mention your name to anyone. And don't you say anything about this, either."

Kiku nodded compliantly, a first for her.

Some time later when she returned to the Gotōya, Kiku ran into Mitsu, her face tight, outside the rear entrance.

"Kiku!" Mitsu stared hard at her rain-soaked cousin. "Where have you been? You ran off without saying anything, and the Mistress and Oyone are really mad. I was so scared! You've got to hurry and apologize, or they'll be just furious!"

"Yeah." She had resigned herself to what awaited her, but still she was frightened to go into the kitchen. She tried to make herself small and peeked cautiously into the room, but the Mistress and Oyone were standing there, gazing at her coldly.

The Mistress callously turned her head away and said with piercing sarcasm, "Oyone. I couldn't say who it is, but we appear to have an important visitor."

"Well, I wonder who this fine lady could be?" Oyone's reply oozed of disdain.

"I really couldn't say. But since she is such an elegant lady, we certainly can't expect her to cook the rice or do any cleaning. She'll be going out to have fun without saying anything to anybody."

The biting exchange continued for some time, and when Kiku tried to apologize, they retorted with feigned surprise, "Oh, *really*? And where did Our Ladyship go? And what was she doing?"

That night when everyone ate dinner, no tray was set for Kiku. She was left alone to clean up in the kitchen, all the while sensing Mitsu's timorous gaze darting sporadically in her direction.

This is all to help Seikichi.

To take her mind off her hunger, Kiku put more than ordinary energy into the hand that swiped the cleaning rag back and forth, her thoughts focused on Seikichi all the while.

Her troubles now had come because she was trying to help Seikichi. But that, paradoxically, was a joy to her. It made her happy.

"Someday, Kiku, you'll understand that I'm not doing anything wrong." That was Seikichi's firm declaration to her as they parted. He was so confident in his assertion that she wanted to believe him. But why would the magistrate want to arrest someone who hadn't done anything wrong?

The only things certain in her mind were that even if Seikichi was a Kirishitan, she could never bring herself to believe that he was a bad person, that she could never despise him, that in fact, her heart was increasingly drawn toward him.

That night, after they had gone to bed, Mitsu poked her and said, "I bet that was really hard for you." She handed Kiku a rice ball. She had made it for Kiku when Oyone wasn't looking.

"It wasn't anything." It wasn't sour grapes, but how Kiku truly felt. Suffering for someone you love "isn't anything" to a young girl. . . .

Once again the rain picked up noisily.

"Padre, you'd better not come to Urakami for a while. The magistrate is keeping a close eye on you."

With gloomy eyes, Petitjean, having heard the full story from Seikichi, nodded his head. His own folly in underestimating the Nagasaki magistrate was now obvious to him. No matter how oblivious Itō Seizaemon had pretended to be, he had, in fact, found out everything.

Most likely Itō had taken his directions from Hondō Shuntarō. The young, wily interpreter had given him veiled warnings, but Petitjean had taken them too lightly.

"But, Seikichi, if I don't go . . . who will hear your *confissão*? Who will perform the *bautismo* for your babies?"

Petitjean's response left Seikichi in a quandary, and all he could do was sigh.

It was certain that if Petitjean stopped going to Urakami, the Kirishitans of Nakano and Motohara and Ieno were the ones who would be left in a quandary. They would have to go back to the old practices of appointing men to such positions as Chōyaku and Mizukata.

It was only after Petitjean pointed it out to the Kirishitans of Urakami, who for so many long years had been without a church or missionaries, that they realized they had introduced a variety of errors into the doctrine and practice of the church as they verbally passed down the teachings through the generations.

Elements of the Shinto purification ceremony had been inserted into their practice of baptism, and they had inappropriately merged the Festival of the Buddha's birth with the Kirishitan Easter. But these were the corruptions of lesser importance. There were numerous ways in which they had erased vital points of doctrine or rendered them ambiguous. If Petitjean stopped visiting them, they would end up back exactly where they had started.

"But we don't have any choice. At least until the pressure is off," Seikichi muttered, but that was merely because he had nothing else to suggest.

Was there no way that Petitjean could make contact with the Urakami Kirishitans without the magistrate detecting it?

Blessed Mother, please give me wisdom. Petitjean turned toward the statue beside the altar and prayed in his heart. Ever since the day he had found *them,* he had been praying to the statue of the Blessed Mother, in much the same way a child depends on its mother. . . . *They . . . they want my help. I don't want to leave them.*

The image of the Immaculata smiled down on Petitjean—like a mother listening to the fervent prayer of a very young child. . . .

You have your kite, don't you? Petitjean could almost hear the clear voice of the Blessed Mother.

"Kite?"

You learned how to fly it, didn't you? It's the season for kite flying in Nagasaki. It's not going to arouse the suspicions of the magistrate if you send up your kite. Use your kite!

Petitjean was certain he had heard the voice of Our Lady, like a mother guiding her child.

Ah, of course! Thank you, Blessed Mother! Petitjean's face lit up, and in jest he winked at Mary's effigy.

"Seikichi, I've had a great idea. We'll use kites to signal each other!"

"Use *kites?*" Seikichi was initially dubious, but after hearing Petitjean's explanation, he said, "Padre, that's a wonderful plan!" and clapped his hands in agreement.

Urakami and Nagasaki were separated by Mount Kompira, which was renowned for kite flying. No one in Nagasaki would be suspicious of a kite sent aloft in this season. Kite flying continued until around the time the new leaves burst forth.

"Seikichi, when you want me to come, send up a red kite. When the magistrate is on the lookout and might be suspicious, use a black kite. Don't you think that flying kites of different colors above Mount Kompira would work?"

Seikichi and Petitjean put their heads together and came up with a variety of kite signals. Using not only colors but also the shapes of kites, they were able to create a quite sophisticated system of communication.

"With this plan," Seikichi said as he was leaving, "the magistrate will never know what we're doing." He made it sound as though this were an exciting game.

The following day Petitjean reinstated his long walks, which he had furloughed for a time. At a set hour, accompanied by the newly arrived Father Laucaigne, he paraded in front of the Nikkanji, where the officials had set up their base camp, wearing a broad smile on his face and bowing politely to Itō Seizaemon's men.

The two priests made a circuit around the streets of Nagasaki. If they paid close attention, they could tell that someone was following them. Depending on the day, the man might be dressed as a craftsman or perhaps as a merchant's apprentice, but the priests had no difficulty discerning that they were spies sent out by the magistrate.

Once they were certain they were being tailed, Petitjean couldn't help but play pranks on them in the French manner. He and Father Laucaigne would stroll into the Chinese residential area and quickly hide behind a house, and when they caught a glimpse of the spies frantically searching for them, they would unexpectedly step out directly in front of them—it was hilarious to see the expressions on the men's faces at such times.

Even as he was pulling these pranks, Petitjean's eyes were ceaselessly fixed on Mount Kompira, which separated Nagasaki from Urakami.

By checking the color and shape of the kite sent up at a set hour, he was able to determine what the Kirishitans of Nakano wanted of him.

An *ago* kite with a black design.

That meant "Warning! Don't come."

Apparently Seikichi and his comrades had decided it was best to be discreet for a while, since they flew a black *ago* kite day after day.

To anyone else's eyes, it was nothing more than a tiny, unexceptional kite. But that little kite floating in the sky had profound meaning for Petitjean and the Japanese Kirishitans. The only other person who knew of this arrangement was Father Laucaigne.

When about seven days had passed, finally it was not a black kite but a paper *shōji* kite shaped like the frame of a paper sliding door that drifted lazily above Mount Kompira.

Please come, Padre. No spies today was the *shōji* kite's message to Petitjean as he looked up at it from the street.

"*Ça y est!*" A cry of victory sprang to Petitjean's lips. The magistrate's spies were not keeping watch today.

That night, after making certain that Okane and her husband had left, Petitjean put on the farming clothes he had stashed away, tied a kerchief under his chin as many Japanese did, and set out. It was already pitch dark when he reached the shortcut that descends from Mount Kompira to Urakami, but a young man from Nakano was waiting there for him, taking care that the flame in his lantern did not go out.

In the shed that they used in place of a church, Petitjean said the Mass. Old and young, male and female, from not only from Nakano but also Ieno and Motohara, had crowded into the shed, and the space reeked from the smells of sweat, body odors, and their expelled breath.

The citizens of Nagasaki thought of Urakami as a foul-smelling village caused by the stench from the animals that were raised there. The smell had gotten worse especially of late, when the villagers began to raise goats and pigs for the foreigners who lived in Nagasaki. As he recited the Mass, Petitjean thought of the horse stable where Jesus had been born. This shed that functioned as a church was similarly filled with the smells of cow dung and urine.

And yet Lord, is there another church this beautiful anywhere in the world? As he intoned the Latin words of the Mass, Petitjean thought of the catacombs where the primitive Christians had secretly assembled during the years of Roman persecution. This shed, with its oppressive air of human and animal smells, seemed as beautiful to him as those catacombs. It was magnificent.

O Lord, these Japanese have endured beyond endurance and employed all manner of stealth to maintain their faith in Thee. Please look upon the faces of these Japanese. Petitjean whispered the words in his heart, and he was unable to suppress the swell of his emotions.

The eyes of every man, woman, elderly lady, and aged male jammed into the shed were fixed on him as he spread his arms wide, made the sign of the cross, and blessed them. They were eyes like those of the parched who plead for water.

When the Mass was finished, he listened to many confessions. On some visits he would also baptize an infant. He was taken to the homes of the sick. Usually by the time he made it back to Mount Kompira, light had already begun to dispel the darkness while the city of Nagasaki continued to sleep.

Unless he returned at that hour, Okane and her husband would grow suspicious, no matter how well Father Laucaigne might try to cover for him. . . .

"*Je suis japonais. Vous êtes français. Il est japonais.*"

Hondō Shuntarō leaned against the window of the Yamazaki Teahouse in Maruyama as he memorized the French verb conjugations that were written on a piece of paper spread across his lap. He was particularly determined to practice over and over again the *L* sound, trying to mimic the way in which Petitjean pronounced it, repeatedly screwing up his face and pointing to his tongue.

"That's so funny . . . ! You look like one of those men who wears a village idiot mask at the festival!" A young geisha named Oyō, who sat beside him watching his struggles, couldn't help but put a hand up to her mouth and laugh.

Oyō, who would later become Shuntarō's wife and one of the most sought-after women at the Rokumeikan,[1] was at this time the most popular of the young geisha working in Maruyama. She was a fair-skinned beauty, buoyant and quick-witted, and she could hold the attention at parties hosted by even the most boorish of customers. It was the custom of the dandies who frequented

---

1. A Western-style building completed in Tokyo in 1883, the Rokumeikan (Deer-Cry Hall) was the scene of many parties and dances for Japan's social elite and became a symbol, for better or for worse, of the rapid Westernization of Meiji Japan.

Maruyama, whenever they wanted to bad-mouth a geisha, to open with "that wildcat . . . !" but not one man was ever heard to snipe about Oyō as "that wildcat"; instead, she was given the pet name of "Snow Queen of Maruyama" because of the exceedingly beautiful whiteness of her skin.

"Like the village idiot, eh?" Shuntarō chuckled. He was a jolly drinker, and when he laughed he twittered like a turtledove, not the sort of laugh one would have anticipated based on his massive bulk.

"So you won't be able to converse with the foreigners unless you make sounds like that?" Oyō taunted him with her eyes. "I hear that the foreigner at the Nambanji who's teaching you these baby noises takes long strolls every day, gives candy to children, flies kites, and seems like an all-around nice man."

"Yeah." Shuntarō nodded and looked through the window at the street below. On this spring evening, the lights of Maruyama flickered seductively. Swaggering by were men with scarves over their heads and their hands thrust into their pockets, as well as the bosses of merchant houses eager to deflower a novice geisha.

Watching them from the second floor, Shuntarō's smile suddenly changed to a gloomy expression and he muttered, "He's a good man. . . . But he's definitely a conniver."

"A conniver?"

"Uh-huh. He seems to be planning to spread the prohibited Kirishitan teachings among the Japanese, and he's making serious problems for the magistrate. It's as though he's rousing the normally docile peasants in Urakami from their slumber. . . . Those things you call his little strolls around Nagasaki . . . they aren't the innocent little outings you think they are."

"If they aren't just walks, what is he up to?"

"I'm . . . I'm not sure yet. But he's up to something. Definitely something . . ."

Oyō's eyes beamed with curiosity. "You mean not even the great Lord Hondō knows what it is yet?"

Shuntarō knew from Itō Seizaemon's reports that Petitjean and Laucaigne went out walking every afternoon. Seizaemon had likely concluded that Petitjean was guiding Laucaigne around Nagasaki, but there was just one thing that didn't make sense to Shuntarō: the fact that they set out on their walks at precisely the same hour every day.

According to Oyō's memoirs from late in her life—

Two or three days after she had this conversation with Shuntarō, she had an errand to run and headed for Kaji-chō on the other side of Shianbashi. As she walked the long road from Kaji-chō toward Teramachi, she noticed two foreigners strolling along, their backs to her.

Curiously enough, the two foreigners were the pair that Shuntarō had labeled "connivers." They walked along in a leisurely manner, glancing up at the temple roofs in Teramachi or calling out to children who were playing beside a fence.

Thinking of what the man she loved had said about these foreigners, Oyō was driven by a desire to somehow be of assistance to Shuntarō, so she followed the two men.

At one point the foreigners turned to look behind them, but they smiled in relief when they saw that the person walking a little ways behind them was merely a young woman.

The sky was cloudless. A few kites hovered in the sky. And just a few moments earlier, a sash-shaped kite had climbed into the sky above Mount Kompira.

Suddenly the two foreigners stopped in their tracks and said something to each other, then quickly turned on their heels and raced back along the road that had brought them to this point.

As their paths crossed that of Oyō, she hastily bowed to them, and they lowered their heads in polite response. . . .

This all comes from Oyō's memoirs, but however clever she may have been, she had no idea at the time that the kite over Mount Kompira served as the mode of communication between Petitjean and the Kirishitans in Urakami.

The sash-shaped kite that had swept through the skies that day was, by prior agreement between Petitjean and Seikichi, a signal of urgency. It meant that there was a gravely ill person close to death in Nakano, and they were waiting frantically for the priest to come and administer the last rites and prayers.

But when he scurried back to the Nambanji in Ōura, Petitjean found Hondō Shuntarō waiting at the entrance for his French lesson.

Mon Dieu! If he didn't reach Nakano quickly, the sick person might die. He had to find some way to slip away from Shuntarō.

"You've been out?" The magistrate's interpreter smiled, feigning ignorance.

"Yes. Father Laucaigne and I have been on one of our long walks."

"You've been particularly diligent about taking those walks lately," Shuntarō said trenchantly. "And they're always at the same hour. . . ."

Petitjean tried to appear unperturbed by this comment, but he sensed that his own complexion had changed. He had been thrust on the defensive, and when Shuntarō said, "Well, shall we get on with the French lesson?" Petitjean could not refuse him. He fidgeted anxiously throughout the lesson, and when Shuntarō made ready to leave, he asked the priest, "What's happened to you? You look as though your mind just isn't here today."

After Shuntarō left, Petitjean rushed to Nakano, but the sick man had already died.

THE CONTEST

THE BLOSSOMS HAVE fallen. . . .

Almost immediately Nagasaki was greeted by a flood of new sprouts. The young leaves sparkled in the early summer sun as though they had been soaked in oil, and homes were filled with the smell of new straw mats.

Kiku was on high alert every morning. She was standing watch in hopes that she would hear Seikichi calling out his wares far in the distance.

"*Takkekuwai!*"—That was what he shouted on days when he was selling bamboo shoots.

Each time she heard that strong voice, Kiku ran to the front of the store, carrying her broom. Sweeping the street in front of the store was one of her assignments, but it was no longer as cold as it had been on wintry mornings, so she would have at least a little time to talk with the man she loved.

But there was more to her anticipation. Each morning when she heard Seikichi's voice, she breathed a sigh of relief. "The magistrate still hasn't arrested him. Whew!"

Seikichi merely laughed at her. "The magistrate can't get his hands on me. Ever since you gave me the warning, me and everybody in the village is being careful so we don't get caught!"

At first she worried, but with each morning that she saw Seikichi striding energetically toward her, Kiku began to feel more and more at ease. Maybe Ichijirō had just been taunting her.

"Kiku, I got this from the padre at the Nambanji." One morning, Seikichi set down his load of goods, wiped the sweat from his brow, and suddenly looked very solemn. He reached into his basket and carefully took out something that looked like a silver coin from some foreign land.

"What is it?"

"It's called a *medaille*, and it's engraved with the image of Santa Maria. It's a very, very important treasure to us Kirishitans. I want you to have it for what you did for me."

"Me?" This was so unexpected that Kiku clutched her broom handle, her eyes sparkling.

"Yeah. But you can't show it to anybody else. If you show somebody, they might accuse you of being a Kirishitan."

The *medaille* he placed in the palm of her hand was engraved with an image of the woman she had seen in the Nambanji. Just like that statue, the woman here wore a crown and cradled an infant.

"I won't show it to anybody. I'll take really really good care of it, since it's from you."

"Ah." Seikichi lowered his eyes in embarrassment. "You know who that woman is, don't you? It's the mother of Lord Jezusu. She's called Maria. . . . If you pray with all your heart to her, she'll listen to you, no matter what it's about. That's what we believe."

A voice called for Kiku from the kitchen, so Seikichi scrambled to hoist his basket full of bamboo shoots onto his shoulder and headed off, calling "*Takkekuwai—!*"

The silver *medaille* shimmered in Kiku's palm. It was the first present she'd ever received from a man, and her only possession that smelled of a foreign land.

She heard footsteps. She swiftly hid her *medaille*.

The fifth month. The month of early planting.

In Nagasaki and the surrounding villages, the most important celebration in the fifth month was the day of the *Pe-ron* competition.

On the fifth and sixth days of the fifth month, during the Boys' Day festival, the young men from villages along the coast—including Magome, Takenokubo, Inasa, Mizunoura, Akunoura, Nishiura, Hiradokoya, and Senowaki—tied cylindrical towels around their heads, fastened their waistbands tightly, and participated in a rowing competition. The residents of each village and township assembled at the beach on those days and cheered on their team until their voices were hoarse. Their support for their teams was so impassioned that bloody fights would often break out.

The Japanese were apparently imitating a competition run by the Chinese residents of Nagasaki, who set up competitions between their barges. There is also speculation that the word *Pe-ron* was the Nagasaki way of pronouncing the name of the *Bailong*—White Dragon Boats—from Guangdong Province. In any case, it appears that the competition got its start in China.

Every year Magome sent a team of young men to compete in the White Dragon Boat Festival, so when the fifth day of the fifth month approached, virtually no young men could be spotted in the village. They all had gone to the seashore to practice their rowing.

Ichijirō was one of the rowers, and he got so busy with practices that he scarcely did any work in the fields.

And it wasn't just the residents of Magome. Everyone in Nagasaki—male and female, elderly and young—grew buoyant in the bright spring weather and looked forward with excitement to the fifth and sixth. Spectators pressed toward the shores in such great numbers that the streets of Nagasaki were basically uninhabited while the boat festival was going on.

"Padre." Seikichi and his comrades described the White Dragon Boat Festival to Petitjean and said, "So, you see, there won't be any spies from the magistrate out that day. Nagasaki will be deserted. You can come openly to Nakano and perform the Mass and hear *confissão*. Please!" Their plan was to take advantage of the boat racing day and assemble all the Kirishitans together.

"Still," Tokusaburō, one of Seikichi's friends, cocked his head curiously, "I don't understand why the magistrate hasn't come to arrest us. Do you think they're just afraid to?"

Thanks to Seikichi's report, they all knew they were being watched, but it seemed strange to them that the officials hadn't raided their gatherings.

"It's probably because they haven't caught us worshipping," a young man named Kisuke responded. "Padre, what do you think?"

Petitjean was puzzled as well. Piecing together some of what Hondō Shuntarō had said, he had concluded that the magistrate, suspicious of the entire region encompassing Nakano, Ieno, and Motohara, had been keeping an eye on them, but it baffled Petitjean that they did nothing more than observe.

Petitjean concluded that perhaps the magistrate's office was holding back out of fear that if they rounded up the Kirishitans, it would provoke the foreign nations who were even then pressing Japan to open its doors unconditionally.

When he expressed this view to Seikichi, Tokusaburō, and Kisuke, they gleefully responded, "So that's why they're so spineless!" To these impoverished farmers, the thought that they had been able to render the magistrate impotent merely served to magnify the delight they felt, since they had never thought such a thing possible.

The fifth day of the fifth month.

The roads from Nagasaki to the Magome inlet were packed with spectators. The White Dragon boats were lined up in the ocean, the stern of each brandishing a flag or banner decorated with the emblem of its village or seaside hamlet. The boats were extremely narrow relative to their length, which ranged from 88 to 118 feet. In the center of each boat was a wooden post festooned with streamers made of white or colored paper braids, as an offering to the Shinto gods. A gong was affixed to the base of the post. Drums had also been provided, and young men who beat the gongs and drums rode in the boats along with the rowers.

Before the boat race began, the beach and the road along the shore filled with people, who raised a tremendous clamor. The tumult swirled into the sky like a waterspout and could be heard all the way to Nakano and Motohara, which were quite a long way from the inlet.

Petitjean and Laucaigne stood in a squalid hut at Motohara. Before them stretched a tight row of faces, each of them exposed over many long years to sweat and mud, poverty and labor, sickness and pain.

Beginning the previous evening, these faces came pressing in one after another to plead with Petitjean. "Padre, please come quickly. I don't think my mother's going to last much longer. She keeps saying that before she dies she'd like the padre to offer *oração* for her." They begged fervently on behalf of infants who needed baptism, sins that needed confessing, and prayers and the Extreme Unction that needed to be performed before death.

Petitjean and Laucaigne hardly slept. Like doctors in a field hospital, they listened to petitions from one location after another, and in response to those requests they spent the entire night making the rounds of Nakano, Motohara, and Ieno.

"Is your mother's illness critical? If not, could you ask her to wait just a little while? The two of us can't get to everybody at once."

"Padre." A man they had never seen before pushed his way to the front of the throng and pleaded with trepidation, "I'm from Shitsu. There are Kirishitans in Shitsu, and there are many hiding out in Sotome as well. Padre, we wait day after day for a padre to come to us."

The shouts from the beach grew more vehement. The boat race had begun. The sounds of the drums and gongs echoed amid the shouting. People were intoxicated by the festivities.

But this room was filled with something other than festivity; it brimmed with human suffering and sorrow. "Greater love hath no man than this, that a man lay down his life for his friends." Petitjean recalled passages from the Bible.

Blessed are they that mourn
For they shall be comforted

He raised one arm and pronounced a blessing on each of these people who had been buffeted by pain and grief.

In this makeshift chapel a baby wailed as though it had been set on fire. Its mother slapped and scolded it. The smells of cow dung and urine blew in on a breeze. In a few moments he would be baptizing this child.

After he performed the infant's baptism, he and Father Laucaigne left their chapel hut and began calling on one house after another. Every house was pitiful and squalid and looked like a squashed animal shed. The smell of dung from pigs, cows, and goats hovered over them, and a flock of children pursued the two priests.

Peering into a dark, grimy house, Petitjean called out to an elderly bedridden woman.

"Forgive us. We couldn't come sooner because we've been occupied since last night."

He sat beside the old woman's bed, surrounded by people of the village. The woman's mucus-caked eyes were tightly shut, and she spoke not a word.

"Padre, for the past three days she hasn't eaten a thing or said a single word. She's beyond help. Please say a final *oração* for her." This came from a woman who sat by the afflicted woman, batting her eyelids.

Petitjean nodded, took the old woman's bony hand, and muttered the Latin prayer. The others in the room seemed to have closed their eyes in prayer as well.

"Padre, how blessed this old lady is. She has a padre to offer this *oração* for her," whispered one man with a sigh. "My mother died without ever being able to hear a padre's *oração*."

Petitjean remembered that day when he had been signaled by the kite to notify him that this man's mother was about to breathe her last, but he hadn't been able to come quickly enough because of Hondō Shuntarō's meddling.

"Padre, my mother ended up being buried with sutras chanted by the Buddhist priest at Shōtokuji. I guess because of that she won't be able to go to Paraíso." The man stared reproachfully at Petitjean.

Petitjean came to realize after his arrival in this country just how vital the Japanese regarded the services for their deceased parents and relatives. The Kirishitans of these villages were no different. Many of the questions they posed to Petitjean involved whether their dead parents and relatives could still be saved in heaven when, under orders from the magistrate, the services had been performed in the Buddhist tradition at their local temple, the Shōtokuji.

"Ever since that day," Petitjean tried to comfort the embittered man, "I have prayed continually for your mother."

"But you weren't here when she died. . . ." The man stubbornly protested.

It is far too bleak here, Petitjean thought. *If only I could help these Japanese develop a hopeful, untroubled faith.*

There was a commotion at the door to the house.

"Officers! Come quickly, padre, it's officers!" A sharp voice cried from behind Petitjean.

He and Father Laucaigne clambered through the back door of the house and raced outside. They were greeted by an outhouse with a lurching roof and a grimy pig tied to a stake. With a shrill cry, a flock of chickens scattered in all directions.

"Padre, come this way!" Kisuke ran ahead of the two priests. They hid in a copse of trees at the base of a hill behind the house.

Petitjean and Father Laucaigne panted for air amid the verdant aroma of the young leaves. From their position they had a view of several farmhouses squeezed together and hills blanketed with terraced fields.

Kisuke, who had concealed himself behind a tree trunk and was scrutinizing the hills, turned back to them and whispered, "Padre, they're over there. The officers . . ."

It was true. A single officer and a man dressed like a detective stood halfway up the hill, looking menacingly toward them. For some reason, they made no move to come down from the hill.

From the distant shoreline they could hear shouts and the beating of drums. The White Dragon Boat competition was still under way.

An insect with flapping wings hovered around Petitjean's face. Time passed oppressively.

The men and women who had fled the makeshift chapel went back inside, their faces radiating blamelessness. The officer and detective who had been watching them climbed to the top of the hill and disappeared in the direction of the village on the opposite side.

Kisuke raced out of the woods and said to a young man named Ichisaburō, "They've gone. Why didn't they come this way?"

"Probably because they don't dare arrest us. You remember what the padre said. . . . If they seize us Kirishitans, the foreigners in Nagasaki will complain. That's why they won't touch us."

Doors opened at a number of houses, and the people who had quickly concealed themselves came outside. They encircled Petitjean and Laucaigne who had emerged from the trees. Like the throng who welcomed Jesus when he entered Jerusalem.

"The officers can't do anything, because we've got the padres here!" When Ichisaburō explained this to the others, they sent up a cheer as though their side had just acquired a million allies. Their cry blended in with the shouts still coming from the White Dragon Boat race at the shore.

As he listened to the chorus, Petitjean suddenly felt a slight uneasiness. The anxiety that agitated his mind was like a black blotch appearing from nowhere in a blue sky.

I wonder if something terrible is going to happen.

His uneasiness had nothing to do with the arrival of the officers. What worried him was the utterly carefree manner in which the Kirishitans were behaving and how boisterously they were celebrating. If they went too far and did something stupid, it would give the magistrate a convenient pretext to take action.

He spread his arms wide and urged caution on the group. "Now everyone, listen carefully to me. Today the officers from the magistrate have gone. But they will surely come again. Please remember that."

The anxiety that had unexpectedly assailed Petitjean's mind at that moment became a reality ten days after the boat races.

On that day, an elderly woman in Motohara died. It was the same woman whose hand Petitjean had held and for whom he had prayed on the day they heard the commotion from the White Dragon Boat races.

She breathed her last in the middle of the night, and her family didn't discover her until the following morning, so Petitjean and Father Laucaigne were not able to be with her or administer the sacrament of Extreme Unction to her.

Toward morning, a man with a self-satisfied look on his face cautioned the deceased's family, "If you have the funeral in the Buddhist way, the old lady might not be able to go to Paraíso." It was, of course, the same man who had not been able to get Petitjean to come on the day his own mother died.

"But there's no telling how much trouble we'll be in if we don't notify the priest at the Shōtokuji." One family member shook his head nervously. When the family member of a peasant in Urakami passed away, they were required to report it to the village headman and to the Shōtokuji, which was their assigned Buddhist parish, and they had to have the funeral services performed by the priest at Shōtokuji. In this manner, the Shōtokuji was able to certify that the family was not Kirishitan and send that report on to the magistrate.

"In trouble? With the priest at Shōtokuji?" The man who had raised the warning sneered, and the men who had come with him likewise sneered. "Nothing to worry about! The officers of the magistrate can't arrest us even if they know we're Kirishitans. And nobody's afraid of the priest at the Shōtokuji!"

This was the attitude that had governed the village since the day of the boat races. Despite both abundant proof that the people of this area were Kirishitans and the information that the padre from the Nambanji had come to visit them, the magistrate hadn't sent a single officer to apprehend them. He couldn't. He couldn't afford to make any trouble for the padre at the Nambanji or for the other foreigners living in Nagasaki. . . .

"We can have the old woman's funeral just among ourselves as Kirishitans. We can ask the padre to perform it."

The family of the deceased ultimately agreed with the crowd's recommendation, eager to send their mother to Paraíso. Consequently, they did not report the death to the Shōtokuji or to the village head. Instead, they decided to send up a kite over Mount Kompira asking Petitjean to come to them.

But word quickly reached the village head that a death had occurred that had not been reported to him. He immediately sent a messenger with that news off to the Shōtokuji and raced over to Motohara.

He assembled all the people out on the road and reproached them, a look of bewilderment on his face. "What kind of reckless game are you playing? If the magistrate finds out about this, you'll be making trouble for more than just yourselves. You'll be implicating all the people in Satogō and Nakano and Urakami, and everyone will be punished. Are you all right with that? Does it matter to you that even your wives and children will be punished?"

But the peasants who had been summoned in from their labors averted their eyes and said nothing.

"I know that you people are Kirishitans. The reason I haven't said anything is because you haven't made any trouble. But if you persist in doing such foolish things, I won't be able to keep silent any longer."

An evening breeze was blowing, and as the sky grew increasingly dark, the warnings and lecture from the village head rambled on and on.

"Do you understand what I'm saying to you? If you do, then you have to report this death to the Shōtokuji immediately." By now he was almost pleading, seemingly having reached the end of his patience. He was fully aware that these peasants were defying him with their silence.

"Excuse me, sir," one woman called out from the group. "I . . . I don't have any use for the priest at the Shōtokuji. My parents and grandparents were all given Buddhist funerals, but I can't bring myself to believe that they're going to hell just because of that. But I . . . As you know, sir, my family's been Kirishitan for a long time. . . . And from now on I'd just like to have our funerals in the Kirishitan way." In the darkness, the woman's face was not clearly visible. But when she finished speaking, voices of assent rose from all around: "We feel the same way!" "Us, too!" Finally, as though it were the summation of everyone's view, some cried, "Sir, please just leave us alone!" Then silence reigned for a time.

"So that's it," the village head said with resignation. "If that's how you feel, then you'll need to send a declaration to that effect to the magistrate. I won't say anything. But I also won't protect you no matter what the magistrate decides to do to you."

"The magistrate?! . . . He can't lay a finger on us!" At that taunt, everyone burst into laughter.

That evening, as the headman tried to placate the infuriated chief priest of the Shōtokuji and encouraged him to write a complaint to the magistrate, the peasants persuaded a calligraphy master who lived in the village to compose a statement for them to send.

"We believe, based on the teachings handed down to us from our ancestors, that no sect other than Christianity offers any hope for the afterlife. Up until now, we have been forced, in accordance with the law, to have last rites for our deceased family members performed at the Shōtokuji, our assigned Buddhist parish. But we have done so only out of duty and not from our hearts. But now a Christian chapel has been built in the foreign settlement, and having heard the teachings there, we find they are in accord with that which we learned from our ancestors, and we embrace it as our faith."

Of course, the language of the statement was not in the colloquial used by the peasants, but in the style of the calligraphy master. Still, these words were the very first attempt by the peasants of Urakami, who for many long years had obediently followed the dictates of the shogunate, to appeal for freedom. For freedom of belief. Freedom of thought. Freedom to live . . .

From that day forward, every morning when she awoke and every evening before she retired, Kiku took out the *medaille* that Seikichi had given her, taking care that no one saw it. Only her cousin Mitsu knew her secret.

"It's wonderful isn't it?"

Mitsu had no choice but to nod and say, "Yeah," but Kiku was oblivious to her opinion in any case. This *medaille* was her most valuable possession because it had been given to her by Seikichi. And because it came from him, the image of the Blessed Mother engraved on it seemed to her the most beautiful thing she had ever seen.

"You mustn't tell anybody that I have this."

"But, Kiku, it scares me. It's like you've become a Kirishitan, too. . . . "

Kiku pretended not to hear. A child like Mitsu still knew nothing of what it meant for a woman to be in love with a man. Seikichi had explained to Kiku that he and the other Kirishitans in Nakano would never dream of causing trouble for anyone else. All they were doing was following the beliefs they'd been taught by their fathers and grandfathers. Why was that so wrong . . . ?

Kiku tried to believe in what Seikichi had said. Her love impelled her to do so. But it wasn't something a young girl like Mitsu could comprehend. . . .

"Kiku, did you eat the pickles I brought you?" Mitsu whispered from her bed. She had swiped some from the dinner table and given them to Kiku.

"Uh-huh."

"I'm so happy. Tomorrow's the day my brother's coming!" Ichijirō appeared outside their shop door on the fifteenth day of every month. It was the happiest day of the month for Mitsu.

Kiku also enjoyed Ichijirō's visits. But this time she was frightened. She had the feeling she'd get into trouble over her feelings for Seikichi.

"You're lucky to have a brother like him, Mitsu," she said in sincere envy.

While the two girls worked the following day, they kept one ear on the back door in case someone should come. Ichijirō always stood and waited by the rear door.

"Ichijirō!" He arrived past noon while Kiku was washing the lunch dishes. Mitsu signaled her with her eyes and she hurried to the back door.

"Hello! Are you both working your fingers to the bone?" Ichijirō laughed gleefully. "Nothing's changed back in Magome, except that Granny's back is hurting her." He went on to boast of how valiantly he and the other young men of Magome had fought in the White Dragon Boat races.

"Our opponent was the dragon boat from Nishidomari, so it was no contest!" Then, as if he had suddenly remembered, he peered intently at Kiku. "But Magome's the only place that's quiet right now. Urakami's in an uproar right now because of what's happened."

"What has happened?"

"Those lousy *Kuros* have caused a real stir," he said quietly, still staring at Kiku. "They sent a ridiculous statement to the magistrate. It said they don't want anything more to do with the Shōtokuji. The word on the street is that the statement horrified the town headman and he went to talk with the magistrate. And even though the chief priest went to Nakano and Motohara a number of times to try to reason with them, they wouldn't listen to him."

Ichijirō's face was unusually calm. But he continued staring at Kiku. She understood the meaning of that gaze better than if he had put it into words. With a stiff face, Kiku focused her eyes on her cousin's mouth. . . .

After a pause, she asked in a soft voice, "Ichijirō. Will the people in Nakano . . . will they be put on trial?"

Ichijirō again responded quietly, "I'm sure they will. If this were the old days, the magistrate's officers would've already raided Nakano and Motohara. But with all the fuss the foreigners are making right now, they've just been watching the situation closely. But the magistrate can't keep silent forever."

Kiku said nothing.

"Kiku," Ichijirō continued. "Not one of us in Magome has ever made any trouble for the Shōtokuji or our village head. A girl from Magome can't marry a *Kuro*."

"Ichijirō, if the Kirishitans get arrested, what will happen to them?"

"They'll be executed for sure." For the first time, Ichijirō spoke passionately, as though he were trying to intimidate his cousin. Kiku's body jerked like a spring.

"But the magistrate can't do anything to them now, can he? So there's hope that they'll be all right, isn't there?" Kiku sounded as though she were pleading with Ichijirō.

But he responded icily, "Hope they'll be all right? No hope at all. There might be if they'd sign an oath that they'd given up being Kirishitans. . . . But they insist they won't do that. . . . The village head doesn't have any idea what to do with them. And now word of all this has reached Nagasaki. The magistrate won't be able to hide it anymore. . . ."

What Ichijirō said was true. He was very familiar with the events because he had heard what the magistrate was doing and what was going on from the chief priest of the Shōtokuji.

"All right, I've got to go." When he had said what he came to say, he turned to his sister Mitsu and said gently, "I'll be back again. Anything you need?"

Kiku said nothing for a long while after Ichijirō left. Mitsu tried to encourage her by saying, "Kiku, you've got to cheer up." Kiku merely nodded, and seemed to be deep in thought.

On that same day—

Lord Tokunaga, ruler of Iwami Province and magistrate of Nagasaki, sent a special summons to Hondō Shuntarō to solicit his opinion. There were at the time two magistrates in Nagasaki; one was Lord Tokunaga of Iwami, the other Lord Nosé, ruler of Ōsumi Province.

The two magistrates were divided in their views. Tokunaga, fearing the impact that the situation in Urakami might have on other villages, took a hard line, insisting that the only way to maintain the dignity of the magistrate's office was to suppress the uprising at once. Nosé, on the other hand, held a more moderate view and, concerned about the enormous implications of having this whole affair become entangled with the ongoing issues in foreign relations, argued that they should adopt a watchful stance and request a judgment from the shogunate. Consequently, Nosé immediately left Nagasaki and headed for the capital to request instructions from the Kyoto marshal.

"Lord Nosé is too soft," Tokunaga sighed. "The upheaval is no longer limited just to Urakami. According to the reports from several village headsmen, some of the Kirishitans who've been hiding out in places like Shitsu and Kurosaki and Inasa are now openly traveling to Urakami, where they meet and talk together and build up each other's morale. The Kirishitans in Urakami continue to boast that they've cut off all association with their Buddhist priest, and their ranks grow by the day. If we do nothing out of fear of France, we'll be guilty of taking this too lightly."

"It's the times we're living in, isn't it?" Hondō Shuntarō folded his arms. If this were still the days of the earlier shoguns, he mused, no one would have dared do anything that challenged the authority of the rulers. But these days, when many of the daimyo domains, especially Chōshū and Satsuma, did not take the shogunate seriously and ignored their bidding, even indigent peasants like these in Urakami were beginning to make a mockery of the central government's power.

"As I've been studying language with Petitjean at the Nambanji, I've been discussing various things with him. I think these attitudes of the Urakami peasants have been fed to them by Petitjean and Laucaigne."

"What have Petitjean and the other priest been telling them?"

"That the shogunate has requested support from France because they can't control Chōshū and Satsuma. And that that's why they can't touch the Kirishitans here, because the religion they follow is the state religion of France. . . ." Hondō watched as the blue veins in the magistrate's temples bulged.

"Can't touch them . . . ? Petitjean came right out and said that?"

"Not in so many words. But he says it in his attitude when he breaks the promise he made with your office when the Nambanji was built here in Nagasaki."

The magistrate nodded bitterly. Then he lowered his eyes and muttered as though to himself, "I understand there are some antiforeign roughnecks who frequent the Maruyama pleasure quarters who'd love to cut down Petitjean. . . ."

Shuntarō had heard the same rumor from the young geisha Oyō. It would be a serious matter for the nation if anyone did something so foolish. He must act before this turned into an international incident.

"I . . . I believe it's time to make a move and arrest the main instigators in Urakami in order to underscore the authority of the magistrate. If we do nothing, these people and Petitjean will grow increasingly cocky, and that will only provoke the antiforeign element. . . ."

HEAVY RAIN

THE THIRTEENTH DAY of the sixth month. Midnight.

Heavy rain.

The fields and forests of Motohara and Nakano were wrapped in silence as sheets of rain pelted the ground.

The doors of every farmhouse were tightly shut, and everyone had long since fallen asleep while outside it was so dark that one could not see even an inch ahead.

In the Motohara chapel—which, in reality, was nothing more than an animal shed—Father Laucaigne was writing in his diary, relying on the light from a rapeseed oil candle that flickered like the wings of a moth.

The surface on which he wrote would, come morning, be transformed into an altar for Mass. Again tomorrow, a large number of Japanese Kirishitans would kneel at the base of that improvised altar. Some would come from Shitsu and Kurosaki. That group was presently asleep in the room adjoining their hut, snoring loudly. . . .

I've neglected writing in my journal for a long while. A dizzying number of things have happened over the past month, and we've been so busy we've scarcely had time to sleep. Father Laucaigne paused in his writing to listen to the sound of the rain. As he lent his ears to the downpour, in his mind he sought to put in order the events that had occurred this past month.

At night, we leave the Ōura Church like bats escaping from a belfry. We remove our vestments and put on Japanese clothing that the Kirishitans have provided for us. Then we put on wigs with a samurai topknot, slip on straw sandals, cover our faces from the tops of our heads to beneath our chins with a scarf, and head out into the silent streets. There's no longer any need to use the kites to contact one another. Even if the officials know that we slip out at night, they can't do anything about it. The young man from Urakami who comes to guide us carries a lantern and starts out ahead of us, with the implements for the Mass in a pack on his back. When we arrive in Urakami . . .

Once more he stopped writing and listened intently. The violent rain had stopped abruptly, and he could hear the croaking of frogs.

"Padre, haven't you gone to sleep yet?" A young believer who had awakened gave a yawn and headed outside. He probably needed to relieve himself.

Everything works in our favor. The long-standing policy of Christian persecution adopted by the Japanese government is, however slowly, becoming a policy in name only. When the Japanese come inside our chapel, the authorities merely blink at it, and a few days ago, when Father Petitjean was installing an image of the Blessed Mother that he had requested from France, those in attendance included not just representatives from various foreign nations but the Nagasaki magistrate himself. He peered curiously around the sanctuary, gazed at the holy image, and even shook hands with us before leaving. With changes like that, I'm certain it won't be long before the Japanese abandon their anti-Christian policy altogether.

The young man returned from outside, said "Good night" to the priest who was engrossed in his writing, and disappeared.

Apparently the rain had now stopped completely. The croaking of the frogs became rather annoying. Father Laucaigne stretched out his back and twisted his weary head to the left and the right. It was almost 3:00 A.M.

At that same hour . . . a black column of officers was climbing the hills from Magome toward Motohara and Nakano, tracing a route alongside the Urakami River. The padre, of course, could not have known anything about this.

The official record states that the number of policemen who raided Urakami that night was approximately 170. The columns of police, led by government officers Andō Ginnosuke, Yatsu Kanshirō, and Hondō Shuntarō, chose this night of fierce downpour to steal undetected into the hamlets of Nakano, Motohara, and Ieno.

By the time the sleeping peasants were awakened by the sounds of footsteps, their houses were already surrounded.

What follows is Father Laucaigne's detailed report of the events of that night:

Saturday and Sunday nights were exceedingly peaceful, with not a single suspicious sound to be heard. Despite the pounding rain, the faithful who had made their preparations for baptism arrived one by one, retired to the chapel or to houses in the neighborhood and calmly fell asleep. But on Monday night, around 3:00 A.M., the doors were suddenly flung rudely open. I heard Ichinosuke cry out, "It's the police! Run! Quickly!!" I pulled a Japanese kimono over my cossack and flew out the rear door. At just that moment, constables came storming in through the front door.

Father Laucaigne escaped to a mountain called Mount Ippongi. Running behind to protect him were Ichinosuke, Tatsuemon, Seikichi, and Yūkichi. The five men ran for their lives, their shoulders heaving, along the rain-soaked road.

"Padre, just a little farther," Yūkichi shouted to the priest as they ran. "Old lady Kira at Ippongi has a hut where you can hide."

Agonizingly the priest replied, "I . . . I left the Mass implements behind!"

The four Japanese Kirishitans stopped in their tracks. The implements for the Mass were of irreplaceable value to them.

Yūkichi muttered decisively, "I'll . . . I'll go back and get them."

"If you're going, I will too!" Seikichi responded. At that, the two men slid down a slope covered with rain-soaked pine trees.

The sky grew light; night was breaking.

"Padre, we must hurry!" Ichinosuke urged the priest, who was still looking absently in the direction the other two young men had fled. The sun was already up by the time they located the two huts near the top of the mountain. A dog barked in the distance.

They dove into the huts and asked old Kira to get them a set of tattered clothes.

"We don't need them. These are for the padre to change into." Ichinosuke and Tatsuemon handed the single set of tatters to the priest and stepped outside the hut to stand watch.

The dog's bark drew closer. Evidently the constables were coming this way.

"Padre, it isn't safe here, either. You've got to escape to the valley or you'll be arrested."

With no time to rest, the three men fled the hut and rushed down to the valley below Mount Ippongi. The trees that sheltered the valley would hide the three men from view.

The rain had stopped, but a milky fog veiled Mount Ippongi, concealing Father Laucaigne, Ichinosuke, and Tatsuemon.

Again a dog yapped in the distance. It had to be a dog belonging to their pursuers. But perhaps they had been discouraged by the heavy fog that blanketed the valley: the barking sounds retreated gradually into the distance.

"I wonder if everybody got away," Tatsuemon mumbled. Then he asked Ichinosuke, "What do you remember happening?"

"I went outside to piss in the middle of the night, and when I opened the door, I saw a big lantern on a pole coming toward us. So I shouted out to the padres to warn them . . ."

"Do you think the other two will make it back?" The priest was concerned about the two young men who had courted danger by going back to the village to retrieve the Mass implements.

"No need to worry about Seikichi and Yūkichi, padre. They're sharp, those boys."

Father Laucaigne closed his eyes and leaned back against a rock. Exhaustion washed over him. He had not slept since the previous night.

Meanwhile, after Seikichi and Yūkichi left Father Laucaigne and the others, they slid down a tree-covered slope. They could hear the gurgling of a mountain stream; it came from the headwaters of the Urakami River that flowed through Motohara.

The two men hid behind the wet trunks of two trees and listened carefully for any sounds. But they could hear nothing other than the murmuring of the river and the plopping of raindrops falling from the branches.

Yūkichi asked, "Do you think they've gone? It's so quiet."

"The fog is so thick, you can't even see the houses or the fields from here," Seikichi nodded. "I think it's OK to go to the bottom of the hill."

They stepped out of the trees. Skirting past the terraced fields, they headed toward a cluster of houses. Their feet were caked in mud, and a wind whipped the fog around, providing them a glimpse of a young woman standing nearby.

"Isn't that Maki from Ichizō's family? What's she doing there?" Yūkichi whispered to Seikichi, then called toward the figure, "Maki!"

Maki turned toward them and cried, "Don't come this way! Run!!"

Several men came bounding through the fog.

Yūkichi tripped and fell to the ground, screaming to Seikichi, "Get away!! Hurry!!"

A man tumbled on top of Yūkichi. Several men kicked him and then bound him in ropes.

Seikichi fled for his life into the trees. He leaped into the swirling fog and tried to hide. His pursuers, totaling nearly ten men, split into three groups in an effort to cut him off.

"You should get some sleep, too," Father Laucaigne called to Ichinosuke and Tatsuemon, who sat with their backs to him. The two men planned to let the priest rest while they waited anxiously to hear the footsteps of Seikichi and Yūkichi returning.

"We will, but those two haven't come back yet. What could have happened to them?" Ichinosuke muttered with concern. "Padre, I'm going to go look for them. Please stay here with Tatsuemon. If you move on, I won't know where to find you when I come back." He paused, then with some discomfort said, "Padre, I have a favor to ask. If I make it back today, I'd like to receive *bautismo*."

Father Laucaigne nodded and watched as the man spun on his heels and disappeared into the fog.

A faint light broke through the overcast sky, enough to weigh heavily on their eyelids. The clouds over Nagasaki cracked open and blue sky appeared. Father Laucaigne shut his eyes and began to pray. Following his example, Tatsuemon also intoned an *oração*, but before long his muttering broke off and he dozed, his head bobbing up and down. The fear and tension of the previous night had drained both him and the priest.

Soon Tatsuemon was awakened by the faint sound of footsteps coming down the mountain path. He put his finger to his lips and whispered, "That's not Ichinosuke. Padre, don't make any noise." The two men froze and listened for movement.

"Hello!" It was a man's voice, but not Ichinosuke's. The priest wondered whether it might be a Kirishitan, but Tatsuemon shook his head sternly, so he did not respond.

"There's nothing to be afraid of. It's Chiyomatsu, I live next door to old lady Kira. She asked me to bring you some sandals and raincoats."

When Tatsuemon finally responded, they again heard footsteps and two farmers appeared from the fog-swathed forest.

"What's happening in the village?"

"We don't really know. But there was a huge uproar before dawn, and then we heard dogs barking."

"That was the officers looking for the padre and us. But it looks like they gave up with all this fog. Yūkichi and Seikichi went to check things out, and Ichinosuke went looking for them, but none of them have come back yet."

"Do you think they were caught?" Chiyomatsu said it as though he blamed Father Laucaigne for all their troubles. "They shouldn't have gone back to the village."

Father Laucaigne lowered his eyes. It was true that if the missionaries had not come to Nagasaki, these Japanese Kirishitans would have been able to live quiet, peaceful lives just as they always had. . . . But because they had come . . .

At that same hour—

The fog was swept away by the wind, and the shapes of thatched roofs and tree branches became clearly visible. From among those houses and trees a group of peasants, male and female, bound with ropes and caked with mud, struggled down the slope, driven like animals. Constables followed behind them.

Motohara was not the only village where arrests were made. Throughout the morning hours the Kirishitans of Nakano and Ieno were also shaken from their sleep; they too had scrambled to escape and been captured.

Many months later, Sen'emon from Motohara reported: "Around 3:00 A.M. there was a loud pounding on the door, so I woke up and went to see who it was, and when I opened the door a whole flock of officers charged into the house. They took me and tied me up, and when I asked 'What crime have I committed?'

they said, 'Rude bastard! You'll find out soon enough!' and then they beat me. As they led me off in ropes, they stopped at Yasaburō's place and then asked me where Taira no Mataichi's house was. But I wouldn't tell them, so one of them shouted 'I'll cut you down!' and whacked me over the head with the side of his sword."

Kanzaburō of Nakano related the following:

The night of the thirteenth, Zennosuke, Kisuke, and I were sleeping in the chapel. But around 2:00 in the morning of the fourteenth, we woke up and saw nearly thirty lanterns with red rising suns printed on them. We realized it was the officers come to arrest us, so we scurried around trying to find a place to hide the Blessed implements, but just then they all came racing in through the front door. . . . I put my hands behind my back and said, "Please tie me up," but they were very frightened and said, "He's trying to work one of their Kirishitan spells on us!" and they threw a lasso around me, and three of them tied me up real tight. But I passed out while they were trying to tie the rope around my neck. They brought me back with some water and smelling salts. . . .

Maki, the daughter of Ichizō of Motohara, was awaked early on the fourteenth by fierce pounding on the door of her house.

"Is that you, padre?" She asked.

"What's a padre? Have you got a foreigner in there?"

When Maki replied that there wasn't, a shuffle of footsteps scrambled up to the chapel where Father Laucaigne was staying. This was soon followed by a storm of noises—pounding on the chapel door, the cracking of the door as it was broken down, shouting voices.

Maki and her father, Ichizō, went outside and looked up toward the chapel. Constables had encircled it in such a throng that a single ant couldn't have broken through.

The constables returned to Maki's house and interrogated her father.

Maki told them, "My father's been home all night. You can see that his clothes aren't wet from the rain."

But a constable jerked open the breast of his kimono, found a scapular of the Blessed Mother hanging from his neck, and immediately tied him up.

By the time dawn broke, a long line of peasants bound in ropes were taken from Motohara and Nakano to the house of the village headman. The number totaled sixty-eight men and women.

Dawn came. Kiku and Mitsu awakened as always along with the other servants the moment light appeared in the sky, got themselves ready, washed their hands, and started in on their various chores. Mitsu and Tome hiked up their skirts and drew water from the well, then lit fires under the several large kettles in the kitchen. As the rice cooked, they dusted and cleaned.

Kiku's assignment in the morning was to tidy up the entryway to the shop. As she swept, her face was constantly turned toward the road that reached into the distance. She waited to hear the bracing voice of Seikichi as he came down the road, calling out to prospective buyers.

Because of the heavy rain the previous night, portions of the road were still wet. But there were no puddles of water in this neighborhood because the shop owners spread sand on the roads.

The sky was still overcast, but tiny patches of blue could be seen between the clouds. It would probably clear by midday.

When Kiku finished her cleaning, she sat down to breakfast. It was the practice in this household for all the apprentices and clerks to gather together and await the arrival of the Master while the Mistress and all the maidservants prepared the morning meal.

It happened after they had all sat down to eat.

Someone raced past the shop entrance, shouting.

That was followed by a number of people racing by and shouting.

The Master was just about to pick up his chopsticks. He looked with concern toward the Mistress and said, "What in the world is going on?" Then he gave an order, "I doubt there's a fire or a brawl this morning. Somebody go outside and see what's happening."

Kiku was the first to dash to the earthen entryway. At such times she was always faster than the apprentices.

When she stepped out onto the street, four or five men and women were racing toward the main road.

Kiku caught one of the women hurrying past and asked, "Excuse me, ma'am, but what's going on?"

The woman stopped and said, "The *Kuros* of Urakami have been arrested, and they're being taken to the magistrate's office right now." The woman quickly ran after her comrades.

The *Kuros of Urakami* . . .

Kiku staggered against the fence, feeling as though her head had been bludgeoned with a club.

Kuros were Kirishitans. And to Kiku, the "*Kuros* of Urakami" had only one meaning: Seikichi.

"The *Kuros* have been arrested . . . !" One apprentice who had followed her outside hurried back into the shop, loudly calling out his report to the Master.

But Kiku had no interest in the shop right now. Completely forgetting that she was supposed to report back to the Master, that she was to have breakfast and clean up afterward, she took off at full speed. Just as on a previous day she had gone out into the rain looking for Seikichi . . . Like a gunshot . . .

Looking at Nagasaki today, it's difficult to conjure up what this district looked like back then. Areas that used to be part of an inlet have been filled in and transformed into residential neighborhoods.

But if you study it carefully, you'll see that traces of the old cape can still be seen along National Highway 34 and in Manzai-machi and that this area was in fact a promontory. The spot where the municipal water works office is now located was, during the Kirishitan period, the site of the famed "Church at the Cape." After the church was destroyed, a jail known as the Sakuramachi Prison was built in its place.

The Kirishitan peasants who were arrested and taken from Urakami would have had to climb over the hill at Nishizaka and then be led to this Sakuramachi Prison. Spectators pushed their way forward, waiting to catch a glimpse of the prisoners when they arrived in Sakuramachi.

"It's divine punishment, serves 'em right if they're executed."

"Yeah, and think of how tough it must've been for the officers to have to go out in that awful rain last night. They'd have been soaking wet as they crossed the hills into Urakami."

Some of the spectators talked as though they had actually witnessed the previous night's events. The consensus among them was that however the magistrate chose to handle the situation, the prisoners deserved whatever they got. The citizens of Nagasaki regarded the peasants of Urakami who believed in the outlawed Kirishitan faith as unlikable and untrustworthy.

Concealed in the crowd, Kiku looked toward the Nishizaka hill. It was the hill that she and her cousin had climbed, in company with the chief priest of the Shōtokuji, the first time they came to Nagasaki. There was an execution ground on the hill that had not been used in many long years, but in the past many criminals had been put to death there.

"I hear that the people of Urakami have been *Kuros* for a long time."

"That's right. They say there's already been three raids on the village."

Kiku overheard the disparaging comments made about Urakami. With each remark, she glared through beautiful, ruthless eyes at those who made such irresponsible statements. Kiku could not countenance those who spoke ill of the village where she had been born and raised.

"Here they come . . . !" someone called out. The heads of every spectator turned as one toward Nishizaka. The procession made its way down the slope, officers of the magistrate at the lead, followed by the prisoners, who were flanked by a company of club-carrying men.

Shouts of surprise arose from the crowd as the column approached. The officers and their prey were covered in mud. Their grimy appearance summoned forth images of the terrifying scene from the previous night.

Most pitiful to see were the men in the group who were nearly naked and the women in torn nightgowns that scarcely covered their bodies. Wrenched from a deep sleep, none had had time to change their clothing.

"Criminals . . . !"

"Fools!"

Relentless insults were hurled like pebbles by the spectators. Under the hail of vulgarities the Kirishitans dragged their muddy feet forward with weary expressions on their faces. Kiku searched those faces frantically to see whether Seikichi was among them.

Seikichi . . . was there.

He walked, somewhat unsteadily, near the middle of the procession, his wrists bound together. Like many of the other men, his clothing was torn, but Kiku nearly cried aloud when she saw that his face was cruelly swollen.

Evidently he had tried to resist his arrestors and was viciously beaten. That was obvious from the dark trails of blood on his cheek.

Licking his swollen upper lip with his tongue he continued walking, staggering occasionally into the man behind him. His eyes seemed unable to focus, as though he were in a trance.

"How dare they mock the temple priests and the buddhas!" An old woman standing next to Kiku commented to a young man beside her. The young man picked up on her scorn and shouted, "Damn you all!!"

That startled Seikichi from his stupor and he looked in the direction the voice had come from. And there he saw Kiku. . . .

Astonishment and humiliation flashed simultaneously on his face. Seikichi hurriedly lifted his bound hands and tried to pull his clothing over his exposed chest.

"To hell with you people from Urakami! You and your beliefs in that Kirishitan claptrap!" When the young man heaped further abuse on the prisoners, Seikichi, aware of Kiku's presence, responded loudly, "What's wrong with being from Urakami? We won't change our beliefs no matter how much we suffer!"

"Ha! You're so bullheaded, you probably think you've got nothing to worry about, but you'll find out differently in jail! Just don't be screaming your head off!"

The procession passed through the gate of the Sakuramachi Prison. A guard holding a long wooden pole waited until the last prisoner had disappeared and then closed the heavy gate.

"That fellow may talk big," the young man who had just exchanged words with Seikichi was still provoked and spat. "Just wait 'til he's made to do the straw coat dance!"

"What's the straw coat dance?" Kiku asked.

"It's one of the ways they punish the Kirishitans. They wrap 'em in a straw raincoat and then set fire to it. They call it the straw coat dance because it gets so hot in there they hop around all over the place." The young man described the tortures in the prison as though he had witnessed them himself.

Fear caused the blood in Kiku's face to drain away. Moments before she had been impressed at how strong Seikichi was when he talked back to this young fellow. But now she could not bear the thought that Seikichi would be facing brutal torture.

Seikichi, why can't you give up this Kirishitan thing?! She wanted to shout the words through the tightly closed gate.

Kiku could not see what was happening beyond the thick prison gate that separated her from Seikichi.

First, the prisoners were divided up by gender and taken to separate cells.

"Strip!"

The officers who had escorted the procession had dispersed, but now the policemen carrying the long poles ordered the prisoners to remove all their clothing.

Once they ascertained that everyone had stripped naked, they unlocked the side gate leading to the cells. When the tiny gate creaked open, they could hear the sounds of other prisoners moving around in the darkness. The area reeked of their sweat and body odors.

"Now, listen carefully. You stick your head in through here, and then you go in slowly." The policeman called out to the young man at the head of the rank. The young man, stripped even of his loincloth, bent, then crouched down and crawled forward like a dog on all fours and poked his head through the tiny cell gate.

At that moment, a large hand reached out from inside the cell and grabbed his hair, and a voice called, "Got him!" The young man was flung faceup into the cell.

"Next!" The second man was also pulled by his hair, dragged through the opening, and tossed into the cell.

This was the initial ritual at the prison. It wasn't limited just to the prison at Sakuramachi in Nagasaki; it was a rite performed in those days among prisoners at many different jails.

Once every new prisoner had been thus incarcerated, the clothing they had removed was examined and then flung in after them. The prisoners who had been lined up in single file were finally able to cover their nakedness, after which they were instructed to sit in front of the chief of the prisoners. The formalities were not yet completed.

"Listen up! Now that you're in here, who's brought me a gift?"

Those who responded that they had no gifts were given a tongue-lashing and ordered to write a letter home asking for money at once. The common practice was for the chief to demand an exorbitant amount, but then a mediator would step in and negotiate a discount to which the newcomers were forced to agree.

But the indigent farmers of Urakami had no means to procure the amount of money he was requiring. Four or five of them hung their heads and pleaded that they could not possibly offer the amount demanded, at which the prisoner chief unexpectedly excused them from their obligation. Perhaps he had been moved by pity when he saw their pathetic, mud-splattered figures. But in exchange, they were ordered to clean the toilet and give him massages.

It was hot inside the prison. The smells of sweat and feces compounded the stuffiness.

Overwhelmed by the sheer numbers of the newcomers, the chief inquired, "What are all of you in here for?"

"For generations, our families have believed in Deus and Jezusu," a young man from Nakano named Moichi replied.

"What's this Deus?"

"We're Kirishitans."

The chief looked puzzled. Someone to his side explained that they were *Kuros*.

"*Kuros*, are you?" The chief said gleefully. "So that's what you were arrested for?"

A CHANCE ENCOUNTER

KIKU TIPTOED THROUGH the service door of the Gotōya and went into the kitchen. She was prepared for a tongue-lashing. She had fled without telling anyone and now was coming back many hours later. She had to be ready for any invectives that were heaped upon her.

Breakfast was long since over and the kitchen was silent. It was deserted, and all the kettles and pots were put back in their normal places, from which they watched Kiku coldly.

She wiped her feet with a rag and stepped up onto the wooden floor. She started toward the room where Tome and Mitsu would be mending clothing, but just then Oyone appeared at the far end of the corridor.

She stopped for a moment when she saw Kiku, but then walked past her without any expression on her face, as though she had seen a stone. From Oyone's taciturn behavior, Kiku could gauge just how angry she and the Mistress were with her.

When she went into the room where Tome and Mitsu were sewing, the two girls looked up at her with trepidation. Without a word, Kiku sat down beside them and picked up her own needle.

"No need to do that." A voice announced behind her. The Mistress and Oyone had materialized there. "Listen, the Gotōya doesn't have any use for girls who fly out of here like a shot and come back whenever they feel like it." The Mistress glared at Kiku. "Get your things together and go back to Urakami at once. You people from Urakami are nothing but a bunch of self-willed troublemakers. I don't suppose you and Mitsu are *Kuros*, are you?"

"Ma'am," Mitsu interjected, half in tears, "please forgive Kiku! Kiku, hurry and apologize."

"She has nothing to apologize for. Even if she did apologize, it wouldn't change how I feel. This isn't the first time Kiku has stepped out of the shop without permission. She's doesn't know the meaning of the word 'obedient.'" She glanced toward Oyone, "Get her things together and give them to her. The priest at Shōtokuji will understand once I explain everything to him." With that the Mistress stomped out of the room.

"You're such an idiot," Oyone gave an exasperated sigh. "If you needed to leave, I might have been able to do something for you if you'd just told me. . . . But when you say nothing and then disappear and don't come back, this is what you get."

"Oyone," Mitsu interjected. "Isn't there some way you can apologize to the Mistress and . . ."

"No. If I did that, I'd be the one who got yelled at." Oyone coldly shook her head. "She's just going to have to pack herself up and go back to Urakami. Plenty of girls go to the Sotome or Ōmura Districts for work."

Tome went with Mitsu to attempt an apology, but the Mistress's wrath wasn't even slightly abated; she merely turned her head to the side and gave no reply.

"The result'll be the same no matter how many times you apologize," Oyone scoffed at Mitsu, who came back to the kitchen deflated. "You can't change the Mistress's mind once she's made it up. All you can do is be silent and accept it."

Kiku seemed to be resigned to the decision, and she began packing in her tiny, second-floor room that had a low ceiling.

"Kiku . . ." As Mitsu stood behind her with tear-filled eyes, Kiku sighed and muttered, "This all happened because I'm always thinking only of myself. I'm sorry that I've made things difficult for you, too, Mitsu."

"Kiku, if you leave here, where will you go?"

"I'll have to go home to Magome." Then Kiku flashed a deliberately cheerful smile. "Actually, I'm relieved. I've never been suited to this kind of work. I'm more the type who's made to farm."

She went downstairs carrying her tiny baggage, smiled at Mitsu who was still sniffling, and said, "Don't cry. . . . Mistress, Oyone, Tome, thank you for everything. I'm sorry I have to leave without thanking the Master."

She bowed properly and stepped into the bright outdoors. The Mistress looked away, and Oyone lowered her eyes, pretending to see nothing.

Outside the shop, Kiku paused. If she took the road to the right, she'd end up in Teramachi; if she turned to the left, she'd come to Shianbashi.

Somehow or other, her feet headed toward Sakuramachi, just as they had this morning, where Seikichi and the others had been thrown into prison.

I wonder if Seikichi is suffering terribly right now? That single thought filled her head. All sorts of people—Chinese, even Caucasian sailors—walked past her, but she no longer dawdled and gawked as she had in former days when she had permission to venture out of the shop. Now she marched straight ahead, looking nowhere but directly in front of her. She didn't even glance at the goods in the stores that lined both sides of the street or at the girl who came out of the dry-goods shop with a woman who seemed to be her nursemaid. Kiku climbed the hill toward the prison.

The spectators who had congregated outside the prison were all gone now. Two guards holding poles stood in front of the gate, and two dogs frisked together.

She continued to stare at the prison until one of the guards noticed and gave her a puzzled look. He grew wary when she didn't move on, so he called out accusingly, "What are you doing there?"

Kiku scurried away from the prison. Now her only option was to return to Urakami.

But she had no desire to return to an Urakami bereft of Seikichi. Leaving Nagasaki while Seikichi languished in a Nagasaki jail felt to her like a betrayal. She wished she could be with him and somehow help him. . . .

In the evening, a hungry and exhausted Kiku sat down on the stone steps of the Suwa Shrine, gazing blankly at the darkening sky. Numberless hosts of Nagasaki's famed cicadas screeched in the grove of trees on the shrine compound.

Kiku wandered the streets of Nagasaki like a stray dog until nightfall. She could not bring herself to go back to Magome.

Children who had been playing nearby returned to their homes. The setting sun that had illuminated her surroundings began to wane.

I guess I'm going to have to . . . go back home.

She was famished, having eaten nothing all day. She tried to stave off hunger by drinking some of the water from the shrine basin that was used for purifying the hands of pilgrims.

Unless something changes, there'll be no way I can help Seikichi.

There would be no succor for Seikichi so long as he refused to abandon his pointless beliefs. And yet this morning he had cried out in a loud voice, "We won't change our beliefs no matter how much we suffer!" What could she do?

She heard footsteps in the compound. She could also hear a conversation being conducted in some unintelligible foreign tongue. Just as she leaped up from the stone steps and turned to look, two foreigners came to a halt, surprised to see her.

Kiku was startled—not because they were not Japanese, but because one of them was definitely the foreigner she had seen at the Nambanji. She was further amazed that the other foreigner was wearing the same mud-covered work clothes that the peasants in Urakami wore.

When he saw Kiku, the foreigner who was dressed in work clothes hurriedly covered his face with the sedge-woven hat he carried in his hand. And the two men, pretending that nothing unusual had happened, continued down the stone steps.

Seikichi's face floated up before Kiku's eyes. Seikichi revered these foreigners from the Nambanji, calling them "Padre."

Maybe these foreigners can help Seikichi. The thought popped into her head. She couldn't say why. But like a drowning person grasping at straws, Kiku threw herself in front of the two foreigners.

"Excuse me . . . !"

The foreigners—Petitjean and Laucaigne—halted as though frightened. Only that afternoon Laucaigne, who had escaped from Mount Ippongi, had finally been able to send a messenger to Petitjean at Ōura.

As soon as he received the news, Petitjean had hurried to the base of Mount Kompira to meet Laucaigne. Now they were crossing through the precincts of the Suwa Shrine on their way to get Laucaigne changed out of the muddy work clothes that betokened the predawn uproar and get him into priestly garb. . . .

"Sirs," Kiku cried, all but kneeling before the two foreigners. "Please help Seikichi. He's in the Sakuramachi Prison because he's a Kirishitan."

"Do you . . ." Finally Petitjean opened his mouth and quietly asked, "Do you know Seikichi?"

"Yes."

"Then you're a Kirishitan?"

"I'm not . . ." When Kiku shook her head forcefully, a look of caution spread across the two priests' faces.

"Why is someone who isn't a Kirishitan . . . asking us to help Seikichi?" Petitjean studied Kiku from head to toe.

Kiku's face flushed crimson. There was no way she could bring herself to confess to these foreigners that she was in love with Seikichi.

But Father Laucaigne was quicker than Petitjean at realizing the truth behind her blushing face and uncomfortable body language, and he whispered to his comrade, "*Elle l'aime.*"

A reassured smile slowly spread across Petitjean's face, and he muttered, "Ah!" Then he asked Kiku, "Are you from Urakami?"

"Yes."

"From Nakano . . . ?"

"Not from Nakano. From Magome."

"It's dangerous for a woman to be heading back to Magome after dark. You're alone . . . ?"

"Yes."

"You don't have an escort?"

Kiku looked up at him and weakly shook her head.

Petitjean looked at her tired face and the bundle she carried in her hands and wondered whether she was running away from home. "You don't have any place to stay, do you?"

Her thoughts having been read, Kiku lowered her eyes and said nothing.

"Did you run away from home after an argument with your parents?"

Still she did not respond.

"Have you had anything to eat?"

"Don't worry about me!" Kiku said angrily. She was so prideful she could not bear anyone taking pity on her for no reason. "I hate Kirishitans. But please help Seikichi!"

Laucaigne shrugged his shoulders and pulled on Petitjean's sleeve. Petitjean nodded and took four or five steps away. But something within would not allow him to abandon Kiku.

"Come with us. We'll give you something to eat. . . . You can stay the night in Ōura and then go back to Urakami tomorrow."

"No thanks. I'm not a Kirishitan." She was still obstinate.

Petitjean stifled an urge to laugh and motioned to her, "Come along."

Laucaigne and Petitjean stepped behind a building and finished changing their clothes, then set off in the darkness down the path from Suwa Shrine to the ocean. From time to time, they glanced casually over their shoulders.

"Is she following us?"

"She is."

Trying not to laugh out loud, the two walked for a time and then suddenly came to a stop.

Petitjean again motioned to Kiku, "There's nothing to be so shy about. Come along. . . . Or are you afraid of me?"

Kiku nodded grudgingly. Her sharp mind quickly calculated whether it would be more to her advantage to go straight back to Urakami or to follow these foreigners. It was obvious that it was best not to return to Urakami right now if she wanted to get help for Seikichi.

With a fixed distance maintained between them, the two priests and Kiku made their way along the beach toward Ōura. With the sun already down, the ocean and sky were already spattered purple while the waves nipped at the shore with a languid sound.

"Bernard," Father Laucaigne said to Petitjean. "Have you contacted M. Leques at the consulate?" Leques was the French consul in Nagasaki.

"Of course. I notified Leques and also sent word to the Prussian consul asking them to demand the release of the prisoners. I suspect they've both already been to the magistrate's office to lodge protests. But . . ."

But . . . Father Laucaigne suddenly thought of Hondō Shuntarō's broad face. A man like Hondō would merely brush aside such a complaint, insisting that this was an internal problem that had nothing to do with them. . . .

"Bernard, I . . . I feel somehow as though we've brought this harm on them," Laucaigne muttered sadly. They could see the fishing lights of several boats in the offing, and the waves continued their monotonous pounding.

"Why?"

"It seems to me that they raised this fracas because we pushed them too hard . . . and now they've been arrested. . . ."

Petitjean had to agree. Their hunger as missionaries to teach the Gospel to the Japanese and their desire to save Japanese souls had stirred up the peasants and set off this confrontation.

"Yet . . . if we think of it as a kind of martyrdom. . . ."

They said nothing for a time. They remained ill at ease in their hearts.

"In any case, first thing tomorrow we've got to start things rolling to obtain their freedom."

"Yes, we must."

Again they stopped walking and looked behind them. Kiku, too, came to a swift halt.

"We're almost there," Petitjean called out gently. "Tonight you should have something delicious to eat and then get some rest."

That evening, Kiku was fed the strangest food she had ever eaten. There was some sort of thick soup that seemed to have flour mixed in with it, and a thing called *pan* that she'd only heard about, slathered with what tasted like hair oil.

It didn't seem the least bit "delicious" to her. With her eyes darting about in astonishment, it took all her effort to force it down her throat.

"This is called *potage*. And this is *beurre*." Petitjean looked on with a smile as Father Laucaigne taught each of the words to Kiku. "Do you like it?"

"Yeah." Her voice sounded like a mosquito when she answered, unable to bring herself to say that it tasted terrible.

"Okane, apparently she doesn't like the kind of food we eat. Do you have anything else?"

Okane, who was serving up the food, looked disgusted, but she brought out some pickled vegetables and rice. She was not happy that the two priests had picked up this dowdy-looking girl.

That night, Kiku was put to bed on a platform they called a *lit*. But she was so nervous that she lay there with her eyes wide open, unable to sleep.

She could hear the sound of the waves. This place where the foreigners lived was a Japanese-style house, but it had a peculiar smell to it. It was an odor just like that of the foreign food that had been pressed on her that evening.

Those foreigners! They eat cows and pigs and drink their blood! Years ago, Granny had struck fear in her with those words. Come to think of it, those two men had been drinking something that was red like blood . . . !

Why would someone like Seikichi go out of his way to believe in the religion of these foreigners? I can't help but hate these Kirishitans!

She thought of Seikichi in his cell. What would he be doing at this hour? She had heard people say that there was a ringleader among the prisoners who swaggered about and taunted the new arrivals. Was Seikichi all right?

Unable to sleep, she got up and took from her bundle of possessions the *medaille* of the Blessed Mother that she kept hidden away.

"I don't like you anymore. It's because of you that Seikichi got put in that prison. Just who *are* you, anyway, you hateful woman?!" She glared at the *medaille* as she voiced her complaint.

Seikichi. You've got to give up this stupid religion. She felt that intensely. She wanted to clasp her hands together and pray to the gods and buddhas that Seikichi would get out of prison quickly, that he would do what the magistrate told him to do, and that he would be freed.

Even as she tormented her mind with these thoughts, Petitjean and Laucaigne were planning how they might secure freedom for the Urakami Kirishitans who were locked away in the Sakuramachi Prison. . . .

The following morning, Kiku had a request for Okane. "Can you get me a job here in these foreigners' house? I'll work really hard!"

Okane looked at Kiku disdainfully, but evidently she realized how desperate Kiku's request was, because she mentioned it to her husband.

"It might be a good idea to hire her. If, like they say, two more foreigners will be arriving here soon, we won't be able to do everything ourselves."

Mosaku's argument made sense. When Petitjean and Laucaigne found out that there were Kirishitans hidden away in Urakami, in various locations throughout the region surrounding Nagasaki, and at Sotome as well, they requested assistance from their compatriots in Yokohama. Before long, two additional priests would be coming to Ōura.

"Fine, but," Petitjean interrogated Kiku closely, "we'll have to get permission from your parents. If we don't, it could lead to trouble for us."

"I . . . I don't have any parents," Kiku lied. "I have a cousin in Nagasaki. I'll have her tell my relatives that I'm working here."

After consulting with Laucaigne, Petitjean hired Kiku temporarily to work at the church. But he took her on only because he recognized that with two additional priests coming, Okane couldn't possibly take care of everything for them.

"Is Seikichi . . . still in jail?" Kiku asked, her eyes filled with tears.

Petitjean nodded glumly and said, "Yes, but not at the Sakuramachi Prison. They've all been moved to a jail in Kojima."

In fact, only two days after their arrest they were transferred from the Sakuramachi Prison to a hastily constructed cell in Kojima.

"Then . . . will Seikichi be released?"

Kiku asked Petitjean question after question. From the desperation in her voice he could tell how much the girl loved Seikichi.

"Of course he will! I pray for that each day, all through the day. Don't you worry."

But Kiku, not being of the Kirishitan faith, was not interested in such whimsies as prayers; she wanted these foreigners to take some sort of concrete action to free Seikichi.

Like a drowning woman grasping at straws, she asked Petitjean, "Will Seikichi really be saved if you just pray?"

"When you pray, your requests are granted," Petitjean consoled the young Japanese woman.

That night, in a tiny house beside the chapel, Kiku tried offering her first prayer. Holding the *medaille* that Seikichi had given her and fixing her eyes on the image of the Blessed Mother Mary engraved on it, she prayed, "I don't know who you are. But you're the woman that Seikichi worships. Since you're a woman, please understand how I feel. I'm asking you. Please arrange it so that nothing terrible happens to Seikichi."

Please arrange it so that nothing terrible happens to Seikichi. . . .

Despite Kiku's agonized prayer, Seikichi and the sixty-seven other Kirishitan men and women from Urakami remained imprisoned in Kojima with no indication that they would be freed.

Each day, one of the shackled prisoners was dragged from his cell, taken to the magistrate's Nishi Bureau that stood on the site of the present Nagasaki Prefectural Offices, and encouraged to abandon his faith. Whether threatened or gently reasoned with, each was ordered to apostatize.[1]

It was not only the men who were grilled. Women, too, had their hands bound behind their backs and were taken to the bureau office.

Initially the officers tried to reason with the prisoners, but often they played on their feelings, making threats that their family members would be made to suffer because of them. If they still gave no response, the interrogating officer would heave a deliberate sigh.

"Have you heard about the tortures we inflict on Kirishitans?"

" . . . "

---

1. In Japanese, *korobu*, a word that literally means "to fall down," was used in this time period to signify apostasy, perhaps something along the lines of "fall away from the faith."

"It's called 'hanging in the pit.' You're hung upside down over a pit filled with filth. You're just left there with no food, no water. The blood pools in your head and comes streaming out of your eyes and nose. They say that even those who can handle it initially end up screaming out in agony after only three days."

". . ."

"Our orders from above are to use this torture on you Kirishitans and get you to return to the right path. We don't want to have to subject you to such painful torment. But if you continue to insist that you won't give up your Kirishitan faith, then you don't leave us any choice—we have to hang you in the pit."

The cunning threats had their impact on the simple peasants.

One evening, when it was brutally hot inside the cell, a policeman brought a man named Kumazō back to the prison from the Nishi Bureau.

"What did they ask you today?" the others inquired, but Kumazō wouldn't look them in the eyes and mumbled a noncommittal answer.

At first they thought he was just exhausted and said nothing further to him. But that night he still seemed listless.

"Kumazō, what's wrong? Did they beat you badly?"

"I . . . I couldn't bear it. . . ." His voice was like an unexpected wail. "I don't have the strength to hold up any longer. I . . . I want to go back to the village."

No one said a word. They all understood too well the cry of Kumazō's heart.

"Why aren't the padres helping us? And why isn't Deus at least helping us?"

They all rebuked Kumazō for his weakness but then tried to encourage him. They were additionally trying to bolster their own resolve, which was beginning to wither.

The next day, Kumazō was again hauled off to the Nishi Bureau and then returned to the prison with a dazed look on his face. He had sworn an oath to the officers that he would abandon his Kirishitan faith.

Then a man named Hisagorō denied his faith. And after Hisagorō, Shigejūrō apostatized. . . .

When one corner of the wall of believers caved in, another five, then ten individuals would collapse like dominoes.

Even after the brutally hot months of July and August passed, the cell was still saturated with the smells of sweat and body odor and feces. The number of believers who abandoned their faith during those two stifling months reached twenty-one.

The magistrate gave no sign of releasing the twenty-one who had apostatized. It was Hondō Shuntarō's suggestion that they keep the fallen imprisoned as a means to persuade those who had yet to abjure their faith.

"Listen, I'm on my knees begging you. I've got a wife and kids to take care of, and if I don't return to my land soon, we won't be able to pay our taxes for this year. Won't you please do what the officers ask you and just think of it as helping me out?" That was the sort of plea that the apostates made to those who had yet to capitulate. Each knew to the depths of his bones how destitute and miserable it was to be a peasant. The entreaties of their friends were more painful to them than threats from the police.

The forty-seven who refused to recant were locked into a room no larger than nine-by-nine feet. They were given only a paltry amount of food. With forty-seven bodies crammed into an eighty square foot cell, there was no room to lie down. They were driven to the verge of madness inside the hot, suffocating enclosure. Seikichi was among them.

Only once during those hellish days did a constable, without gaining authorization from the officials, allow three women from Nakano to meet with the prisoners. It was of course the bribe money that the women had collected from others in the village that persuaded the constable to give them a short time to converse in secret with the prisoners.

"This must be so difficult for you! So difficult!" The women repeated the words many times, tears streaming down their cheeks. Clinging to pillars in the cell, the prisoners begged for information about their families and their fields.

"Everyone is offering *oraçio* for you. The padres are talking with the magistrate, and they've sent a messenger to Edo trying to rally all the foreigners in Japan to help the Kirishitans. You just need to be patient a little longer. . . ." The women wept even more. Some of those in the cell sobbed loudly as they listened to what the women had to say.

"Both Father Petitjean and Father Laucaigne are saying prayers to Santa Maria for you."

The constable appeared and announced that it was time to conclude the meeting. The three women handed out food and clothing that had been provided by the prisoners' families, and then said to Seikichi, "Father Petitjean said to give you this," and handed him a small parcel.

Seikichi summoned the courage to open the parcel in a corner of the cell after the women had left. It contained a few rice cakes, a small crucifix, and a single sheet of paper.

The paper was a letter that Kiku had apparently had someone write for her.

"I know this is very hard for you. I came by the jail hoping to see your face, but they wouldn't let me come near. Right now I'm staying at the Nambanji in Ōura. I'm saying prayers for you."

As he read the letter, the warmth of the young woman's zeal ran through him from head to toe like a flaming arrow.

He had regarded her as a young girl until now. But here in his hands was proof of how much she worried about him and how much she thought of him. Feelings of euphoria and joy beyond words swept through him. He recalled with clarity Kiku's almond eyes as she swept the street in front of the shop that he walked by every morning.

She loves me this much. His face flushed. He tucked the letter into his pocket, cautiously avoiding the gaze of the others whose bodies pressed against his.

He repeated to himself something Kiku had added to her letter: "I'm not a Kirishitan, so I don't know how to pray the way you do. But every night I ask your Santa Maria to help you."

Yes, Blessed Mother. Please do as she asks, please help me, he muttered.

The following morning—

"Next ones out!" The constable poked his face through the cell door and shouted. The summons was for Seishirō and Taira no Mataichi of Motohara, and for Seikichi.

In the same manner as those who had preceded them, the three men squeezed from the cell with their hands tied behind them. They were to be interrogated at the Nishi Bureau.

This temporary release from the jail for questioning was the sole opportunity the prisoners had to breathe the air of the outside world.

It was an autumn morning, but the heat lingered and cicadas shrieked from every direction. Yet, when the three men emerged from a cell that reeked of sweat and urine and body odors, they were delighted to be free to breathe in as much of the fresh air as they wanted.

Mataichi puffed out his chest and said merrily, "Oh, that's so sweet!" The autumn air truly was . . . truly was delicious.

They were taken to the courthouse at the Nishi Bureau and bombarded with the familiar dogged warnings to apostatize.

"You only have to do it outwardly. After that we'll leave you alone. Just say publicly that you've given up being a Kirishitan!" The two officers were so frustrated they were willing to accept a compromise. But Seikichi, Mataichi, and Seishirō stared at the floor and said nothing.

"You're still going to remain obstinate?!"

No response.

The officers looked at one other and muttered, "You leave us no choice. . . ."

"You leave us no choice" did not mean they had given up. It meant they were left with no choice but to inflict torture.

"Stand up!" The constable barked at the three men. The prisoners still had no idea at that point what would be done with them. It had not actually occurred to them that they could be tortured.

A light as piercing as molten tin streamed through a transom to illuminate a darkened corridor. The light made even the grains of wood in the floorboards visible.

"In there!" The constable pushed the three men into a large room on the left side of the corridor. The room had a wooden floor and only one window.

The constable had them kneel in formal posture and made one final attempt to reason with them. His voice sounded like that of an exhausted man heaving a sigh. "You'd better brace yourselves, we'll be causing you a great deal of pain. When you can't take the pain anymore, all you have to do is say, 'I now apostatize.'"

The three men kept their eyes down and said nothing.

"Then you won't recant?"

The silence continued.

The constable left the room without another word. He returned with five of his comrades.

The officers stood behind Seishirō, Mataichi, and Seikichi and ordered them, "Put both hands behind your back!"

Their wrists were bound together so tightly it seemed their bones might break. Then the ropes were tossed over a beam near the ceiling and the bodies of the three men were pulled into midair.

"Bet that hurts! But there's even worse pain to come. Of course we'll set you free if you swear an oath of apostasy. . . ."

The three silent prisoners seemed insolent to the officers, who became all the more infuriated with them.

Bamboo poles made a harsh sound as they beat mercilessly against the three bodies. The poles slashed through the air with a whistle and then a crack as they struck the bodies.

Initially the men grit their teeth to endure the pain and tried to utter no sound. But as the number of blows from the poles reached ten, then fifteen, screams began to escape through their clenched teeth.

Their screams changed from a restrained "Uh!" to agonized cries of "Ah! Ah!" when the number of blows passed thirty. With each howl the ropes that suspended them coiled and spun the three bodies with them.

Footsteps sounded in the hall and an official came into the room. It was Itō Seizaemon. With a deliberate yawn, he asked, "Have they apostatized yet?"

"They're stubborn as hell." One of the constables massaged his tired arms as he replied.

"Then pour water on the ropes," Itō ordered.

When the ropes became damp, they shrank and bit into the flesh. For this "wet rope" method of torture ordered by Seizaemon, the officers took water from a bucket that was kept on hand to revive prisoners who had fainted and poured it onto the ropes that bound the three men.

At that same hour, Kiku was offering a prayer to the Blessed Mother engraved in her *medaille*. "Please don't let Seikichi suffer."

Through the wooden wall the screams of the three men were clearly audible in the hallway. Another six Kirishitans knelt in the hallway in formal fashion, awaiting their turn to be tortured.

The cries of the men being tortured, like the howling of wild beasts. The sporadic wails. In between, the angry shouts of the policemen. The whack of the poles.

Each of these sounds produced its desired effect on the six men in the hallway who were awaiting their own ordeal. With their hands bound behind their backs, they stared at the ground, quivering.

Finally the officers came out of the room, dragging by their legs the three blood-spattered bodies of the men who had blacked out.

With a grin, Itō Seizaemon called out to the six prisoners in the hall, "Open your eyes and take a good look at them. This is what the Nagasaki magistrate does for amusement . . . ! Anybody feel like apostatizing now?"

"Yes, sir." One of the Kirishitans answered in a mosquito-like voice. "I was wrong. I will change my heart!"

A smile of victory slowly spread across Itō Seizaemon's face. "You will, eh? So you've seen the light? If you do change your heart, we will do nothing to harm you." He signaled the constable with his eyes.

The abused bodies of the three men were dumped outside the gate of the jail. They were placed as an example for the other Kirishitans, who were taken from the Kojima jail to look at them.

The naked bodies of the three men, prostrate on the ground and soaked with blood in the lingering heat of the sun. Even though flies were already swarming around their faces and the wounds on their bodies, none of them had the strength to shoo them away. The only indication that they were still alive was the groans spilling from their swollen lips. The officers hauled the other Kirishitan men and women from their cells and forced them to look from a distance on this gruesome scene. . . .

"I . . . I can't do this anymore!" One woman cried. "I'm sorry to all of you, but I can't bear it any longer!"

No one reacted against her words. They had all lost the confidence to do so.

"Why doesn't Deus come to help us? Why does he say nothing about these horrid acts?!"

The bonds of commonality that had linked these people together collapsed at this point. Sensing what had just taken place, Itō Seizaemon hurried back to the magistrate's office and reported it to Hondō Shuntarō and the others.

"I can't say that torturing them was the best of all possible methods . . ." Hondō tried to dispel the bitter aftertaste, "but in this case they left us no choice." Tonight at Maruyama with his lover Oyō, he would have to drink himself into a stupor.

Again that day, knowing nothing that had transpired, Kiku prayed for Seikichi. As she served Petitjean his meal, she asked, "If I ask this Lady Mary, will she give me everything I ask for? Will Seikichi be spared any harm?"

Petitjean nodded vigorously. "I promise she will grant your petitions."

THE SETTING OF THE SUN

IN ORDER TO reach Maruyama, the pleasure quarters of Nagasaki, one had to cross over the Shian Bridge, the "Bridge of Pondering," which no longer stands, thanks to land reclamation.

Beyond this bridge lay a smaller bridge, commonly known as the Omoikiri Bridge, or the "Bridge of Resolution." A single willow tree had been planted on the approach to the bridge, similar to the Mikaeri willow, the "Glancing Back" willow[1] at the Yoshiwara quarters in Edo.

In *Love Letters from Maruyama* of 1684, there is a passage that reads:

Once you pass through the gateway
The aroma of lotus and musk delight the nose,
And the rustle of fine silk sleeves strikes the ear

Once a client has crossed the Bridge of Resolution, the atmosphere of the pleasure quarters is unmistakable.

From the window of the Yamazaki Teahouse at twilight, Hondō Shuntarō enjoyed watching the people on the street below who were caught up in the hedonistic mood of the quarter. Especially these days, with the burden of his assignment at the magistrate's office to force the Urakami Kirishitans into

---

1. The "Glancing Back" willow was at the gateway of the old pleasure quarters in what is now Tokyo. Male patrons who had spent the night in pleasure were said to pause at the tree and glance back longingly toward the women from whom they had just parted.

apostasy even if it meant resorting to torture, he was eager to dispel his feelings of gloom by enjoying the spectacle of the pleasure quarters in the evenings as he drank his saké. . . .

Oyō continued to press liquor on him, but the images of the naked, blood-covered Kirishitan peasants lingered before his eyes no matter how much he gulped down. It was true that he had not laid his own hands on them, but he could forget neither the cruel sounds of the police beating the prisoners nor the sounds of the prisoners' cries.

"But nearly all the *Kuros* of Urakami have given up their vile religion, haven't they? Then please look a little happier!"

"No, there's one who's still immovable." Shuntarō had, of course, said nothing to Oyō about the tortures. In her ignorance she believed that the Kirishitan peasants had submitted to the orders of the magistrate thanks to verbal persuasion.

However—

There was still one immovable man. He was a peasant from Nakano by the name of Sen'emon, who refused to listen to any of the entreaties from the officials. He would not change his views under any form of threat or plea. He boldly answered the officers' questions, and his responses were exceedingly lucid, making it difficult to regard him as a peasant.

Hondō still had vivid memories of the interrogation he had conducted with Sen'emon two days earlier.

"Now let me ask you: Do the Kirishitans teach you to go against the orders of your superiors?"

Sen'emon replied, "No. The padres told us that we must follow the shogun as long as it didn't go against the laws of Deus. For generations, my family has been encouraged to pay its taxes, to work hard, and we've been doing our very best to follow that. It's just that . . .we can't worship anybody other than Deus."

"I understand you've lost your wife and that you have children at home. Surely it will bring grief and pain to your children if you're tortured and then have to return to them with a broken body. You'd better give that some thought."

"Thank you for those words. But no matter how much pain I have to suffer in the flesh, it's nothing compared to losing my soul. Those are my feelings."

Hondō Shuntarō was moved by what Sen'emon said. He was impressed that this humble man would not abandon his resolve. Did faith really make a person that strong . . . ?

When Shuntarō related this experience with Sen'emon to Oyō, rather than being impressed by it she responded with something like distaste, "That's scary! Men who are that stubborn frighten me!"

"Well, I admire him. His courage is enviable, but that's a problem for us. Looking at him, I can fully understand why even a mere peasant like him doesn't fear death or danger because of his faith and devotion. That's why years ago, even Lord Hideyoshi and Lord Ieyasu were at a loss how to deal with sectarian rebellions[2] and why the peasant insurgents of Amakusa fought so ferociously against the military power of several daimyo in the Shimabara Rebellion.[3] . . . What I fear now is that something similar might occur here."

Hondō Shuntarō had not intended to describe the current domestic perils to Oyō. But even Oyō would have had some vague awareness of Japan's present situation.

To begin with, the shogunate was on the verge of collapse. Hondō knew that they were rapidly losing the authority they had held for many long years. And a number of foreign nations, led by the United States, were using a combination of threats, warnings, and proposals to force the shogunate into opening Japan's doors.

Compared with these tumultuous domestic affairs, perhaps this petty uprising by the Urakami Kirishitans was of little significance.

And yet—

And yet the decision by the Nagasaki magistrate to imprison Kirishitan peasants and force them to apostatize gave Christian nations such as the United States and France an excuse to interfere in Japanese affairs and fanned their animosity toward Japan. That was the real problem.

In Shuntarō's view, Japan needed to display firm resolve and poise to these foreign powers. He was in favor of opening the country's doors, but he felt it was absolutely essential that Japan spurn these attempts by foreign nations to intervene in its domestic affairs. That is why he had urged the magistrate to brandish his authority convincingly against the intolerable activities of the Urakami Kirishitans.

"Oyō, there's a possibility that that insignificant little village of Urakami just might have a powerful impact on Japan's future. . . ." Oyō was stretched out

2. Throughout the late sixteenth and early seventeenth centuries, the warlords who eventually united Japan had to struggle with uprisings by militant Buddhist sects that feared—rightly—that they would be stripped of their power and wealth.

3. In 1637 and 1638, peasants in the former Arima fief, suffering from brutal taxation and starvation, rose up in rebellion against the anti-Christian government. The fief had originally been home to a Jesuit seminary and printing press, and although most of the peasants had publicly renounced their Kirishitan faith, once the rebellion broke out, they declared themselves followers of Christ and fought vigorously until nearly 35,000 were killed in the siege of Hara Castle.

beside him, and as he spoke, he reached his hand into the folds at the neck of her kimono.

Oyō's breasts, said to resemble snowballs, were milky white, warm, and soft. Hondō Shuntarō had acquired the unusual habit of fondling Oyō's strawberry-colored nipples whenever he talked to her about Japan. As he stroked them, inspired ideas would somehow float into his head. And as he caressed her, she narrowed her eyes as if she was experiencing pleasure as well and did not move a muscle.

Ever since the Urakami Kirishitans were arrested, consuls and ministers from France, Portugal, and the United States had come knocking one after another at the Nagasaki magistrate's office to lodge protests and demand their release. One of the magistrates, Governor Tokunaga of Iwami, had repeatedly rejected their demands, citing the laws of the land as a shield.

But once rumors circulated that the magistrate was torturing the Kirishitans, the protests from other nations grew louder, and a few consuls even demanded the dismissal of the magistrate.

"We . . . we can't give in. The law is the law. We can't release peasants who have violated our laws that proscribe Kirishitan belief." As he muttered the words, Shuntarō pinched Oyō's nipple roughly.

Despite his feelings toward the Kirishitans, Hondō Shuntarō did not neglect his visits to Petitjean to study French.

He was convinced that from here on out, a man would be of no use to Japan if he could not communicate with those in foreign lands. That was one of the motivations for his visits to Petitjean, but he also wanted to keep a discreet eye on the activities of this foreigner, who could well be considered the chief instigator of the recent unpleasantness.

For his part, Petitjean was determined to ferret out the real intentions of the magistrate as he exchanged casual conversation with Hondō.

Hondō climbed from the shore at Ōura up the slope that was surrounded by cultivated fields. When he stepped through the gate of the Nambanji, he encountered a young woman who was weeding the garden. An attractive face met his when she turned her towel-wrapped head toward him beneath a blazing sun.

So . . . Petitjean has a young woman at his place. . . .

He took his customary route leading past the rear of the church and walked toward the Japanese-style house where Petitjean lived along with the other French *bateren*.[4]

The lessons began in the room overlooking Nagasaki Harbor where they always met. Hondō had advanced to the point where he could carry on a basic conversation in French.

4. *Bateren* was the Japanese pronunciation of the Portuguese word *padre*.

"I saw a young woman working outside there. . . ." As they chatted after the lesson, Hondō probed, to which Petitjean nodded his head.

"Yes. With another two Frenchmen coming to live here, we needed a new *bonne*—that's French for 'maid.'"

"Are those additional Frenchmen coming with the intent to teach your Kirishitan beliefs to the Japanese?" Hondō asked sarcastically. "That is strictly prohibited, as you know. . . . Why are you trying to force a religion that we despise onto us?"

Petitjean raised his head with conviction and replied, "We . . . we believe that the teachings of the Kirishitan faith will bring salvation to the Japanese people. Our aim is for your salvation."

Hondō sat up straight and said, "Lord Petitjean. What we're trying to make you understand is that this is an annoyance to us. We would like you to leave Japan alone. You see, the Japanese have been able to live happily for a very long while without knowing anything about your Kirishitan teachings. . . . In spite of that, today . . . well, and even three hundred years ago, you come from Europe to stir up Japan and make trouble for us. That's why Japan closed its doors."

"You're saying that the Europeans came to stir up trouble in Japan three hundred years ago?" Petitjean asked defiantly. "We came to engage in trade and to share the teachings of Christianity that we believe to be true."

"Lord Petitjean, let's be honest here." A fierce look flashed across Hondō's face. It was the first time Petitjean had seen this perpetually jovial man look so ruthless. "Of course, there were some who came to Japan for trade and some who came to teach the Kirishitan beliefs. I know that from reading through documents in the magistrate's office. There's no question that there were virtuous *bateren* and *iruman*[5] who provided free medical care for the Japanese. But in exchange, during their voyage to Japan the Europeans attacked parts of China and India, subjected them to their own rule, and robbed them of their lands. . . . That is what Japan feared. The Japanese did not ban your teachings because they were Kirishitan. It was because they feared the avarice of the Western nations that sought to take over Japan with the help of the local Kirishitans."

Petitjean blushed unwittingly. Hondō Shuntarō had obviously just struck at something that was highly painful and embarrassing for Petitjean.

"But . . . ," Petitjean hoarsely protested, "but it's wrong for you to think that the mistakes made by Kirishitan nations like Spain or Portugal were inspired by Kirishitan teachings. The Kirishitan faith did not teach people to pilfer land in India or China or to take control of those countries." There was a lack of

5. *Iruman* is from the Portuguese word *irmãos*, brothers who ranked just after the padres. Initially most were European, but under Alessandro Valignano (1539–1606), visitor for the Jesuit missions in Asia, the number of Japanese *iruman* increased significantly.

confidence in Petitjean's strained voice. Neither he nor Father Laucaigne believed it was in any way proper that the Christian nations in the sixteen and seventeenth centuries had invaded Asia and Africa and turned them into colonies. Petitjean could not help but feel that this Asian man, Hondō, had every right to be critical of those actions.

"Lord Petitjean." Obvious contempt showed on Hondō's broad face. He was fully aware that this particular issue was one that was painful to the missionary and one he wished to keep buried. "I can't agree with your rationalizations. If what you said were true, why did your Kirishitan *papa* say nothing and disregard the fact that the Kirishitan nations were stealing Asian lands, invading our countries, and killing our people?"

"His Holiness did protest."

"With his lips only. But I'm certain that behind the scenes he approved of spreading the Kirishitan teachings in the vanquished countries. Or would it be more accurate to say that he turned a blind eye to those activities in order to spread your Kirishitan teachings? Lord Petitjean, why can't you just say that it was a mistake perpetrated by Kirishitans? Lord Petitjean, you've instigated an uprising in Japan right now so that you can share your Kirishitan teachings. You're no different from the *bateren* of the past."

Recoiling from Shuntarō's arguments, Petitjean made an attempt to argue that at least he himself had no such intentions. But with cold precision Hondō struck the fatal blow by asking, "Well, then, why is it that while the Urakami Kirishitans are suffering in prison, you snugly enjoy your little haven here at the Nambanji?"

Hondō Shuntarō realized he had gone too far. Petitjean's pallid face made it evident that he was struggling desperately to repress his anger. But Hondō had no desire to amend his statement.

"Lord Petitjean, allow me to teach you something. . . . All but one of the Urakami Kirishitans has sworn an oath that they reject your religion. Eventually we intend to free them."

With a sallow face Petitjean muttered, "You have brutally tortured those poor peasants."

"A few of them, yes. We had no choice. We had to do it as a warning for the others. . . ." Clutching the sheath of his sword in his right hand, Shuntarō bowed and left the room. Normally Petitjean would have seen him to the door, but today he sat motionless in his chair.

The sun still baked the garden of the Nambanji. Cicadas screeched violently. And the girl with the towel-wrapped head was still tugging at weeds.

"It's good of you to work so hard. It must be difficult to weed when the sun's so hot," Hondō gently consoled the girl. "Do the foreigners here treat you well?"

"Yes."

"Are you . . . a Kirishitan?"

"No!" Kiku quickly shook her head.

"Ah. Well, that's good." He nodded and started off when an urgent voice from behind called out to him.

"Excuse me!" When he turned around, Kiku picked up a cloth to wipe her hands and asked, "Since your lordship is an official of the magistrate's office, if you know what's happened to the people from Nakano, then maybe you know a man named Seikichi . . . ?" She could say no more. Hondō stood where he was, regarding Kiku as he repeated his question, "Are you . . . one of the Urakami Kirishitans?"

"I'm not from Nakano. I was born in Magome. There's not a single Kirishitan in Magome."

"Is that so? Then listen carefully to me. It's fine for you to work here, but you must never become a Kirishitan. Their religion is illegal. That's why the people of Nakano have been arrested by the magistrate and been subjected to severe torture."

"Torture?" Kiku's face went pale.

"That's right. Some suffer so much pain they come back covered in blood. And it's because they believe in a heretical religion. Do you understand?"

Shuntarō did not say this to Kiku to threaten or torment her. He merely wished to give a stern warning against becoming a Kirishitan to this woman who worked at the Nambanji.

He could have had no idea what a shock his news inflicted on this young woman. He set off walking toward the grove of trees where the cicadas screeched noisily. . . .

Kiku was trembling, quivering. *Seikichi is being tortured.* . . .

Fear and torment racked her body. She had no idea what forms of torture were used by the magistrate's office. But she could almost see before her eyes the pathetic, unresisting body of Seikichi as the officers and constables cursed and kicked and stomped on him and beat him repeatedly with their fists. The man she loved was at that very moment suffering humiliation and agony.

That knowledge caused her to feel the same torment he was experiencing. That's the way with a woman. And Kiku had become that kind of woman.

"Ahh!" She covered her face with both hands and crouched down on the ground. Overhead, a swarm of large brown cicadas nesting in a large camphor tree shrieked as if to mock her.

Why did you have to become a Christian? She lifted her head resolutely. It's not Seikichi's fault. He's a good person. It's that Kirishitan religion that has jumbled his mind and brought this cruel punishment on him.

No mother considers her own child bad. She tries desperately to believe that someone else ruined her child. Kiku, too, was overcome by the same sort of agonized feelings shared by all women.

The Kirishitan faith—for Kiku, it came down to that one woman. That woman, of course, was the Santa Maria that Seikichi so adored. He had given Kiku a *medaille* engraved with that woman's image. And once, he had knelt with a look of rapture on his face before her statue in the Nambanji.

This is all her fault. She's to blame for everything that's happened.

Defiantly she marched straight to the door of the church. She put her weight against the door to open it.

With Mass completed, the chapel was empty, dark, and silent. Once it became known that the Urakami Kirishitans had been arrested, spectators suddenly stopped appearing on the church grounds.

To the side of the altar flickered a tiny light fueled with rapeseed oil. It was a sign that the Eucharist representing Christ's body had been placed at the altar.

To the side of the altar was that woman: the statue of Santa Maria stared fixedly toward Kiku. The statue of the Blessed Mother that Seikichi had gazed on with such rapture. . . .

It's your fault! Kiku glared at the other woman. Even when frowning, her face was beautiful.

You're a woman, too. So you must understand how I feel. I prayed to you every single day that nothing terrible would happen to Seikichi. . . . But . . . but you made terrible things happen to him. Since you're a woman . . . you must understand how sad . . . how painful . . . how painful . . . Tears poured in a deluge from Kiku's eyes. There was nothing else . . . nothing else Kiku could say. She looked up at the statue of the woman, her eyes brimming with resentment.

Since you're a woman . . . you must understand how sad . . .

Heaving with sobs, groaning, her shoulders shaking, Kiku continued to remonstrate with the statue. She muttered protests. Since she was not a Kirishitan, she knew nothing about prayers to the Blessed Mother, but her protests and her sobs were surely one form of human prayer.

The statue of the Blessed Mother Mary looked down at Kiku with wide eyes. With her large eyes open wide, she listened carefully to Kiku's prayers of anger, of protests, and of curses.

Since you're a woman . . . you must understand how sad . . .

Kiku did not know that the Blessed Mother also had had someone she loved very much taken from her. The one she loved, like Seikichi, had been arrested and beaten, had bled, and had died on a cross—but Kiku did not know that. Kiku did not know that just as she herself was doing now, this woman had also once wept in pain and torment.

It was silent in the chapel that afternoon. In the silence, all that could be heard was Kiku's intermittent, seemingly interminable sobbing. In the light of day, the streets of Nagasaki were like a desert; the black shadows of houses dozed along the roadways; a man in front of the gate shared by the magistrate's office and the Sakuramachi Prison sat on his haunches and gnawed on a melon; and in Nagasaki Bay the waves lapped languidly at the shore.

Nagasaki Bay was also visible from Petitjean's room. Unaware that Kiku was in the chapel, Petitjean sat with his head resting in both hands, struggling to rid himself of the anger he had felt since his conversation with Hondō.

As he gazed at the bay of Nagasaki, which glimmered in the sun like the sparkle of countless needles, his anger gradually abated, and he reached a point that he could ponder coolly what Hondō Shuntarō had said.

If I were a Japanese . . . Petitjean was a fair-minded priest, and he tried to consider the matter from the standpoint of the Japanese . . . *I might feel just the way Hondō does about this.*

Potent Western nations had invaded the countries of Asia. Petitjean could not deny that. His own homeland of France had actually been more active in occupying parts of Africa. The justification used for the invasions was that they were efforts to bring modern civilization and culture to primitive lands, and the Christian church had been tacitly complicit in their actions.

But if he were an Asian from one of the plundered countries who had had his pride deeply wounded, Petitjean would surely have sensed hypocrisy in the attitude of the Christian church for granting unspoken approval to all this, turning a blind eye, and conveniently benefiting from all the coercive tactics. Without question, it had been a grave error, even a sin, on the part of the Christian church.

Why are you causing disruptions here in Japan? Why are you stirring things up in Urakami Village? And here you are, not in prison, but sitting back carefree in your room!

Petitjean could vividly recall Hondō's words. The words stung, but he could not ignore the jabs of his conscience.

Petitjean hung his head, his hands still over his face. In a separate place, Kiku's shoulders shook with sobs. . . .

What tormented Petitjean the most was the fact that of the sixty-eight men and women held in prison, every one except Sen'emon had apostatized out of fear of the gruesome tortures. Hondō Shuntarō had casually and triumphantly reported to him that the Urakami Kirishitans had been broken. That the believers had abandoned God.

Petitjean had to admit his bitter defeat. The elation he had felt when he found the Kirishitans hidden in Japan had changed into this unspeakable pain of remorse and regret.

O Lord, Thy ways are . . . are unfathomable to me. Thou hast granted me the flowers of delight . . . only to suddenly destroy them.

He heard Okane call his name. "Lord Petitjean, when will Lord Laucaigne be returning?"

"This evening."

Laucaigne had once again gone to visit the homes in Nakano, Motohara, and Ieno, where he offered comfort to the women whose husbands or sons had been taken off to prison. But those same husbands and sons, having abandoned their faith, would eventually be set free.

He decided to kneel in prayer in the chapel, which was his heart's refuge. He wanted to be alone in the chapel to pray and ponder to know whether the things he had done were approved or misguided.

But as he was about to step into the sanctuary through a door behind the altar, Petitjean saw Kiku standing there alone. She was looking up at the statue of the Blessed Mother and weeping.

"Kiku. What . . . what are you doing there?"

Startled that Petitjean had called to her, Kiku began to flee.

"Kiku, I have something to tell you."

She paused.

"Seikichi is . . . I've heard that Seikichi will soon be released from prison."

Kiku stood with her mouth open, almost as though she couldn't understand what the words meant. Then color returned to her tear-stained face and with a look exuding joy, she responded, "Seikichi is going to be released . . . ?"

"Yes."

"The magistrate has pardoned Seikichi?"

"That's right . . ." Petitjean nodded, tasting an emotion as bitter as his own gastric juices.

"Then he'll be going back to Urakami?"

"Yes . . ."

"Oh, Santa Maria!" Without warning, Kiku turned her face toward the statue of the Blessed Mother and, to Petitjean's astonishment, cried out, "You're wonderful! I'm sorry for hating you. Forgive me? Thanks to you, Seikichi has cut his ties with the evil Kirishitan faith!"

It looked as though it would rain that day.

Beneath the leaden sky, a procession of vagrants trudged its way up Nishizaka Hill toward the Togitsu Highway. Every man and woman in the column looked haggard, but from their expressions it appeared not that they were physically exhausted but had lost all will to live.

They were the Urakami Kirishitans, who had been released by the magistrate after many months in prison. But it was no longer correct to call them Kirishitans. They had abandoned their faith. They had apostatized.

When they passed by the Shōtokuji, the chief priest was waiting for them. His apprentices had set out earthenware teapots and teacups for them, intending to treat them to a drink of tea, but not one of them accepted the offering.

"Well done, well done! After thinking it over, you've had a change of heart!" The chief priest tried to encourage and cheer each one individually, almost to the point of patting them on their backs, but the apostates kept their faces averted and walked past the priest without uttering a word.

They came to Magome. Mitsu's brother Ichijirō was in the field with his father and other relatives, just beginning to harvest the rice. Noticing the ghostly looking band, he shouted, "Hey, it's the *Kuros* of Nakano and Motohara!" Then he muttered, "Just look at them. Looks like they were treated pretty badly!" Inwardly he was ashamed of buckling under to the officials at the magistrate's office and the priest of the Shōtokuji and spying on Nakano village. He didn't like the *Kuros*, but he also disliked having to act like a spy.

Beneath the dark gray sky, the column passed through Magome and finally set foot in their beloved village of Nakano. The groves of trees, the terraced rice paddies, the colors of the earth, and the smell of the soil—all these they had thought about and dreamed about while in prison. When one person at the front of the column came to a stop, they all stopped walking. Some of the women began to weep.

They were looking at their own houses, each as tiny as an animal shed. The doors were tightly shut, and all was still. There was not a sign of a single person on the road. Not a single child was at play.

Where is everybody? Seikichi thought, and without even a parting word to the others, he set off for his own house. The rest followed suit and dispersed in various directions. It was painful to look into each other's faces. In those faces they could see their own likeness: a traitor.

The door of Seikichi's house was also tightly shut.

"Mother, it's me!" he called softly, knocking on the door. The house was stubbornly unresponsive.

"Mother, it's Seikichi!" he called in a louder voice. Finally he could hear the door being unlocked from within, and an elderly woman poked her face out.

"Mother!"

"Come in quickly!" his mother said rapidly. "Once they heard that you'd apostatized, the villagers decided not to have anything to do with you."

"Nothing to do with me? They told you that?"

"That's . . . that's what they all decided. The padres were opposed to it, but . . ."

Seikichi's father was stretched out on a woven mat they used in place of a tatami. His legs had been bothering him ever since he took a fall while working in the fields. Sitting in the dark, dank room blackened by smoke from the hearth, Seikichi and his parents conversed in whispers, as though fearing they might be heard outside.

"They said you had all betrayed Deus. That you'd turned your backs on the village. Turned your backs on what our village and our families have believed in for generations. . . . That's what everybody said. They decided that even if you returned to the village, they wouldn't associate with you for fear of angering God."

"That's a damned fine thing for them to say! People who know absolutely nothing about the horrible pain we suffered, strutting around like they're the only ones with real faith . . . !" Seikichi spat the words out angrily, but his heart was bursting with the feeling that he was in fact a cowardly traitor, an apostate.

"Won't you go to the village head and tell him you want to return to the faith?" From his sickbed, Seikichi's father asked between coughing fits. "Returning to the faith" meant, of course, for one who has separated himself from the Kirishitan faith to come back to the church.

"If you don't," his mother sighed, "I doubt the people of the village will ever forgive you."

"Are you telling me to return to the faith so that I can be tortured again? Mother, look at these scars." Seikichi stripped his kimono down to his waist and showed them the deep red scars on his back that witnessed the torture he had undergone. "People only say what suits their own convenience."

A misty rain began to fall outside. Both his father and mother hung their heads and said nothing further. Gazing at their sorry postures, Seikichi's chest tightened with agonizing emotion. He got to his feet and brusquely left the house. He had decided to show his wounded body to someone in the village and, together with some of the others who had just been released from jail, to protest this ostracism.

When he got outside, he saw through the misty rain that two men had emerged from their houses and were walking toward him. Both men, Seishirō and Mataichi, had been tortured along with him.

"Seikichi, I guess you've heard what they're saying?" Mataichi asked, almost in tears.

"They told me that if I didn't come back to the church, I'd be an outcast. I've never heard anything so ridiculous."

"But Seikichi, we've rejected Lord Jezusu and Santa Maria. I can put up with being shunned. But I can't bear having promised to turn my back on Lord Jezusu and Santa Maria."

Seikichi could not dispute what Mataichi said. He felt the same way himself. His heart was seared as though with molten lead for abandoning what he had been taught from childhood was the most beautiful, most pure, and most true of all things.

"Are you suggesting we should go to the village head and tell him we want to return to our Kirishitan faith?" he muttered weakly, with a sigh.

The light rain drizzled over the three men. But they stood motionless, like cows that have been left standing in the field.

As the trio headed through the rain toward the village head's house, they saw the hazy gray figures of several other people moving through the fog. When they drew near, they recognized another three who had apostatized: Mojū, his wife Kisa, and their son Shigeichi.

At this point, they knew without asking why this family was going to the village head's house. The six now trudged wordlessly along the wet road.

Catching sight of them, a dog tethered in the village head's garden began to bark. At the sound, the village head, Kanjūrō, stuck his head out the door and said, "Ah, you're back home!" Unaware of their intentions, he seemed to think they had come to offer their apologies, and with a forced smile on his face he said, "Well, come in, come in! How terrible that you've had such a rough time." Once Seikichi, with a weak shake of his head, explained their desires to return to the Kirishitan faith, his look changed to one of shock and despondency.

"What?!" He was at a loss for words.

One after another, men and women assembled through the mist at the village head's house. Each of them had heard about the ostracism and had come to ask permission to return to the church.

"I see . . ." Breaking his long silence, he stammered, "Well, I . . . Because of my position, I'll have to report this to the magistrate. I assume you have no objection?"

"There's no other choice."

"You'll have to go back to prison."

No one responded. Their wretched life in jail came vividly back to mind. But their minds were thrown into confusion by the threat of ostracism, the agonizing prospect of being separated once again from their families, and their guilt at having betrayed Lord Jezusu and Santa Maria.

Someone cried out, "Sen'emon is still in prison by himself. If Sen'emon can endure it, we can, too!"

"Is that so?" The village head nodded. "You know, it's possible that the magistrate won't have any more time to deal with you. . . . The domains of Satsuma and Chōshū have joined forces with a pledge to attack Edo. Things will change if the shogun loses that battle. And who knows what will happen to the magistrate?"

Seikichi and the other peasants had a hard time understanding what the village head was saying. Of course, even living unobtrusively as Kirishitans in the shadow of the Urakami hills, they had heard something about a conflict between the emperor and the shogun, but they were utterly in the dark regarding the specifics of the situation.

"Ah-hah." Comprehending nothing, they merely nodded.

The rain grew fierce.

"You want to return to your faith no matter what?"

"Yes, sir."

The village head heaved a sigh.

It's possible that the magistrate won't have any more time to deal with you— This bleak pronouncement by the village head also made oblique reference to the fact that peasant uprisings similar to the one here in Urakami were erupting in various parts of Japan.

For the past two or three years, peasants and merchants in areas of the country plagued with unrest had been abandoning their centuries-old postures of submission and had incited riots. In Osaka and Edo, in Musashi, and in Shinobu of Mutsu Province, farmers had been raising cries of "Reform!" as they stormed the homes of the wealthy and held rallies, and though the officials had finally been able to subdue them, for a time they were completely unmanageable.

In addition to these uprisings, this was also the period in which bizarre dances known as "Ee ja nai ka"—"Who cares?"—became the rage among the masses. Men dressed as women, and women dressed as men filled the streets, dancing in a manner similar to the Awa Dances and chanting:

Who cares? Who cares?
Spread some paper over whatever stinks,
If the paper rips, spread some more!
Who cares? Who cares?

Dancing with abandon, they paraded through the streets. The dance swept like a tsunami across the land, from Kantō in the east to Kamigata in the west.

The rebellion of the Urakami Kirishitans and their return to the faith were of an entirely different nature from the peasant rebellions in other parts of the country and the Ee ja nai ka Dance phenomenon, but that was because the vague premonition that "it's pretty much all over for the shogun" had made its way to this impoverished village.

They knew nothing concrete about such matters, but in fact the shogun had already decided to surrender his political power.

The magistrate's office in Nagasaki was thrown into disarray as these pieces of news arrived one after another. Just as the village head had predicted, when the magistrate was notified that there was more trouble among the Urakami Kirishitans, who should have been stifled by now, he was at his wit's end. *They're in revolt again?!*

Itō Seizaemon, with a dumbfounded look on his face, went to seek advice from Hondō Shuntarō. "Lord Hondō, what should we do about this?"

But with a sardonic smile Hondō replied, "It's no longer a question of what to do. Of far more interest to me than the Urakami peasants is the problem of what will become of us, Lord Itō."

"What do you mean, 'what will become of us'?"

"If the shogunate falls, there will be no more military class. What will you do then, Lord Itō?"

With a tragicomic look on his face, all Itō could say was, "Hmph."

In the tenth month of the third year of the Keiō period, the shogunate restored ruling power to the emperor. By the Western calendar, the date was November 1867.

THE REUNION

THE SHOGUNS WHO had ruled Japan for more than two hundred years had been defeated by the emperor. . . .

When this news arrived, Nagasaki was flung into a spiral of confusion. Unlike surrounding domains, this province was under the direct control of the shogunate, a privilege that had been a source of pride to the residents for many years. For that very reason, when a rumor ("They're saying that those ruffians from Satsuma are going to attack us!") spread around the city that the military forces of Satsuma, which was part of the imperial faction, were marching on Nagasaki, the citizens trembled in fear. The ferocity of the military forces of the Shimazu clan in Satsuma had been legendary throughout Kyushu ever since the wars of unification in the sixteenth century.

Impulsive merchants threw together their belongings and fled in search of refuge. Some houses shut their doors tightly and huddled behind them, as though violence and pillage would break out in the city at any moment.

The Gotōya shop was one such place.

In hushed tones the Master and Mistress discussed whether the best precaution might be to escape to their ancestral home on the Gotō Islands.

"If they close down the shop, what will happen to us?" Tome asked Oyone.

"Obviously they'll just throw us out," Oyone replied resentfully.

"Mitsu has a home to go to, so she'll be all right. But my family's so poor, I can't even think of going back there," Tome mumbled disconsolately.

Mitsu was filled with pity for Tome, who had once told her, "There's lots of families as poor as mine who have to sell their daughters as servants." Mitsu's nature was just a bit different from Kiku's: whenever Mitsu saw a sad, unfortunate person, she was filled with an overwhelming compassion toward them.

"I wonder what Kiku will do?" Tome asked. Mitsu knew that Kiku had not gone back to Urakami but that, for who knows what reason, had ended up working as a maidservant at the Nambanji. One early morning as Mitsu was sweeping at the entrance to the store, Kiku had come running breathlessly up to her. After explaining briefly that she had ended up working at the Nambanji, Kiku said, "So could you tell Ichijirō that that's what I'm doing? I'll take care of myself, so there's no need to worry." Then, announcing she had to fix breakfast for Lord Petitjean and Lord Laucaigne, she ran off like a shot from a gun.

"There really isn't any reason to worry about her; she is Kiku, after all," Mitsu thought. Kiku was the sort of woman who would choose and pursue her own life's course.

But I'll never be like Kiku. From childhood, Mitsu couldn't help but envy the outgoing Kiku. But one day she came to the realization that she was not Kiku. That "one day" was the day Kiku was booted out of the Gotōya.

For her part, Kiku was working with all her might at the Nambanji. Petitjean and the other foreign missionaries, as well as Okane and her husband, all thought very highly of her.

It was a real advantage for Kiku to be well liked here rather than having to return to her home in Magome. Were she to go back to Magome, she would have no way of knowing what was happening to Seikichi. Kiku had been told from her youth that even though Magome was right next to the Kirishitan village of Nakano, there was an invisible and impassable chasm separating them.

Staying here, however, it was easy for Kiku to learn what was happening to Seikichi and his fellow believers. Petitjean and Father Laucaigne were kind enough to keep her informed.

It made no difference to Kiku that the shogun had fallen or that the emperor had taken the reins of government. It was of far greater importance to her as a woman that Seikichi be happy and that she might one day have the good fortune of becoming his wife.

"Kiku. Seikichi and the others have returned to Nakano." When Petitjean gave her that news, the clouds lifted from her face, and it suddenly became so light around her that it seemed as though sunlight was pouring down onto the flower garden.

But then he went on. "Kiku. Seikichi and his friends showed up unexpectedly at the village head's house, saying they wanted to become Kirishitans again."

The blood rushed from her face. She hurried to the chapel and once again began spewing a stream of complaints to the statue of the Blessed Mother.

The magistrate's office, however, was on the verge of collapse itself and had no time to be bothered with the likes of Seikichi and his comrades. Joy returned to

Kiku's face when she learned that the magistrate had decided to put them under watch and allow them to live their normal lives.

If that's the case . . . then one day soon he'll be coming here to the Nambanji, she thought intuitively. Gradually that thought became a conviction in her mind.

"Kiku," one day Petitjean smiled and asked her, "would you be interested in going with me to France?"

In amazement, she responded, "France?"

"I'm only kidding, Kiku. But actually I am going back to France. I'll return to Japan soon. . . ."

Petitjean and the other Christian missionaries living in Japan shared the view that with the fall of the shogunate, the new government that was being formed would likely be more tolerant of Christian proselytizing. As a result, they needed to confer with the church leadership in their homeland regarding the proper response to these new circumstances, and Petitjean had been chosen to perform that assignment.

"But you'll be coming back to Japan soon?"

"I will. Japan is now my home, Kiku."

Although Kiku detested the Kirishitan teachings, she was fond of the priests at the Nambanji. She liked Petitjean especially because he was the one who brought her here. Though she definitely disliked the way he reeked of butter, and she didn't care for the beard on his face. . . .

The second month of the year came.

During the winter in Nagasaki, the morning peddlers sold sea cucumbers called *tōrago*. Other men walked about hawking Chinese cabbage.

About this time the troops from Satsuma and Chōshū stormed in to occupy Nagasaki, blowing pipes and beating drums. The citizens bolted their doors, fearing random violence; the foreigners, preparing for any exigency, summoned aid from the warships anchored at sea while sailors were brought to land and positioned to defend the mouth of the harbor leading to Ōura.

I hear the magistrate has fled the city! The rumor spread like a flash throughout the city. The magistrate, Kawazu Sukekuni,[1] had disappeared.

Several young men of promise from Satsuma and Chōshū took charge at the leaderless magistrate's office and assumed the role of preserving peace in the city. Included among them were men such as Matsukata Masayoshi

---

1. Kawazu Sukekuni (d. 1868) served the shogunate in a variety of positions; his title at this time was governor of Izu. In 1863 he sailed as deputy delegate to Europe to participate in talks regarding the opening of the country. He was the last magistrate of Nagasaki, fleeing the city as described here when he received news of the defeat of the shogunal army.

and Machida Minbu,[2] who would become prominent leaders during the
Meiji period.

Because they had feared violent behavior or looting, the anxious citizens
of Nagasaki were relieved to discover how well disciplined the Satsuma and
Chōshū soldiers were. Shops that had locked their doors once again opened for
business.

Every day when Kiku had some free time, she would stand in front of the
Nambanji, stretching as tall as she could make herself and peering toward the
beach, wondering whether perhaps Seikichi might be climbing the hill.

On cloudy days the inlet was cold and forlorn. On such days her feelings were
also cold and forlorn. She was cheered somewhat on clear days by the sound of
the waves pressing in on the shore. Those were the days when she had hope that
Seikichi just might appear.

One day—

The person Kiku saw climbing the hill to the Nambanji was not Seikichi but
a samurai. It was Itō Seizaemon, looking particularly down in the mouth. Once
he loses the backing he so grandly boasted of, such a man comes to look startlingly unkempt.

He walked past Kiku, apparently preoccupied. Kiku, of course, had no idea
he had been the mastermind behind the painful tortures inflicted on Seikichi.

"Well, if it isn't Lord Itō!" With a slightly acidic smile, Laucaigne greeted the
man who had been spying on the priests.

"I'm sorry to bother you. The truth is that I've had to swallow my pride and
come to beg a favor from you." Itō smiled awkwardly and bowed his head ser-
vilely. He went on to explain that thanks to the generous good offices of Matsukata
Masayoshi, he had been permitted to continue his work at the magistrate's office,
but ultimately he would have to look for other employment. No one is as pathetic
as a government worker who has lost his stipend. So his request was for the priests
to help him get a position as a guard at some foreign country's consulate.

"I don't have the talents or the quick wit of someone like Hondō Shuntarō.
I hear that he made a quick getaway to Yokohama and is up to something
there. . . ." There was spite toward Hondō in his voice.

Striving to contain his amusement, Father Laucaigne promised Itō he would
try to find him work. When the man left the Nambanji, the priest spotted
another man climbing up from the shore. It was Seikichi.

2. Matsukata Masayoshi (1835–1934) served the Meiji government as finance minister, as founder of the Bank of Japan, and as the sixth prime minister of the modern
nation. In 1865 Machida Minbu (1838–1897) traveled to England with a group of fourteen
other gifted young men to study for three years. He was the first director of the National
Museum in Tokyo and, in later years, took Buddhist vows.

Itō, walking with his head down and engrossed in thoughts about his own future, didn't see Seikichi coming from the opposite direction. But when Seikichi spotted Itō, he quickly hid himself behind the trunk of a camphor tree. Once the man was gone, he scrambled up to the Nambanji.

"Father Petitjean!" Happy but breathless, he called out for the priest. He did not know that Petitjean had left Japan for a brief time.

Laucaigne came outside and, reflexively calling out in French, "*Quelle surprise!*" gave Seikichi a bear hug. Not one Kirishitan had come to the church since the terrifying crackdown. Seeing Seikichi made Laucaigne's joy all the sweeter.

"We're being watched," Seikichi began. "Every single day, there's someone hiding out at the end of the Togitsu Highway. They're constantly watching to see where we Kirishitans go."

Seikichi's report on his experiences in prison, his release, and his return to the faith came gushing out of his mouth like the words of a man who has had no one to talk to for a very long time. Laucaigne summoned his brethren, Father Cousin and Father Ridel,[3] to hear Seikichi's account.

"But since the magistrate's office shut down, they've let up on following us. . . . I think the officials don't really know how to deal with us. After all, I hear that the magistrate himself has gone missing." Seikichi seemed pleased with himself at the final comment and grinned as he spoke, showing his white teeth. He was brimming with the confidence and feelings of victory that came from belonging to a group of impoverished farmers who had won out over the magistrate.

"Padre, everybody's waiting for you to come. We want to receive the Mass. And some children have been born, so they want you to baptize them."

"Tell them I'll come by night as soon as I can," Laucaigne agreed.

As they conversed, the priest sensed someone behind them. When he turned to look, he saw Kiku standing a bit away from them, watching them intently. No—Laucaigne quickly realized she was not watching "them"—only Seikichi.

How much she must love him. Laucaigne and Petitjean were well aware of what was going on. They noticed that Kiku hadn't missed a word they'd said about the Kirishitans who were in prison, and they knew that Kiku was secretly praying for Seikichi's safety to the statue of the Blessed Mother in the chapel.

3. Both men, like Petitjean and Laucaigne, were priests of the Société des Missions-Étrangères de Paris. Jules-Alphone Cousin (1842–1911) served as bishop of Nagasaki from 1891 until his death. Félix-Clair Ridel (1830–1884) did missionary work in Korea in the 1860s when the religion was still banned by the king. In 1866, when another missionary was executed along with around eight thousand Korean converts, Ridel fled to China and notified the French authorities about the massacre. A retaliatory French fleet moved on Seoul but was defeated by Korean forces.

"Kiku." Laucaigne beckoned to her. "Come here. Seikichi, Kiku has been continuously concerned about your welfare."

Kiku stiffened, lowered her eyes, and did not move.

"Kiku, why don't you go out to the garden and have a good talk with Seikichi?" Laucaigne tactfully signaled the other priests with his eyes, indicating that they should leave the young lovers to themselves. The French priest thought it would be best for Seikichi and Kiku to talk together alone, just as young people in France would do.

But—

Once the priests in their display of tactfulness disappeared, Seikichi and Kiku felt even more constrained and embarrassed and said nothing to each other.

Kiku could have talked freely with him if he were just the Seikichi who came peddling in front of the rear door of the Gotōya. And Seikichi would have been able to speak to her without reservation if he could have thought of her simply as a young woman who, like him, was from Urakami.

But their mind-set now was quite different. The letter he had received from Kiku while he was in prison had given him a sense of her single-minded ardor. And even before her expulsion from the Gotōya, Kiku had realized just how completely he consumed her thoughts.

Fully cognizant of their own feelings, they looked away from each other with an almost angry look on their faces.

"So I understand you work here." Seikichi sullenly asked the obvious.

"Uh-huh."

"I imagine the padres are kind to you."

"Uh-huh."

They lapsed into silence again.

Suddenly Kiku spoke. "The prison . . . I guess it was pretty difficult."

"Hmm. It wasn't all that bad, I wasn't there by myself. And the magistrate didn't treat us so badly."

"But I heard you were tortured terribly."

"Yeah, it took its toll. But I was able to bear it by thinking about the sufferings of the Inferno."

"But, Seikichi, are you sure you won't be punished for coming like this to the Nambanji?" Kiku looked up worriedly at Seikichi. She did not mention to him that every day she had been petitioning, pleading, cursing, railing at, and complaining to the statue of the Blessed Mother Mary in the chapel. It was, after all, too embarrassing for her to confess. . . .

"There's nothing to worry about." Seikichi became suddenly spirited. "I'm sure you've already heard the news. There's no more magistrate's office, the magistrate himself has vanished, and now the emperor is in charge. Everybody's been saying that Kirishitan countries like America and France can now start letting people know that what we believe is true, so we won't have to practice our Kirishitan teachings in hiding anymore. They say we'll be able to march right up to His Majesty and declare in a loud voice that we're Kirishitans!"

"Oh!" Kiku had no interest in what those Kirishitan teachings were. But it thrilled her to think that the time had come when the people running the country would recognize something that Seikichi believed in so fervently. "That's wonderful, Seikichi!" She smiled like a girl sharing in the joy of her older siblings.

Everything seemed like a dream to Kiku.

Complex matters were beyond her grasp. But even if she didn't understand everything, as she listened to what Seikichi was saying, she felt that the days ahead would be joyful and free. In any case, the magistrate's office that had been so frightening until now had lost all its power. And Seikichi and the others from Nakano could live from now on without reproach.

Perhaps now the people of Magome could get rid of some of their antipathy toward the residents of Nakano, who would no longer bear the mark of blame on their shoulders. And surely her cousin Ichijirō and Granny and her parents would stop calling the Nakano people *Kuros* and not consider them weird anymore.

When that happens—

Her heart puffed up like a balloon.

When that happens, maybe I can become Seikichi's wife. Realizing what she was daydreaming about, Kiku unwittingly blushed.

"You still have it, don't you?" Seikichi suddenly asked.

"What?"

"What I gave you. The Santa Maria . . ."

"I take special care of it," Kiku nodded happily. "I talk to her every day."

"Talk?" Seikichi was startled. "How do you talk to her?"

"Well, not talking, really. . . . I blamed her. I hated her, knowing that it was because you worshipped her that you were suffering so much. So I kept telling her how much I disliked her. . . . But it's all right now. Cause you're out of prison now."

"How could you have done something so evil?" Seikichi cried, seemingly horrified. "Our Lady Santa Maria is the mother of Lord Jezusu. To say hateful things to His mother . . . It's terrible!"

"Who is Lord Jezusu? The strange words you Kirishitans use sound like Chinese gibberish. . . ."

"Lord Jezusu is the Son of Deus. And Mary is Lord Jezusu's mother."

"So Deus and Mary are husband and wife?"

Seikichi rolled his eyes. "Husband and wife?! No, they're not husband and wife! Deus doesn't have a wife!"

"That's ridiculous! How was this Jezusu born if they weren't husband and wife?"

"Mary got pregnant when she was a virgin."

Stunned, Kiku opened her eyes wide and then flushed crimson. Even *she* knew that there wasn't any way a virgin could be with child. What kind of foolish stories did Seikichi believe in, anyway!?

Seikichi did his best to recite for Kiku the stories he knew from the Bible.

The Virgin Mary conceived a child and gave birth to Jezusu. Mary, though she remained a virgin throughout her life, was the wife of the carpenter Joseph and the mother of Jezusu. Jezusu was killed by evil men who hated him, but before long he came back to life and appeared before his disciples. . . .

The more he talked, the more disenchanted Kiku became, and with a look in her eyes that indicated that she thought he was making fun of her, she muttered, "I'm amazed you believe such nonsense!"

"What can't you believe about it?"

"There's no way I can believe that this virgin married a carpenter and stayed a virgin until she died."

"You have to admire a man who can be that kind of husband."

"So, if you got married you wouldn't do anything with your wife, huh? And you honestly think she could have a baby while still a virgin, do you?"

At this point, Kiku lost all sympathy for Seikichi, even though she loved him. As a child she had been so precociously adept at winning arguments that even Ichijirō couldn't get in the last word. She did not lose any of her glibness after she matured into a young woman.

"What are you saying?!" Seikichi was angry. "I can't believe I'm hearing something so shameful coming from a woman's mouth!"

"Stupid things are stupid whether they come from a woman or a man. I suppose if you got married, you'd be a husband just like that carpenter and never lay a finger on your wife!" As she spoke, she suddenly pictured herself as Seikichi's bride. Would he really never touch her? Kiku turned bright red at the thought. "I don't get it! I just don't understand it."

Seikichi, unable to grasp the workings of a woman's mind, said nervously, "Are you mocking us Kirishitans?"

"No, I'm not mocking you. But it all sounds so strange. That a dead man could come back to life—what kind of person would tell you something that's so obviously made up?"

"It's exactly what the padre said."

"Lord Petitjean did? I don't suppose Lord Petitjean actually saw all this happen? Talking about things you've never seen, and then believing in it—you Kirishitans really are strange people."

"Shut up! I hate people who mock us Kirishitans the way you are!" Seikichi shouted as Kiku kept firing away at him like a machine gun. Their voices echoed so loudly that even Father Laucaigne and the others could hear them inside their house.

"*Qu'est-ce qu'il y a?*" Father Laucaigne stood up in surprise. He had hoped to give the two lovers some time alone. And now they were apparently engaged in a ferocious argument.

When Laucaigne rushed out into the garden, Seikichi had just stomped away.

"Kiku, what has happened?"

"I hate him! I hate men like that!" she shouted. And then she began to wail. . . .

This was the first time Kiku had ever been in love. And because Seikichi was the object of her love, she had been utterly captivated by him and had been completely forthright in expressing her affection for him. During his incarceration, she had experienced his sufferings as though the tortures were being inflicted on her own body.

And yet, he understood nothing of how she felt, and had gone so far as to lash out at her with "I hate people who mock us Kirishitans like you are!"

I'm not going to see him again. I'll never speak to a man like that again. She had made up her mind. Father Laucaigne and his comrades tried to elicit the details of their argument from her, but no matter how they tried to pacify her, she kept stubbornly repeating, "I'm done with him. I don't ever want to see his face again!"

Laucaigne was as tenderhearted as Petitjean, so he tried to assuage her anger, but he ended up only flustered. Having been educated at a seminary where women were off-limits, after all, he knew nothing of the subtle workings of a woman's heart.

As she had done so often before, Kiku went into the chapel, stood in front of the statue of that woman, and spilled out the feelings of her heart that she could reveal to no one else.

"All of this, everything is your fault. Seikichi's going around telling lies about how you gave birth to a child when you were still a virgin. He believes nonsense about you having a husband but living out your whole life as a virgin. And he even argued with me about it. This is all your fault!"

As always, the Blessed Mother Mary peered back at Kiku. But her face resembled that of an exasperated woman who has just been argued into silence by her younger sister. It was also reminiscent of the face of a frustrated young mother whose child has just thrown a tantrum.

"Since this is all your fault, I won't forgive you unless you put everything back the way it was before. I'll be really mad at you if you do something to ruin my relationship with Seikichi!" Kiku pointed a finger as though to threaten the

Blessed Mother. "But if you help me to marry Seikichi . . ." She became conscious of the look of bliss on her own face and blushed. " . . . I'll do anything you want. I'll bring you gifts of pretty flowers and rice cakes. . . . I'll even become a Kirishitan. I don't like the Kirishitans. But if you help me become Seikichi's wife, I don't mind becoming Kirishitan."

The statue of the Blessed Mother to which Kiku made this promise still stands in the Ōura Catholic Church in Nagasaki. Her cherubic, unsullied face seems to change expressions depending on the angle from which she is viewed, the intensity of the light shining on her, or the feelings in the heart of the petitioner offering prayers to her.

Kiku was able to converse with her like a little girl talking with her doll, even though she did not believe even slightly in the Kirishitan faith. . . .

The emperor dispatched a governor-general from the new administration to assist with the pacification of Kyushu. His name was Sawa Nobuyoshi, and he would later become the Minister of Foreign Affairs.[4] His assistant was Inoue Monta, later known as Inoue Kaoru.[5]

Matsukata Masayoshi, Machida Minbu, and Sasaki Sanshirō had already taken over the vacated offices of the magistrate and functioned as the leaders of the city government, and they were joined by Inoue Monta. Inoue was informed by Matsukata and the others that Nagasaki, like Yokohama, was a foreign concession, leading to an incident that had involved the Kirishitans hidden in Urakami Village.

"Japan has no other gods beside His Imperial Highness. Lord Sawa has been very clear on that point," Inoue explained to his fellow officers.

Matsukata and his allies were also well aware that Sawa was a prominent exponent of expelling the foreigners from Japan.

Sawa gave firm directions to Inoue and the others: "For a variety of reasons, the shogunate sought aid from France, and so they were unable to come out strongly against the Kirishitans. But we have an obligation to teach the citizens and the peasants that they must rely solely upon His Imperial Highness." The officers immediately set about to implement them.

4. Sawa Nobuyoshi (1836–1873) also served as governor of Nagasaki and was one of the most ardent persecutors of the Kirishitans. He died of an illness at the age of thirty-seven.

5. Inoue Monta (1836–1915) was initially an antiforeign activist who joined with others to set fire to the British legation in 1863. A close ally of Itō Hirobumi, the first Meiji prime minister, Inoue studied in London and later served the Meiji government as Minister of Foreign Affairs, Minister of Agriculture and Commerce, Home Minister, and Minister of Finance.

Notices were posted in every prominent location throughout the city of Nagasaki under the signature of the Grand Council of State:

1. The people are to properly observe the five filial relationships of Confucianism.[6]
2. The organizing of factions to make direct petition to the daimyo or to lead others from the villages is prohibited.
3. Acts of violence against foreigners are prohibited.
4. Fleeing from the village is prohibited.
5. The Kirishitan faith, as in the past, is strictly prohibited.

These new bulletin boards, still smelling of freshly cut wood, were placed where in earlier days the notices from the magistrate's office had been posted, and people gathered round to read them.

"What's this about 'fleeing from the village'?"

"It means you can't leave Nagasaki without permission and go to live somewhere else."

"I suppose the folks in Urakami are really upset that they're still treating the Kirishitan faith as a heretical religion."

The citizens of Nagasaki actually gloated a bit among themselves when they read the notice reaffirming the ban on the Kirishitan faith. A majority of the residents did not have positive feelings toward the peasants who were followers of a nonsensical cult that made trouble for the magistrate's office.

"Don't worry about it." On the other hand, when the Kirishitans of Nakano and Motohara and Ieno read the notice, they paid it little heed. They believed that just as had been the case with the magistrate, the new officials sent by His Majesty would be restrained by the views of foreigners and would not make a move against them. And the upshot of recent events gave them the courage to believe that Deus would not leave them to be slaughtered.

Their calculations proved correct. Several foreign attachés were quick to launch complaints against the new government. Of particular significance was the fact that Harry Smith Parkes, the ambassador from Great Britain, was among the protestors, since his government had thrown its support behind the new Japanese administration.

The new government was thoroughly flustered by Great Britain's participation in the protest against the Kirishitan suppression. But the Meiji leaders had made up their minds that they would maintain the shogunate's posture toward Christianity as part of their new regime's religious policy.

6. The five relationships are subject to ruler, child to father, wife to husband, younger siblings to elder sibling, and friend to friend.

In March, orders unexpectedly came from the local government office for twenty-four of the leading Kirishitans in Urakami to surrender themselves to the police.

The name of the Nagasaki magistrate's office had been changed to the "government office." The name change, however, did not signify that the new administration was planning to change the shogunate's policy of prohibiting Christianity.

Included among the twenty-four was, of course, Sen'emon, who had clung to his beliefs to the bitter end, as well as others such as Seikichi who had initially apostatized but then returned to their faith.

This time we won't get away with just a beating as we did before. Maybe they'll kill us.

When the village head notified them of the surrender order, the faces of those whose names were read out turned pale. The blood similarly drained from the faces of their family members.

"Lord Deus, Lord Jezusu, and Santa Maria will be with us!" Sen'emon was qualified to encourage the others because he alone had endured the previous round of tortures. Everyone had been showing respect to this unassuming man because of his courage.

"No matter what happens, Santa Maria will protect us. We all just have to continue offering our *oraçió* to her and put all our trust in her."

On the morning of their surrender, however, each of the twenty-four felt somber, as though they were bidding their final farewells to their families.

The mountains were wrapped in a spring haze, and the flowers were in bloom. For the Kirishitans, this was the month that they would be celebrating the resurrection of Jezusu on Easter Sunday. But it was simultaneously a time of great sorrow—it was also the month when Jesus died.

They had no way of knowing whether their fate would lead them to death or restore them to life. When the twenty-four left their homes, their families followed behind, intoning prayers. Their numbers swelled from one hundred to two hundred, then from two hundred to three hundred.

"Go back to your homes now," the village head and the government officials ordered the crowd, but they shook their heads and formed into ranks that walked all the way to Nagasaki.

At the gate leading to the government office—the same gate through which they had earlier entered the magistrate's office—the twenty-four prisoners turned back to their families and called, "Don't worry! This time we won't reject Lord Jezusu and Santa Maria no matter what!" And then they disappeared through the gate that summoned up such painful memories for them.

Even then the families did not withdraw but crouched down quietly and waited. One, then two, of the curious onlookers went away, until finally all were gone. But the Kirishitan men and women refused to budge from where they sat.

It was a peculiar scene beneath the warm spring sun. Many hours passed.

Near nightfall, the gate opened once again, and the twenty-four Kirishitans, with Sen'emon at their head, emerged with triumphant, joyful smiles on their faces.

"Not one of us apostatized! We told the officials there was no way we would abandon our Kirishitan faith. Absolutely never abandon it!" Seikichi puffed out his chest and explained to the crowd.

Another summons came from the government office a month later. Unlike the previous summons of twenty-four individuals, this time the heads of every household were ordered to surrender to the police.

As a result, 180 Kirishitan peasants from Nakano, Ieno, and Motohara set out for Nagasaki, once again in the early morning. Nearly four hundred family members followed behind, but on this day it was rainy and muggy.

The interrogating and admonishing dragged on for many hours in the presence of Governor-General Sawa Nobuyoshi. Rain beat mercilessly down on the faces and bodies of the peasants as they sat on white gravel in the courtyard listening to the remonstrations. The rain reminded them of the night of the downpour when they all had been viciously beaten.

One by one, each of the officials—Ōkuma Hachitarō, Matsukata Masayoshi, Machida Minbu, and Inoue Monta—took turns questioning and warning the prisoners to abandon their faith. They alternated between reproaching the prisoners for violating the laws of the land and insisting that they had been deceived by the missionaries, or else they would let their anger get the best of them and begin threatening the Kirishitans with violence in their voices.

However—

The peasants of Urakami stubbornly refused to give in. On this occasion they did not employ the silent resistance typical of farmers; instead they became defiant, openly contesting and arguing with their interrogators. *If you're going to threaten us, go ahead and kill us,* they responded. *Even if you get all worked up, our way of life is just different from yours,* they retorted.

One of the interrogators, Ōkuma Hachitarō—later known as Count Ōkuma Shigenobu[7]—would later report on these events as follows:

"The firmness of their faith was like gold and iron. One young woman of a weak and mild countenance responded to the inspector's questions, his threats,

---

7. Ōkuma Hachitarō (1838–1922) was one of the most active and influential of the oligarchs who helped establish the Meiji government. Influenced by his reading of the New Testament and the American Declaration of Independence, he pushed for the shogun to cede power to the emperor, was elected to the first representative Diet of the new era, served as Minister of Finance and Minister of Foreign Affairs, and twice served as prime minister (for four months in 1898, and from 1914 to 1916). He also founded the forerunner of Waseda University and served as its president.

and his admonitions with calm presence of mind and not a hint of fear." He went on to admit, "Of the interrogators, Inoue Kaoru was the one who was most zealously participating in the inquiry, but he was at a loss for how to deal with the young woman's manner: he grew impatient with her, thundered at her, and was almost beside himself, but the more impassioned he became, the more serene she appeared. The logic of her responses was beyond dispute, and he couldn't do anything to attack her cogent rationality. He had quite a rough time of it!"

Thanks to their experiences in prison and then the interrogation in the third month, the Kirishitan peasants of Urakami had a clear notion of the kinds of logic the officials would try to use to persuade them. They had probably already discussed among themselves how to answer when questioned in a particular manner and how to argue back when they were threatened in a certain way, and they had thought carefully through every single response they would give.

Consequently, it was only natural that they were able to outwit men like Ōkuma Shigenobu and Inoue Kaoru, having seen through their ploys. Skilled as they were in political disputation, these officials underestimated these totally illiterate peasants, certain that they would be crushed by the power of their glibness. They were dead wrong.

Once again, the government office that had summoned the Urakami Kirishitans was forced to send them back to their homes. Needless to say, the officials could not push them any harder owing to the tenacious protests from foreign legations in Japan, who adopted the same attitude toward them as they had toward the shogunate.

The peasants of Urakami were bursting with self-confidence. The rain had already stopped when they emerged in high spirits from the government office.

A blue sky was visible in the west, a sign that the weather was going to improve.

Just as before, the many families who had followed their loved ones from Urakami stood outside the gate, and when their relatives came out of the interrogation, they waved their hands and cheered loudly.

Seikichi was part of the procession that came through the gate as someone at the front of the line, most likely Sen'emon, began singing a hymn.

Let us go, let us go
Let us go to the temple of Paraíso!

As they filed out one after another, they all joined in the singing; the family members who followed behind them also began to sing.

Seikichi relished an indescribable feeling of joy as he sang while he walked along the rain-drenched road. He was proud of the other Kirishitans who walked beside him. What they believed in was true. What they believed in had proven stronger than either the magistrate's office or the government office. . . .

He strode forward, staring up at the blue sky visible between the gray clouds. It didn't matter that his legs and body were being splashed by mud. And he didn't even bother glancing at the spectators who stood on both sides of the road.

But then he caught sight of Laucaigne and the other priests from Ōura standing amid the crowd. At their side was Kiku.

People of every land, bless the holy name of the Lord
Forever and ever.

As he whispered the Latin prayer, Laucaigne gazed at the feet of the Kirishitans; they were covered in mud from walking along the road after the rain.

Kiku, for her part, stared only at Seikichi.

Seikichi is so strong. . . . Seikichi, who had not despaired despite what he had experienced at the magistrate's office and the government office. Seikichi, who had not faltered. Kiku was even more powerfully drawn to Seikichi's strength. . . . If only he weren't a Kirishitan!

Seikichi really is a man.

Let us go, let us go
Let us go to the temple of Paraíso!

The triumphant singing voices were of course audible in the government office. Their interrogators—Inoue Monta, Machida Minbu, and Matsukata Masayoshi—also heard their singing.

They each had a bitter look on their faces, but Governor-General Sawa Nobuyoshi was in an especially foul mood.

"They've really gone too far," Machida Minbu sputtered. "For mere peasants, they seem to understand our weaknesses all too well. I'm sure that's because of what the Namban clerics have filled their ears with. . . ."

Inoue Monta also shared his views with Sawa. "If we do nothing to them, they're bound to get cocky. What have you decided?"

"Matsukata, what do you think?" Sawa asked.

After thinking for a few moments, Matsukata proposed, "It seems to me we can't really decide this here in the Nagasaki office. I think that Inoue and I should go to Osaka and seek the sanction of Lord Kido[8] before we do anything. . . ."

8. Kido Takayoshi (1833–1877) was an imperial loyalist who helped initiate many of the moves toward modernization under the Meiji government. He traveled with the Iwakura Mission (1871–1873) to the United States and Europe and pushed for the creation of a constitutional government. As an adviser to the throne, he oversaw the young Emperor Meiji's education.

A man had been skulking in front of the Nambanji for nearly half an hour.

He stood stock-still, staring nervously at the church behind its fence. To avoid arousing suspicion he would leave for a while, then return to the same spot.

It was Kiku who discovered him; every day between chores she looked toward the door of the church, earnestly hoping that Seikichi would make an appearance.

Abruptly she cried out, "Ichijirō!" It was her cousin she had not seen in a long while. She raced outside and called through the fence, "Isn't that you, Ichijirō?"

"Ah!" In relief he wiped the sweat from his brow. "So you're here after all. Just like Mitsu said."

"Mitsu's still working hard at the Gotōya, isn't she?"

"Working her heart out." Then abruptly Ichijirō gave her a dour look. He was not happy with this cousin; unlike his hardworking sister Mitsu, Kiku had stolen away from the Gotōya. "Why didn't you send word to Magome that you were here?" His voice was menacing. "Do you have any idea how worried your mom and dad and Granny have been since you disappeared . . . ? You probably haven't given that even a single thought."

"But I knew they'd all be really mad at me if I told them. . . . Mitsu's the only one I told that I'm working here."

She kept her eyes lowered as she tried to defend herself, but Ichijirō kept pressing her. "Have you . . . have you done something that would make everyone mad at you?"

Kiku said nothing.

"Why aren't you answering? How am I supposed to know what's going on if you won't talk to me?" But Ichijirō knew full well the reason for her silence. He had heard everything from his sister.

Still Kiku had nothing to say.

"Are you still love struck with that boy from Nakano? That *Kuro* fellow?"

"Ichijirō, what's so bad about being Kirishitan?" Kiku suddenly raised her head defiantly and challenged him. "You probably don't know that the times have changed, and one day soon the Kirishitans will be able to walk the streets freely. That's why even when the government people called them in, they just let them go."

It angered Ichijirō to have his young cousin jabber at him like this, but he stifled his emotions. Kiku's parents and Granny had told him in no uncertain terms that he was to bring Kiku back to Magome.

"Even I know that much," he nodded reluctantly. Then, after a pause, he said, "But not a single woman from Magome has ever married a *Kuro* from Nakano or Ieno. If you did something like that, everyone would point fingers at you."

"Point fingers? Why?"

"Because they'd say you married a *Kuro*."

"I don't care!" She spoke triumphantly, even proudly. "I don't care what any-body says. I'm not doing anything bad. Pointing fingers at someone who hasn't done anything wrong just means there's something wrong with their heads!"

"Listen, Kiku." Ichijirō sensed that he was no match verbally for his cousin. "Doesn't it bother you that you're causing your parents and Granny to worry so much? Everybody is very concerned about you. There's all kinds of good places to work without having to serve at this foreign temple. Come back to Magome for a while. . . . "

"I'm not coming back." She flung her refusal back at him. "If I come back to Magome, they won't let me marry a *Kuro*, so I'm not coming home."

"Kiku . . ." Ichijirō was stunned. "Do you really love him that much?"

"I do love him . . ." *I do love him.* Kiku spoke the words forcefully, proudly.

"Why?"

"I don't know myself. But I know I love him."

"You won't give him up, no matter what happens?"

"I won't."

Ichijirō involuntarily heaved a deep sigh. Since childhood it had been Kiku's nature to persist obdurately in having things her way once she had made up her mind. If she said she wasn't going to give Seikichi up, there was no way she ever would. If she announced she wasn't going back to Magome, she would not be going back.

"I see." In reality, Ichijirō felt remorse in the depths of his heart. He had the distasteful memory of spying on the peasants of Nakano at the urging of the magistrate's officers and the chief priest of the Shōtokuji. That regret now changed his attitude toward Kiku somewhat. "I see. . . . If you're that deter-mined, I'll pass the word along to your father."

"Then . . ." Kiku looked happy for the first time. "Then you'll help me?"

"I'm not saying I'll help you. But . . ."

But seeing the look on Ichijirō's face, Kiku sensed that ultimately this cousin would become her ally. It was her woman's intuition.

Joy surged through her entire body.

Now I can become Seikichi's wife . . . !

Kiku had no idea how Seikichi's parents would feel about this. But she was happy. She was truly happy. . . .

SEPARATION

THE CHERRY BLOSSOMS at Nakagawa were in full bloom, as though they were a manifestation of Kiku's happiness. At night the blossoms were hazily lit by paper lanterns, and crowds of spectators passed beneath them.

The calls of peddlers as they walked the streets selling cockles and clams were audible throughout the day. The month for the Kite Competition had again come to Nagasaki.

In the fourth month, the new government in Tokyo, in receipt of a report from Sawa Nobuyoshi, held one of their frequent council meetings in the presence of the emperor and finally set out a policy for dealing with the Urakami Kirishitans.

With this decision in hand, Kido Takayoshi arrived in Nagasaki as a government representative on the thirtieth of the fourth month to consult with Sawa, who had just been appointed governor of Nagasaki, on the best method to put the policy into practice.

The decision was a cruel one that dashed the overly optimistic expectations of the Kirishitans. Even though it meant setting aside the objections from foreign diplomats, the government had decided to exile the Urakami peasants who were followers of the outlawed religion. The proposal of the hard-liners in the government, including Prince Arisugawa, Ōkubo Toshimichi, and Kuroda

Nagatomo,[1] had emerged victorious: the Kirishitans were to be punished decisively, first, as part of their plan to create a Shinto-based national polity centered
on the emperor and, second, to assert the country's sovereign rights.

Before departing from Nagasaki, Kido gave orders to Sawa to select 114 of the
Kirishitans who had not apostatized and banish them to the three domains of
Hagi, Tsuwano, and Fukuyama.[2]

On May 21, without any notice, orders to surrender were transmitted via the
village heads to households in Motohara, Nakano, and Ieno.

"You are ordered to report to the Nishi Bureau tomorrow morning at
6:00 A.M."

When the notices arrived, Seikichi and some of the other young men
merely laughed it off. "This is ridiculous! Just one more time we have to argue
them down, and they won't be able to do anything to us!" The fact that they
had come back unscathed after their second interrogation had bolstered their
confidence.

Before dawn the following morning they set out for Nagasaki, accompanied,
as they had been before, by family members. They passed over Nishizaka Hill
and arrived at the Nishi Bureau in Nagasaki, but the gate was tightly shut.

"Wait here!" Barked an official whom they recognized when he came out
through the gate.

"Lord Itō, we were commanded to be here at 6:00 A.M.," Kumazō responded
snidely. Kumazō was the first man who had apostatized during their initial
incarceration, but now he was set on treating the officers as fools.

"I don't know anything about that. All I know is that the orders from the
governor are that you are to wait here." With that, Itō disappeared.

Noon came and went. Still they were ignored. Evening came. The gate still did
not open. Some of the Kirishitans seated on the ground began to mutter and
complain. Just then, Itō Seizaemon reemerged.

---

1. Prince Arisugawa Takahito (1835–1895), a member of the Imperial Household, was
a close adviser to the emperor, a general in the Imperial Army, and lord president of the
Council of State. Ōkubo Toshimichi (1830–1878), like his comrade Kido Takayoshi, was
instrumental in founding the new Meiji government; traveled with the Iwakura Mission
(1871–1873); and served as Home Minister and, later, Minister of Finance. Because he led
the troops against the insurrection of his old friend Saigō Takamori in 1877, Ōkubo was
assassinated by loyalists, who regarded him as a traitor. Kuroda Nagatomo (1839–1902)
was the last daimyo of the Fukuoka domain and its first governor after the changes in
political structure following the Meiji Restoration.

2. Hagi, in present-day Yamaguchi Prefecture, lies on the Sea of Japan. Tsuwano is
located in what is now Shimane Prefecture, also near the Sea of Japan. Fukuyama is
today a part of Hiroshima Prefecture.

"We have no business with any of you who did not receive a summons. Go back to your homes right away. Leave!"

But even after the 114 Kirishitans had gone into the government office, their families remained stubbornly in place. Without warning, several policemen armed with bludgeons came rushing out. Amid screams and angry shouts, the family members were driven away like animals. Nothing was the same as it had been the previous time.

The 114 who passed through the gate of the government office also sensed inside that everything about the atmosphere this time was different from before.

On the previous occasion, there had really been nothing harsh in the attitudes of the police. But this time they snarled, "Get out there!"

They were taken to the courtyard and ordered to sit on the gravel. Soon an official appeared, opened up a scroll of paper with both hands, and began to read.

"Whereas you are believers in a heretical religion and are in violation of Imperial law, there is every reason to punish you severely, but because you are illiterate peasants, out of the good graces of His Majesty you will be held in custody in distant domains."

He looked around at the group, then called out, "Sen'emon!"

"Yes, sir?"

"Sen'emon and twenty-seven others will be held in custody by Lord Kamei, Governor of Oki and holder of a 43,000 *koku*[3] stipend in Iwami Province. . . . Mojū!"

Mojū did not respond.

"Mojū and sixty-five others will be held in custody by the government steward, Lord Mōri, holder of a 370,000 *koku* stipend in Suō and Nagato Provinces. . . . Moichi and nineteen others will be confined under the direction of Lord Abe, Chief Paymaster and holder of 110,000 *koku* in Bingo Province."

The 114 prisoners listened blankly to the official's voice. What they were being told did not feel the least bit real to them. It felt as though they were having a nightmare.

"On your feet!" The entire group stood up, but several of them staggered.

We're being sent to a far-off province. . . .

None of these 114 peasants had ever seen a place outside Urakami and Nagasaki. The hills and forests and terraced fields, the only scenery that Nakano and Ieno and Motohara had to offer, were an inseparable part of their daily activities, their very lives, in the same way that a snail cannot be separated from its shell. Their fathers and mothers, even their grandfathers and grandmothers,

---

3. *Koku* is a measure for rice, the rough equivalent of what one adult could eat in one year, and was the standard measure of a daimyo's wealth and prestige.

were born and raised, toiled and died, in these villages. Not one of them ever considered the possibility of leaving Urakami.

"Move!"

The group was herded out the gate. Beyond the gate, a column of soldiers carrying guns had appeared from nowhere. The family members who had followed them from Urakami had vanished like vapors.

"Where . . . where are we going?" Sen'emon inquired of an officer who walked beside him.

"You'll be getting on a ship, so we're heading straight for Ōhato." The officer pointed toward the harbor.

"We're going to get on the ship right now?"

"That's right. Didn't they just tell you that . . . ?"

This was the first moment it became real to them that they were being torn away from Urakami for the rest of their lives. The pain in their breasts felt as though they had been stabbed with a knife.

The ocean at twilight was black, and Mount Inasa rose like a purple dome before them.

"Runaways!!" An officer at the rear of the rank suddenly shouted. Three of the peasants had managed to escape.

"Get them!"

The three fugitives quickly ran between houses and tried to hide themselves in the encroaching evening haze. Several policemen pursued them.

The remaining prisoners were taken directly from the government office to the boat dock at Ōhato.

The wind was strong, and the harbor waves were rough. At Ōhato several barges bobbing in the water awaited them.

"On board! Quickly!!"

The 111 peasants climbed one after another into the barges.

"These fools tried to escape!" Two of the fugitives, their hands lashed behind them, were shoved to the edge of the water by policemen. As the others looked on, they were beaten and kicked, and finally were the last men put on board.

"Kumazō got away!" One of the captured men whispered quietly to his fellow believers. "He can run fast, so he disappeared right away. I wonder where he's hiding right now."

Apparently the officers and the police had given up chasing Kumazō; they ordered the boatmen to untie the mooring lines. The four barges, splashed by the waves, headed toward a steamship waiting in the middle of the harbor.

The evening haze gave way to night. Lights flickered faintly from the base of Mount Inasa and the streets of Nagasaki. It was pitch black in the vicinity of Urakami. But the gaze of every one of the 113 prisoners was directed toward that darkened village of Urakami.

They might not ever return home again. Perhaps they would be taken off somewhere and executed. If so, they would never again set foot on the soil of Urakami.

And what about their family members who had followed them all the way to the government office? Where were their wives and children, their fathers and mothers, in that thick darkness? Did they have any idea that right now their loved ones were being loaded onto a ship and taken far from them?

Every manner of thoughts clutched at their hearts. In earlier times the padres had told the ancestors of these peasants that God would grant happiness and triumph to those who believed in him, but in reality, all they had received was exile from their homes and separation from their families.

The waves lapped noisily against the barges. Eventually they drew near to the black hull of the steamship, its sails billowing.

"Mary full of grace . . ." As soon as one of the prisoners began to recite the *oração* to the Blessed Mother Mary, everyone else joined in. The officers and police who rode with them on the barges uttered no word of complaint.

"Look! There's a light at Urakami!" At that cry, everyone turned toward Urakami. There could be no doubt that the light was coming from the Ōura Church where they practiced their faith.

"Say, do you think the padres know that we're being led away like this?" someone asked. His voice was filled with loneliness and desolation.

"They don't know yet. If they did, they couldn't abandon us like this."

"That's true." They all looked down and were silent for a time.

But at that same moment, the priests at Ōura were in fact watching as the prisoners were transported on barges to the steamship.

Three women had come stumbling into the church to notify them what was happening.

The women were relatives of the 113 Kirishitans who were being hustled away. Some of them had been among the families and relatives of the prisoners who had been driven off by policemen with bludgeons but, not wanting to return to Urakami, had hidden and waited for their loved ones to reemerge from the government office.

When these women saw their own husbands or siblings being taken to Ōhato and loaded onto barges, they raced along the beach to Ōura to seek help from the priests.

As soon as he received the report, Laucaigne rushed to the French consulate in Nagasaki, but his efforts at intercession were fruitless. Governor Sawa stubbornly deflected all objections.

All the other priests stood in the church's garden gazing at the harbor. When they saw the barges lurching through the dark waters of the harbor toward the steamship, they rushed back to their house and ignited lights in the windows to let the prisoners know they were there. Those were the lights that the 113 Kirishitans saw. . . .

The priests' view of the port was cut off by the darkness of the night. By now the harbor and Mount Inasa had all been dyed the same blackish color, and they could no longer see anything. They couldn't even locate the steamship carrying the Kirishitans.

Father Laucaigne returned from the consulate in a state of utter exhaustion. At his report, all the priests felt powerless, realizing there was now nothing they could do.

"If only Petitjean were here . . ." At times like this, Laucaigne always wished that Petitjean were here. His timing was only a little off: he would be returning to Japan in another two or three days. . . .

"Let us pray for them."

All the priests knelt on the ground. Laucaigne prayed, "If it be possible, please let me take the place of these Japanese Kirishitans. These simple peasants are about to suffer in Thy name. Please include me in their suffering. . . ."

He thought he heard something far off in the distance, and he lifted his head. Father Cousin also seemed to have noticed, and he was straining to hear what it might be.

"*Écoutez!*" Laucaigne pointed toward the harbor.

They could hear faint voices mingled with the sound of the waves. It was the voices of many men singing.

Let us go, let us go
Let us go to the temple of Paraíso.
Let us go, let us go
Let us go to the temple of Paraíso.

Their voices were muffled by the waves, then audible again.

It was them! They were standing on the deck of the ship and raising their voices in song toward the church on the hill.

"Let's sing with them!" Father Cousin urged the others. The priests lifted their voices toward the shadowy harbor. Loud enough for the men in the boat to hear them. . . .

As for Kiku—

Right then she was crouched down in the night-swathed garden. Laucaigne and the other priests had completely forgotten about her.

She was motionless as a statue. With both hands covering her face, she braced herself to listen to the poignant hymn echoing quietly from the dark ocean in the distance.

Seikichi was one of the men singing that hymn.

There was no doubt about it. She had asked one of the women who had come running to the temple, "Was Seikichi with them?"

"Seikichi? Yes, he was there. You mean Seikichi from Nakano, right?" The response came down on Kiku's head like a giant tree crashing on top of her.

Everything had been smashed. The dreams Kiku had woven up until yesterday all tumbled like a falling tower, kicking up a cloud of dust.

Even her cousin Ichijirō had decided it would be all right for her to marry Seikichi. With his support, eventually her father and mother and Granny would have a change of heart as well.

Each morning when she awoke, and each night in her bed, Kiku had savored this fantasy just as an infant nurses for a seemingly endless time at its mother's breast. Her dream of happiness had known no bounds. In her fantasies, Kiku had imagined herself nestled against Seikichi as they walked through a meadow of lotus flowers. She had even pictured them working side by side in the fields.

And now it was all gone. Everything had been obliterated. At that very moment, Seikichi was being held prisoner on a ship in the inlet just below her eyes, being taken to some unknown place.

Seikichi. Hurry and talk to the officers. Tell them you'll abandon your Kirishitan beliefs. When you do, the officers will immediately let you off the boat and return you to the shore. Hurry and talk to them! Quickly! Quickly!

Kiku kept screaming inwardly. She couldn't bear hearing the singing of that hymn any longer. So long as the singing remained audible, Seikichi would feel pressured by the others and would not abandon his Kirishitan faith. She stuffed her fingers in her ears and tried to blot out the voices.

This is all because of that evil woman. That woman!

Once again the face of that woman danced before her eyes. That alien woman called Santa Maria. That woman had ensnared Seikichi with some mysterious power and would not let him go. She had muddled his mind and led him down an evil path.

You'd better remember this! If you don't bring Seikichi back to me as soon as tomorrow, I'll get even with you! She directed the words toward that woman. *I'm not surrendering to the likes of you!*

She stood up and raced toward the chapel. An urge to smash the statue to pieces had swept over her.

Candles flickered at the altar in the chapel. Father Laucaigne and the other priests had just knelt and commenced their prayers.

Dawn broke. Kiku awoke to the chilly air and realized she was huddled in a corner of the chapel, sleeping like a puppy.

No one else was in the chapel. Evidently Laucaigne and the other priests had withdrawn without noticing Kiku.

Kiku suddenly came to herself. What had become of the ship that Seikichi had boarded? In the stillness of dawn, she could no longer hear the singing voices.

She ran outside in a daze.

The waters of the harbor were calm again today, and the surrounding hills were wrapped in a milky morning mist. But there was no sign of the ship.

Tears streamed from her eyes like water gushing from a well. She wept loudly. *Why does Seikichi have to experience so much pain? What evil has he ever done?*

She wanted to scream the words through the streets of Nagasaki from her spot on the hilltop. She wanted to shout them to the people who were still sound asleep in the spring dawn. She wanted to shout them to the ocean and to the sky.

Awakened by her wailing and sobbing, the priests rushed out of their house. Laucaigne held her in his arms and did his best to console her.

Throughout that day, the fathers demanded through the French consulate that the Japanese government provide them information on where the 113 Urakami believers had been sent, but their demands were rejected. Governor Sawa had adopted a rigid attitude toward foreign petitions.

"It's frightening. I hear that the *Kuros* were taken to the open sea and tossed into the ocean!"

"I heard that they'd been sent to Sado to work in the gold mines."

Such rumors began to pop up one after another in the streets of Nagasaki that very day.

Kiku stayed in her bed throughout the day like an invalid. The priests could read in her hollow eyes and unfocused gaze how much she really loved Seikichi.

She refused any food, leading Okane to snap disagreeably, "You seem pretty comfortable for somebody dying of love," but Kiku just stared blankly into space, as though she did not hear.

Seikichi often appeared in her dreams.

Seikichi would be walking along, his hands bound behind him, with a policeman shouting at him. Kiku would rail at the policeman in hopes of rescuing Seikichi.

She also saw scenes of Magome, the lotus flower in bloom. Kiku would be playing with Mitsu and some other friends, making garlands of flowers.

"If you want to see flowers, they're in full bloom in Nakano!" she would tell the others, but none had been willing to follow her to Nakano.

"Kiku, what's wrong?" She was roused from her dreams by a familiar voice calling to her through the sliding screen. In the hallway stood Petitjean, who had been absent from Japan for some time. Kiku did not recognize the young foreign man standing to his side.

This young Frenchman, Father De Rotz,[4] was later to be venerated by the Japanese as the saint of the Sotome region.

4. Marc Marie De Rotz (1840–1914), born in Normandy to an aristocratic family, was brought to Japan by Father Petitjean in 1868. He became parish priest in Shitsu (located in the Sotome region outside Nagasaki) in 1879. He freely parted with his own considerable wealth in order to assist the Christian peasants, built churches for them, established a printing operation, constructed roads and dikes, taught techniques of sewing and dyeing and set up a production factory, built a medical clinic and pharmacy, established a Latin seminary school, and fostered the training of Japanese nuns. He is buried in Shitsu, and a memorial museum was established to celebrate his contributions.

THE CROWD

"**THAT MITSU IS** a real worker! She gives you an honest day's labor," the Mistress of the Gotōya often flattered Mitsu.

The praise thrilled the shy girl. At the same time, though, she wished the Mistress would also say something kind about Tome, who worked alongside her. And she wished that the Mistress would stop making the occasional derogatory comment about Kiku.

"Compared with you, that Kiku was a real handful. I hear she's serving now at the Nambanji . . . but I'm sure I don't know just what *sort* of service she's rendering."

The Mistress, who loathed Kirishitans, and Oyone both disparaged the Urakami Kirishitans for their defiance of orders from the magistrate's office and for adamantly refusing to alter their beliefs.

Consequently, it appeared that the Mistress was annoyed at the very thought that Kiku was working at the Nambanji.

It was painful for Mitsu to hear the Mistress grousing about Kiku. Being reserved and timid, she said nothing, but her face bespoke her sadness.

Mitsu was in fact a very hard worker. She accepted the weight of responsibility for Kiku's desertion and tried to work twice as hard herself. She pushed herself to the point that Oyone and even Tome cautioned her, "If you don't slow down a little, you'll ruin your health."

On a brisk day in the fifth month, the Suwa Festival gets under way, and the rhythmic sounds of flute ensembles echo through the streets of the town. Carp streamers stir in the greenery-laden wind, and men who stroll about selling cakes wrapped in bamboo or oak leaves take breaks in the shade of the earthen walls in Teramachi. Once the dragon boat races conclude, the rains finally begin. It is the start of the rainy season.

One evening when a rain that felt like a precursor to the rainy season quietly soaked the roofs of the houses and the roads, Mitsu went on an errand for Oyone and was on her way back to the shop when she noticed a beggarly looking man in a state of complete exhaustion huddled beside the rear door of the shop.

Frightened, Mitsu stood back and watched him from a distance. The man lifted his pale face toward her and said feebly, "Miss, could you let me rest here for a while? I won't stay long."

Mitsu detected an Urakami accent in his speech and asked, "Are you from Urakami?"

"No!" He shook his head energetically. "No!" And then he asked, "I'm sorry, but . . . could you give me a cup of water? I haven't put anything in my mouth since morning."

By nature, Mitsu could not bear to see miserable or pitiful people. Gazing now at the weary face of this man begging for water from the well and licking his lips as though from hunger, Mitsu felt great compassion toward him and replied, "Of course."

She hurried into the kitchen through the rear door. It was drizzling outside, and the kitchen was darker than usual. Oyone and Tome were nowhere to be seen.

Quickly she took some rice from the bottom of the kettle and made two rice balls and ran back outside with them.

"I think this might be better than water."

The man stared at her in astonishment. A tear-like sparkle glistened in his eyes.

"You're very kind, miss." He greedily stuffed a rice ball into his mouth.

As she watched him eat, Mitsu said, "I'll give you something to eat tomorrow, too, so come here in the afternoon."

Early afternoon was the least busy time at the shop. And since lunch would be finished, there would likely be some food left over after the Master and the clerks had finished eating.

The following day, in response to her invitation, the man appeared at the rear entrance. And Mitsu, as she had promised, slipped him a rice ball and some pickled vegetables.

"Miss?"

"Yes?"

"Please give me some job I can help with. Getting this food for nothing, acting like a beggar . . . it just doesn't feel right."

"Some job . . . ? I'm afraid I'm just an employee here myself."

"I'll do anything—chopping firewood or weeding. Could you ask your boss? All I'd need in return . . . is something to eat."

Mitsu felt a little uncomfortable, but the man was pleading and nearly in tears, so she went directly to the Mistress to convey his request.

"If we brought a man we know nothing about into the shop, we could end up with something stolen and him running away." At first the Mistress flat-out refused, but Mitsu kept repeating, "But he's such a good-hearted person," so the Mistress finally went out the rear door to have a look at him.

Ultimately, he was hired on the condition that his only compensation would be food. His name was Kumazō.

"Where are you from?"

"Ma'am, I'm from over by Sotome." But beyond that, he was for some reason noncommittal.

Chores were heaped on Kumazō, but he worked hard and didn't utter a word of complaint. Of course, if he were booted out of here, he would have to go back to begging again, so he could hardly grumble no matter what chores he was assigned.

He weeded, he drew water, he loaded merchandise from the store onto a cart, and he delivered it. His only free time was during meals, and then he was fed in a corner of the kitchen separate from the family and the other employees.

Thanks to him, the burden was lifted considerably from the female employees, including Oyone, Tome, and Mitsu. All they had to do was ask, "Kuma-san, would you mind?"—even with chores that were difficult for them, such as fetching water or chopping wood—and he never complained.

"Well, of course he doesn't. We picked him up off the street, didn't we?" Oyone said, but somehow Mitsu couldn't help feeling sorry for Kumazō.

"Isn't he from Urakami?" Oyone asked Mitsu.

"He says he was born in Sotome, but his accent is like somebody from Urakami," Mitsu observed.

For whatever reason, Mitsu felt certain that Kumazō had come from Urakami Village. He was certainly not from Magome, so he must be from Nakano, or perhaps Motohara . . . ?

"That Kumazō isn't a *Kuro*, is he?" Oyone and the Mistress began to have suspicions about him. On one occasion, the Mistress had asked him, "I don't suppose you're a *Kuro*, are you?"

Kumazō's complexion changed abruptly and in a loud voice he disavowed: "A Kirishitan? No, I'm no Kirishitan. I hate the likes of them!"

"Well, then, that's fine. We don't like Kirishitans here, and we made the decision we wouldn't hire any Kirishitans no matter what the circumstances," the Mistress nodded, relieved.

Not long after Kumazō began working at the shop, summer arrived. Summers in Nagasaki are scorching. Some nights there is no breeze at all after the sun sets. On those nights, one could hear people throughout the house fanning themselves and turning over in bed, time after time.

Autumn began; it deepened, then turned to winter.

Employees at the shop received only two days of vacation during the New Year festivities. That was sufficient for someone like Oyone, but there was no way that Tome from the Gotō Islands could go home and back in only two days.

"Tome, why don't you come home with me?" Mitsu decided to invite Tome to her home in Magome. Tome was delighted.

They worked until late on the first day of the year, finally getting time off on the second. Tome and Mitsu left Nagasaki together early in the morning.

Near the summit of the Nishizaka Hill, they passed several women heading toward Nagasaki from the direction of Urakami. The women moved in a line, and as they walked along they chanted words that Mitsu could not understand.

"They're Kirishitans," Tome told Mitsu. Tome knew that there were homes in Gotō where people recited *oraçiō* in that manner.

The Kirishitans that Tome and Mitsu crossed paths with on the Togitsu Highway were, of course, women from Nakano and Motohara. They were headed for the Ōura Church to seek the Lord's help on behalf of their husbands and sons and brothers who had been transported far, far away.

Back home after a long absence. Though it was a mere two days, everything about it—with one exception—was joyful and comfortable for Mitsu.

The only thing that bothered her was that Kiku was nowhere to be seen. Her parents wouldn't even mention Kiku's name, as though it were somehow taboo. Perhaps Kiku's relatives felt ashamed toward the other villagers for having produced a girl who had, of all things, fallen in love with a Kirishitan boy.

But when the two-day holiday came to an end, on the morning when they had to return to Nagasaki, Granny called for Mitsu and asked, "Would you give this . . . to Kiku?" She furtively produced a bundle of dried persimmons. "And tell her if there's anything she needs, I'll have Ichijirō get it to her. . . . Tell her that, will you?"

"OK." Mitsu nodded, almost in tears. She was overjoyed that Granny did, after all, worry about Kiku.

She returned to the Gotōya that evening with Tome.

"Well, aren't we just the little princesses? Getting yourselves a little chance to rest up," Oyone said sarcastically, but Mitsu and Tome both were used to her insults.

"This morning we ran into some Kirishitan women on the Togitsu Highway," Tome told Oyone.

"Probably the wives of the exiled *Kuros*."

At that moment, the sound of the ax chopping firewood in a corner of the kitchen abruptly stopped. Kumazō was silently listening in on their conversation.

His face seemed to contort with inexpressible anguish. He stared at the ground, struggling against the pain of his loneliness, but when he noticed Mitsu looking at him, he quickly raised his ax once again.

Once the New Year holidays were over, Mitsu, making sure the Mistress and Oyone didn't discover them, persuaded Tome to dash with her early one morning to deliver the dried persimmons from Granny to Ōura.

Kiku was sweeping in front of the gate of the Nambanji, just as she had at the Gotōya. Catching sight of Mitsu climbing breathlessly up the hill from the beach, she shouted, "Mitsu!" and rushed to her. Mitsu gave her the dried persimmons, exchanged only a few words of conversation with her, and then with painful reluctance announced that she had to get back to the shop.

"Mitsu." Just as Mitsu was leaving, Kiku suddenly blurted out something unexpected: "If you come to see me again, I may not be here." She whirled around and disappeared inside the Nambanji.

After glancing over her shoulder to check the spot where Kiku had gone, Mitsu raced back to the Gotōya. She was worried by what Kiku had said as they parted. Did it mean she shouldn't come too often, because Kiku was busy? Or did it mean that Kiku intended to leave the Nambanji and go somewhere else? It was hard for Mitsu to decide what it meant.

Kiku herself was struggling to decide. Should she follow Seikichi and go to be where he was?

Listening in on conversations between Petitjean and Laucaigne, she found out that the priests had received word that the Kirishitans—113 of them, including Sen'emon and Seikichi—had been taken by boat to Shimonoseki, but they seemed to have no information about what had become of the men after that. They did not know how much farther the prisoners might have gone after they were carted off the boat at Shimonoseki.

One morning, Kiku abruptly went to say good-bye to Petitjean. "I'm sorry I've been nothing but trouble."

Stunned, Petitjean asked, "Kiku, if you leave here, where will you go?"

"Sir, I haven't thought about that yet. But I'm going to find out where Seikichi is."

"What are you saying?" Petitjean emphatically shook his head. "If we can't find out where he is, there isn't any way that you'll be able to track him down, Kiku. Stay here for a while longer. The number of padres here is increasing, and we need at least one other person to look after them. If you stay here, we'll surely find out where Seikichi has gone."

Kiku listened without responding. In her heart, she felt that what Petitjean said was true.

To begin with, she had no money to travel to Shimonoseki. Even if she did make it there, how in the world would she go about locating him?

And so summer ended and fall came. Autumn foliage flourished around the Ōura Church. Seeing the Chinese bellflowers and the wild chrysanthemums, Kiku longed from the depths of her heart for her home in Magome. But more powerful still was the yearning to see Seikichi.

Each day as she cleaned the chapel, she hurled words of rage at the statue of the Blessed Mother Mary. "You're really a horrible, devilish woman! Now that you've separated Seikichi and me . . . are you happy?" She had no one else on whom to vent her anger, her resentment, and her sorrow other than to fling them at this statue.

"You're a devil of a woman!"

Yet, for a devilish woman, the statue of the Immaculata merely stared back at Kiku mournfully.

"I won't be asking the likes of you for any more help. I'm going to find Seikichi myself!" she said spitefully.

Then one day in the ninth month, Father Laucaigne came to her beaming with news.

"Kiku. Kiku! We've found out where Seikichi and the others are! They're in Tsuwano of Iwami Province. Do you know it? Tsuwano?"

Kiku listened to the words in utter amazement.

Tsuwano of Iwami Province.

Raised in the sleepy village of Urakami, she had no idea where Tsuwano might be. It certainly sounded like a place far, far away.

But now it was affirmed that however far away, Seikichi was alive and living there. What was he doing that very moment? What was he thinking about? Was he thinking of me?

What if they weren't giving him anything to eat, and what if he were ill? What if he were being beaten by guards at the prison?

With thoughts such as these, not even brandished weapons could hold Kiku back. "I have to see him!"

A few days later she walked out of the church and down to the beach that skirted the bay. With a leaf clenched between her teeth, she closed her eyes and tried to let the sound of the waves calm her surging emotions.

But the ardent desire to rush to Seikichi drove her to walk along the beach toward Nagasaki. Though there was no likelihood of meeting up with Seikichi in Nagasaki, she could not sit still.

The streets of Nagasaki were bustling that afternoon. She continued walking aimlessly until she came to the Dōza-machi district where many Chinese people lived.

When she reached Dōza, she saw Chinese men and women standing in front of their houses conversing. One of the houses was a butcher shop where pigs' heads hung from the rafters, while another was a Chinese ceramics store stocked with vases and plates. In the street some men were stretched out on wooden platforms where they were being poked with acupuncture needles.

Kiku swallowed hard as she studied the unfamiliar surroundings and started up a hill toward Maruyama, walking along a street that smelled of cooking oil.

"Young lady!" Someone abruptly called out to her. A man with yellowed teeth stood there alone. "Young lady!" he called. "Young lady . . . do you by chance work at the Gotōya? . . . I feel like I've seen you somewhere near the Gotōya."

"Yes, I worked there," Kiku nodded cautiously.

"That's what I thought. . . . So you're out on an errand today?"

"No . . . I'm not at the Gotōya anymore." She spoke quickly and tried to walk away.

"Is that right? You quit, did you? What are you doing now?"

"Sorry, I'm in a hurry." She gave a slight bow and picked up her pace. But the man seemed headed in the same direction, and he followed her.

"Where do you work now?" he had the nerve to inquire.

"Me? I'm at the Nambanji in Ōura."

"Where the foreigners live?" The man's eyes flashed with curiosity. "You're a Kirishitan, are you?"

"No." Kiku was becoming uneasy at this man's familiarity, and with an aloof look she headed into the entertainment quarters at Maruyama.

"Young lady, I can get you a job a lot better than working at the Nambanji," he called unexpectedly from behind her. "Why don't you come with me, young lady? You don't need to be afraid of me. Why, I've helped out those foreigners at the Nambanji where you work."

Kiku was trying to ignore the man and his words, but his last remark pricked her curiosity.

"No, you haven't!"

"I wouldn't lie to you. Those foreigners spent a lot of time searching for Kirishitans hidden here in Nagasaki. . . . And I helped them."

Kiku had heard from the other priests how Petitjean had walked the streets of Nagasaki until he found Kirishitans.

"You really did?"

"I really did. That's why I'm telling you that I can get you a good job."

"What kind of job?" Kiku stopped walking and peered into the man's face. Truth be told, she was desperate for some money. Enough money to travel to be near Seikichi. The money to go to a place called Tsuwano . . . She was provided with food and a place to sleep at the Nambanji, but they didn't give her enough money to do that. . . .

"Will you wait here for a minute?" The man left Kiku standing there and disappeared into the Maruyama throng.

What should I do?

Confused, she remained at the side of the road.

To abandon the Nambanji—she felt it wasn't fair to Petitjean and Laucaigne, who had always treated her with kindness. But she couldn't remain there forever. Nothing would change if she stayed there. Seikichi had been shuffled from Urakami to some distant place. And the foreigners at the Nambanji hadn't been able to do anything about it.

"Well, you've waited here patiently!" The man came scrambling down the hill, and once he determined that Kiku was still there, he looked behind him and called to someone, "Ma'am?"

A middle-aged woman nodded at his words and followed him down the hill.

"Ma'am, this is the girl I told you about. With just a little polishing, she'll be a real prize. You don't see many girls this pretty these days."

The woman studied Kiku and smiled affably at her. Then somewhat forcefully she said to the man, "Why don't you leave?"

"Me? Why?"

"You've introduced me now, so just leave."

Grudgingly the man disappeared.

"Now, dear," the woman spoke gently to Kiku. "You look so very sad. . . . Have you had some troubles?"

"No, no troubles." Bewildered, Kiku shook her head.

"Well, that's fine, then. . . . But if you walk around the streets in Dōza or Maruyama with such a gloomy face, you'll have lowlifes like that fellow who brought me here calling out to you. You'll be all right now that I'm here, but if one of those bad men got hold of you, they'd sell you off."

"Sell me off? Really?!"

"Really. The slave traffic has picked up lately." The woman smiled and nodded. "I understand you've been working at the Nambanji."

"Yes."

"And why were you with those foreigners?"

This level-headed woman did not seem like a bad type to Kiku, but she still did not respond to the question.

The woman peered at Kiku and said, "Why don't you come with me for a bit? Have a cup of tea and then you can go back to Ōura."

Kiku was escorted to the Yamazaki Teahouse in Maruyama.

"Ma'am, what is this place?" Kiku was taken and seated in front of a rectangular hibachi brazier, and her eyes opened wide in wonderment at the delicious flavor of the steamed cakes she was served. Having never in her life eaten anything sweet other than dried persimmons in Urakami, this was a new taste experience for her.

"It's a Chinese pastry called *xiang bing*." As the woman poured tea for Kiku, she kept carefully examining the girl's face. The almond eyes. The tiny lips. There was no doubt she would make money for them once they shined her up a bit.

"Now, why did you say you were working at the Nambanji?"

Kiku could no longer avoid giving a response. As Kiku explained her situation, the woman listened carefully, nodding along the way.

"You've had some painful experiences, too, haven't you? The man you love being a *Kuro* . . . and then being taken off somewhere far away."

"Ma'am, what kind of place is Tsuwano?"

"Tsuwano is the domain of Lord Kamei. Just think of it as being between Yamaguchi and Matsue."

That still gave Kiku no idea where Tsuwano was. She narrowed her eyes and seemed to be gazing at something far in the distance.

"And you're sure this Seikichi of yours is in Tsuwano?"

"Yes. That's what the foreigners at the Nambanji said."

"Kiku . . . It was Kiku, wasn't it? Why don't you work here for a while? Some very important men from the Nishi Bureau in Nagasaki come here for entertainment. We often see such men as Lord Inoue and Lord Matsukata. You could get to know them and then plead with them for Seikichi's life."

In spite of what this woman said, Kiku's mind was in commotion. She felt as though working here would be a slap in the face to Petitjean or Laucaigne. But since it was all for Seikichi . . .

TSUWANO

TSUWANO, IN THE province of Iwami.

Unlike Nagasaki, there was no blue ocean anywhere in sight. It didn't matter which way you looked: there were mountains to the east, mountains to the west, and mountains to the south. Among them were Tokusaga Peak, Mount Aono, and Shiroyama, which was crowned by a castle.[1]

It was summer, and the mountains were still blanketed in green when Sei-kichi and the other men were brought here from Shimonoseki, accompanied and guarded by Itō Seizaemon from the Nagasaki government office. Pure white cumulonimbus clouds drifted up from the shadows of the green mountains. In a tiny basin surrounded by these mountains squatted a village as serene as a napping pet.

Here was none of the liveliness found in the bay of Nagasaki, where boats were always coming and going. There was not a single Westerner with strangely colored hair and eyes, or even a Chinese person to be spotted. Instead of the bustling traffic, this village was subdued and still, and irrigation canals reflecting the sun's rays traversed it in all directions. The villagers washed their clothes and themselves in these canals, and throngs of carp swam in them, the sounds of their splashing deepening the silence of the town.

Lord Kamei, who had been daimyo of this province until the end of the shogunal reign, worked to foster men of talent through an emphasis on education and training, and as a result Tsuwano produced a succession of scholars and

1. Iwakuni Castle, which is included in the "top 100" castles of Japan.

literati. It is well known that such men as Nishi Amane and Mori Ōgai[2] were brought up here.

Tsuwano was chosen as the place of exile for twenty-eight of the Urakami Kirishitans because Kamei Koremi, the former lord of the domain, had expressed to the Meiji government his opinion that "the Kirishitans should be converted through the use of reason," and it was determined that this approach should in fact be attempted here in Tsuwano, enclosed by mountains.

Sen'emon, Seikichi, and twenty-six other prisoners were sent to the Kōrinji Temple, a vacant Buddhist temple on the outskirts of town.

Initially they were treated so well that it felt almost eerie. One of the exiles, Kanzaburō, recorded in his notes:

Our lodgings at the temple were surrounded by a bamboo fence. Tatami mats cover the floor of the great room, there is a hibachi brazier, and the cook was extremely polite and greeted us by saying, "I look forward to serving you."

The quality of the food was also good for prisoner fare. Even the rice was served in small individual wood containers. This was all part of the strategy of the authorities, probably a manifestation of their desire to "persuade through the use of reason."

Despite the favorable treatment, however, the peasants of Urakami had absolutely no intention of abandoning their Kirishitan faith.

This isn't going to continue forever, Itō Seizaemon, in his role as their guard, chuckled to himself at the magnanimous treatment. *It won't be long before we see just how stubborn the Kuros of Urakami really are. One day soon things will get rough.*

The Tsuwano authorities paid them no heed for about a month, but eventually the officers began their attempts at persuasion. Even a Shinto priest was brought in to assist.

It seemed to the Kirishitans that they were endlessly asked the same questions they had been asked at the Nagasaki government office and harangued with sermons of the same gist as before. But the twenty-eight Kirishitans by now were veterans at refuting the lectures and throwing the questions back at their interrogators.

---

2. Nishi Amane (1829–1897) studied at the University of Leiden and, after returning to Japan, introduced such Western philosophies as utilitarianism and empiricism. He also published an encyclopedia, headed the Tokyo Academy, and was a member of the House of Peers. Mori Ōgai (1862–1922) was one of the great titans of Meiji literature. He studied medical hygiene in Germany; served as surgeon general of the Japanese army; and, in a separate career, translated many European and Scandinavian novels, poems, and plays, and produced his own original works, one of the most famous being *Gan* (*The Wild Goose*, 1911–1913; trans. 1995).

The officers based their admonitions to apostasy in the logic of National Learning[3] and Confucianism, but not one of the prisoners was swayed by this approach.

The green of the Tsuwano mountain range gradually began to change into autumnal colors. The mornings and evenings became increasingly chilly.

"Right about now, they should be starting to harvest the rice," Seikichi mumbled, and everyone listened wordlessly to his comment. The faces of the relatives they had left behind floated before each individual pair of eyes.

The manner in which they were treated changed overnight. The officials switched to the mode of persuasion preferred by Itō Seizaemon.

One morning, just as the prisoners were finishing breakfast, Itō Seizaemon suddenly appeared, and with a thin smile on his lips said, "Everyone listen carefully. It's been decided that I will return to Nagasaki, so you won't be seeing me for a while. Every single day I've been waiting patiently here in Tsuwano for you men to change your minds, but since you continue to be headstrong, even I can't protect you from the officials here any longer."

The men listened quietly, but none of them believed that he had been protecting them from the rulers of Tsuwano.

"Once I'm gone, things are going to get rough for you. Soon you'll be tortured. Take my advice: you'd better hurry and have a change of heart. . . ." With a smirk and those parting words of counsel, Itō departed.

"What a pest! Him and his snooty sermons!" the men mocked.

"Yeah, but somehow when I see him I feel sorry for him. Why would that be?"

All the men shared Seikichi's opinion. Spineless and cowardly though he was, and though he strutted about acting like some important administrator, Itō was still somehow laughable, and they couldn't bring themselves to despise him.

But there was nothing untrue in his words.

Two days later, several men swarmed into the temple, and without a word they began removing the tatami mats from the main building.

"What are you doing?" When Sen'emon, the presumed leader of the men, asked in surprise, one man responded, "We're under orders from Lord Kanamori. Starting tonight, you won't be using any bedding. You're to sleep on these thin little woven rugs." He pointed at a stack of straw rugs they had brought.

---

3. *Kokugaku* (National Learning) was a philosophical and scholarly reaction against the prevailing intellectual and political preoccupation with Chinese Confucian and Buddhist texts. Some scholars in the mid-nineteenth century turned their attention instead to the earliest Japanese classics—the *Kojiki* and *Nihon shoki* (early-eighth-century collections of native myths) and the first great poetry anthology, the *Man'yōshū* (late eighth century)—in a quest for a "purer" Japaneseness that predated Chinese influence.

After their tatami mats were removed and their original bedding was carted away, the five cups of rice they had been receiving each day were reduced to two. Their soup became water with a little salt and no trace of even a vegetable leaf. The treatment they had received up to this point was completely overturned.

The interrogations, which until now had been gentle, suddenly turned fierce. If they talked back, they were beaten mercilessly. And they were beaten if they remained silent.

During the interrogations, two of the three attending officers employed violence and one showed sympathy. Once the two officers had finished punching and kicking the prisoners, the third would offer tender words of comfort. "Listen, we don't want to have to do this to you. If you'll just give up your heresies, we'll have them release you from this temple, and we'll even give you money to return home." At other times, he would prey on their longing for their families in their attempts to sway them: "Wouldn't you like to see your mothers and your wives back home? You can't imagine how they worry about you. It's time to stop shirking your duty to your parents."

The captives could still endure the pummeling and the kicking. And they labored to turn a deaf ear to all the appealing enticements. But the steadily increasing cold of late autumn and the hunger they suffered began to weaken the bodies of these twenty-eight prisoners.

When they were punched and kicked, they mustered their courage by feeling anger at the unjust treatment. Or they put up with it knowing that if they endured it for only a time, the brutality would eventually have to end.

But starvation was not a temporary condition. Hunger continued day after day, like a rainy season with no letup, and it took its toll on their bodies. Some staggered when they stood up, others often felt dizzy.

"Look how thin my cheeks have gotten! I've turned into quite a handsome fellow!" Initially Seikichi and the others showed their faces to one another and chuckled feebly, but they began to realize that it wasn't just their cheeks that had dropped flesh; their arms and thighs were also progressively wasting away. As they grew even thinner, their skin turned opaque and rough, as though sprinkled with flour. Before long, their bellies began to swell abnormally. They were beginning to show signs of malnutrition.

In addition—

In addition, no matter what the activity—even shifting their bodies slightly— all movement became a torment. The listless desire to lie down, unalleviated feelings of exhaustion, as though their bodies were encased in lead—these feelings continued throughout each day. If there was anything they thought about, it was eating.

They tried to chew the meager daily ration of rice for as long a period of time as possible and then swallow it with their spittle. That was Sen'emon's suggestion.

But an unbearable hunger seized them in the middle of the night, which they could only put at bay by drinking some of the water they had put aside.

"Do you think the men who were taken to other places are going through the same kinds of struggles that we are?"

The 113 men exiled from Urakami had been dispersed to Tsuwano and also to Hagi and Fukuyama. They had no way to find out the fate of those who had been shipped off to the other two locations.

Soon they no longer had the strength even to think. Young Seikichi initially thought about Kiku from time to time, but soon it became like a dream and lost all sense of reality. He couldn't imagine any reason why a woman would continue to have feelings for an outcast such as him.

I imagine . . . I imagine even she has forgotten all about me by now. . . .

He felt neither regret nor sorrow. It seemed perfectly natural; in any case, he was suffering far more because of starvation than because of her.

"Sen'emon, we can't bear this anymore. Please talk to the officers!"

Surrendering to the entreaties of the other men, Sen'emon pleaded frantically with one of the officers. "If this goes on much longer, we'll all die!"

The officer curled up his lip. "Why are you worrying about your lives? I thought you believed that this life means nothing to you!" he mockingly responded. "And don't you claim your Deus or whoever he is will give you anything you want? Why don't you ask your Deus for help? Tell him you'd like more to eat!"

This officer assumed they would eventually admit defeat.

These men from Nagasaki were unfamiliar with the winters in the San'in region in northwestern Honshu. They were ignorant of the depths that the snows can reach in Tsuwano. The officials speculated that the prisoners would be unable to endure the freezing winter on top of their hunger and before long would cave in.

It unfolded just as they had thought it would—

Winter crept up on the prisoners. Autumn, with its bright colors ablaze on the hills surrounding the village, fled at a gallop, and Mount Aono and Mount Shiroyama grew desolate. Nights became intolerably cold.

The men had no bedding. It had all been taken from them. All they had been given in its place was a single thin straw rug each. It would be impossible to tolerate the cold with only that one little rug.

They decided to sleep in groups of two, clinging to each other beneath a pair of the rugs. Their hope was that they could warm each other with their body heat. They no longer cared anything about awkwardness or appearances.

Still, by the middle of the night, it grew too cold to sleep. Wrapped in each other's arms, they were somehow able to keep their abdomens warm, thanks to their body heat, but the chill wind on their backs was unbearable.

Next they tried sleeping back to back. Then their abdomens became cold as ice. In the darkness they coughed, turned over repeatedly on the floor, dozed off from time to time, and waited for the dawn to break.

"Let's say an *oraçiō*!" Trying to hearten the men who seemed on the brink of breaking, Sen'emon began to pray aloud and bid the others to join in chorus. The voices of the men united in prayer in the darkness sounded almost like groans.

"What is wrong with this Deus of yours?" From time to time an officer would stop by to taunt them. "What has he done for you? Do you still believe in your Deus who won't even give you a mattress?"

Such words had a more powerful effect on these starved, semiconscious prisoners than the enticements of Satan.

Why do we have to go through all this? Surely Lord Jezusu and Santa Maria know how much we're suffering. But they do nothing to help us. Occasionally such thoughts flickered through their minds.

One night, the cold was painful beyond words. They could tell it was snowing outside. In the dark they heard a man weeping.

"What are you blubbering about?!" Sen'emon asked with deliberate harshness. "Lord Jezusu endured even more pain as he carried his cross!"

The rest of the men listened in silence to the tongue-lashing. But every one of them felt alone. They had to battle starvation and cold on their own.

At dawn they had their first glimpse of what the snows in Tsuwano were actually like. Snow had never piled up this much in Nagasaki or Urakami. The snow had quit falling, but there were mountains of snow everywhere, everything was white, and the cold was intense.

"No food this morning. Just an interrogation," a prison guard dressed in a straw coat called out from amid the snow.

What could they possibly still have to ask us?

But they could not disobey an order. As they formed a row and walked down the hallway to a back room of the vacant temple where other officers were just waking up, they appeared to every eye like a procession of ghosts.

They were ordered to sit on the icy wooden floor at the front of the room. A hibachi with red coals smoldering inside had been placed in the room, and there three officers seemed to relish the warm breakfast they were eating.

The scent of steaming miso soup, and the sound of pickled radishes being chewed. Forcing the starving Kirishitans to smell and hear these things was inhuman torture. Even if they lowered their eyes and tried not to look, the sound of hot tea being slurped and the smell of the soup mercilessly provoked their empty stomachs. They wanted to scream.

An elderly official sipped his tea and asked, "You'd like some of this? Of course you would! We aren't devils, you know. Seeing you so skinny and shaking, naturally we're moved to compassion. We'd like to give you something to eat. We wish we could offer you some winter clothing. But we have orders from our leaders that we can't show you any form of mercy until you reject the heathen teachings. . . . We'll have to continue the cruel treatment." His voice sounded almost bewildered. "Stop being so endlessly stubborn and making things difficult for us. All you have to say is 'I've had a change of heart' . . . and, look here, we'll give you all the warm rice you can eat. We'll move you to another temple right away and give you warm bedding to sleep in."

He set down his teacup and looked around at the men with steely eyes. "I understand. . . . None of you who'd like to have this over with can say the words while you're all here together. We'll have you come one by one into the next room, and you can whisper to me whether you will continue in your beliefs or reject them. Those who recant will be given food in a separate room so none of the others knows. But those who remain adamant will be taken back to their cells."

He got to his feet, opened the sliding door to the next room, and vanished within.

Their names were called one by one. One by one, they went into the neighboring room. The man asking the question and the man answering spoke in low voices so that no one would know how anybody responded.

I will keep my faith. After each man made this declaration, he returned on wobbly legs to the wretched room where they were held prisoner. Those who had already completed the ritual and returned to the cell rubbed their hands together and flashed each man who rejoined them a sad smile.

They returned, one, then another, then yet another. But of the twenty-eight, eight did not come back. Those eight had apostatized.

"Dammit!" Seikichi shouted angrily. Even he didn't know who he was angry with. Was it with the eight who had apostatized? Was it with the officers whose methods were so heartless? Was it with some invisible power? Or was it with God, who said nothing . . . ?

MARUYAMA

WHILE THE PRISONERS groaned from cold and starvation in Tsuwano . . .

In the ninth month of the preceding year, the new Meiji era was ushered in. Kyoto, which had been the capital city for many long years, was replaced by Edo, whose name was changed to Tokyo. A series of reforms in domestic administration was carried out, their radical nature creating chaos in various parts of the country and spawning several acts of terrorism.

On Christmas in the second year of Meiji—Christmas was observed at the Ōura Church according to the solar calendar for the foreign residents[1]— women and children who had walked all the way from Urakami participated in the Mass.

By now everyone in Nagasaki knew that these women were *Kuros*. They made no attempt to conceal the fact that they were Kirishitans. These wives and sisters of men who had been sentenced to exile formed a procession, as though they hoped to be arrested themselves, and paraded along the Togitsu Highway toward Nagasaki, following the shoreline until they reached the Ōura Church.

In the Christmas Mass, Petitjean looked into the faces of these women whose eyes were fixed on him and spoke:

"You are suffering much."

The faces of women burnished by the sweat of daylong labor. The faces of women who had borne babies, nurtured children, and toiled alongside their

---

1. Although the Japanese began using the Western calendar during the Meiji period, the Asian lunar calendar remained in common use until after World War II.

husbands. The faces of women who, having their husbands torn from them, had nowhere but here to turn for relief.

"I'm sure you question why the Lord has granted you such trials. But please consider carefully. Without suffering, one individual can never be fully connected to another. Think of those times when your children have fallen ill. I'm sure that you and your husbands grieved and worried together and cared for that child through the night together. No doubt it was in such times that your heart and the heart of your husband were joined as one. Do you see? Suffering links people to one another. I believe that your present pain has caused you to love your husbands more than ever before. And I am certain that your husbands in faraway Tsuwano or Hagi think about you each and every day. Suffering has thus bound you as a couple together powerfully, tightly."

Tears in their eyes, the women nodded at Petitjean's words.

"I assure you that none of you is alone. That Man is always at your side. Because he, too, suffered terrible pains, he knows more than anyone your current suffering and pain. I myself . . . yesterday I visited with M. Outrey of France and Mr. Parkes of England, and we joined hands and promised that we would continue our petitions to the Japanese government."

When he finished his sermon, Petitjean returned to the altar and resumed the Mass. The flames from the candles on the altar flickered like the wings of moths. Eventually the women began singing a hymn in voices of lamentation.

Ah, this spring, this spring!
The blossoms of the cherry shall fall.
Again next spring,
The same flowers will open their buds.

Ah, Mount Shiba, Mount Shiba!
Today it is a vale of tears.
But in coming days
It will be the path to deliverance.

The voices of the Urakami women singing the hymn were audible in the house where Kiku and Okane lived.

"That is so sad!" Even Okane was deeply moved with sympathy. "Here it is almost New Year's, and those women will be spending a lonely holiday. Their husbands who've been taken so far away won't have a New Year's Day or anything, will they?"

As Kiku listened to the singing of the hymn from the chapel, she thought of Seikichi.

Again next spring,
The same flowers will open their buds. . . .

Would Seikichi be coming back next spring?
Neither Laucaigne nor Petitjean was able to obtain any information that would have answered her question. Precisely because they were foreigners, the government office in Nagasaki remained tight-lipped and would tell them nothing.

"Why don't you work here for a while? Some very important men from the government office come here for entertainment." Kiku still had fresh memories of what the madam of the Yamazaki Teahouse had said to her. "You could get to know them."

Despite the madam's invitation, Kiku had returned to the Ōura Church. When all was said and done, she felt an obligation to Petitjean and Laucaigne.

Even though the holiday was still a month away, the streets were lined with stalls selling New Year's decorations such as ropes made of rice straw, pine branches to decorate doorways, small pine trees with roots attached, bitter oranges, and persimmons, and the calls of the hawkers echoed through every neighborhood. There were even some houses where the families got a head-start on pounding rice for *mochi*, their mallets hammering away.

On the first day of the twelfth month, Father Laucaigne returned to the church, his face twisted with anger. At the doorway he shouted for Father Petitjean and the others and began screaming something in French.

After hearing Laucaigne's news, Father Petitjean raced into Nagasaki with an alarmed expression on his face.

"Padre, what has happened?" Okane asked in surprise.

Twisting up his sallow face, Laucaigne replied, "Another seven hundred Kirishitans are being arrested! They've been ordered to assemble at the Tateyama Bureau on the third."

"Seven hundred!"

"Yes."

"Then, women and children too?"

"Women and children . . . yes, them too." Father Laucaigne pointed to several boats moored in Nagasaki Bay. "I suspect the government has prepared those ships to carry these seven hundred away," he muttered in a voice that was more a moan.

When Kiku heard these words, her mind was made up.
I can't help Seikichi if I stay here.
If she wanted to help Seikichi, she'd have to go to Maruyama. There was no option other than to accept the invitation from the madam of the Yamazaki Teahouse. Kiku was convinced of it. That very evening, she left the church. . . .

Following urgent pleas from the missionaries, the French consul Dury, the American consul Mangum, and the British consul Enslie went to the prefectural office and requested an audience with Governor Nomura Sōshichi. This time their protest was not based on religious grounds; rather, they argued on humanitarian grounds that it was unconscionable to exile so many men and women.

Nomura responded that he was acting on orders from the Grand Council of State that could not be disobeyed.

"These are Japanese internal affairs," Nomura repeated the customary cliché through his translator, Hondō Shuntarō, who had returned to Nagasaki after a stint in Tokyo. Shuntarō had undertaken further study of French in Yokohama and now held a position with the Foreign Affairs Ministry. "I beg you not to interfere in internal matters."

The consuls took turns registering objections, but Governor Nomura sat with his eyes closed, saying nothing.

"The Japanese government has already sent 113 Christians to Chōshū and Iwami." Unable to maintain his composure, U.S. Consul Mangum inquired, "Do you intend to exile similar numbers again this time?"

Finally Nomura opened his eyes and asked Shuntarō to translate: "This time we'll be banishing six times that number. To be specific, the number is 729. But there are still three thousand Kirishitans in Urakami."

"And is it your ultimate intention to exile those three thousand as well?"

"I assume that so long as they continue to believe in a religion that is banned under the laws of the country, our government will adopt stern measures against them."

Again Nomura closed his eyes and sat motionless. This stone statue of a man had no further interest in dealing with the complaints of these foreign diplomats.

Governor Nomura could take such a cold, obstinate stance not merely because he detested the interference of foreign powers in domestic matters but also because the Meiji government had decided that their policy toward religion would hinge on a revitalization of Shinto and its shrines in an effort to establish a system that unified church and state under the emperor. To recognize the Kirishitans would violate that policy. This approach toward the foreign religion differed markedly from that of the Tokugawa shogunate, though the upshot in both cases was the banning of Christianity.

On the fourth day of the twelfth month, initially only the males among the 729 were loaded onto waiting ships. On the fifth, the families of those men who had been exiled the previous year were lodged at the Nishi Bureau, and that evening they were put onto ships.

On the seventh and the eighth, all the Kirishitans from Nakano, Satogō, Motohara, and Ieno were herded together in Togitsu, Omotaka in Nishi Sonogi District, and in Nagasaki.

It was snowing that day in Nagasaki. The women, with loads on their backs and children at their sides, were brought to the homes of the village heads in the outlying regions and then forced to walk from there to Nagasaki through the snow, the yellow and white scarves on their heads standing out like signal flags. The houses they left behind were strewn with dishes and other possessions, as though in the aftermath of utter destruction. A cow abandoned by its master lowed mournfully in the snow.

They thought perhaps they would never see their village again. In later years they referred to this banishment as "The Journey." A journey. A journey to eternity. A journey to Paradise. That's what their hymn described:

Let us go, let us go,
Let us go to the Temple of Paraíso!

And this was that Journey, they thought.

Father Villion, one of the missionaries laboring at the Ōura Church at the time, records this dreadful scene in his journal of the twelfth month. He writes in part:

7th. Following yesterday's official orders, it appears that the women and children were put into ships in the middle of the night. We saw several barges, their lamps aflicker, plying the harbor. We're told the rest of them will be summoned today and put onto the ships.

At four in the afternoon, the barges slowly traversed the harbor and sidled up to the steamship that was moored in the distance. Nearly fifty women sat in the center of each barge, with baggage stacked around them, and children crouched between. There were one or two officers in each barge.

Every one of the Kirishitans was gazing up toward our church here in Ōura. Some made the sign of the cross. Each of the women, in a public declaration of her faith, wore the white veil that had covered her head when she was baptized.

What a scene!

Three of the barges pulled alongside a large ship flying the flag of the Satsuma domain while the remaining barges moved up to other ships. We watched all this dumbfounded. We had been left behind, unable to share the joy of confinement with them.

8th. Officers wearing two swords broke into the church. They made as if to draw their swords, but after talking together, perhaps anxious that there would be trouble for them if they wounded any foreigners, they exchanged glances with one another and departed.

At seven o'clock, the first steamship weighed anchor and left the harbor.

We understand that more than two thousand Kirishitans are aboard those ships. At eight, the large Satsuma ship set off, and at two in the afternoon, the steamship from the Chikuzen domain also departed.

This was Father Villion's detailed description of the scene as every Kirishitan from Urakami was transported far from Nagasaki Bay.

These believers were in fact divided into groups and taken to the Tōhoku region in the north, to Kyushu, to Shikoku, and to the Hokuriku region. The exiled were sent to Kōchi, Takamatsu Matsue, Okayama, Nagoya, Tsu, Himeji, Hiroshima, Kagoshima, Kanazawa, Matsuyama, Wakayama, Kōriyama, Daishōji, Fukuoka, Tottori, Tokushima, Tsuwano, and Fukuyama.

On the seventeenth, Father Villion was finally able to visit Nakano and Ieno, which were now utterly deserted.

From the far side of the harbor I climbed the hill, then following along the edge of the basin I went down the slope and arrived in Ippongi. All around me was devastation, followed by even more devastation.

The houses were empty, their doors beaten down, with shards of bowls and plates scattered about. Not a single soul remained. I have no words to describe the appearance of this village tucked away in the mountains, its houses arranged in a ring like a circular theater stage. Every house has its doors thrown open, and not a single tatami mat is left on the floors. All that reaches my eyes is wreckage and cold death and absolute silence.

All that reaches my eyes is wreckage and cold death and silence.

The people who had lived here until the previous day now suffered aboard wave-tossed ships. Some muttered prayers; some threw up; children wept; and their mothers scolded them. This was the beginning of their "Journey."

Maruyama was lively and frenzied before New Year's Eve. In every house, preparations were made for the pounding of the ceremonial rice and the arrival of the male patrons.

As the mallets began to pound energetically in the mortars that had been placed in the spacious earthen entryways, the middle-aged madams, the geisha, and their male assistants commenced a spirited plucking of samisens in time to the mallets and chanted:

Let's celebrate! How festive!
We pine for the strong young men
Who come as the young pines bud.

It was the custom in Nagasaki to take the last rice pounded in the mortar, form it into a ball, and affix it to the central pillar of the house. They called this "pillar *mochi*," and on the fifteenth of the first month it was heated and eaten.

Just as they finished up the rice pounding, they would also amuse themselves by scrambling to smear their faces with soot from the iron kettle. When the laughter died down, débutante geisha, accompanied by men who carried their samisens and displayed large placards with the women's names, would make the rounds of each house to convey their New Year greetings.

The morning of New Year's Day arrived after these various events had been held. The streets of Maruyama, which normally were bustling with activity, fell eerily silent during the morning hours, but the silence was broken on many streets in the afternoon by the whirring of shuttlecock rackets, and before long, Daikoku performers, whose dances portended good fortune, as well as dancing monkeys and pipers playing the double-reed charamela, began circulating from door to door.

"Kiku." The madam of the Yamazaki Teahouse said consolingly to Kiku, who had started feverishly wiping down the kitchen on the second day of the New Year, "You don't need to work that hard from first thing in the morning. It won't be long before we'll be so busy our eyes will swim. You've got to rest up during this three-day holiday." Then suddenly she lowered her voice and said, "I want to tell you something I happened to hear. Those Kirishitans who were exiled were divided up and sent all the way from Ōshū in the north to as far south as Shikoku and Hokuriku."

"Who did you hear that from?"

"Our geisha Oyō heard it and told me about it. She has a customer from a long time back, named Lord Hondō. He's an official with the Foreign Ministry now and has ended up back here in Nagasaki. He's the one who told her."

"Ma'am?" Kiku abruptly lifted her face. "Could you ask that Lord Hondō if he would bring Seikichi back from Tsuwano?"

The unexpected request put the madam in an awkward position. "Kiku, you can't be in such a hurry. There's such a thing as a right time for everything. Once they've had the Nanakusa celebration[2] and eaten their herb porridge, Lord Hondō and many other influential officials will start flocking in here. I'll make your request when they're in a grand mood," she said with mild reproof.

If you're off to have fun,
Tap on the doors of the Kagetsu,
The Naka-no Teahouse
Or the Plum Garden
As you stroll around Maruyama

2. It has long been the custom in Japan to eat *nanakusa kayu*, a rice porridge with seven herbs intermixed, on the seventh day of the first month of the year in the belief that it will help digestion and protect from illness throughout the coming year.

Hondō Shuntarō smiled and hummed the melody to this "Yatachū song" while Oyō played the samisen.

Although physically he was as enormous as a stone mortar, Hondō didn't hold his liquor particularly well. Once he became tipsy, it wasn't unusual for him to begin humming the Yatachū melody or the Kankan Dance song with its lyrics in Chinese. Now that he had been elevated to a position of responsibility in the Ministry of Foreign Affairs, those songs probably brought back fond memories of the time he spent in Nagasaki.

Suddenly Shuntarō grew somber and said, "Oyō, this is likely to be something off in the future, but . . . I may end up going to some distant lands like America or England as an attendant to Lord Iwakura."

"America or England?" Oyō gripped her samisen tightly and responded in surprise.

"Now, I'm not saying it will be right away. But this expedition will have enormous significance for the future of Japan, and for my future, too. Imagine how valuable my foreign language skills will be to Lord Iwakura and the others. . . . And besides, I really want to see what things are like in the advanced nations."

"But if you're going to travel to those distant places, you'll be gone for five or six years, won't you?"

"Silly!" Shuntarō chuckled. "These days you can travel to America in two months if you take a large steamship. I can go around the world and be back in a year or a year and a half."

Oyō seemed relieved to hear that. "Then I can wait. If it's something that will help you advance in your career, then it makes me happy, too!" Then, as though she had suddenly remembered, "What's happened to Lord Itō? He hasn't come by yet."

"I don't want to talk about him."

"He said he was going to Tsuwano again, and that he traveled back and forth all the time between Nagasaki and Tsuwano."

"It's his job," Shuntarō said, looking a little miffed. Even though they had worked at the same magistrate's office in Nagasaki, a large gulf had opened up between them: Hondō had gone to Nagasaki and taken the first steps up the ladder of success in the new government, while Itō remained a low-ranking official who made visits to keep an eye on the exiled Kirishitans.

"Oh. And one more thing . . . " As she was putting her samisen away, Oyō clapped her hands, having remembered something else she wanted to ask. "When do you think the Urakami Kirishitans will be pardoned?"

"When? Why are you asking such a thing?"

"There's a girl from Urakami working here as a maid, and she keeps insisting that I ask you."

"Not even I know the answer to that. I can't imagine it will happen in the next two or three years," Hondō muttered disinterestedly.

The fate of someone as inconsequential as the Urakami Kirishitans held no interest for Hondō, who was ascending the ladder of success step by step. They were nothing more than a gang of malcontents who had risen in opposition to the new government. Leaders of an insurrection against the new order. In Shuntarō's view, at a time when it was essential for Japan to mature into a modern nation so that it could stand up to foreign powers, anyone—even a mere peasant—who disrupted the system had to be punished.

Soon there was the sound of footsteps on the stairs.

"Ma'am?" A woman's voice called to Oyō. "I've brought the saké."

When Oyō heard the voice, she looked at Shuntarō and said, "This is the girl I was just telling you about." Then she said, "Come in!"

Sliding the door open, Kiku came into the room, bowed, and brought in a tray from the hallway. She did everything as she had been instructed by the madam.

Shuntarō stared at Kiku and thought, *A remarkable face for such a young thing.*

Kiku set down the tray with its saké bottles and tiny bowls, again bowed her head deferentially, and started to leave the room.

Just then a voice called out "I'm here!" and Itō Seizaemon poked his droopy-eyed face through the open doorway. Perhaps because of all the traveling he had to do, Seizaemon looked far more worn out than he had the last time they met.

"I'm not interrupting anything, am I?" he said sarcastically, glancing toward Oyō.

"What are you talking about? No trouble at all! Haven't seen you for a while. Let's have some drinks together tonight," Hondō said with a deliberately controlled face. "Bring another tray," he ordered Kiku as she headed out of the room.

"Are you off to Tsuwano again?"

"I am. It's so cold there in the winter! A Nagasaki boy like me can hardly bear it. But compared to me, you've risen in the world by leaps and bounds now that Lord Sawa has become the foreign minister. I'm jealous!"

Once he'd aired his grievance, Seizaemon sniffed and took the saké cup handed to him. Oyō poured him a drink.

"So, has the Tsuwano domain managed to change the minds of those Kirishitans?" Hondō asked. "I understand that Governor Kamei Koremi claimed he could persuade them with reason."

"High-class gentlemen like him with their fine educations can't spout off anything besides hot air. Kirishitan peasants who gave the magistrate such a hard time aren't going to cave in that easily. They're at their wits' end over there."

"I'm sure they are. . . . Say, that serving girl who just brought your tray is from Urakami. Evidently one of her relatives was arrested, and she's all worried about what's going on in Tsuwano."

"Hmmm." Itō Seizaemon gulped down the contents of his cup disinterestedly. But when he saw Kiku come in with another tray, his drooping eyes suddenly flashed strangely. "You're from Urakami, are you?" he asked Kiku in a soft voice.

"Yes, from Magome."

"Then are you a Kirishitan?"

"No, we aren't Kirishitans, sir."

"In that case, is one of your Kirishitan relatives in Tsuwano?"

"He's not a relative. But Nakano and Magome are very close to each other, so I know a lot of people from there," Kiku deftly glossed over the details.

"Kiku," Oyō interjected, "this gentleman is Lord Itō, and he goes frequently to Tsuwano on government business, so why don't you ask him? Lord Itō, this girl is engaged to a young man who was banished to Tsuwano."

Kiku's eyes flashed when she heard that Itō worked for the Nagasaki government, and she adjusted her posture.

"Oyō!" Hondō Shuntarō reprimanded her with a look of disgust on his face. "Lord Itō and I are here tonight to renew old acquaintances. You can talk about those things later."

At the reproof from a man she loved, even Oyō, known throughout the quarter as the "Snow Queen of Maruyama," flushed and hung her head. She had no choice but to signal to Kiku and have her leave the room.

Although she worked in the Maruyama district, Oyō was a geisha, not a prostitute. Geisha were called *geiko* in Nagasaki, and in local parlance they were referred to as "wildcats," possibly because the samisens they played were made from cat hides.

The *geiko*, unlike prostitutes, were indistinguishable from women born and raised in Nagasaki, but they were reviled by litterateurs visiting from Edo for being not as quick-witted or sophisticated as their Edo counterparts. Oyō, however, was an exception, skilled at both the arts and conversation, and she had a beautiful, vividly white face. When her lover Shuntarō rebuked her, however, she became anything but a "wildcat," responding instead with the docility of a lamb.

"I'd like to get out of Nagasaki and go up to Yokohama or Tokyo," Itō grumbled. "It's boring here. They're talking as though foreign ships will start docking in Yokohama instead of Nagasaki, so we'll fall even further behind the times."

"Now, hold on a minute. Don't be in such a rush. Even if you go to Tokyo now, every important government position is monopolized by men from Satsuma and Chōshū. It's not that easy for someone from another province to get his foot in the door. I'll keep my eye out for the right opportunity and try to come up with something for you."

To some degree Shuntarō was fed up with Itō, who sniffed up snot as he moaned and whined, so Shuntarō kept plying him with saké.

Eventually Itō, his eyes blurry from drink, staggered to his feet and headed for the bathroom. Oyō followed him out of the room, and while he was relieving himself, she weighed the circumstances and went to fetch Kiku.

When Itō emerged from the toilet, dragging the hems of his formal skirt behind him, Kiku was holding out a basin for him to wash his hands. He gaped at her with dissolute, drooping eyes and whispered, "Hey, how about it? Why don't you come to bed with me? Then I'll see what I can do for your fellow in Tsuwano."

Kiku turned bright red and scowled reflexively at him.

"That angry face of yours makes you look even more beautiful. You're a fine girl, now aren't you?" With a chuckle he returned to the room.

For a time, the rage lingered in her breast. This was the first time the innocent young woman had ever been insulted in such vulgar terms.

"Silly child, to get upset over something so trivial," the madam smilingly took her to task. "We don't have any harlots here, but we're a house where gentlemen come to amuse themselves with *geiko*. You've got to learn to laugh off a few harmless jokes." She then instructed Kiku to take more saké bottles upstairs.

When the inebriated Itō saw Kiku, he called to her as though he had forgotten that Hondō and Oyō were in the room. "Com'ere! Over here! Whyn't you pour me a drink?"

"Here, I'll pour for you," Oyō responded in place of Kiku. "Please tell this girl whether her friend is doing all right in Tsuwano."

"Her friend? Wha's 'is name?"

"Seikichi," Kiku answered, her knees tightly pressed together as though in self-defense.

"Seikichi. Hmmm, seems like there was a fellow with that name. Yeah. I remember now. One of the pushy bastards. I imagine right about now he's prob'ly ready to give in 'cause of the cold."

"Is it that cold a place?" Oyō asked.

"It's a little village surrounded by the San'in Mountains, so it's a lot colder than you can imagine here in Nagasaki. In the morning there's icicles hanging from every roof. At night the snow freezes over, and it's hard to even walk. The ones who cave in get fed all the rice they want, and they give 'em bedding. But the stubborn bastards like this girl's friend get nothing but a little straw rug. They don't feed 'em more than two cups of rice a day."

"Two cups of rice? That's horrible!" Oyō cried instinctively. "That's the same as letting them starve to death."

"Can't be helped," Hondō, who had remained silent until now, interjected. "Those who don't follow orders from their leaders must be sternly punished. The ban on Christianity is one of the core policies of the new government."

Oyō easily acquiesced to words spoken by the man she loved. On the one hand, she felt sorry for the Urakami Kirishitans, but on the other, she felt there were no alternatives, since they had gone against the will of the government. Feeling thus conflicted, she said nothing.

Suddenly Kiku leaped up and stumbled from the room.

Outside the room, she leaned against the wall of the staircase and wept aloud.

Two cups of rice a day. Seikichi has nothing to sleep on, so he has to wrap himself in a thin little rug. And in such bitter cold . . .

But there was nothing she could do to help him. She had no money to travel to Tsuwano. She had no way to help him.

Before long Itō had fallen asleep, snoring vulgarly.

"Bring something to cover him. Can't let him catch a cold," Hondō said to Oyō, smiling sardonically as he looked into the face of this man, drooling into the unkempt whiskers that had sprouted around his mouth. "No matter how you look at him, he's a pathetic soul."

"Why pathetic?"

"He's good-natured enough. But it's because of his good nature that he'll never amount to anything his whole life."

Sitting with his arms folded while Oyō massaged his shoulders, Hondō pondered the difference between himself and Seizaemon.

Hondō had been born into an underprivileged, low-ranking samurai family, so the points of departure for him and Itō were essentially the same. They had previously worked together at the Nagasaki magistrate's office. But Hondō was the type who looked to the future, and while he was assiduously studying foreign languages, Itō remained oblivious to the shifts and flows in the times and carried on, being far too much devoted to his official duties. Those differences had now created a wide gap between the two of them.

"About the Urakami Kirishitans. A short time ago, there was a heated debate in Tokyo, at a place called Takanawa, between several foreign envoys on one side and Chancellor Sanjō[3] and Minister of the Right Iwakura representing Japan. I acted as interpreter," he added with some self-importance.

Hondō remembered that day clearly. The British envoy, Parkes; the French ambassador, Outrey; the American chargé d'affaires, DeLong; and the Dutch envoy, Von Brandt, complained vehemently to the Ministry of Foreign Affairs about the wholesale banishment of the Urakami Christians. The gist of the protest from these foreign legacies was "If foreigners hear that these people have been punished because of their religious faith, it could damage the friendship

---

3. Sanjō Sanetomi (1837–1891) also served the Meiji government as Lord Keeper of the Privy Seal and briefly in 1889 as interim prime minister.

that has been fostered between us," and "If you don't modify your handling of this situation, your country will be despised by the entire world."

In the meeting room at Takanawa where Hondō participated as interpreter alongside Prince Iwakura, Prince Sanjō, Councillor Soejima, and Minister of Foreign Affairs Sawa, Hondō was able to renew an old acquaintance with Dr. Siebold, who was also present as interpreter for the opposing side.

Hondō's precise manner of translating on that occasion enabled him to make a favorable impression not only on the Japanese representatives but also on the foreign delegation. Perhaps for that reason, two or three days later Hondō was singled out for commendation by Chief Councillor of State Iwakura.

"Even Siebold applauded your linguistic abilities," Prince Iwakura said as he handed Hondō a glass of imported wine. "In the near future—that is to say, probably in another two or three years—would you be interested in going to America?"

"To ... America?"

"Yes. Our country signed a pact with America in the 1850s, but resentment over its terms is tremendous. We are planning to travel to America to sound them out on possible revisions. I'm considering taking you along as interpreter."

Shuntarō's face flushed as he bowed his head. The joy of that moment still cascaded through his heart.

But right now, here before his eyes Itō Seizaemon was fast asleep, drooling. Framed in scruffy whiskers, his face, exhausted and muddied from his visits to Tsuwano ...

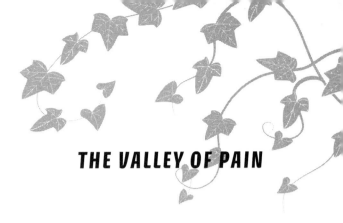

THE VALLEY OF PAIN

SEVERAL BOYS HAD finished their midwinter training exercises at the Tsu-wano clan school and were walking home, the bags that held their fencing sticks propped on their shoulders, their breath white in the frigid air, and frost crystals crunching under their feet. The clan school was named the Yōrōkan and had been built by the earlier rulers of the domain, who placed a high premium on education.

One of the boys whispered furtively to a classmate, a short fellow they called "Rin-saa," as though he were passing along some great secret, "Say, Rin-saa, did you hear? The Kirishitans at the Kōrinji were thrown in the frozen lake."

Rin-saa looked up in surprise and said, "In the lake?"

"That's right. That's what happens to people who don't do what they're told."

The Kirishitans were confined at the Kōrinji Temple on the outskirts of town. Even young children in this tiny village of Tsuwano knew about them. The children sensed something frightening about this situation, but at the same time they were in their own way curious and interested in it.

When Rin-saa got home, he set down his fencing stick and told his mother what he had just heard.

"You children don't need to know anything about this," his mother chided him, her brows knit.

But they tell us at school that people who don't know the right path should be taught it with kindness and reason, so why would they be so cruel as to throw them into a frozen lake? With glum eyes, he pondered this to himself.

The young man's real name was Mori Rintarō, who later became known as Mori Ōgai. In his biography of the literary giant, Yamasaki Kuninori demonstrates persuasively that the brutal treatment of the Kirishitans at the Kōrinji, which Ōgai knew about while he attended the Yōrōkan School, left traumatic wounds in the writer's heart.

After eight men at the Kōrinji apostatized when they could no longer bear the hunger and cold, the authorities inflicted even more ruthless punishments on the twenty who still stood firm.

First, those who had renounced their faith were moved to a nunnery known as the Hōshin-an. They were taken to a stream in front of the Hachiman Shrine and there subjected to a ritual purification to memorialize the vow they had made to abandon their Kirishitan beliefs. Afterward, they were given warm clothing and warm food, and every day they received an allowance of seventy-one *mon*,[1] were allowed to move about outside the nunnery, and were granted the opportunity to do piecework.

In contrast, the twenty men who refused to apostatize had their allotment of food reduced even further. Occasionally they were called out three at a time and taken to observe the traitors at the Hōshin-an savoring copious amounts of food and living in comfortable rooms.

The apostates naturally averted their eyes when their former brethren were herded in to see how they were living. They were ashamed of their own weakness. Somewhere in their hearts they despised those who resolutely maintained their convictions. They could not have coped with their own emotions had they not scorned those who were strong.

The apostates tried to sway those who were brought to observe them: "Even if you try to stand up to them, what's the point of wasting away and dying here? Jezusu and Santa Maria aren't coming to help you. Don't you think it's better to pretend to apostatize and go on living so we can go back to Urakami? You've been duped by Sen'emon and Kanzaburō."

Those who had apostatized singled out Sen'emon and Kanzaburō from among the stalwarts as the targets of their loathing, while the officers waited for them to begin squabbling among themselves. . . .

Why do we have to endure all this suffering?

At times, when the captives would lie awake in the middle of the night, unable to sleep because of the severe cold, such questions would assail their minds. These questions were accompanied by terrifying doubts about the love of God and the validity of their faith. Doubts stabbed like a sharp knife at their chests, inflicting excruciating pain.

---

1. The smallest unit of Japanese currency at the time, *mon* were coins cast in copper or iron. They were replaced by the yen in the early 1870s.

When these thoughts arose, their teeth began to chatter—and not merely because of the cold. It was also because of the dark, chilling feelings of loneliness that come when one's faith wavers.

"Lord Jezusu suffered even more than we are. Think of that and don't give up!" Sen'emon tried to encourage them all. But even his steadfast encouragement had no impact on their vacillating minds. Jesus's sufferings ended after a single day. But there was no way to tell when their own torment and hunger would cease. . . .

Seikichi was among those struggling against uncertainty. In his darker moments he would recall happy scenes from the past in an effort to dispel his feelings of loneliness: those mornings when he would stroll through the streets of Nagasaki, selling whatever might be in season. Seikichi was proud of the resonance in his vendor's call.

"Such a lovely voice!" He was often complimented by the women who stood outside their doors waiting for him. Among those women . . . yes, Kiku was one of them.

I wonder what that plucky girl is up to right now. Was she still working at the padres' house in Ōura? Or had she ended up working somewhere else?

But the details of Kiku's face and figure had grown hazy in his weary mind. He could not imagine that she was still in love with him. This emaciated, grimy body with hair and whiskers growing in wild disarray. In his condition he no longer had the leisure to even think about a woman.

"Come here!" One day, Seikichi was unexpectedly beckoned by an officer. It seemed strange that he would be summoned by himself, but he did as he was told.

"You're still so young. Don't you think it would be a waste for someone as young as you to spend your whole life here like these other men? If you'll just apostatize, I'll pretty much let you do what you please." The officer's face was perfectly serious. Even though they had pushed eight of the others to renounce their faith, they were losing patience with the ones who were still unshakable.

Seikichi did not respond. Even the words this officer spoke lacked a sense of reality for him, and he felt as though he were hearing them from the distance.

"I see. So you won't comply no matter what we do, eh?" The officer sounded resigned, but then he gave orders to several policemen, who forced Seikichi into a tiny box. It was a mere three feet in width and height, with thick planks of pine wood for walls. A single hole had been cut in the roof to pass items through. Seikichi was unable either to stand or to stretch out his legs.

"If you just say, 'I give it up,'" he heard the officer's voice through the hole in the roof, "I'll let you out of here. Give it some thought."

Inside the box, his sense of the passage of time went amok. One second came to seem like an hour, and an hour felt longer than an entire day.

White, threadlike slivers of sunlight seeped between the cracks in the planks of wood that served as walls. They were his only connection with the outside world. Since he could neither lie down nor stand up, he had to remain in the same position all day long.

Before long his hips and back began to ache, and he could no longer contain the urge to urinate. A dull pain flared through his neck. He massaged his neck with his right hand and let the urine spray out. The warm liquid drenched his immobilized knees and legs.

The square door in the roof opened, and by turns two policemen poked their leering faces inside. Their names were Takahashi and Deguchi—and for the rest of his life Seikichi would remember those two names along with the pain he suffered in that three-foot box. Takahashi had a round face that made him look like a raccoon dog, while Deguchi resembled a fox or a badger.

"What do you think? Nice little house, isn't it?" The two took turns amusing themselves. "Have you taken a liking to it? If you've taken a fancy to it, you can stay there as long as you like. Nobody will complain."

Along with their taunts, they passed two tiny rice balls and a single dried plum through the hole each day.

"Lord Itō will be coming back to Tsuwano soon. When he gets here, your little box won't be the worst of your problems."

Takahashi and Deguchi seemed to be cut from the same cloth as Itō Seizaemon, and they behaved like his underlings whenever he paid a visit from Nagasaki.

After suffering five days of torment in this narrow box, Seikichi, covered in excrement and barely half alive, was dragged out and returned to the cell with the others. Takahashi scrambled to cover his face with a cloth to keep him from dying of trauma when the light of the sun suddenly struck him. That is how wasted his body had become.

"Think maybe that had a little effect?" Deguchi said hatefully, his eyes beady like a badger's.

Sen'emon and the others cared for Seikichi throughout the night.

Because he was still young, Seikichi somehow recovered, but the next man crammed into the box, a man from Ieno named Wasaburō, was older than Seikichi and had not been in good health for some time, so the men worried what the outcome might be.

"I'm not so sure Wasaburō can survive in a place like that." Sen'emon and Kanzaburō, having heard from Seikichi about the torment of the three-foot box, conferred with the other men about possible steps they might take to help Wasaburō.

No one had any good ideas. They recognized that pleas to the officials or the guards would be of no avail.

"We can't die without making it back to Urakami." With closed eyes, Sen'emon mumbled as though to himself. In his heart he was praying fervently to be blessed with a stroke of inspiration. "We can't let Wasaburō die."

He was not alone in his feeling. Wasaburō was docile and self-effacing, and he was kind to everyone and loved by all.

"Is there any way we could slip out of here . . . and sneak over to the box?"

No one had an answer. It didn't seem possible.

For the entire day, Sen'emon sat in a corner of the room hugging his knees and sunk in thought. Everyone knew what their leader was brooding over, so they left him alone and did not try to speak to him.

Near evening—

Abruptly he spoke. "Kunitarō! You had a copper coin, didn't you?"

"Yeah. Did you want me to give to a guard and ask him to help?"

"Naw," Sen'emon shook his head. "D'you think you could use the coin as a tool to make a knife?"

He explained himself. Back in Nakano, every now and then a farmer would dig up a knife-shaped rock in the fields. They assumed that people in former times had ground these rocks and used them as knives.

"So when we're taken out for questioning, I think we should be able to pick up a roof tile from the courtyard. We'll use the copper coin to grind it and make it into a knife. Once we have a knife, we can cut through these floorboards and dig a hole to the outside."

"That's too dangerous!" Several voices rose in opposition. If an officer or a guard were to discover what they were doing, they'd be in serious trouble. Their food rations would be cut back even further, and they might be subjected to severe torture. Several of the men were opposed to the plan.

"I don't suppose you have any other ideas, do you? Or are you saying you just want to leave Wasaburō in that box to die?" Seikichi retorted, casting a sharp glance toward the cowards. "I know the pain of being in that box! We can't abandon Wasaburō!"

Seikichi's entreaty led to the adoption of the hard-liner plan.

Taking care not to be seen by the officials and guards, the men swiped a roof tile and carved it into a stone knife. To drown out the noise of their efforts, several of the men, by design, sang in loud voices.

The knife was finished. Taking turns, they hacked away at the floorboards. That was the easy part. By the third day they had made a hole large enough to poke one finger through; then, squeezing one hand through the gap, they managed to pull up the floorboard and commenced to dig out the soil beneath the wall of their cell. Somehow or other they managed to create a tunnel to the outside.

"Sen'emon!" That night, each man contributed the meager allotment of rice he had received for that day to make two rice balls, which they gave to Sen'emon. "Give this to Wasaburō to eat."

In the darkness Sen'emon slid down beneath the floor and crawled out through the hole they had excavated.

The night in Tsuwano was icy cold, and the mountains and houses were all darkened. The guards appeared to be unconcerned and noticed nothing.

When he reached the three-foot cell, Sen'emon pressed his face against its wall and whispered, "Wasaburō! Wasaburō! It's Sen'emon. It's me!"

He sensed a faint stirring inside the box.

"I know this is hard for you. But you've got to pray and hold on just a little longer. I'm giving you some rice balls through the hole up top."

There was no response.

"What's happened to you? Wasaburō!"

"Yes." His voice was feeble. It was clear that he had been worn down.

If he's left like this, he'll die!

As Sen'emon turned from the three-foot cell and started back toward the tunnel, Wasaburō's voice still lingered in his ears. He muttered to himself, *Lord Jezusu! If this goes on any longer, Wasaburō will die!*

There was still some time before dawn. The darkness was thick, Mount Aono towered blackly to the rear, and the cold wind was brutal. But Sen'emon couldn't bring himself to return to the others. He cut across the frozen garden of the temple and came to the bamboo fence that enclosed the compound. He wanted somehow to get outside. . . .

Please help me, Lord Jezusu!

When he pushed gently at the gate, it creaked softly and moved. The careless guards had neglected to secure the latch.

With quiet steps Sen'emon climbed down the hill. There was no danger of anyone seeing him at this hour, but he feared that a dog, hearing his footsteps, might begin barking. If a dog barked, someone might wake up.

Sen'emon decided to go to the Hōshin-an where the apostates were lodged. He knew that the eight apostates felt very ambivalent toward those who still clung to their principles.

But he had to enlist their aid in order to help Wasaburō. Sen'emon's own feelings were conflicted right now.

Since the Hōshin-an was a nunnery, it had no imposing walls. Even so, he sustained a few cuts on his arms and legs from the hedge as he pushed his way into the courtyard.

"Motosuke! Motosuke!" He placed his mouth up to a crack in the storm shutters and called out, but since he spoke softly from the fear of being overheard, there was no response.

"Motosuke . . . !"

He heard a cough; apparently someone had awakened. But perhaps having heard Sen'emon's voice, there was silence for a few moments.

"Who . . . who is it?"

"It's Sen'emon. Can you open this shutter?"

The shutter opened a crack, and two dark faces peered out at him.

"It really is Sen'emon! Did you escape?"

"No, I didn't. Wasaburō is close to death. They've stuck him in a little box they call the three-foot cell and he's covered in his own filth. . . ."

Lowering his voice, Sen'emon described the agony of the tiny cell and Wasaburō's grim condition.

"And we . . . we can't do anything to help him. I thought maybe if you could share a little of your food . . . that's what I've come to ask for. Motosuke, Satoichi—you're both from Urakami, too. Can you think of some way to help?"

The other six men had awakened and listened quietly to what Sen'emon had to say. No one uttered a word in reply.

"It's going to start getting light. . . . I've got to go back."

"Would you . . . would you take this to him?" Someone stood up in the darkness and held out several rice cakes to Sen'emon. "This is all I've got tonight. But if you can come back tomorrow, I'll save up some food to give you," the man whispered. . . .

But Sen'emon knew full well that Wasaburō's debilitation was growing more critical with each passing day. Wasaburō could evidently no longer swallow the food that the apostates at the Hōshin-an were willing to provide out of pity.

When Sen'emon returned through the passage they had dug, he reported in a lifeless voice, "He's not going to make it. He can't even answer me anymore."

On the twentieth day after Wasaburō was put into the three-foot cell—

A guard came to summon Sen'emon: "The man says he wants to talk to you."

Sen'emon raced to the cell, where Wasaburō's emaciated appendages poked out from under a straw rug.

His body was soiled revoltingly with the feces he had to live with every day. Sen'emon swallowed hard at the extreme wretchedness of his friend.

"Sen'emon," Wasaburō pleaded in a faint voice. "Don't let them burn my body, OK . . . ? When the rest of you are executed, please carry my body to that same spot. . . ."

"I understand," Sen'emon nodded through his tears. "Even if we die, all of us from Urakami will be together in Paraíso. Our ancestors are waiting for us there."

Let us go, let us go,
Let us go to the Temple of Paraíso.
Though it's called the Temple of Paraíso . . .

Knowing that Wasaburō would soon die, the other men began to sing from their cell inside the temple. The officials and guards said nothing, even as their melancholy voices grew gradually louder.

When the officers began to carry Wasaburō's corpse out of the boxlike cell, the nineteen remaining prisoners, aware of their friend's dying wish, began to shout at them. One man named Kunitarō became particularly desperate and continued to argue with the officers who yelled and barked orders at him.

But all their protests were in vain. Two days later, Wasaburō's body was carted off to some unknown location, and no one had any idea where it had been disposed of.

Overnight the three-foot cell was transformed into the most painful and frightening location the remaining nineteen men could imagine. Being placed in there signified death. And it was a death in which a man breathed his last in horrible pain and smothered in his own excrement.

The next to be cast into the three-foot cell was a man named Yasutarō. Kanzaburō, Kunitarō's second son, wrote in his reminiscences:

This man Yasutarō was a man of faith and humility who did all the nasty jobs that other men hated to do, and he often reduced his own ration of food in order to feed it to someone weak in his fides. . . .

Yasutarō was periodically dragged from his three-foot cell to the courtyard amid the falling snow, and attempts were made to force him to apostatize. He, too, wasted away, sullied with diarrhea.

This time it was Kanzaburō's turn to make use of the tunnel they had dug to give encouragement to Yasutarō.

I pulled up the floorboards in our cell . . . and made my way outside, reaching the three-foot cell sometime after midnight, Kanzaburō recorded. *I called out, "Yasutarō! Yasutarō!" one or two times until he responded in a faint voice. I said, "Being in this little cell must be awfully lonely for you," but he answered, "I'm not lonely between ten o'clock and twelve. Just after ten, a woman in a blue kimono with a blue scarf around her head, looking just like the pictures of Santa Maria, comes and tells me stories, so I'm not lonely at all then." But he told me not to mention this to anyone while he was still alive. Three nights later the moon was truly beautiful. I think he was a real saint.*

It was not long before Yasutarō, reduced to only skin and bones, breathed his last. The remaining eighteen prisoners, each absorbed in his own personal thoughts, gazed down at the wasted corpse laid out on a straw rug. Some were deeply moved; others felt only fear. A few chewed on their lips in anger and remorse, while some were gripped with apprehension.

Around this time Itō Seizaemon resurfaced in Tsuwano. He had not seen the Urakami Kirishitans in quite a while, and he greeted them with uncharacteristic gentleness: "I've brought you a present." He pulled a heavy cloth bag from the pocket of his kimono. "Do you know what this is . . . ? It's some of the soil from Urakami. It's soil from your hometown of Urakami. Give it a whiff. You'll recognize it."

There was no doubt that the soil that spilled from the cloth bag had come from Urakami. Having cultivated this soil for so many long years, these farmers recognized it instinctively.

"Go ahead and scoop it up in your hands. No need to hesitate."

After the first man responded to Itō's offer and touched the soil with trembling hands, the rest of the men excitedly reached their hands out, too. They brought it up to their noses and kept their eyes shut for a long, long while.

Itō glanced around at the faces of the Kirishitans with a broad smile and asked, "Is there a Seikichi here?" When Seikichi responded, he said, "I see. So you're Seikichi, are you . . . ? Do you happen to know a place called the Yamazaki Teahouse in Maruyama?"

"I certainly don't."

"Don't lie to me. A maid that works there, name of Kiku . . . she's very worried about you. . . . She says she wants you back in Urakami soon. I wouldn't make something like that up. I'm sure you'd like to smell the soil of your home again, wouldn't you? Or would you prefer to die in your own shit in that little box?"

Seikichi's face flushed. Itō's comments were his usual blend of part aggravation and partly his habit of preying on the men's weaknesses, but this time, for once, his words appeared to have some impact.

Several days later, six of the eighteen men quietly declared their apostasy. Ultimately they were defeated by the smell of the soil of Urakami and their fear of the three-foot cell.

TWO KINDS OF LOVE

MITSU SAW SOMETHING unusual at the Gotōya one day. She ran across Kumazō sobbing in a corner of the kitchen.

It happened on the same morning that all the Urakami Kirishitans, including women and children, were driven from their homes and scattered to various locations.

The rout had been the subject of gossip at the Gotōya since the previous day. It started to snow that morning, and throughout Nagasaki, people watched as Kirishitan women, their heads covered with yellow or white scarves to shield them from the snow, headed up the hill toward the Nishi Bureau carrying belongings on their backs and leading their children by the hand.

"I wonder if your family is going to be OK," Oyone said sarcastically to Mitsu. "They live in the same town of Urakami . . ."

"But why are those people so pigheaded?" the Mistress sighed. "They lose their houses and their land, and they're exiled to some unfamiliar place. . . . Don't they see what they're giving up here?"

Mitsu and Tome, bracing themselves against the cold, climbed up on the poles used for drying laundry and tried to watch as the steamships bobbing in the harbor took on these refugees and departed. As a native of Urakami herself, Mitsu felt unbearably sad for them. She was especially overcome with pity when one of the shop clerks reported that he overheard a young child, who had no idea what was happening, whining incessantly as her mother led her by the hand along the snowy road to the Nishi Bureau: "Mom! Let's go home! Let's go home!!"

The next morning when Mitsu went into the kitchen to perform her normal chores of preparing breakfast and cleaning, she discovered Kumazō beside the hearth, his back toward her, weeping. When he realized that Mitsu was standing behind him, Kumazō fled outside.

Mitsu went out to the well. Her burdens had been made somewhat lighter since Kumazō came to the shop, as he would draw the water from the well and carry it in buckets to the kitchen, but today he had not brought any water in.

Kumazō turned his face away from Mitsu as she approached. She said nothing but picked up the bucket of water that Kumazō had drawn so she could carry it to the kitchen herself.

"Mitsu!" Kumazō, his head still bowed, muttered abruptly. "You saw me crying just now, didn't you?"

Mitsu could only nod her head. Then Kumazō said in a raspy voice, "Could you please not tell anybody else?"

"I won't."

They said nothing further for a time. Then Kumazō suddenly broke the silence. "Mitsu, I'm a Kirishitan from Nakano. But I was scared to be sent off to some distant land, so when the boats were leaving, I ran away. I went to the officials and told them I'd give up my Kirishitan beliefs. So here I am, a 'pardoned' apostate! This morning, they told me that the people from my village of Nakano and from Motohara had all been put on those ships in the bay that headed out to sea. . . . And I . . . and I'm left here alone!" He spat the words out, clutching to his chest the bucket he had taken from Mitsu's hands.

Mitsu told Kumazō's secret to no one. She didn't even reveal it to her friend Tome. As a result, an unseen connection developed between Mitsu and Kumazō.

He really shouldn't punish himself so much. . . .

Since she wasn't a Kirishitan herself, Mitsu couldn't really understand why Kumazō felt so guilty about abandoning his Kirishitan faith. When she mentioned this to Kumazō, he said sadly, "You wouldn't understand," and turned away to swing his ax into a piece of firewood.

Mitsu stared at the back of her forlorn friend and felt tremendous sorrow for him. Seeing someone or something miserable or unfortunate was usually more than she could handle.

The New Year came around again.

"Kumazō, I'm sorry." Mitsu felt somehow guilty toward Kumazō; although he also was from Urakami, he had no place to go home to for the holiday.

"Nobody's left in Nakano, so I can't go back there. But I'd like to go to Ōura just once," he responded.

"To Ōura?"

"Yes. I wish I could at least go to the church there and tell Santa Maria how sorry I am for my weak resolve. Mitsu, would you slip away with me and go to Ōura? And could you keep watch while I tell Santa Maria I'm sorry?"

She empathized with Kumazō's agony, and Mitsu realized she could use this opportunity to see Kiku again.

On the afternoon of the third day of the first month, the two finally got some time off and left the Gotōya. Kumazō tied a kerchief over his head and knotted it under his chin so he wouldn't be recognized. The streets were jammed with people visiting shrines and temples, but the beach at Ōura was deserted. When he spotted the cross atop the church, Kumazō kept his head down as he climbed the hill toward it.

Mitsu stood at the entrance to the church as he instructed her and stood guard while Kumazō went inside. She could not hear even the faintest sound from the sanctuary after he disappeared into it.

When he finally emerged with tears in his eyes, Mitsu said, "OK, now will you wait at the beach for me? I'm going to go see Kiku." She set off in search of Kiku, but she soon learned from Okane that Kiku had run away.

"She's gone off to Tsuwano, probably following some man," Okane said spitefully.

Kiku toiled doggedly at the Yamazaki Teahouse. She needed to get to Tsuwano as quickly as possible to give encouragement to Seikichi. But she needed money to do that. Never before had she wanted money so badly.

The New Year holidays passed, and following the customs of the day, on the fourteenth the Mole-Pounding Ceremony[1] was held. Children gathered into groups of five or six each, and using bamboo sticks wrapped in rope, they went around to each house, pounding on the stepping-stones at the entrance as they sang:

It's mole pounding on the fourteenth!
Hurray! Three times with the stick—
Whack! Whack! Whack!

On the fourteenth, with the singing voices of the children echoing all around, an incident occurred at the Karatsu Teahouse, which was not far from the Yamazaki. A courtesan from the Karatsu named Wakamatsu ran away with a client.

It was common practice in Nagasaki when a person took flight or came up missing for everyone in the city to go out searching for them. On this occasion, groups of young men sent to track down the couple divided up and raced

---

1. The *mogura-uchi* is celebrated most commonly in Kyushu, with the pounding of sticks on the ground symbolizing the extermination of moles, which were the bane of a farmer's existence. Similar to the custom at Halloween, the children usually received candy, tangerines, or coins from the houses they visited.

through the mountain forests, beating gongs and drums and calling out, "Bring her back! Bring her back!"

"Still haven't found her, eh?" The madam of the Yamazaki Teahouse went outside repeatedly and conversed with those who had gathered to discuss the matter. Even the children out mole pounding joined in the search, half for the fun of it.

Near nightfall the two were discovered. In a cemetery they had bound their bodies tightly together with rope and had committed lovers' suicide.

That night, the government office boorishly enough suspended all activities in the Maruyama district so they could conduct their investigation. Eventually the two corpses were carted in. The man turned out to be a merchant named Shōsaburō from Motoshikkui-machi in Nagasaki.

"They didn't have to die like that," the madam apprehensively described the scene she had just witnessed to Kiku. Apparently the deceased man and woman were clutching each other's hands firmly, and no effort to separate them met with success.

I envy them. . . . In her heart, Kiku was unspeakably jealous of Wakamatsu and Shōsaburō. As a courtesan, Wakamatsu was constrained in both body and heart and could never hope to be united for life with the man she loved. Her grief and Shōsaburō's ardor for her had led the two of them to die in protest of their helpless fate.

Kiku felt that her own circumstances were just like those of a courtesan. Seikichi was a Kirishitan and therefore a criminal who had violated orders from their leaders, and she never knew when she might be able to see him again. It was identical to the situation that Wakamatsu and Shōsaburō had found themselves in. And so their love suicide seemed to Kiku less pitiful than it was infinitely beautiful.

I wonder if he's forgotten all about me by now.

Wracked by anxiety, Kiku asked Oyō, "Can you teach me how to write?" She had made up her mind to learn how to write so that she could compose a letter to Seikichi and ask Itō Seizaemon to take it to him in Tsuwano on his next visit.

Oyō taught her how to write the characters as though she were her own little sister. Being bright, Kiku quickly learned the characters she was taught.

Mornings commenced in Maruyama just as they did throughout Nagasaki, with the calls of street vendors. Even the clients at the pleasure houses, sound asleep with exhaustion from their night of revelry, were awakened by the vendors' calls:

Whiiite-fish! Whiiite—

The young men called out robustly as they walked about selling whitefish.

Every time Kiku heard the voices of the fish peddlers she thought of Sei-kichi's voice. How she had waited with her heart pounding to hear that pleasing voice from far down the road when she worked at the Gotōya!

Seikichi's voice was wonderful, a joy to listen to. Kiku had listened to it with real admiration.

But Seikichi no longer walked any of these streets.

Before she went to bed each night, she read and reread her letter to Seikichi that she had finally half completed with Oyō's help. She had struggled to write:

Im sure your having a hard time. I was hopeing to see you so I wanted to come to tsuwano, but I couldnt so well have to talk in letters. Be brave.

She had to figure out some way to get this letter to Itō Seizaemon. Ironically enough, right now Seizaemon was the only person who could provide her with any information about the man she loved.

"When will Lord Itō be back from Tsuwano?" she repeatedly asked Oyō and the madam.

"He said he'd be back when winter ends, so I'm sure it will be soon."

With that information, she began to wish earnestly that the spring sun would quickly shine on Nagasaki Bay, which right now was still frigid.

The third month finally came. As the Peach Blossom Festival[2] approached, the young street vendors began strolling about calling "Festival dumplings! Cold saké laced with flowers!"

The festival was near its end when the madam came racing into the kitchen calling, "Kiku! Kiku! Lord Itō is here!"

With a broad smile the madam welcomed him. "Lord Itō, Kiku has been counting the days until you came again."

Apparently Itō mistook what the madam was saying and gave a vulgar chuckle. "So she's been looking forward to my return, has she? Excellent, excellent! Bring me some saké right away. And would you call that girl for me?"

"Lord Itō, Kiku isn't a hostess here," flustered, the madam responded. "I'll get Oyō for you."

"I don't want Oyō!" He shook his head vigorously. "I want Kiku to pour for me."

On orders from the madam, Kiku carried a saké bottle and a side dish to the room on the second floor. Seizaemon had stretched himself out on the floor, using his arm as a pillow, and watched with great interest out of one eye as Kiku's white arms rose and fell.

---

2. *Momo no sekku*—literally, "Peach Blossom Festival"—is today more commonly called *Hina matsuri*, or Girls' Day. Traditionally, it was held on the third day of the third month by the lunar calendar and marked the passing of winter to spring. Dolls representing the imperial court of the Heian period are put on display.

Kiku being who she was—

She was painfully conscious of Itō Seizaemon's gaze from behind her as she arranged the bottle and cup and dishes on the table. She knew that his eyes were drinking in the movements of her neck, her back, her hips, her feet. It gave her an unpleasant feeling that sent a shudder through her.

"There's this place they call the three-foot cell," Itō abruptly muttered, as though to himself. "Stay there and just listen for a minute. A three-foot cell, it's called. Once you're stuffed in there, you can't stand or even move about. It's three feet high and three feet wide. There's only enough room for one adult body to fill up every bit of space. It's got a small opening in the roof, and once a day they push two tiny little rice balls in. That's all the prisoner gets to eat for the whole day."

Kiku's body stiffened as though petrified. Itō gave a thin smile as he watched her back become rigid and continued his description.

"Since they can't move a muscle, they have to just relieve themselves where they are. I imagine their bodies start to ache the very first day. By the second day the pain is unbearable. Day after day goes by as they sit in their own body waste. Can't be helped. That's what happens to people who won't follow orders from above and refuse to give up their perverse beliefs no matter what you say to them. Hey, pour me another drink!"

Kiku turned her pallid face toward him. Her eyes cringed with anger and pain.

"Hey, why's your hand shaking? Seems like I frightened you a bit with my little story. But your friend Seikichi . . ."

"Was Seikichi put in that tiny cell?"

"Only for a little while. It was just as a warning to the others." Still reclined on the floor, Itō brought the cup to his dry lips, closed his eyes, and savored the saké. "But listen to this: he got out because I was clever enough to arrange it so that he was punished for only two days. I did it all for you. If I hadn't taken care of him . . ." He picked up the bottle himself and refilled his cup. "'Cause already two of them took sick in the little cell and died."

"I beg you. Please don't put Seikichi in that horrible cell again!"

"Well, that . . . That all depends on what you're willing to do now." He spoke in a deliberate voice that was a curious mixture of hope and dejection. "What you're willing to do . . . What you're willing to do."

"What is it . . . that I need to do?"

"I think you know. . . ." He leered at her, relishing the game. "Working here as you do, I think you must know what goes on between Hondō Shuntarō and Oyō when they're alone together. What does her voice sound like . . . when they're going at it?" Itō reached out his hand and clutched Kiku's ankle.

"No!" Kiku cried. "Stop it!"

She wrenched her body and tried to push Itō away with her right hand. Suddenly a ferocious look swept across his face.

"What? Is it that disagreeable to have me touch you?"

Kiku said nothing.

"I'm not going to force myself on anybody who doesn't want it. At Tsuwano all I ever do is torment people against their will and then report on what they say. But hey, hold on a minute. Next time I come back to Nagasaki, as my gift to you I'll let you know what's happened to Seikichi."

He brought the cup to his mouth and drained out the saké. Drops of the liquor spilled from his mouth ringed with scruffy whiskers and soaked his collar.

"Go downstairs!" He spat at Kiku. "And tell the boss . . . tell her to get me a more cooperative girl. A cooperative girl, for your information, is a girl who'll give me her body with a smile when I touch her."

He couldn't tell whether or not Kiku heard him: she was immobile, staring at a spot in the air as though in a daze. Itō, of course, had no clue what she was thinking.

"Hey! Didn't you hear me tell you to go downstairs? Useless girl . . ."

Still Kiku did not speak.

"What are you looking so idiotic about?"

"Lord Itō," Kiku suddenly looked up at Itō and responded, "If . . . If I . . . If I do as you say . . . will you send Seikichi back to Nagasaki?"

"Back to Nagasaki?" Itō's droopy eyes widened in surprise. And then he inadvertently let show the good in himself and answered honestly, "What are you talking about? I don't have that kind of power. But I can certainly make things easier for him in his cell at Tsuwano."

"Make it easier—how?"

"I can slip him a little extra to eat. If you give me some money, I can get that to him. Even in prison, there's times when money is king. A man can even get his time spent in hell shortened with a few coins."

"Even the time in the three-foot cell?"

"Well, if I give them the word . . . he can probably avoid the place altogether."

Kiku was silent. As she pondered what to do, Itō's eyes hungrily studied her profile.

"Lord Itō?"

"Yes."

"Then . . . I'll do . . . I'll do whatever you want me to do." At that, she closed her eyes, almost as though she were about to stretch out on an operating table.

"If you're going to be so prim about it . . . it sort of takes away the fun. Hold on—I'm going to have another bottle or two to drink." Itō brought the cup to his lips, eager to become intoxicated as quickly as possible.

In that instant, two distinct images appeared on the screen of Kiku's closed eyelids.

One was of herself, dressed up as a new bride. She was so happy, walking alongside Seikichi through the fields of lotus flowers in Urakami. . . .

The other was an image of Seikichi, his arms tied behind his back, crammed into that box-like little cell. With froth seeping from his mouth, he gave a low moan. He had been seated in that same position for days, in a box that hardly any sunlight could pierce.

Seikichi, please stay strong! I'm going to do something to help you right now!

She had made up her mind, even though helping Seikichi meant doing what Itō Seizaemon told her to do. And doing his bidding meant defiling her body. It also meant abandoning forever her dream of becoming Seikichi's bride.

"Aaah . . . !" A groan escaped through Kiku's lips. Itō, his face flushed with arousal and alcohol, impatiently insinuated his right hand between the hems of her kimono and tried to push her body back onto the floor with his left.

"Aaah . . . !" Her groan was filled with pain and disgust and grief. There was not the slightest trace in her cry of the pleasure a woman feels when she gives her body to a man she loves. In that moment, she had to abandon her dream of happiness, her dream of spending her life at Seikichi's side, walking together through the lotus fields of Urakami. She had to discard her dream of busily working as his wife and becoming the mother of his children. . . .

Soy flour! Say—come get your flour here!

Outside, the street vendors raised their monotone voices loudly as they passed by. Children were kicking stones along the road—it was exactly the same kind of game that Kiku and Mitsu had played years ago in Magome.

Seikichi! Seikichi! Seikichi!

Inwardly, Kiku desperately repeated Seikichi's name first as Itō's body covered hers, his drunken breaths coming faster until he was almost gasping for air, and again as she clenched her teeth to endure the searing pain that tore through her body. Seikichi's name was all she had to cling to.

A long time passed. When finally Itō ceased his protracted labors, he pulled his body away from hers. But Kiku did not stir; she merely gazed absently at the ceiling.

Eventually—Eventually pallid tears slowly flowed from her almond eyes, then slowly dribbled along her cheeks.

Soy flour! Say—come get your flour here!

The droning voice of the vendor was back, clearly audible.

One potato, two potato, three potato, four!
We got no treats from the lady next door.
Her kids'll all be devils from the day they're born,
And her grandkids'll all have a long sharp horn!

The children sang as they kicked rocks. Just as Kiku and Mitsu had sung as young girls in Magome.

The lotus flowers that covered the fields, back when they were innocent, and her dream of becoming Seikichi's wife had all flown off far into the distance. An unending stream of tears welled in Kiku's eyes, then flowed down her cheeks. . . .

After a while—

When Itō Seizaemon stood up, he glanced awkwardly at Kiku, then suddenly in a gentle voice said, "I'll be back again. Before then, think of any messages you'd like to send to that fellow in Tsuwano. You can send money if you want. . . ." With that, he fled down the stairs.

"Oh, are you leaving . . . ?" The madam looked at Itō with a strained smile, then winked and said, "So, how was Kiku?"

"Umm . . . OK." Itō hastily went out the door.

After watching him leave rather downcast, the madam quietly went up to the second floor. Kiku had her back to the door and was quietly gathering up the scattered bottles and bowls.

"Once you've finished cleaning up, why don't you take a little break until this evening? We won't have any more customers until after dark." She spoke to Kiku with greater compassion than usual.

That night, two or three groups of customers came in, and at one point Oyō came downstairs to speak to the madam. "Mama, there's something funny about Kiku tonight."

"Funny how?"

"I can't really say, but she's a lot quieter than usual. Did something happen in Tsuwano?"

"Not that I know of," the madam feigned ignorance.

Two or three days later, the madam unexpectedly asked Kiku, "Kiku, this isn't something I'm trying to force you into, so please just relax and listen, OK? Have you given any thought to becoming a *geiko* like Oyō?"

Kiku said nothing.

"A girl as pretty as you with just a little work could become the top *geiko* in Maruyama. You'd make good money for a long, long while, and you could use it to help your man in Tsuwano. . . ."

Kiku still did not reply. Dark currents of fate had swept her up and were carrying her toward some unknown destination. No matter how hard she struggled against those currents, ultimately she would be borne away. . . . That was the sort of acquiescence that governed her heart right now.

Itō came back to the teahouse another two or three times. He was careful to choose the afternoon hours, when no other clients were about, to make his appearance. As a house, they were not particularly grateful to have him for a customer, but since he was an official at the Nishi Bureau, the madam had no choice but to welcome him with a smile.

He always drank saké in the same room on the second floor, and then he would pull Kiku, who sat silently pouring his drinks, into his arms. Wordlessly Kiku laid back, and Itō climbed on top of her.

But when he was finished with her, he would leave with a strangely uncomfortable look on his face, as though he were ashamed of himself.

Clients were still few in number when Itō climbed down the slope from Maruyama, now lit by the declining western sun, and he muttered to himself, "I'm . . . I'm a despicable man. A truly despicable man."

He blinked his eyes.

A MAN NAMED ITŌ

OF THE TWENTY-EIGHT men who had originally come to Tsuwano, fourteen had apostatized and two others had died in the three-foot cell. Only twelve continued to insist that they would not abandon their Kirishitan faith.

One evening the twelve prisoners heard the sound of digging in the garden. Sen'emon peeked out and saw several men using hoes to dig a hole.

The workers realized they were being watched, so they began talking to one another loudly enough to be heard: "Anyways, it's a grave for men with no hope of becoming buddhas, so we can make it shallow enough so's that wild dogs won't have no trouble diggin' 'em up!"

The prisoners could then visualize the grave that was being dug.

Maybe it won't be long before we're beheaded. That was the consensus among the captives, but strangely, they were no longer afraid of execution; it had begun to seem like a sweet release to them. If all they had to look forward to was one painful day after another and the fear of the three-foot cell, they would prefer to have their heads lopped off sooner rather than later so they could go to Paraíso.

A heavy snow fell on the third day after the hole was dug. Late that night Sen'emon caught the chills, but at dawn while the prisoners were still sleeping a policeman arrived and summoned all twelve to an interrogation, "You're all wanted!"

"I can't go." Sen'emon demurred, suffering from a severe headache.

"Why is that?"

"I'm sick. I can't walk."

"If you can't walk, somebody'll have to carry you. You're coming! Is that clear?" Underscoring the order, the policeman disappeared.

Assisted by Kanzaburō, Sen'emon walked slowly behind the others down the long hallway of the temple. The temple edifice was right next to the building where they were interrogated.

The atmosphere in the room was different from usual. Today, an older man who looked like he might be a physician sat beside the interrogating officers, along with several other men seated stiffly, wearing swords and dressed sharply in formal kimono trousers and robes with their sleeves tied up with cords.

Maybe we will be executed after all. . . . The mood in the room gave all twelve men the sense that their time had come.

"Still no wish to change your beliefs?" It was the same question they were always asked by the officials. When no one replied, they were queried individually.

"Sen'emon, what about you?"

"I don't wish to."

"And you, Kanzaburō?"

"I won't change my beliefs."

The men in formal attire, who seemed to be expecting those replies, scrambled to their feet.

"Sen'emon, Kanzaburō—outside!" An officer ordered the door to be opened. Through the opening they could see the courtyard blanketed in pure white snow.

All the men were convinced that these two men would be the first to be executed. Both men felt the same way as they got to their feet. Kanzaburō held on to Sen'emon, whose legs were shaky because of his fever.

The doctor and the official led the way out into the drifts of snow and stopped in the courtyard.

"Take off your clothes! Then come over here!" The official ordered brusquely.

The men removed their clothing and stepped across the snow to where the official stood.

They hadn't seen it from the distance, but the official and the doctor were standing at the edge of a pond. Because the pond was covered with a thin white layer of ice, they had not been able to distinguish it from the snow-blanketed ground.

"I told you to take off your clothes . . . !" the official screamed at Sen'emon and Kanzaburō, who were hugging their bodies with both arms. "Take off those loincloths, too!"

The moment the two prisoners submitted and removed their loincloths, the men in formal attire hurled themselves without warning against the bodies of both men. Thrown off balance, Sen'emon and Kanzaburō tumbled into the icy pond with a splash.

A spray of water shot up as the ice shattered. The two men's bodies were sucked into the dark water, then bobbed to the surface again. Their hair was disheveled.

The ice broke, and we tried to swim around, Kanzaburō later recalled his painful memories of that day. *Our feet didn't reach the bottom of the pond, but it was shallower in the middle, so I was able to keep my chin above the surface. I lifted my eyes to heaven and clasped my hands and pleaded to Santa Maria to intercede. I begged for Jezusu to be with me, while Sen'emon prayed the "Our Father." I offered up a devotional prayer. Then an officer mocked us, saying, "Sen'emon, Kanzaburō, can you see your heavenly Lord? Eh? How about it?!"*

The officers mercilessly scooped up water in a long-handled ladle and poured it over the two men's faces. As a result, they could barely catch their breath.

My body was freezing, I was shuddering, and my teeth were chattering. Sen'emon said to me, "Kanzaburō, how are you holding up? I can't see anymore. The world is spinning. Please don't forsake me!" He was about to draw his last breath when the official ordered, "Come out now!" and one of the guards yelled, 'Hurry out!' I was at the point of saying "I can make the climb to heaven but I can't climb out of this lake" when they brought a six-foot-long bamboo pole with a hook on the end and wrapped our hair around the hook and pulled as hard as they could. They dragged us up out of the ice, brushed the snow off us, and built fires with two bundles of brushwood and some logs. Then six of them surrounded our two bodies, warmed us by the fire, and gave us some warm liquid to revive us.

They were not the only two prisoners tortured in the frozen pond. On that day alone, Kanzaburō's father, Kunitarō, and Tomohachi were subjected to the same punishment. As soon as Kanzaburō was pulled from the pond, he was jammed into the three-foot cell. The officials had concluded that unlike the aging Sen'emon, they could shove young Kanzaburō in the tiny enclosure without fear of his dying.

Despite these torments that were heaped on them one after another, not one of the twelve men apostatized.

But even though their spirits could not be broken, these tortures, when added to the cold and starvation, led to the deaths of two of the men. A man named Seishirō muttered words of encouragement to his friends as he died.

At around that same time—

A procession of men and women, led along by officers, was making its way along the cold, snowy road toward Tsuwano.

The procession included not just women and children but even elderly people and infants. It was obvious from their baggy clothes that they brought only what they wore. Some mothers carried their infants on their backs. Behind them climbed the elderly, scarcely able to breathe.

Young children walked beside their grandparents.

These were 125 of the Urakami Kirishitans who had been driven from their homes a month earlier and were relatives of the men and who were already suffering in agony in Tsuwano. They had initially been taken to Mikuriya Village in the Hirado domain rather than to Nagasaki; from there they had been loaded onto boats and taken to Onomichi. They had then been separated out from those being exiled to Hiroshima and were now heading toward Tsuwano under armed guard.

We'll be able to see our husbands and fathers again.

Although they feared what might lie ahead, still their hearts thrilled at the prospect of being reunited with their husbands, fathers, and other relatives, about whom they had heard no news.

I wonder how they've been treated.

They were less worried about what would be happening to themselves than they were about the well-being of their husbands and fathers. Had they been ill? Had they been subjected to terrible tortures?

Even the women and children felt that they could endure whatever suffering lay ahead if only they could be with their husbands and fathers from whom they had been so long separated. They had no way of knowing that some of those husbands and fathers had already apostatized.

News of this procession quickly reached the cell in Tsuwano. As one day after another passed, the emotions of the prisoners were a mixture of joy and pity.

How inhuman! They didn't have to drive our wives and children from the village!

I didn't want them to have to endure the hunger and cold and the three-foot cell here!

Anger and anxiety clutched at their hearts.

The sounds of trees being cut down and stakes being driven into the ground echoed every day from the garden of the temple.

"You men will be moving over there," one guard secretively alerted them. "Your wives and children will live here."

The men were moved into the new cell as soon as it was completed. On the evening of the following day, they were startled by sounds of crying children and conversing women. They heard an elderly person coughing.

"They must have arrived." As one, the men pressed their ears against the newly completed mud wall. One man picked up a brick from the ground and gouged a hole in the wall. "Ah—they are here!" Unbidden tears flowed from his sunken eyes. As the father of one of the young children who had been led here from Urakami by her mother, the man could not help but weep.

"What are you doing?! Peeking through that hole?!" An officer caught them observing the new arrivals and had one of the guards fill up the hole with mud. The clamor continued for some time, but finally night approached.

"I've just had a horrible thought!" Sen'emon suddenly voiced a concern to his cellmates. "The officers are going to lie to our wives and children. They'll tell them that we apostatized a long time ago, so they might as well go ahead and apostatize, too!"

Sen'emon's fears were right on the mark. They knew that the officers would use any possible means to persuade them to abandon their faith.

"There's nothing to worry about!" Kanzaburō said with a laugh. "I left a note on the floor of the privy telling them that the twelve of us haven't left the faith!"

"You did?"

"I did!"

Coincidentally enough, it was Kanzaburō's younger sister, Matsu, who found the note he had left in the privy. When she discovered the note in the familiar scrawl of her brother, she hurried to tell the others that the twelve men had not apostatized.

"But what about all the others?" Through the heart of every woman passed both the fear that her own husband or father had apostatized and a feeling akin to a prayer that her own relatives were still holding firm.

Among the 125 new prisoners, sixteen were children age five or younger, and there were ten adults who were at least sixty-one. The officers moved all the men over the age of fifteen to a room separated from the women and younger children.

Once they had been assigned to their cells, a voice called out, "Mealtime!"

Their meals consisted solely of a small quantity of food served on a tray. The side dish was a clump of miso the size of one's thumb and a pinch of salt.

Dauntless by nature, Matsu asked a guard named Takahashi, "Is this all there is?"

Takahashi, who had a face like a ferret, taunted her, "That's all. But if you apostatize, you can stuff yourself full."

Everyone was silent as they chewed their food. But the mothers in the group gave their meager portions to their young children.

"This must be how they've treated my husband the whole time." One woman set down her chopsticks and was choked with tears. It was as though something that had been held within suddenly burst out.

"Why are you crying?" the staunch Matsu, who was twenty-seven, tried to cheer up the woman. "If that's true, all the more reason that we've got to endure this. . . ."

When they finished eating, Matsu led the women in prayer. They could tell that the men were also praying in the adjoining room.

Their first night in Tsuwano was bitterly cold. Since there were elderly people and children in the group, the officers gave them old, threadbare bedding instead of tiny rugs, but even when they snuggled under them, the chill pierced their skin as the night deepened.

"I'm cold! I'm so cold!!" Children clung to their mothers; old men coughed incessantly. That was how the first night passed for these 125. But the women took courage from their joy at being in the same location as their husbands and fathers.

Three months later—

Everyone was on the verge of starvation. With the scant daily ration of three-quarters of a cup of rice and the remonstrations to apostatize that were heaped on each member of the family day after day, the bodies of the elderly were the first to weaken.

According to the historical records, thirty-one of the 125 new prisoners, equivalent to one-quarter of the total, had died within a mere sixteen months of their arrival. One in four died of starvation. Their single greatest tormentor was hunger.

As an aside, an examination of the death records reveals that nearly twice as many men as women died there—twelve women and twenty-two men. A significant percentage of those who died were elderly, with twelve of them being over the age of fifty, along with seven deaths among those in their twenties and thirties. This may indicate that many of the prisoners were in these age brackets and that the tortures were concentrated on them.

Nearly every day, entire families were summoned for questioning. They were most likely interrogated in groups because the officers were fully aware of the Japanese tendency to act as a family unit, with either the entire family apostatizing or all of them maintaining their faith.

In the early stages, no matter how much they were persuaded, everyone staunchly refused to change. At that point, the officers merely responded, "I see. Well, think it over carefully."

The officers knew from previous experience that some time would have to pass before they would hear screams come from the Kirishitans. Over time, the daily ration of three-quarters of a cup of food would sap the Kirishitans' physical strength and their wills, so the best plan was to wait patiently until their energy had drained away.

Winter came to an end and spring arrived.

Because it's surrounded by mountains, spring in Tsuwano is heralded by cotton-hued clouds that drift lightly over Mount Aono and Shiroyama. Unlike winter clouds, these are neither cold nor ashen in color.

Then a spring mist rises over the mountains, and the locals make preparations to gather bracken and wild plants. They begin commenting that the cherry blossoms at the horse-riding track of the Washihara Hachiman Shrine have changed color. These are the first intimations of spring in Tsuwano.

Toward the end of spring, with a call of "Greetings!" Itō Seizaemon, back after a long absence, showed his face at the cell holding Sen'emon, Kanzaburō, Seikichi, and the others. Behind him stood the two policemen, Takahashi and Deguchi, now assuming roles as his henchmen, their faces still looking respectively like a raccoon dog and a badger.

"You're a stubborn bunch! What's the point of making so much trouble for me and the Tsuwano domain? Don't you think it's about time you put an end to this nonsense and went back home to Urakami?" Itō grinned cynically as he looked around at the men. "I have to thank you for all the trouble you've caused me."

He flung down the oil paper-wrapped package he held in his hand. "Seikichi," he called. "This is a letter from your girl in Maruyama. Want to read it? If you do, all you have to say is that you'll give up your Kirishitan beliefs." He spoke half in jest and kicked the package toward Seikichi. Wrapped in paper that Kiku had made herself were a letter, a summer robe, and some bleached cloth. But Itō did not give Seikichi the money that Kiku had earned.

That evening, Itō used the money that Kiku had sent for Seikichi to treat Takahashi and Deguchi at a grimy little restaurant from which they could hear the flow of the Nishiki River.

"Drink up! No need to be timid!"

"This is very unusual, having Mr. Itō buy for us!"

The three men, their faces vivid red, repeatedly went outside to urinate along the bank of the Nishiki River, then came back into the restaurant.

"Take a look at this! This coin here, this coin is no bogus battle coin!" He pulled a gold one-*ryo* coin from his pocket and held it out for the others to see. During the fighting preceding the Meiji Restoration, the armies of the Satsuma and Chōshū domains were in need of war funds and had issued emergency coins that, though now worthless, remained in circulation; the public called them "bogus battle coins."

"It's an honest-to-goodness gold coin! This coin . . . this coin was earned through the hard labors of . . . the hard labors of Seikichi's woman . . . to give to Seikichi." He stared unblinking at the coin. "You and I are having these drinks right now . . . thanks to this money!" he muttered mostly to himself.

Takahashi laughed, "Mr. Itō, you're quite the man! After all, it's against the law to give money to a Kirishitan."

"Yeah . . . but don't forget that we're knocking drinks back . . . on money that a woman made selling her body." Then Itō glared angrily at Takahashi and Deguchi. "That's the kind of black-hearted bastards we are! We're men who drink our liquor by stomping on women's hearts."

"Mr. Itō, what're you saying? That we're no better than villains?"

"And are you suggesting I'm some kind of saint?!" Inflamed by drink, Itō continued, "I've stolen the money that Seikichi's woman earned for him. That's the kind of wretch I am."

"You're drunk. Let's get out of here."

"Lemme alone! I loathe the kind of man I am. But it's too late to change. I was born this way. You can't change a man's nature. . . ."

Takahashi hastily tried to calm Itō down. "A man responsible for handling these Kirishitans can only damage his position by blubbering like this. C'mon, let's go!"

But Itō remained with his head bowed and made no effort to stand. He could almost picture that room lit by the afternoon sun, and the face of Kiku as she lay beneath his body, staring at a point in space, waiting for it all to be over.

"Damned weepy woman!" He tried using disgust to sweep the image of Kiku's face from his memory. He had remembered the single thread of pale tears that had flowed slowly from her eyes.

A sharp pain raced through his heart.

"Another drink!" He drank more to mask the pain in his heart. Takahashi and Deguchi watched him with fear in their eyes.

One strange trait of this man named Itō was the fact that even though the previous night he had been wracked with guilt and emotional pain, the very next day he would harness that same measure of pain and use it to torment the prisoners.

The morning after Itō got drunk on the money Kiku had entrusted to him and then bought a prostitute, he poked his head into the women's cell and, pointing to a young mother holding an infant on her lap, said, "You there! Come outside, will you?"

He chose this woman because something about her reminded him of Kiku. She was from Motohara, and her husband had been one of the men brought here along with Sen'emon and the others, but he had apostatized some time ago and was no longer around.

Itō made the woman sit on the bamboo-floored veranda and shouted at her, "So which do you choose: your husband or your Kirishitan beliefs?" Part of his strategy hinged on his knowledge that a person's legs became agonizingly painful after sitting formally on this bamboo floor for a long while. "Will it be your husband? Or your Lord Jezusu? Of course, choosing Jezusu over your husband is the height of infidelity! Are you going to be faithless to your husband and still choose your Jezusu?"

His logic was preposterous, but at this moment Itō cared nothing for logic.

"Take off your clothes! Strip down!!"

When he saw the startled look on the young mother's face and the fact that he had rendered her speechless, Itō was gripped by an urge to inflict even greater pain on her, and he hollered, "Don't expect me to pamper you people. If I treat you kindly, you'll turn into a bunch of spoiled shit-kickers. What makes you shit-kickers think you can go against your superiors?!"

Itō's furious shouts were audible to all the prisoners incarcerated at the temple.

"Take off the underskirt too!" Itō callously ordered the woman, who squirmed and clutched her infant to her body.

"Are you embarrassed? Lord Jezusu will hide your nakedness, so there's nothing to be embarrassed about. I'll bet your husband would be delighted to see you in this disgusting posture!"

When the young mother began to weep loudly, the child she held also began to wail as though he had been set afire.

"So, will you forsake you faith . . . ? How about it? If you do, I won't make you take off your underskirt."

Like a cat tormenting a mouse, Itō sat with his chin in his hand, staring down at the sobbing woman.

"What's your choice?"

Still sobbing, she answered in a low voice. "I . . . I will . . . give up my faith."

"Splendid! You should have said that sooner."

That night, Itō drank himself into a stupor at the Daruma House and said agonizingly to the prostitute beside him, "Would you be kind enough to spit in my face?"

"Why?!"

"Because I'm . . . I'm the sort of man who ought to have his face spit into. Again today I did something terrible to a woman," he muttered, his face twisted in pain.

THE BLESSED AND THE UNBLESSED

SUMMER APPROACHED.

There are those in this world who are blessed by fortune and those whose fortunes seem cursed. Some achieve acclaim, while others cannot find success in the world and merely squirm in the mud.

These two types were evident in the differences between Itō Seizaemon and Hondō Shuntarō. Shuntarō attracted the notice of Count Iwakura and ascended to a post as an official in the Ministry of Foreign Affairs, but Itō never became anything other than a low-level administrator at the Nishi Bureau who spent his days shuttling back and forth between Tsuwano and Nagasaki.

Would I be better off getting myself involved in this revolt?

Such thoughts crossed Itō's mind from time to time as he pillowed his face on a prostitute's wispy chest.

The various branches of the military in Chōshū domain had been ordered to demobilize because of economic exigencies, but some of the soldiers had risen up in revolt, which in turn ignited an insurrection among the samurai in northern Kyushu who had harbored pent-up resentment toward the new government. It was an explosion of malcontent among those who had fallen behind the times and had not attained success in the new society. The third year of the Meiji era, 1870, was a time of many tests for the new government as it tried to solidify a foundation for its rule.

"I wonder what that Hondō fellow is doing up in Yokohama."

Itō could not stand the thought that Hondō was now of such stature that he could amuse himself with first-class geisha at first-class houses while he was stuck here in the mountains enclosing Tsuwano, swatting away mosquitoes as he slept with this flat-chested whore.

"What was your name again?"

"Hideko."

"With shriveled breasts like these, there's nothing for a baby to latch onto," Itō belittled the prostitute. He thought of Kiku's beautiful round breasts and strawberry nipples. "Ah, I want to get back to Nagasaki! They must already be celebrating the Kiyomizu Temple festival."

Nagasaki hosted a variety of festivals from season to season. The sixth month marked the advent of the Gion Festival[1] and the start of the Thousand-Day Festival at the Kiyomizu Temple.[2] Custom dictated that the streets along Shin-shikkui-machi and Imashikkui-machi near the road to the shrine be purified by the hanging of sacred ropes and *sakaki* evergreens, and each house prepared to welcome guests with dishes of raw fish and vegetables seasoned in vinegar and *mochi* that had been frozen and dried.

As he recalled those celebrations, Itō Seizaemon missed them so desperately he was at the point of tears.

Around the time of the Gion Festival, in Nagasaki—

At long last, Shuntarō bought out Oyō's contract with the Yamazaki Teahouse, and she boarded a ship bound for Yokohama.

It was swelteringly hot that day, but the madam, Kiku, and several other women from the teahouse set out to the dock to send off Oyō, whose face shone with joy. Male attendants had already loaded her baggage onto a tiny skiff at the dock.

With a smile, Oyō tried to buoy up Kiku. "Kiku, I know something good is going to happen to you soon, so just be patient, OK?"

Gazing out at the ocean lit by rays of the sun spilling between the clouds, Kiku nodded her head.

Something good is going to happen.

But she had no news of Seikichi. Had Itō actually given her letter and money to him?

1. The Gion Festival originally provided an opportunity to pray for protection from plagues, for tranquillity at home, and for peace in the nation. Night stalls selling a variety of wares were set up around the Yasaka Shrine, and on the fourteenth and fifteenth, the courtesans of Maruyama formed a procession to worship there.

2. Popular legend had it that an individual who made a pilgrimage to the Kiyomizu Temple to worship Kannon on this day would receive merits equivalent to 46,000 days of worship.

There are those in this world who are blessed by fortune and those who are not. As she looked at Oyō, Kiku felt just as Itō had toward Shuntarō.

Oyō stepped into the little skiff and waved her hand at those who had come to see her off. The skiff would transport her to the black steamship that waited in the offing. And the steamship would deliver her to her beloved, Hondō Shuntarō.

Oyō's white face beamed with happiness. Shafts of sunlight seeping between the clouds warmed her back, and as she slowly pulled away from the wharf she smiled cheerfully, bowing her head toward these friends she would miss seeing.

"Well, she's gone," the madam sighed as the skiff receded into the distance. "She's going to be so happy. Lord Hondō fell for her, and now she'll be marrying into wealth and status. One day she'll find herself the wife of an important government official."

The madam started out walking, and the others followed along behind her. But Kiku remained standing at the wharf, looking out toward the silvery ocean in the offing. Oyō, setting off toward happiness. She was incredibly envious.

"Kiku!" Someone called her name. When she turned around, one of the male attendants who had delivered Oyō's baggage to the boat was standing there. It was the yellow-toothed man she had met on the streets of Maruyama before she started working at the Yamazaki Teahouse. He was one of those men always skulking around the Maruyama district looking for odd jobs that would bring in a little spending money.

"Kiku, have you made up your mind that you want to become a *geiko*?" he asked with a smirk. "I'm sure you've figured out why the madam at the Yamazaki lent you two *ryo* in cash? She's setting you up so you'll be stuck there when you can't pay back the loan."

Kiku looked up at the man in surprise. Why would this little hoodlum know about that? It was true, though, that she had borrowed two *ryo* from the madam. Before Itō Seizaemon left for Tsuwano, he promised he would pass it along to Seikichi.

"Of course, if you want Seikichi's life to be made easier, he'll have to provide a little gift to the officials in Tsuwano. Probably take two or three gold coins." Seizaemon had stroked his chin as he mumbled the words. The madam lent her the two *ryo* out of sympathy.

"That two *ryo* comes with interest, you know," the hoodlum said softly. "Two becomes three *ryo*, and then the three snowballs into four. You'll be way over your head by then. What are you going to do, Kiku?"

She had no response.

"Listen, I know a way for you to earn that two *ryo*."

Still nothing from Kiku.

"I'm telling you the truth. And in only two nights of work!"

"What . . . would I have to do?"

"You just need to come to the Nakajuku brokerage house in Honkago-machi. Actually, there's this rich Chinese fellow . . . One look at you and he'll be ready to explode! All you have to do is be his companion. He'll give you the two *ryo*."

Kiku angrily set out walking. Just what kind of person does he think I am?!

Once her anger had subsided, she was filled with a loneliness that almost led her to tears. Ever since Itō had taken everything from her, she knew exactly how she was viewed by the madam and the others.

Each time she had found herself in Itō's arms, she had plunged another level. She had been plummeting to the depths of the earth, from which she would never be able to crawl her way back to Seikichi's world. This was still the most painful of all for Kiku.

That field of flowers, blanketed with lotus flowers. Her youth, when skylarks had shrieked through the skies. Those mornings in early summer when she waited, her heart pounding, to hear Seikichi's voice from the distance as he advertised his wares. Where had it all gone?

She wanted to be by herself. Gradually she fell behind the group that was following the madam as they returned from the dock, then suddenly slipped away between two houses. Once everyone had disappeared in the direction of Maruyama, she began walking down the road along the waterfront.

She had no destination in mind. Because she had nowhere in particular to go, her feet began to lead her toward Ōura, a place that was crowded with memories for her.

The steamship was still just barely visible in the offing. Surely Oyō had already reached and boarded that ship.

Kiku deliberately averted her eyes from the ship. It was too painful for her to look at a symbol of happiness that was forever beyond her grasp.

The Ōura Church was directly above. The church Seikichi had attended. The church where Petitjean and Laucaigne had treated her with such kindness. But she knew full well that she was no longer the sort of person who could look those missionaries in the eye.

She approached the church, careful that no one saw her. The tranquillity of afternoon reigned over the fields and farmhouses adjacent to the church.

She gently pushed the heavy door open and peeked inside. It was exceedingly quiet in there as well. Only that woman's statue stood forlornly next to the altar.

Kiku looked at the woman sorrowfully and muttered, "It's me. You remember me, don't you?"

Kiku resumed the kind of solitary monologue beside the statue that she had so often recited in the past.

"You must remember Seikichi, too. Right now Seikichi is suffering horribly every day, but you do nothing for him. But I'm no different. I can't do anything for him either. It's sad. So very sad! I can't do a thing for him. . . ."

She paused and bit her lip. "All I could do for Seikichi was . . . was make a little money to send him. But to get the money . . . I had to disgrace my body."

Kiku would never forget the terrible, stinging pain and humiliation she experienced the first time Itō Seizaemon climbed on top of her.

"You . . . you don't know anything about that kind of pain, do you? You . . . you never had a man do that to you, did you?"

Just then, she heard the faint sound of footsteps. Kiku quickly hid herself behind a column. At a time like this, she did not want to meet Petitjean or Laucaigne.

But it wasn't either of the priests. A shabby-looking man appeared from behind the creaking door, and behind him a woman stepped quietly into the chapel.

Mitsu . . . !

Kiku nearly cried out in surprise. It was definitely Mitsu who was walking behind the man toward the altar.

Neither she nor the man realized that Kiku was watching them as they knelt before the statue of the Blessed Mother Mary. The man lifted his head and crossed himself, after which Mitsu imitated him and clumsily moved her hands in the shape of a cross.

"Hail Mary, full of grace, the Lord is with thee . . ." The man spoke the prayer that all the Kirishitans invoked to the Blessed Mother, but Mitsu apparently had not yet memorized the prayer and was silent.

Even after he finished praying, the man remained where he was for a long while, his drooping head supported by both hands. Looking at his despondent posture, Kiku sensed that the man carried a heavy burden in his heart, though she couldn't imagine what it was.

"You don't need to punish yourself anymore," Mitsu tried to console the man. "Someday they'll understand how you feel. Sometime I'll tell them how long you've suffered such terrible guilt for what you did."

"Even if they all forgive me, Deus won't forgive me."

"How do you know that? Even if he won't, though, this Mary you believe in will smooth things over for you with Lord Deus. You've always said that Mary is the mother of all people. . . ."

"She is."

"If she's a mother, then there's no way she can just ignore her children when they're suffering. No mother can turn a deaf ear to the pleas of her own child."

Kiku had never heard the Mitsu she knew speak with such intensity. Mitsu was trying so desperately to console this man.

Since their childhood together, Mitsu had never been able to turn away from anything pitiful or unfortunate that she encountered. She was the type who would hide her own food and give it to stray dogs or cats, no matter how much her brother or Kiku reprimanded her. With that same intensity she was now trying to comfort this man. . . .

"Let's go," the man muttered as he got to his feet.

"Mitsu!" Kiku could no longer stifle her feelings of affection for Mitsu and finally called out. In astonishment, both Mitsu and the man turned toward her. When she recognized a smiling Kiku standing beside the column, Mitsu's eyes widened and she cried, "What! What are you doing here? Kiku, oh, I've searched and searched for you! Ichijirō's been going all over the place trying to find out where you are. He's come here again and again . . . But the foreigners always just shake their heads. . . ."

Kiku dodged Mitsu's unspoken question. "You're looking well. I hear you're still working at the Gotōya."

Monotonously the waves nipped at the shore, then retreated. The steamship that had until just minutes before floated in the offing had now carried a blissful Oyō out of sight. The canopy of gray rain clouds broke open, and light from the sun steamed on the surface of the sea.

"So . . . have you decided you want to marry him?" Kiku asked Mitsu, glancing toward Kumazō, who was sitting on the shore a ways away from them with his head bowed. "Of course, you've talked to your brother and your parents about it, right?"

Mitsu shook her head. "No. Even if I did talk to them, they wouldn't approve of him. . . . That's kind of what I've assumed, so I haven't said anything to them."

"That's so like you. You've always been the sort of girl who can't bring herself to turn away somebody you feel sorry for. . . ."

"I just feel like if I can do even a little something to help take the pain from his heart . . ."

"Funny, isn't it? You and I never imagined we'd wind up in these relationships with Kirishitan men. . . ." Kiku scooped up some sand in her palm, and as she let it trickle through her fingers, she said earnestly, "We both have pretty difficult associations with our men, don't we?"

"Yeah. But, Kiku, where in Maruyama are you working?"

"It's better not to ask," Kiku said forlornly. "I've ended up in a place you're better off not knowing anything about. I'm not like you anymore—I'm a filthy woman."

"A filthy woman?"

Anxiety clouded Kiku's brow as she let the sand slip from between her fingers. "Kiku, don't you feel like coming back to Magome?"

"No, I don't. There's no reason to go back home. I mean, I don't regret what I've done." Kiku said with determination as she stared at the offing. "I don't regret it. After I fell in love with Seikichi, I became a filthy woman just so I could help him, so I don't feel bad about it. I believe with all my heart that a woman wants to do anything for the man she loves. You understand that feeling, don't you?"

Mitsu nodded. All she had to do to understand how Kiku felt was to compare her own situation with that of a passionate woman like Kiku and she could visualize what would happen when such a woman fell in love with a man. Kiku brushed the sand off her lap and stood up.

"I've got to get back to the house. It gets very busy in Maruyama at night. And I bet you'll be in trouble with the Mistress at the Gotōya if you don't get back, too."

"I'll see you again, won't I, Kiku?" Mitsu asked uneasily. Kiku gave a sisterly smile and said, "I'm not sure. I might end up going to Tsuwano. 'Bye!"

"'Bye!" And with that, Kiku began the climb up the road from the beach without even looking behind her. Mitsu understood that Kiku did not turn back to look at her from want of feeling but because she was determined to devote herself completely to her love.

Summer came. In Nagasaki, summer nights are almost unbearably hot. There is absolutely no breeze, and it is hard to sleep even in the middle of the night.

A famous event in Nagasaki, when boats are floated on the water as offerings to the spirits of the dead,[3] is held on one of those humid summer nights. On the fourteenth of the seventh month, families spread straw mats on the ground in temple cemeteries throughout the city and hold drinking parties, then eat a dish called *p'eihsin* and agar-agar formed into the shape of a plate, which they also present as offerings at the family grave sites. From midnight of the following day, the harbor is jammed with crowds of people.

Many people place lighted candles in their "spirit boats" and release them into the sea. The myriad lights—jostling on the waves, then hidden by the waves, then floating atop the waves—create an indescribably beautiful world of illusion.

---

3. This ritual is the Nagasaki version of the famous Obon celebrations held throughout Japan in the summer. Interestingly, it was only one year after this story took place that the Meiji government banned the floating of these boats in Nagasaki Bay, citing some deaths among those who towed the boats through the water, as well as instances of the candles in the boats starting fires in ships docked in the harbor.

That evening, the customers at the Yamazaki Teahouse took the madam and her *geiko* to watch the floating of the spirit boats, while Kiku was left behind to care for the house.

The heat was so stifling that she broke into a sweat even when she tried to stay perfectly still. She finished doing the wash, sat down on the step leading to the entryway, and turned her thoughts vaguely toward Tsuwano.

This heat! They said Tsuwano sat in a mountain basin, so it might be even hotter than Nagasaki. How intolerable it must be in their cell! With that thought, in deference to Seikichi she lost all desire to cool herself with a fan and simply endured the rivulets of perspiration that coursed down her cheeks.

She heard a sound. Someone was coming into the house unannounced. Caught off guard, she stood up.

"It's me." With a broad grin on his ruddy face, Itō Seizaemon entered. "Did I surprise you? I got back from Tsuwano a couple of days ago. I wanted to come see you right away, but I didn't have time. I can't believe how hot it is for Obon this year. The crowds at the dock just now were overwhelming, but I ran into your madam there. When I heard you were here holding down the shop all by yourself, I came hurrying over. Would you get me some water? My throat's so dry!"

He gulped down the cup of water Kiku hurriedly brought to him and said, "Now some saké too!"

"OK. But I'll bring it to you here. We're not going upstairs."

As Kiku scurried to get him a bottle, he scanned her body from the top of her head to the ends of her toes and said, "Here's just fine. You don't have to treat me like a customer. But you're still a fine-looking woman, you know. After nothing but sluts stinking of horse dung to sleep with in Tsuwano, there's too many beautiful women to choose from back here in Nagasaki."

"Umm . . ." As she heated the bottle of saké over the oblong hibachi, Kiku softly asked, "About the letter and the money . . ."

"I gave it to him. The letter and the two *ryo* . . . I put them right into your fellow's hands. Not even someone like me is supposed to do that sort of thing, so I went out of my way for you."

"And did Seikichi give you any kind of—?"

"Reply? That's not allowed. No, no reply." Itō shifted his gaze away from Kiku, perhaps ashamed at his lie, and snapped almost angrily. "Where's my saké?"

He began drinking in silence. It was hot in the room, and raucous shouts could be heard from the distance. Unsightly sweat coursed down Itō's rust-colored face.

Normally after a few drinks, Itō's bloodshot eyes would steal over Kiku's back, and he would stretch out his arms and pull her body to the floor.

But he had made no advances yet tonight. For some time he sat deep in thought, nursing his drink with the cup pressed against his lips. In the light of the lantern his bat-like figure cast an unsightly shadow on the wall.

"Listen." As though he had made up his mind to something, he gulped down the saliva in his mouth and called to Kiku. "If I'm going to continue treating Seikichi kindly . . . it's going to take some money."

He muttered the words almost to himself alone. Kiku listened without responding.

"The Tsuwano domain has three interrogating officers—Chiba, Morioka, and Kanamori. And then there's the Shinto priest, Saeki. If I'm going to ask those four to take it a little easy on Seikichi, I can't go to them empty-handed. I think you understand what I'm saying. . . ."

Since Kiku still said nothing, he continued, "Normally it'd take ten *ryo*, but with just five I'll somehow manage to persuade them. . . . If five is impossible, three *ryo* would work. You can wrap up one *ryo* for each of the three officers. . . . Don't think you can get that much? Remember, it's all for Seikichi."

Having said that, he began knocking down one drink after another to drown his own guilty conscience.

Shrieks of delight sounded in the distance again. By now an endless number of spirit boats were probably floating and drifting and sparkling like the lights from a swarm of fireflies in Nagasaki Bay.

Sweat poured down Itō's drunken face.

"What do you say? Don't you think you can make three *ryo* for Seikichi? I'm not saying it has to be right away. As long as you've got it when I go back to Tsuwano at the end of autumn. Winter comes early in Tsuwano, you know. And winters must be awfully tough on those men."

Kiku listened to Itō's menacing words with her eyes shut. She didn't know how much she could trust him. But she had no choice but to rely on this man in order to make life easier for Seikichi.

Behind her closed eyes hovered the image of the statue of the Blessed Mother in the Ōura Church.

Kiku. Please help Seikichi. You haven't done enough yet. Those men are suffering for you, so there's still more for you to do. How can you sit here doing nothing, keeping your body undefiled while they suffer so?

Keeping my body undefiled??! She wanted to throw the words back at the Blessed Mother Mary. *Some women in this world can't ever attain love without defiling their bodies. You don't know anything about the suffering of those women! They say you lived your whole life a virgin, so you never had to sleep with a man who sickened you. You've never been groped by a disgusting man, never been toyed with by a disgusting man, never been soiled to the very depths of your body by a disgusting man!*

"I'll . . . I'll somehow come up with the money," Kiku whispered.

"You will? You know . . . ," Itō said with relief, "you're a good woman. I'm honestly jealous of Seikichi for having your love." He spoke almost out of character.

Still, it wasn't long before he placed his hand on Kiku's shoulder. Pushed onto her back, Kiku looked blankly, emotionlessly into the face above her that breathed fiercely.

"I'll . . . I'll somehow come up with the money."

No, not "somehow." If Seikichi was going to be treated harshly this winter in Tsuwano unless she did something, then she must find a way to raise the three *ryo*.

She would borrow it from the madam. But she'd already borrowed two *ryo* from her. Whatever the madam's true intentions might be in lending her the money, it pained her to ask to borrow even more when she had no idea how to repay it. That obnoxious man she met on the street once told her that the madam planned to bind her with debt, but Kiku simply couldn't bring herself to believe that.

What should I do?

For a woman like Kiku with no other viable options, there was only one possible way. Out of love, she would have to surrender her body, to offer herself as a sacrifice. . . .

That night, after Itō had left, the madam came back to the house with a group of customers and *geiko*. They drank and played the samisen until deep into the night, then finally went to bed.

Strangely, Kiku felt no hesitation or indecision. . . .

"Really?!" The following day, after the man heard what Kiku had to say, he scratched his chest and said, "That's fine! But if you want to become a *geiko*, it'll end up costing you a lot of money because of the way the Maruyama quarter operates. It'd be simplest if you became a companion to the Tang fellow I told you about." The man offered no further explanation, but he was obviously referring to a Chinese resident of Nagasaki; the Chinese were still collectively referred to as "Tangs" in the early years of the Meiji period.[4]

During the Edo period, the Chinese, like the Dutch in Dejima, were confined to one predetermined section of the city, and for a time they were prohibited from wandering at will outside their quarter. The Japanese referred to the quarter as the "Chinese Estates" or the "Chinese Settlement." But with the end of the Edo period and the transition into Meiji, this restrictive segregation was eliminated.

"So, when can you come to the Nakajuku brokerage house?"

---

4. In Japanese, *Tōjin*—literally, a "person from Tang-dynasty China"—but the word came to have pejorative connotations.

The Nakajuku brokerage house was located in what was once called Honkago-machi; it was the rendezvous spot for prostitutes who had authorization to work inside the Chinese Estates. Since both the Chinese and the Dutch were barred from entering Maruyama in search of entertainment, it became the practice for a restricted number of prostitutes to go to the brokerage house and wait for a call from a customer.

"I'm busy every night," Kiku answered quietly. "The only time I can leave the teahouse is during the day."

The man replied that he would have to consult with his client. "You'll be paid one *ryo* for a single night as his companion. And you won't have to spend time with other clients, so it's the best possible situation for you. My client is ridiculously rich, so it doesn't get any better than this!" He went on to boast about how he had gotten to know the Chinese man.

On the afternoon of the appointed day, Kiku left the Yamazaki Teahouse under the pretense that she was going shopping and set out in search of the brokerage house at Nakajuku. The man was standing in front of a Chinese temple known as the Dojindō, located in Kannai-machi.

The distinctive smell of the Chinese filled the neighborhood: pork, oil, incense, and garlic. They all blended together to produce an odor that had permeated the houses and even the streets.

"Kiku, I'm over here!" The man raised a bony arm from his worn-out kimono.

The histories say that originally this Chinese Settlement was enclosed by a bamboo fence or, at times, a moat, and that traffic through the main or inner gate was closely supervised. But such precautions had been done away with by the beginning of the Meiji period.

Although the restrictions had been lifted, the atmosphere in the Chinese quarter was utterly different from that in Maruyama. The brilliant vermilion colors of such buildings as the Dokōshi, the Kanteibyō, and the Kannondō were unusual, as were the rows of tiny shops selling Chinese liquors and confections, each with signs written in characters that Kiku could not decipher. She could hear the sound of flutes being played inside those shops.

"My Chinese client doesn't know much Japanese," the man said, walking along with his hands in his pockets. "It'd be a good idea for you to learn some Chinese words."

"What sorts of words?"

"Our clients here are called *shinkan-san*. *Shinkan-san* means 'an important person.' 'What would you like?' is *in-mou?* 'Good woman' is *ei-gii.*"

The man taught her several Chinese words of dubious accuracy that he had picked up secondhand, but Kiku had no wish to exert herself to listen to them. Her head was filled with thoughts only of the three *ryo* that Itō Seizaemon had demanded of her.

They went into one of the shops. It displayed a skillfully penned sign reading, "The Kōgei Pavilion," but Kiku could not read it.

The man nodded his head toward a young Chinese man sipping tea inside the shop and introduced him to Kiku. "This fellow will act as your interpreter. . . . I have to go now, but I'm leaving everything to him, so you've got nothing to worry about."

The young Chinese set down his teacup and said to Kiku, "Your client is upstairs. He's there waiting for you."

"Yes, sir."

He led her upstairs. A plump Chinese man with a healthy complexion sat in a room with an open window, fanning himself with a large fan and sipping tea.

"Can you read?" the young Chinese asked Kiku.

"No."

"This gentleman says he wants to talk with you by writing down his questions and your answers. . . ."

The customer held out a piece of paper for Kiku to see.

"敢問娘子尊名."

"What in the world does that mean?" Confounded, Kiku asked the young man.

"He's asking what your name is."

"Kiku."

The customer nodded casually, and again his brush scurried across the paper.

"青是多少. 容貌票至生得出塵."

"He's asking how old you are, and he says you're charming."

The sounds of the Chinese quarter streamed through the open window. The ocean was visible beyond the quarter.

As the young man and the client exchanged words incomprehensible to Kiku, she stared out at the ocean and suddenly thought of Oyō. What feelings did Oyō experience as she looked out at the ocean alongside Yokohama?

As the saying goes, Oyō was spending each day "enfolded in flowers of happiness."

Yokohama. Although it was a harbor town just like Nagasaki, it was more alive with energy. The masts of foreign ships in the harbor lined up like trees in a grove, and while some cargo was unloaded, other cargo was loaded onto the ships, and at the pier and elsewhere sailors and boatmen swaggered about. They were surrounded by row upon row of stalls set up by the Japanese to cater to the foreigners.

The sounds of active building construction echoed from many quarters. These were the sounds of sledgehammers knocking down old, dilapidated Japanese houses before erecting foreign-looking buildings in their place. Those sounds, so novel they seemed to waft the fragrance of new wood through the neighborhood, were an audible announcement that a new age was dawning.

The breeze blew invigoratingly through the second floor windows of the house on the bluff that Hondō had rented for Oyō. Pointing toward the ships and the sea, Hondō said cheerfully, "Look! From now on, our eyes have to be focused in that direction. By 'that direction,' I mean the wide ocean. America lies across that ocean. And there's England and France. I know you're a woman, but . . . but it's exactly because you're a woman that it won't be enough for you in the future to just study sewing and housekeeping. I've heard that our leaders are considering sending several of the daughters of former daimyo to America to have them learn about their customs and manners and language."

"Sending young women to . . . to America?" Oyō's eyes opened wide in surprise. In Nagasaki where Oyō was raised, it used to be that the only young women who went to foreign countries were those who were sold into prostitution.

"That's right. It's so they can learn things over there and then teach them to the women of Japan."

"And will these young ladies be traveling on the same ship as you?" Oyō asked, feeling faintly apprehensive. Next year, Hondō would be journeying to America with Prince Iwakura Tomomi. Oyō was jealous that he would be making the long voyage in the company of young women.

"Well, I don't know," he simpered. "Does that bother you?"

"Yes. It didn't take you long to make moves on me," Oyō chuckled, remembering those days.

"Don't you worry. We've pledged ourselves to each other as husband and wife. I have no women but you."

That seems almost too good to be true, Oyō thought, but still it made her happy. Because Hondō had such a large body and a childlike face, she had not imagined he would be so energetically amorous, but she was provided every night with evidence of how exceedingly lecherous he actually was.

"In the middle of the day . . . ?" When she tried to rebuff him as he suddenly plunged one chubby hand down the front of her kimono, he rejoined with a magisterial look on his face, "We're husband and wife, aren't we? I've got to stock up, after all. Once I go to America, we won't be able to do this for a year or more. So we've got to build up a surplus while we have the chance!"

As he fondled her nipple, Oyō narrowed her eyes like a cat. She had already forgotten the jealousy she had felt only moments before. And most certainly there was not a single trace of a memory in her mind of that girl at the Yamazaki Teahouse in Nagasaki named Kiku. Oyō was so intoxicated with her own joy. . . .

OTOME PASS

ANOTHER AUTUMN CAME to Tsuwano. The foliage atop Otome Pass,[1] which rose to the rear of the temple compound, gradually changed colors, and from their cells the prisoners watched each day with anxious eyes as the autumn leaves eventually turned a deep amber.

The prisoners knew the bitterness of winters in Tsuwano to the very cores of their bones. The end of summer and the coming of autumn represented a palpable threat to them.

Some made preparations to stave off the cold of winter by taking the single sheets of paper they were given each day and pasting them together with rice grains to make something resembling paper garments. They thought that something of that nature might help ward off the cold just a bit.

Around the time the chill of late autumn started taking an increasingly greater toll on their bodies, the officers inflicted a particularly gruesome torture on one young man.

They selected a juvenile rather than one of the adults to torment in an attempt to strike fear into the hearts of the other prisoners, to weaken their resolve, and to push them to the point of apostasy.

The young man's name was Yūjirō. He was the younger brother of Kanzaburō and Matsu, and at the time he was fifteen years old.

"You're being punished like this because your brother and sister are too pigheaded. So if you're going to hate anybody, hate your brother and sister." With that, the officer stripped Yūjirō naked, bound his hands behind his back, and sat

1. The word *otome* means "maiden, virgin."

him down on a bamboo-floored veranda. The prisoners knew that a person's legs and knees would begin to ache after sitting this way for a long time, and that the pain would grow progressively unbearable.

But the object of the officials in using this particular mode of torture was not merely to coerce the young man to abandon his faith, but also to force his parents to listen to his screams.

"Heat up the bathwater!" The officer intentionally chose Yūjirō's brother, Kanzaburō, to stoke the fires under the bath that day. The opening where the fires were kindled was near the bamboo veranda, and from where Kanzaburō crouched to perform his assignment, the shouts of the officer and the wails of his younger brother were acutely audible.

"Are you hungry? Cold? Embarrassed to be sitting there naked? But we're not finished yet! We've whipped up a real feast, and we want you to have your fill of it!"

At an order from the officer, Takahashi and Deguchi took turns beating the boy with whips.

"That's not real whipping! Don't hold back thinking he's a child! Put all your strength into it!!" The officer rebuked the two men for taking their victim's youthful age into consideration. Eventually a brutally aberrant light flashed in Takahashi's oval eyes and Deguchi's sunken eyes as they flailed Yūjirō with their whips.

With his hands bound behind him and his body lashed to a pillar, Yūjirō writhed and howled—"Ah! Ah! Ah!"—each time the whips gave a dull crack in the air and then smacked against his head or back or arms. Kanzaburō heard each of his brother's shrieks as he heated up the bathwater. He gritted his teeth and shut his eyes tightly to bear up under the agony. Throughout all of this, in her cell where a stony silence prevailed, Yūjirō's sister Matsu, encircled by all the other women, buried her face in her hands and prayed earnestly for her brother.

"Still no effect?!"

The tips of the whips that Takahashi and Deguchi took turns swinging at Yūjirō tore into his nose and mouth. When his nose and mouth were completely swathed in blood, even the officer had to avert his eyes and exclaim, "That's enough!" He spoke to Yūjirō. "Yūjirō, you have until tomorrow to think this over carefully. If you haven't changed your mind tomorrow, you'll be in for worse than you got today."

That night, a stark-naked Yūjirō remained tied to the pillar and exposed to the frigid air of late autumn.

The next day, and the day after, and the day after that—

Yūjirō remained, naked and bound, sprawled atop the bamboo veranda. His cries during the tortures each evening made it known that the young man's body was weakening with each passing day owing to the bitter nights and the daily beatings. The screams he emitted as he was struck and kicked gradually grew fainter and fainter.

From time to time, however, the other prisoners would hear him let out a blood-curdling scream, a tear-choked wail that sounded like an infant being set to the torch. The officers had poured water on the boy and then beat him with whips.

Even after the tortures were finished for the day, an endless stream of low moans could be heard. A cold rain fell throughout the night, and the groaning never ceased amid the darkness and the freezing rain.

On the fourteenth day of torture—

"Quick! Summon Lord Morioka!" The officers had panicked for some reason and rushed off to call an authority. Eventually the official appeared, and a discussion was held.

"Matsu!" Takahashi and Deguchi poked their heads into the women's cell. "Your brother's sick. Go move him." They scurried away.

Three or four women raced alongside Matsu to the courtyard. There they saw the pitiful sight of the boy, stretched out on the bamboo veranda like a grub worm.

His entire body had swollen up a sickly blue color, dark splotches of blood clung everywhere to him, and in some places they could see purple bruises where he had hemorrhaged. His face, too, was swollen, reducing his eyes to threadlike slits.

"Yūjirō!"

From the narrow eyes in the swollen face flowed a single thread of tears. Matsu and the other women wept aloud.

They helped Yūjirō to the women's cell, but Matsu had no medicines to treat him. All she could do was massage his body and moisten his lips with water.

"Matsu . . ." It was the middle of the night before he spoke, and in a faint voice he said, "I . . . I didn't want to cry out when they beat me. But . . . it hurt so much . . . I couldn't . . . I couldn't help shouting."

"It's all right. It's all right." Matsu wept as she massaged his body and repeatedly nodded her head. "I'm so proud of you. You put up with it so bravely."

"By the eighth day, I couldn't take it anymore. But . . . but then I looked up at the roof across the way, and I saw a sparrow bringing food to her babies and putting it in their mouths. And then I thought of Santa Maria. I thought, someday Santa Maria will help me. . . ."

Late that night, the young man's body began to convulse. Although men were prohibited from setting foot in the women's cell, they sent for Kanzaburō, who came quietly through the darkness. Everyone was awake, praying for the young man.

"The children . . ." Yūjirō whispered. "Don't let them make the children cry. They mustn't hurt the children. . . . I'll pray for all of you in Paraíso."

They mustn't make the children cry. . . . Those were the slaughtered Yūjirō's last words.

But the abuse of the children did not cease. The officers were convinced that they would be easily frightened by violence and would submit.

Twelve-year-old Suekichi. Suekichi was from Ieno, a child orphaned after both parents and his siblings died.

"Come with me!"

It's said that when Takahashi came for him and took Suekichi to the interrogation room, the boy kept glancing back over his shoulder, pleading with his eyes for help from the adults who were watching him.

"Suekichi! Pray to Santa Maria! Santa Maria will protect you!!" The women all cried in one voice to the child. He paused and nodded his head in agreement.

The three officers in the dim interrogation room were intentionally chewing on candy, putting on a deliberate show for the starving Suekichi.

"So you're Suekichi? This candy is delicious, it just melts in your mouth!"

One of the officers smiled fawningly and brought a piece of candy up to Suekichi's face. "You're a bright boy. Being that you're so bright, listen to me carefully. Some evil grownups have lied to you. Nothing good will come from believing in this Kirishitan nonsense. In fact, it'll end up leading you down the wrong path. The proper path . . . it's to do your duty to your parents and be devoted to your country—the dual paths of loyalty and filiality. The Kirishitans are on the wrong path because they don't follow the rules of our country."

Suekichi stood stock still, his eyes glazed over.

"If you'd like some candy, you're welcome to it. Don't be afraid, go ahead and eat it."

Although Suekichi took the candy in his hand, he still looked dazed and made no move to put it in his mouth.

"Do you think it's poisoned?" the officer laughed.

But when Suekichi remained frozen in place and gave no response after continued urgings, the officers finally understood what was going through the child's mind. Suekichi was no different from the adult Kirishitans from Urakami.

"All right. Hold out your hands!"

When he thrust out both of the hands that were clutching the candy, one of the officers poured lamp oil over them.

"Do you understand that this is oil?" The officer thrust a rolled up piece of paper into the hibachi and then removed it. The smell of fire and a thread of white smoke rose from the paper, and a tiny flame flickered like the wings of a moth.

"If you don't give up this Kirishitan stuff, I'll set fire to your hands."

Even then, Suekichi stood unflinching with his arms outstretched, as though he had heard nothing.

The flames sputtered above his hands.

"Stop it!" Another officer shouted. Evidently it was too much for him to see a twelve-year-old's hands set on fire.

"Go back to your cell!"

Suekichi gave the officers a vacant look and left the room.

Late that autumn, Itō returned to Tsuwano after a long absence and gave the package that Kiku had wrapped in oil paper to Seikichi, but as before, he retained the three *ryo* for himself.

In addition to a letter, the parcel contained several items that Kiku had collected. *Mochi*, needles, thread, bleached cotton cloth, a salve for wounds, dried potatoes. Studying the items closely, one at a time, Seikichi had an aching desire to see Kiku.

Before he came to Tsuwano, and even after his arrival here, Seikichi had not developed a sharp mental image in his mind of how Kiku looked. In part it was because he didn't have the mental leisure to focus exclusively on Kiku, and in part it was because the ongoing days of starvation robbed him of the physical and mental energy to think about her. He was certain that she had long ago forgotten all about him, and that seemed only normal to him. He couldn't bring himself to believe that Kiku would continue to love a criminal who had been driven from Urakami and banished to a distant spot like Tsuwano.

But Kiku had not forgotten him. In fact, she had entrusted a touching letter and all these items to Itō to bring to him.

What she had to offer an Urakami Kirishitan who did not expect aid from any person was a love that transcended sectarian dogma. That realization prompted an earnest desire in Seikichi's heart: "To live . . . to see her again."

"Lord Itō?" One day, he quietly asked Itō, who had looked into his room, "That woman . . . is she really in Maruyama now?"

"She certainly is. Didn't you know that?"

"Maruyama is the red-light district. What could she be doing in . . . in a red-light district?"

As a Kirishitan, he didn't want to consider the possibility that the woman who loved him worked in such an area. Surely she hadn't become a prostitute who sells her body to men?

"You want to know what she's doing? She works as a maid at a place called the Yamazaki Teahouse."

Seikichi nodded at Itō's reply. He could accept the fact that she was a maid.

"Lord Itō, when . . . when will you be going back to Nagasaki?"

"Before the New Year. I have no desire to spend the holidays up here in these mountains. I don't care what my duties are—if I can't at least spend New Year in Nagasaki, then it's not worth what they're paying me."

Then Itō realized what Seikichi was thinking and gave a thin smile. "Ah? So you want to ask me to deliver a message, eh? What did you want me to say? That when you return to Nagasaki you'll be able to marry her, so please be patient?"

Seikichi did not respond.

"It's not likely you'll be returning to Nagasaki, you know. Our orders from up top are that anyone who doesn't renounce their heretical beliefs will stay locked up in a Tsuwano cell until they die. If you want to see that woman again, the first thing you've got to do is dump this religion of yours."

". . . That's not . . . not what I want to say to her," Seikichi muttered, with his eyes fixed on the ground.

"Then what *do* you want to say?"

"I want her to forget about me . . . and find a good man to marry. . . . That's what I want you to tell her."

Itō saw a tear glisten in Seikichi's eyes. When he saw the tear, Itō felt both an overwhelming compassion for and an urge to treat Seikichi brutally.

"I see. A good man to marry? Is that how you really feel?"

Seikichi said nothing. In all honesty, the agonizing torture he was experiencing right now was worse than any physical abuse he had suffered.

"Such a waste!" Itō feigned a deep sigh as he launched a taunt at Seikichi. "She's a charming girl, you know. A nice face. A nice body. Spending the rest of your life here, never able to hold such a girl in your arms . . . why were you even born into this world?"

Seikichi had no response.

"Fine. I understand. You know, every time I go to Maruyama, I see Kiku . . . and it's only the thought that she's your woman that's kept me from laying a hand on her. . . . But now I guess I don't have to hesitate to do whatever I want with her. Besides, the madam at the Yamazaki Teahouse has been asking me to initiate one of her girls into the ways of the flesh."

"Kiku . . ." Seikichi glared at Itō in predictable anger. "Kiku isn't that kind of girl!"

"Oh, and how do you know that? Listen to me. No matter how deeply a woman falls for a man, in time her love will grow cold if the man can't return her affection. No matter how faithfully she's maintained her chastity for you, once she realizes it's all been to no avail, Kiku's resolve will crumble. Once she starts to slide, it'll turn into an avalanche. And when that happens, I know just how to use my fingers to make her melt. . . ."

Itō smiled as he relished the way his words hurt and made a mock of Seikichi, who had never known a woman and who understood nothing of a woman's heart.

He left Seikichi in that state and stopped by the women's cell.

Some of the women had gathered to offer prayers, while others looked after their children or talked quietly together. When they saw Itō, they quickly sat up with proper formality and stopped talking.

In a gentle voice, Itō said, "How are you—is everyone well today? It's going to be terribly cold today. It looks as though it will snow in the mountains to the north." As he spoke, his droopy eyes searched the group for the woman who resembled Kiku.

"You there!" He called after locating the woman. "What's your name?"

"It's . . . Shima."

"Shima? Come outside with me for a bit."

Before long, he was once again inflicting on her the same humiliation as before. He always had the women remove their clothing on the bamboo veranda or on top of the rocks in the garden, and then he made them sit down. It was customary for him to inflict spiritual torture in addition to physical abuse. More than a few women had tearfully apostatized as a result.

The men who apostatized were moved to the Hōshin-an nunnery, but the apostate women were shifted to a separate room.

Ample quantities of food were provided to the apostates, and they were allowed to do handwork and labor outside the compound.

Occasionally an apostate man or woman would secretly share some of their food with those in other cells. According to the historical records, that gesture provided great encouragement to those who continued to sustain their Kirishitan faith.

Sometimes Itō was strangely gentle with the Kirishitan prisoners, but at other times he behaved with such cruelty that he seemed a completely different person. The prisoners and even his underlings Takahashi and Deguchi considered him capricious, but the feelings of these two low-ranking officers toward him were in their own way complicated.

Late on those days when he had tortured prisoners—especially female prisoners—Itō invariably went out drinking with Takahashi and Deguchi. They always went to the same bar, and after he got so drunk that Takahashi and Deguchi found him revolting, he would begin to weep and throw up.

"There's people who have good fortune and those with bad. The unlucky ones, no matter how hard they struggle, can never crawl out of the muck. The fortunate ones always have things go their way, whatever the odds."

That was Itō's trademark pronouncement once he got drunk.

"This fellow named Hondō that I worked with—he's not all that bright, but since he has good luck, he wound up as an official at Foreign Affairs. And I've heard rumors that some high-and-mighty took note of him and soon he'll be heading to America as an interpreter. And then there's me. . . ." Itō's eyes would pool with tears at such thoughts. Occasionally he would stare at his drinking partners as though a thought had just occurred to him and ask, "What do you guys think about those Kirishitans?"

"What do I think . . . ? I think they're a bunch of idiots," Takahashi replied.

But Itō shook his head. "Idiots . . . ? How could idiots put up with all the horrible tortures we're inflicting on them and still cling to their beliefs? They're no idiots. They're a strong bunch . . . strong . . . ! If I were forced into their position, I could never be as strong as they are." Then, in a solemn voice he muttered, "Do you think there's any chance . . . any chance that this God they believe in is real?"

"Don't be ridiculous!" Takahashi chuckled. "We'll have real problems if even you start thinking like that!"

"But when I see how fervent they are, I start wondering what this being they believe in could be. It's like the intensity of a woman's love when she's completely fallen for a man. When a woman gives her heart to a man, she'll give up absolutely everything and put her whole body and soul into it."

"Are there really women like that?" Deguchi spoke mockingly, but Itō snapped back at him.

"There are! There are women who are like that. Women who will surrender everything they have for the man they love, even if it means ruining themselves in the process."

He closed his eyes and seemed to be deep in thought about something. But Takahashi and Deguchi had no idea what Itō might be thinking about.

It was at the beginning of the twelfth month of that year, when the first snows had fallen on this castle town nestled between the mountains, that Itō was summoned by an official of the Tsuwano domain.

The official, named Chiba, stared at the palms of his hands as he held them over the hibachi and muttered, "We have problems."

The Japanese government had retained its policy of suppressing the Kirishitans and had banished the Urakami followers to several locations, where they were abused on a daily basis. Protests over this treatment of the Kirishitans came primarily from the British chargé d'affaires, Mr. Adams, and had reached the point that the government could no longer turn a deaf ear to his complaints.

"There are rumors that our leaders have no choice but to launch an inquiry into the situations of the Kirishitans in each province. . . ."

"What will they be looking at?"

"How the prisoners are being handled."

"And so . . . ?"

"So when you return to Nagasaki next month, would you be good enough to determine whether this rumor about inquiries is true and also to find out exactly what the foreigners are up to? Especially find out how much the foreigners know of what's going on here in Tsuwano. After all, Nagasaki is one of those places like Yokohama where a lot of foreigners are living. I'll see that you're suitably rewarded."

"I don't need a reward. Instead of a reward . . ." Itō gazed unblinking at the officer's profile. "I have a request. Could you . . . could you use the influence of the domain to see if I could get a job in Tokyo sometime?"

"Tokyo?"

"I've heard that there are some men from Tsuwano who have some influence in the Ministry of Divinities,[2] so couldn't they pull some strings to get me a position in Tokyo or Yokohama?"

Itō was thinking of the impressive standing of Hondō Shuntarō. His heart was transfixed by the hope that if he ended up in Tokyo or Yokohama, his luck might change for the better, just as it had for Hondō.

"We'll consider it." Chiba nodded as he continued to warm his hands. "But given the current situation, Mr. Itō, I think it would be best if you didn't discipline the prisoners quite so viciously for the time being."

Once Itō left the station, the officials in the room exchanged meaningful glances.

"He's a pathetic soul. Doesn't know a thing that's going on," said one with a faint smile.

Chiba picked up a pair of fire tongs, and as he scribbled something in the ashes of the hibachi, he said as though to himself, "He is pathetic, but it can't be helped. In this world of ours, we need some men like that."

2. The Shingishō was created in 1871 as part of the Meiji government's attempts to shift the people's focus from Buddhism to Shinto. A national hierarchy of Shinto shrines was created, with the Ise Shrine—closely linked to the Imperial family because their mythological ancestor, Amaterasu, was enshrined there—occupying the foremost position. The Ministry of Divinities survived for only one year, being replaced by the Ministry of Religion, but it played a role in the formation of the "State Shinto" philosophy, which was used by the government to unify the country under a supposedly "divine" emperor.

THE THIRD WINTER

THE OFFICIAL FROM the Tsuwano domain had been right—

Diplomats from several foreign nations had picked up sketchy details about the abuse of the Urakami Kirishitans in the regions to which they had been exiled. The British chargé d'affaires, Francis Adams,[1] began to take special interest in this matter, and immediately after the New Year holidays, he urged Sawa Nobuyoshi, the Minister of Foreign Affairs, to put an end to these atrocities.

"How did Lord Sawa respond?" Itō, who returned to Nagasaki at the beginning of the year, inquired of one of his superiors at the Nishi Bureau.

Foreign Minister Sawa had been directly involved in the exile of the Urakami Kirishitans from the outset. When he served as military proconsul of Kyushu, he summoned 180 Kirishitan peasants from Urakami Village to the Nishi Bureau, where he tried to persuade them to convert from Christianity; during his stint as governor, after conferring with Kido Takayoshi, he made the decision to banish 114 of them. Consequently, Itō's superiors at the Nishi Bureau knew the particulars of the negotiations between Sawa and Adams.

"Lord Sawa adamantly denied that any such things had occurred."

"Of course." Itō nodded in relief. He had worried that if this problem mushroomed, even he might be implicated.

After the New Year holidays, he decided to make a predusk visit to Maruyama, something he had not done in a long while. In earlier years, the coming of a

---

1. Francis Ottiwell Adams (1825–1889) served as secretary to the British legation during a brief interval when Harry Smith Parkes was on leave in the United Kingdom.

new year had been the time to gather together all the quarter's prostitutes and require them to trample on the sacred Kirishitan images, but by now the custom had been abolished.

"It's me. It's Itō!" he called out as he entered the Yamazaki Teahouse.

"Well!" The madam had just stepped into the entry hall. "I'd heard you were coming back last month, but I began to worry when we didn't see anything of you."

"I've been busy. I don't have that much time today, either." Itō laughed, then held up the little finger of his left hand, a gesture signifying a woman, and asked, "How is she?"

"Actually . . ." The madam lowered her voice. "She's been sick in bed since yesterday."

"Sick?"

"Oh, it's nothing to worry about. She'll be back on her feet soon. Here, why don't you come upstairs?"

"Hmm." Itō snorted as he climbed the creaky stairs and went into a room on the second floor.

The room was unchanged except for the sound of an iron kettle noisily boiling water on the hibachi. This was the room where he had first pressed Kiku to the floor and clambered on top of her. Pale tears had trickled from her eyes that day. . . .

The moment he stepped into the room, the memory of her profile as the tears streamed down her cheeks surfaced in his mind, and he felt a pain like that of a needle jabbing into his chest.

Even so, he knew that ultimately he was very likely to repeat the same activities again today.

That's the kind of man I am. . . . He said to himself as he plopped down on the tatami.

He was made to wait a long while before he heard the stairs creaking again.

Kiku's face appeared at the doorway. Itō was startled at how colorless her face had become. Only her cheeks radiated redly, as though she had a fever.

"I heard you've been ill. What happened?" Itō sat up and took a hard look at Kiku.

"Yes, I have a slight fever."

"When did it start?"

"Four or five days ago . . ." Kiku lied. She had been laid up with a fever for far longer than four or five days. Her body had begun to feel languid during the twelfth month. She was so weary it felt as though her body were weighted down with lead. Her fever rose every afternoon.

"I'll bet you're exhausted. The madam here makes you work too hard."

It was not merely exhaustion. It had started at the first of the twelfth month. On her way back from a rendezvous with the Chinese man she had been set up with, she got caught in the rain and was soaked by the time she made it back to the Yamazaki Teahouse. She had caught a cold but had pushed through it and continued working.

When she finished her customary chores of setting out saké bottles and dishes on the table, Kiku coughed two or three times. It was an unpleasantly dry cough.

"Seikichi is doing well. Yes, that money was very helpful for him, and he's being treated much more compassionately now. You've got nothing to worry about." It was Itō's turn to lie as he drained one cup after another. An unanticipated wave of pity washed over him and he decided to be kind to her, even if in word only.

"Nothing . . . to worry about." Kiku nodded dejectedly. A place beyond her reach—that's where Seikichi was.

"Yeah."

When she opened a second bottle, she asked, "Would you like more?"

"No. No more to drink."

Without a word, Kiku lay back on the tatami. She knew without asking what Itō had come to get from her.

It was twilight, and it looked as though a gentle rain was falling outside. Itō rolled on top of Kiku, and as he watched her gape like a stone statue at the ceiling, waiting motionless for a man's lust to dissipate, he felt an ineffable futility. Guilt, bitterness, and loneliness—the emotions swelled one after another through his breast.

"Enough. That's enough."

Kiku silently stood up and straightened her disheveled robes. Then she coughed. Itō caught a glimpse of reddish blood on the tissue she used to wipe her mouth.

"Have you . . . have you got consumption?!" He slid away from her, crying out in an excess of fear. At the time, consumption was a dreaded, incurable disease.

"Please . . . please don't say anything to the madam. If she finds out, I'll have to leave here." Kiku pleaded with tears in her eyes.

Even Itō's heart was gripped with pain at the sadly pathetic woman's plea.

But aside from his pity for her, the egotism that dominated the other half of his heart made him want to have no further association with a woman suffering from consumption. Unsure which of these two conflicting emotions to give sway to, Itō could only stare in incredulity at Kiku.

"You've got to take care of yourself. If you're this sick, you should have stayed in bed and not come to be with me." That was as much as Itō could bring himself to say right now.

"I'm sorry, but . . . when will you be going back to Tsuwano?"

"When? I just came here for the holidays, and I've got to go back at the end of the month."

"How much money do I need to come up with for Seikichi this time?" Kiku coughed another couple of times, but she was determined to find out how much money she needed to send to Seikichi. She genuinely believed that the money she gave helped in some small way to release Seikichi from some of the pains of life in captivity. And she never even dreamed that all the money she had provided to this point had been pocketed by Itō.

"Money?" With discomfort written in his eyes, Itō retreated even further from her. "We don't need any more money. What I gave to the officials last time was more than enough. . . . I don't need your money." He no longer had the nerve to extort even more money from this afflicted woman.

"But . . . but please take at least one or two *ryo*."

"Well, I guess I could take it. . . ."

"Didn't Seikichi have any messages for me?"

Itō remembered the message Seikichi had asked him to deliver to Kiku. His pitiful message asking her to forget about a man like him and marry some good fellow . . .

"Seikichi was . . ." Itō averted his eyes and lied, ". . . he was pleased by your thoughtfulness. Very pleased."

"Really?"

"Uh-huh." This was the first sign of life he had seen in her feverish face. She smiled happily.

This was too much for him. He could bear it no longer. "I've got to go." Itō scrambled to his feet and fled down the stairs. On his way out, he ran into the madam. "She's very ill. It's cruel of you to make her get out of bed and work!"

Disgorging an angry outburst sufficient to dumbfound the madam, Itō slipped on his geta that waited in the entryway and hurried outside.

While clients of the pleasure quarter still tottered about in a festive New Year's humor, Itō's feet carried him swiftly away, his mind preoccupied.

As he scurried along, thoughts of what he had done and what he had just now seen tore at this craven man's heart.

Choking back bitter drafts of shame, self-loathing, and even self-vindication, his feet took him unawares past the Chinese settlement and toward the ocean.

The noise of the streets and the swarms of people were, for some reason, intolerable to him in his present state of mind. Along the way he bought himself a bottle of saké and brought it up to his mouth from time to time as he walked.

Whenever he drank himself to the point of intoxication, he was somehow able to rationalize his behavior. He could tell himself, *I'm not the only man who does this. Everybody does!* Or *When you get right down to it, this is all the fault of those Kirishitans. If they had just laid low, I wouldn't have had to do the things I've done!*

But the loneliness and the self-hatred gouged at his chest once he sobered up. Itō frequently suffered those pangs on nights in Tsuwano. When he tortured a young woman stripped naked who offered no resistance, or when he impatiently abused men and women who raised no protest, he never thought of it as something for which he was accountable. It was the exhilaration and the impulses that he could not restrain that drove him to do it.

He walked out onto the beach. There was no wind, but still it was cold. Itō squatted down behind a scrapped boat that had been dragged onto the beach and drank straight out of the saké bottle.

I wonder if she's going to die.

Kiku probably would die. Itō loved her. He loved her even though he knew that she could never love a revolting man like him. He tormented her because he loved her. And even though he tortured her, he knew better than anyone else the gemlike heart of this girl who loved Seikichi.

Ahh, she mustn't die!

He grabbed a handful of sand and hurled it in anger and resentment.

In that same moment, he caught sight of a tall foreigner walking toward him from the Ōura beach.

He recognized the man as Petitjean. Petitjean was walking this way with his head bowed—most likely in prayer.

Itō stiffened. Even though he had been sent to determine how much this foreigner knew about the abusive treatment of the Kirishitans in custody, for some reason Itō was frightened of being seen by him right now.

"Ah!" But Petitjean had noticed this Japanese fellow scampering like a mouse to find a hiding place. "Ah! Lord Itō!"

"Well, it being New Year and all, I've just been here having a drink at the beach. Would you care for some?"

"I don't drink." Petitjean sat down beside him.

Petitjean had just returned to Japan from Rome. Though still young, because of the quality of his earlier work he had been appointed the bishop in charge of missionary labors in Japan, and he had entrusted the care of his beloved Ōura Church to his younger companions, Fathers Laucaigne, Poirier, and Villion, with the intention of moving to Yokohama where he could consider proselytizing in Japan from a broader base.

Seeing the beggarly face of Itō for the first time in a while brought a rush of memories back to his recollection. Petitjean remembered this minor official slinking around the Ōura Church to spy on them and setting up camp in the neighboring Nikkanji Temple to keep watch on their movements. But somehow or other, he could not bring himself to hate this vulgar, pusillanimous fellow.

He's a rogue, but he's no devil, he often told his brethren.

"Lord Itō, I thought you were in Tsuwano?" Petitjean asked, puzzled. And he sought some means to gather information about the Urakami Kirishitans from this fellow.

"At the very least, I always insist on being able to celebrate the New Year in Nagasaki. But it's painful to think I'm going to have to return to that village way off in the mountains. Of course, that's all because those Kirishitans are so obstinate!" Itō said with a sarcastic smile.

Petitjean's face suddenly lit up with delight. "So they remain obstinate, do they? They're still following the Kirishitan teachings, are they?" Nothing could have made Petitjean happier. Every piece of news he received regarding the Kirishitans banished to various parts of Japan was distressing, dark, and painful. Tsuwano was not the only place where the faithful were suffering torture.

One hundred seventy-nine were confined in Hiroshima. The food they were given amounted to just over three and a half ounces per day. As a result, many had apostatized, and forty had died.

The 117 packed off to Okayama also suffered starvation from the quarter ounce of rice given to them each day, and in addition they were forced into painful physical labor, leading to eighteen deaths and fifty-five apostasies.

Of the eighty-four held in Matsue, eighty-one had abandoned their faith.

Reports on the sufferings of the faithful that were conveyed one after another to Petitjean and Laucaigne sometimes provoked feelings akin to despair. But just now, whether in sarcasm or as a joke, Itō had claimed that "those Kirishitans are so obstinate!"

That meant that even during this frigid winter, there still were some in Tsuwano who had not abandoned their principles and departed from the faith.

"Lord Petitjean." With the bottle of saké to his mouth, Itō suddenly looked serious. "There's something I want to ask you."

"What is it?" Itō's face was so earnest that Petitjean nodded.

"You Kirishitans . . . why do you put up with all this meaningless suffering?" And then, as though spewing out the words, he asked, "And do you hate me? With these hands of mine I've beaten and abused and brought pain to many Kirishitans. But they've endured it all. Despite their daily sufferings, they won't utter a word of apostasy. Why is that? Why are they so stubborn? If they'd just for appearance's sake say the words 'I apostatize' . . . on that very same day they could return to a comfortable life like any ordinary person."

With his eyes closed, Petitjean moved his lips almost imperceptibly. It appeared he was praying for each of the prisoners who currently were groaning in Tsuwano.

"God . . . God never does any evil to us." The whispered words seeped like a moan from Petitjean's lips. Why had God given such painful trials to these peasants from Urakami? Why didn't God use his power to rescue them? Did God ignore those who suffered for his sake?

Those doubts plagued Petitjean every day after his meeting with Itō. Dark shadows were occasionally cast across his believing heart. But ultimately he made every effort to believe that God could never do anything evil but would only provide good things for man.

"God . . . Lord Itō, God works only good for mankind."

"So you're telling me that the horrible suffering of the Kirishitans in Tsuwano, that this God of yours regards those sufferings as *good*?!" Itō scoffed. Only a religious fanatic or an idiot could ever give the answer that Petitjean just gave. Little wonder that Itō laughed in scorn.

"Yes."

"Their sufferings are good?"

"Right now they don't seem like good to us. But the day will come when we will realize that it was all for the best."

"That's ridiculous!" Itō noisily gulped down his saké. "How can you know something like that?"

"It is contrary to reason. But the knowledge and the workings of God are far, far beyond our comprehension. What I'm telling you is true. It's because they believe this that the Urakami Kirishitans are able to endure such torments, and they believe and pray and regard the workings of the Lord just as we do."

"Hmm. So you're saying their sufferings will one day bring about something good? Well, I'm willing to bet that nothing good will result. I'll wager my head on it." Itō stood up angrily to contest Petitjean's declaration. "If this God of yours doesn't really exist—and I don't think he does—then you and those prisoners are living totally pointless lives."

If there is no God, you and the Urakami Kirishitans are living totally pointless lives—Itō's assertion struck at the very heart of the most frightening, most cruel, of all spiritual dilemmas.

If there is no God, then it was absolutely meaningless for Sen'emon and Seikichi and Kanzaburō and the others in Tsuwano to have endured those brutal tortures. It would render Petitjean's arduous journey across the seas to this distant land of Japan an act of futility. Perhaps God did exist, and perhaps he didn't. Certainly many people believe that God is the product human imaginings and desires. . . .

"You're right." His eyes closed, Petitjean muttered, "If there is no God . . . then I and the prisoners at Tsuwano . . . we have indeed lived cruelly meaningless lives."

"And yet even knowing there is that possibility, you still endure such hardships? What exactly is the bearing of such pain supposed to lead to?"

"I don't know. But I know with absolute certainty that God will not let their sufferings come to naught. You'll realize that someday. I am certain you will realize it."

Fanatical bastard. Itō looked with pity at the sorrowing face of the foreigner. It was futile to try to say anything to men beguiled by such fossilized thinking. They rebuff any attempts at persuasion.

It was more important now to take this opportunity to find out what the official of the Tsuwano domain had asked him to determine.

"I hear that you foreigners persist in lodging complaints to the authorities about the harsh treatment the Kirishitans are receiving."

"That's right. We continue to request through our ministers and consulates that the violence be stopped and that they be given a bit more to eat."

"And do I understand that you're demanding that people like me who treat the prisoners roughly must be punished?"

"I wouldn't know about that. That's something your Japanese courts will have to consider."

"You do a fine job of evading the issue."

Itō sneered. This is how these missionaries always behave. They protect themselves so effectively that the ultimate responsibility for things doesn't fall on them. The missionaries stirred up the Urakami peasants to revolt, but after the protestors were arrested, they went on living their carefree lives.

"Why haven't you gone to Tsuwano? Why haven't you gone there to experience the same torment as those peasants? You put on such a good face. . . . You're just like Hondō Shuntarō."

"I have suffered sometimes—no, frequently over that very question. On chilly nights, I think about how I'm sleeping in my own house while those farmers are shivering in the cold, and it pains me deeply."

"Spare me the fancy words!" Itō said angrily. "You're no different from Hondō Shuntarō. All you have is a gift for getting on well in the world. Without ever dirtying your own hands. Hondō's never struck a single criminal. He orders somebody else to beat them and watches from a distance. I'm the one that has to strike the blows. . . ." His eyes filled with tears, Itō cried, "I'll bet you don't know the first thing about the pains of those who are beaten. And you know nothing of the torment of those who administer the torture!"

Then Petitjean said something completely unexpected. "No, I don't know those pains. But I do know that God loves you more than he loves Lord Hondō."

Itō looked up at Petitjean's face in amazement. He thought perhaps he was being mocked, ridiculed.

"You say this God of yours . . . loves me more than Hondō? A man who's tortured and inflicted pain on you Kirishitans?"

"You are suffering. But Lord Hondō feels no anguish in his heart. His heart is filled with the dream of taking advantage of the mounting opportunities in this age of Meiji and making a success of himself."

"And what . . . what's so wrong with that? I'm . . . if anything, I'm jealous of the success Hondō is having."

"But it's your jaundiced, wounded heart that God is trying to penetrate, not Hondō's. God has no interest in a man like Lord Hondō, who is inflamed right now with the lust for success. He is drawn instead to a heart like yours."

Hatefully Itō said, "I really despise the kind of nonsense you people use to trick the hearts of men. You prey on a man's weaknesses, but no matter how hard you try to charm me with your Kirishitan babble, I'm not falling for your lofty words and schemes. I see exactly what you're up to."

"You're wrong." Petitjean shook his head vigorously. "Someday you'll understand. By inflicting pain on the Urakami Kirishitans, you're splattering your own body with blood."

"Listen, I'm not that kind of man! Someone like me—I enjoy torturing them. It's nothing more than torture. I hurt them because I find it amusing to hurt them—that's all there is to it!" Itō protested, his eyes flashing with rage and the spittle rising in his mouth. He was determined not to allow Petitjean to see through his weaknesses. He could not forgive this foreigner with the all-knowing look who had rudely penetrated into the depths of his heart.

"Then go ahead and torment them all you want."

"What are you saying?"

"Pain will give birth to love among them. Without pain, Lord Itō . . . love cannot come into being."

Itō couldn't understand half of what Petitjean was saying. But the remaining half of his words echoed through his heart with a weight that he had never sensed in words before.

"Hmmph!" He stood up from the sand in a deliberate show of scorn. "So you're saying that this God or whoever loves me more than he loves Hondō? What a peculiar religion!" Sneering, he made his way down the beach.

A man as base and cowardly, cunning and selfish, and incapable of curbing his lusts as himself was no better than a worm. What could Petitjean's bizarre statement possibly mean—that such a worm had vastly more worth in the eyes of God than did Hondō Shuntarō?

SNOW. AND THE BLESSED MOTHER

ON THAT DAY—

The cold was more biting than usual. It seemed as though at any moment, snow would begin to fall from a cloudy sky that was the color of faded cotton. The madam of the Yamazaki Teahouse had gone to participate in the Shinto Fire Festival at the Suwa Shrine, leaving Kiku to mind the shop. As a result, Kiku was able to rest until evening came.

After Kiku fell ill, the madam began taking verbal jabs at her. "We're not like other places of business—we can't afford to support people who can't work. I can't have you do nothing but lie around all day."

It incensed a determined woman like Kiku to listen to such sarcasm, so she would work through her fever, toiling in the kitchen and dusting the shop. But while working that hard, she sometimes had dizzy spells or became so lethargic she felt like crouching down where she stood.

On this particular day she was unusually exhausted. It felt as though leaden weights were pressing down on her body, and she could tell that she was running a fever.

"You're such a fortunate girl. I hear that they stop feeding a courtesan who ends up unable to work because of lung problems." Recalling the madam's spiteful words, she worked until nearly noon. When she lay down to rest a bit at midday, the man with the yellow teeth slid the back door open with a rattle.

"You again?"

"Yep. Can you come see a client? He's a Chinese merchant, and he's the kind of guy who won't take no for an answer when he wants a woman. He says he'll pay handsomely."

"I can't today." Kiku feebly shook her head. "I don't feel well, and I'm in a lot of pain."

"That's too bad! But it won't take long. And he says he's willing to pay two *ryo*."

"Why don't you just send for one of the Jūzenji girls?" Kiku whispered.

The "Jūzenji girls" were the prostitutes who serviced the Chinese; they were considered lower in status than the women at Maruyama who entertained the Dutch. "Jūzenji girls" was used as an epithet to describe them.[1]

"But your reputation is so high among the Chinese men. A beautiful face, they say, and a good heart, too!" The man was determined to win her over with flattery. No doubt he had boasted around Nakajuku that he would bring Kiku back without fail.

"It's two *ryo*! Aren't many Chinese who'll pay as much as two *ryo*!"

Kiku wanted to earn at least one or two *ryo* for Seikichi before Itō returned to Tsuwano. She had the feeling that with her body this enervated, she would not live much longer anyway.

And for that reason—

For that reason, she needed to muster the last of her strength and give her all for her love of Seikichi. Kiku was the kind of woman who simply had to give love.

She locked up the shop and left the Yamazaki Teahouse to accompany the yellow-toothed man. The sky was overcast, and the penetrating cold stabbed into her body.

"Looks like it might snow," the man muttered, looking up at the gray skies.

"I have to get back as soon as possible. The madam will be coming back from the Fire Festival soon, and then clients will be coming this evening. If they start arriving before the *geiko* are there . . . that would be a disaster!"

"I know. I know!" With a knowing look, the man started down the Maruyama slope ahead of Kiku.

The ocean was dark today. Conspicuously black clouds pressed in from behind Mount Inasa.

Today's client was a young Chinese merchant with a slim figure and protruding cheekbones. He was impatient to get his hands on Kiku's body.

"衣裳斉整. 容貌嫖致," he exclaimed when he saw Kiku. He may have been correct in saying 容貌嫖致 (What a beautiful woman!), but it was idle flattery for him to say 衣裳斉整 (Such a charming outfit!) when she had come without even taking the time to change her clothes.

The Chinese man who was acting as interpreter lied and told the client, "She's one of the top two women of the quarter right now," to which the client voiced his gratitude, "多謝多謝."

---

1. Many Chinese residences were located in the Jūzenji sector of Nagasaki.

Large snowflakes began to fall outside the window. The cold grew even more intense. As she poured the drinks and joined in singing the Chinese songs, Kiku's body became feverish and she felt terrible. Seeing her red, feverish face, the Chinese merchant mistook it for intoxication and the flush of desire, and he quickly moved her into bed.

So sluggish. She wanted this laborious chore to be over quickly. While the slender Chinese man moved his body unremittingly above her, Kiku endured by imagining Seikichi's face. She struggled to remind herself that however much she had to undergo, Seikichi was suffering far greater pain. And she hoped that if there were a God, he would lessen Seikichi's suffering by exactly the amount of suffering she was subjected to.

The image that suddenly popped into her mind was the angelic face of the woman in the Nambanji. That Blessed Mother whom Seikichi revered and worshipped.

I don't care how much I have to suffer, please just make things easier for him in Tsuwano. With her eyes closed, she pleaded in her heart to that woman. It was less a plea than it was a prayer. As she repeated the prayer in her heart, the body of the slender man shuddered; she heard his heavy breathing, his face with its bloodshot eyes was directly above her, and the torrent of his lust coursed powerfully into her body.

In that moment, Kiku coughed violently. It felt as though some object like a fishbone was caught in her throat, so she tried to force it out, with the result that a bloody liquid filled her mouth.

It was fresh blood. The blood spilled from her lips and stained the tatami.

The startled Chinese man wrenched his naked body away from her and shouted frantically for the man who was waiting for him at the bottom of the stairs.

The Chinese men were kind to her. They let her remain lying down and, before long, brought some warm medicine in a cup and had her drink it.

"It's a sedative and something to stop the bleeding," the man who was acting as interpreter, with a face whiter than a sheet of paper, explained to Kiku. The brown medicinal drink had a strong aroma, but when she drank it, she could tell that the tightness in her chest was gradually abating, and she no longer felt nauseous.

I have to go back. It must be about the time the madam will be returning. Those were her first thoughts, but her leaden body would not move. The medicinal potion they had given her must have contained a sleeping drug, since she fell into a light sleep.

Her dream was the same as usual. A gentle spring in Magome. Skylarks twittered overhead, and then the field carpeted in lotus flowers. She was playing with Mitsu and some other girls. Seikichi was there, too. And Kiku, excessively mindful of Seikichi's presence, was purposely standoffish, moving far away from him at times. When she did, Seikichi looked very, very sad.

She woke up. It was a dark, solitary evening. Outside enormous snowflakes were falling. The roofs of the houses had turned starkly white.

Kiku forced herself to get up and staggered slowly down the stairs. Three or four men, including the slender Chinese man, were drinking and playing a Chinese version of paper-rock-scissors.

"You should have slept longer," said the one who could speak Japanese.

"I'm sorry for all the trouble. I'll come back again to give a proper apology, but for today, please excuse me."

"You've got to take care of yourself!"

The Chinese merchant had paid her two *ryo*, but she tried to return one *ryo* to him as an apology for coughing up blood.

"Don't worry about it. Keep it," he said gently, shaking his head.

She tried to make her way back to Maruyama through the large flakes of falling snow. And she began pondering how she might make her excuses. She knew that she would be found out no matter how hard she tried to conceal her activities, and there was every possibility that the madam already had some vague idea of what Kiku had been doing.

She walked through the snow, her heart heavy. It was dark along the road and there were no other people to be seen. Her fever sent shivers racing from her shoulders to her back from time to time, and her head was extremely hot.

Again she felt like throwing up. She stopped and spit out whatever was caught in her throat. Bright red blood stained the snow.

Staring at the blood, she decided she could never return to the Yamazaki Teahouse. Maruyama was not so indulgent a place as to let a woman who could not work obtain her food and lodgings for free.

Could she go back to her home in Magome? Her pride would not allow it. It was too painful to consider the pain she would cause Granny and her parents when they saw her wasted body.

I don't think I have much longer to live. In that moment, she sensed the certain brevity of her own life. And she realized that there was really only one place she could go—the Nambanji at Ōura, where she could recall how Seikichi had looked when she saw him there.

Seikichi had always said that no place was more valuable to him than the Nambanji. And it was there he had worshipped that woman.

The dark ocean. The dark beach. Kiku walked along the deserted road toward Ōura.

The snow fluttered in the wind. The ocean was tinged a deep purple hue, and the road alongside the beach had already turned white. Kiku had no umbrella, so the innumerable snowflakes grazed past her hair and shoulders or landed on them.

Strangely she felt no pain. For whatever reason, her last strength came from the hope that if she could make it to the Nambanji in Ōura, she would find Seikichi there.

Panting for breath, stopping occasionally and coughing every time she stopped, she climbed the slope. Snow had already started to bury the slanting path, making it difficult to walk. She kicked off her geta and continued barefoot.

By the time she reached the crest of the hill, her energy was gone. She coughed violently and leaned against the earthen wall of the church to catch her breath. That earthen wall she leaned against has become a corner of the Tōkyū Hotel today, but the church still looks essentially the way it did that day.

Through the white veil of snow, she could see the Nambanji directly in front of her. Enfolded in that veil, she was swept up in the illusion that Seikichi was waiting for her right now inside the church. Spring in Urakami. Young girls at play. Days filled with such joy. Wispy memories of Seikichi's clear voice as he sold his wares those mornings in early summer, and the brief opportunity she had to talk with him at this church.

Those recollections twirled inside her head like images in a revolving lantern.

She stumbled up the stone steps of the Nambanji. Looking very much like a porcelain doll, she pushed open the door and went into the sanctuary.

Tiny flames fueled by rapeseed oil glimmered at the spot where the Eucharist was laid out. When she had worked here, one of her jobs had been to refill the oil so that the flame was never extinguished.

She dropped at the base of the woman's statue and coughed. A spot of blood tinged the hand she held to her mouth. With wide eyes the statue of the Blessed Mother watched Kiku as she coughed.

Well, I've ended up here again. After all, you're the only person I can talk to about Seikichi. Between coughs, she murmured to the Blessed Mother. *I hated you, you know. Seikichi thought more of you than he did of me. I was jealous of you and tried to draw his heart in my direction.*

She coughed violently.

But it didn't work. I lost everything. Unlike you, this body of mine has been repeatedly, totally violated.

Tears poured from Kiku's eyes as she railed at the statue. They were the same as the tears she shed the day she was raped by Itō.

I can't . . . I can't be close to Seikichi ever again. But I really did love him!

She coughed up blood and collapsed with her face toward the floor. It was quiet in the chapel, and outside the snow fell noiselessly. When the sound of her coughing ceased, her body no longer moved.

Translucent tears just like those of Kiku welled up in the large eyes of the Blessed Mother. The tears spilled down her cheeks and dampened her robes. She wept for Kiku, who lay facedown, motionless; she wept for this woman who had loved one man with everything she had; she wept for Kiku, who had given all for her lover, even to the point of defiling her own body.

I . . . I really did love him!

The Blessed Mother heard Kiku's cry distinctly. With tears pooling in her large eyes, the statue of the Immaculata nodded in strong affirmation.

But unlike you, this body of mine has been repeatedly, totally violated. . . .

In response to Kiku's moan filled with such sorrow and pain, the weeping Blessed Mother shook her head vigorously.

No. You are not violated in the least. Even though you gave your body to other men . . . you did it for just one man. The sorrow and misery you felt at those times . . . has cleansed everything. You are not the least bit defiled. You lived in this world in order to love, just as my son did.

Stretched out on the floor, Kiku's body was depleted of all energy and did not even stir.

This snow will probably continue all night long. This much snow will purify everything stained, everything foul. Ultimately the streets of Nagasaki will become a land of pure whiteness. And just as this pure white snow will conceal all the blemishes and lewdness and pains and sins of humanity, your love will obliterate all the filth from the men who have touched you.

Then the Blessed Mother urged Kiku: *Come, fear not. Come with me. . . .*

Time passed in utter silence. Outside the church, the large flakes of snow continued to fall.

When Petitjean came to the chapel to pray after darkness fell, he discovered Kiku collapsed on the floor directly beside the altar. The area around her down-turned face was darkly stained with the immense quantities of blood she had disgorged, and her body had already stiffened and drawn its last breath. The hemorrhaging from her lungs had suffocated her.

Petitjean summoned Okane and her husband and brought Laucaigne and the other priests into the chapel. Okane's husband hurried through the snow to notify the Nishi Bureau.

The candles on the altar were lit. Although Kiku had not been a Kirishitan, Petitjean and the others priests offered the Kirishitan prayer for the dead on her behalf.

"*Requiem aeternam dona eis, Domine.* Grant her eternal rest, O Lord," Petitjean recited, moving his lips faintly. "*Et lux perpetua luceat eis. Requiescat in pace.* And may eternal light shine upon her, and grant her eternal rest." As he whispered the Latin words of the *Requiescat in pace,* an unbearable grief clenched at Petitjean's heart.

He knew that Kiku had loved Seikichi. He also knew how much she had suffered because Seikichi had been locked away in distant Tsuwano. And he felt as though he understood why she had died here before this altar, soaked through like a stray cat and coughing up blood.

But then he recalled the conversation he had held a few days ago on the beach with Itō, who had wondered what sort of meaning God would assign to all this death and suffering.

Late that night, several policemen carrying lanterns came from the Nishi Bureau, accompanied by an official sent to investigate the death. The official was Itō Seizaemon.

Itō looked down at Kiku's dead face, then fixed his eyes on the stains from the enormous amount of blood Kiku had coughed up. He stood stiff as a rod. The priests and Okane and Mosaku watched the wordless man from several paces away.

Since Itō said nothing, one of the policemen asked Okane and Mosaku, "Do you know this woman's identity?"

"Yes, her name is Kiku, and she's from Magome in Urakami Village. She was employed here for a short time, but like the wife and me, she wasn't a Kirishitan." Mosaku emphasized the fact that she was not a Kirishitan, not so much for Kiku's benefit, but to protect himself and his wife.

"How was she hired here?"

"I'll answer that." Petitjean gave a summary explanation of how he first met Kiku that day in the sixth month and the circumstances under which he had brought her here. However, he adroitly avoided mention of the fact that it had been the same morning that Father Laucaigne had been entangled in the arrest of the Urakami Kirishitans and had fled over the mountains.

"And why did she quit working here?"

"I don't know," Petitjean said, but Okane deliberately interjected, "I heard she went to Maruyama. . . . Because it's got to be more fun for a young woman to work in Maruyama instead of at a place like this."

"If she was in Maruyama . . . did she become a prostitute?"

"I wouldn't know. But since they said she was working in Maruyama, I guess she must have done the same things as the other women there, don't you think?" Because Okane hadn't been fond of Kiku, there was a note of derision in her voice.

"Then she was a whore, was she?" The policeman muttered with a sneer. "But why did she come all the way back here to die?"

Casting a glance in Petitjean's direction, Okane responded, "Once a girl gets this sick, nobody'll have anything to do with her. After all, at Maruyama the women disgrace their bodies every night with men, so once your body's no good, you're done for there."

Okane grinned obsequiously as she spoke, but suddenly Itō whirled in her direction and shouted, "Shut your mouth! What the hell do you . . . do any of you know?!"

He shouted with such rage that Okane and her husband and even the policemen looked startled.

"What in hell do you know about this woman?! She . . . she was not that kind of woman. Compared to her, you and I . . . we're so much filthier than she was!"

He stopped, shocked by what he had just blurted out. A look of panic washed across his face when he realized what he had just admitted. . . .

"Let's get out of here. Work with her family in Magome to make sure her body is buried with all proper respect. I said *proper respect*! Do you understand me? *Proper respect!!*"

Those were Itō's parting words. . . .

GOING HOME

THE MEIJI GOVERNMENT ultimately acceded to persistent demands from the foreign diplomatic community and launched an investigation into the treatment of the Urakami Kirishitans who had been banished to various parts of the country. It was fifth month of 1871.

In the latter part of that month, an inspection team set out for Tsuwano, led by Kusumoto Masataka, an appointed official from the Ministry of Foreign Affairs, along with Katō Naozumi and Uemura Yoshihisa.

The new leaves of early summer are beautiful in Tsuwano. It feels as though the color and fragrance of those young leaves adhere themselves to every feature of the scenery.

At the home of Yae Kan'emon, where the inspectors were lodged, Kusumoto and Katō received a visit from the men who were responsible for the handling of the Kirishitans.

Kusumoto explained the reason for their investigation to Chiba, Kanamori, and other representatives of the Tsuwano domain. "As you know, gentlemen, our government is planning negotiations with several foreign nations at the end of this year to press for revisions in the unequal treaties that were forced on us. Should there be any mistakes made in the treatment of the Kirishitans at this juncture, it could create difficulties for the negotiations."

There was neither reproof nor undue probing in Kusumoto's outline of the purposes for their observation tour. Harsh treatment of the Kirishitans had, from the outset, been the Meiji government's approach to religion, one it had inherited from the Tokugawa shogunate. The attitude of the investigating team was so relaxed that Kusumoto and his colleagues were up late into the night entertaining Chiba and Kanamori with food and drink.

The following day, the inspection team was scheduled to examine the prison where the Kirishitans were being held. The only two locations they toured were the Kōrinji Temple, where those who had shown no intention of abandoning their faith were confined, and the nunnery that housed those who had apostatized.

"Have you inflicted any severe punishments on them?" Kusumoto asked the prescribed question of the officers in charge of the jails. It was obvious to him from a single glance at the children—so emaciated that their eyes alone appeared large, their arms and legs as thin as wire—how they had been treated.

"The Tsuwano domain has strictly prohibited anything even resembling harsh punishment," an officer responded just as he had been ordered to do. "But there is a possibility that some excessive coercion may have taken place outside our supervision."

"What do you mean by . . . 'some excessive coercion'?" Kusumoto and Katō displayed prearranged suspicion on their faces.

"We of the Tsuwano domain aren't the only ones who've been charged with caring for and persuading these prisoners. They've also been interrogated by a man from the Nishi Bureau in Nagasaki," the officer said, as though he were reciting a memorized speech. With this response, the Tsuwano domain was released from any fear that the central government might reprimand or hold them responsible for abusive treatment of the Kirishitans.

"Are you saying that in the unlikely scenario that excessive force was used, it was done by someone from the Nishi Bureau in Nagasaki?" Katō asked with a fierce expression, but the officers stared at the ground and said nothing further. Their silence was meant to be interpreted as an affirmative answer to the question.

"What is the man's name?"

"Sir . . . It's Lord Itō. Itō Seizaemon."

Two weeks later, Itō received notice that he was being dismissed from his position at the Nishi Bureau in Nagasaki.

"Lord Itō, all of this . . ." Glancing up intermittently to check Itō's reaction and looking very sympathetic, Itō's superior, Noguchi, muttered, ". . . all of this is on orders from Lord Sawa. . . . We don't understand it at all. . . . Evidently they feel it was wrong for you to have interrogated the *Kuros* in Tsuwano so roughly. The foreigners heard about it, and so Lord Sawa, as foreign minister, probably had no choice but to take these measures."

His face crimson with anger, Itō shouted, "This is unfair! From the very beginning, wasn't it on orders from the higher-ups that I interrogated them harshly? And it wasn't . . . I wasn't the only one who was hard on them. The officers in Tsuwano did even worse things than I did, throwing them in the icy water and shoving them in that three-foot cell!"

"Clearly." Noguchi hurriedly nodded his head. He was in the habit of saying "Clearly" in place of "I understand."

"So it's completely unfair that I'm the only one being punished, don't you think?!"

"Clearly. But this is what our superiors have decided, so petty little bureaucrats like us can't do anything about it. For now, just be patient and we'll come up with something." "We'll come up with something" was another of Noguchi's stock phrases.

"And just what will you 'come up with'?! Damn it all!!" Itō was frustrated to the point of tears.

Somewhat unpromisingly, Noguchi replied, "What I mean by 'come up with something' . . . is that I plan to ask Lord Hondō Shuntarō if he would intercede with Lord Sawa and ask for some leniency."

"Hondō?" Yet again Itō was forced to acknowledge, with frustration and envy, the enormous gap between his life and that of Hondō. But at this point he had no options other than rely on Hondō, even if it meant having to treat him obsequiously. "Lord Hondō, is it? Well, please do what you can."

"Clearly. We'll come up with something."

A misty rain fell in Nagasaki throughout the day. As he watched the rain, Itō reflected that there are distinct categories of people in the world: the strong and the weak, the fortunate and the unfortunate, the glamorous and the wretched. While he cursed his own ill fortune, he hung his head as he thought of how Kiku had desecrated her own body by believing in his deceptions.

I couldn't help it . . . Those were the first words Itō had muttered to an ephemeral vision of Kiku. *Can you forgive me?*

Still, he knew full well that his own weaknesses would drive him back into the same sort of behavior, perhaps even as early as tomorrow.

Hondō received the letter that a kindly Noguchi had sent him on behalf of Itō Seizaemon.

"He's no end of trouble, that Itō . . . ," he said, showing the letter to Oyō, who was now his wife.

Their home in Aoyama was circled by thick groves of trees and bamboo. At her husband's behest, Oyō was regularly visiting the home of a British family in Kōji-machi, where she took lessons in English conversation and European cooking from the lady of the house. In Hondō's view, the wife of an up-and-coming high-ranking government official had to be able to speak English and be skilled in Western table manners.

"What are you going to do about this?" Oyō asked.

"Nothing. When it comes right down to it, the man is just not the lucky sort. No matter how hard you try to help someone that ill fated, it's the same as pouring water into a bottomless bucket. But, Oyō, more important than that . . . you're still speaking in the Nagasaki dialect," he cautioned her. He was perpetually admonishing her that the wife of a high-ranking official must not speak in a provincial dialect. "I'm a busy man. It's too late for me to be worrying about someone like Itō." With that, he shifted his eyes back to the Western book he had been reading. Realizing the conversation was at an end, Oyō quietly left the room.

He wadded up Noguchi's letter and threw it in the wastebasket. Determined to walk the road to success at full tilt, Hondō was not inclined to give any thought to some low-level drunkard he had gotten to know during his time in Nagasaki. It annoyed him that a country bumpkin could be so insensitive as to ask something so out of keeping with his place in society, on the dubious grounds that they had had some minor interactions in the distant past.

His head was filled with plans for his imminent journey to America. The diplomatic mission seeking treaty revisions, to be led by Prince Iwakura Tomomi, was set to leave Japan in the eleventh month, and one of the distinguished members of the delegation was Hondō, who would be serving as Second Secretary.

The decision to send a delegation to negotiate for treaty revisions was complicated by a power struggle between Kido Takayoshi and Ōkubo Toshimichi, and the corps of translators also was caught up in the vortex of this rivalry, but a prudent Hondō had adopted a wait-and-see attitude that kept him aloof from either faction. Wisely, he felt instinctively that the path to worldly success lay in not playing out his hand until the last possible moment.

Once the eleventh month came, there seemed to be farewell parties every night, and each night Oyō waited up late for her buoyant husband to return home so that she could nurse him through his intoxication.

With the twelfth day of the eleventh month set as the day the delegation would set sail, the couple spent the night of the tenth alone together, consoling each other over their temporary separation. Oyō played the samisen while Shuntarō lifted the saké cup to his mouth with a fleshy hand.

"Sitting like this together reminds me of those days in Maruyama."

"It does, doesn't it."

"Now that I think about it, there was a girl at the Yamazaki Teahouse named Kiku, wasn't there . . . ?"

"Yes."

Of course, flushed as they were in their own happiness, neither Hondō nor Oyō spent any further time discussing the Kirishitans in Tsuwano, much less Itō. Those people no longer had anything to do with their lives.

"Oyō . . . This voyage is going to make my career!" Hondō smiled triumphantly at his wife.

On the twelfth,[1] a clear autumn morning, Hondō Shuntarō left the port of Yokohama aboard the S.S. *America* as part of the forty-eight-member Iwakura Mission.

They were not the only passengers on the ship. At 10:00 A.M. that same morning, Mr. DeLong, having concluded his term as minister to Japan, along with his wife, were joined by fifty-nine Japanese exchange students, including five women, bound for Europe and the United States; they all stood on deck waving farewell to their loved ones. As thirty-four gunshots saluted them, the 4,554-ton *America* quietly set out into the Pacific Ocean.

Hondō leaned against the deck rail and looked out at the great ocean frothing with whitecaps. This was the first time in his life he had seen the vast ocean surrounding him in every direction.

Japan is poised to become a great nation. And I will rise in the world along with my country. Taking a deep breath of the ocean breeze, Hondō reassured himself. He considered Western civilization to be the path to progress, and he had not the slightest doubt that the study of Western civilization meant progress for Japan and the Japanese people.

The sparkle of the dazzling ocean before his eyes. The blue sky, swept clear by the strong winds. Right now Hondō was completely detached from the bleakness, the incurable sorrow, the cowardice, the baseness, the impurity of heart that defined lives like that of Itō. As a result, it was just as Petitjean had said: Hondō had no need of God. He was able to steep himself in the optimism of the modern age, so fully removed from God.

This industrious man wasted not a moment of time. He tirelessly roamed the foreign ship, recording everything there was to learn, everything there was to know in his diary:

The twenty-first of the eleventh month is January 1, 1872, by the Western calendar. So last night the European and American passengers all got together. Champagne and brandy were brought out on silver trays, and several other liquors were mixed together in something they called "punch," which they drank as they talked with one another late into the night. The skirts of the women's dresses are very long, and they wear a wiry lantern-shaped contraption they call a "corset," while they puff out their hips with a hoop made of something like thin strips of bamboo. The husbands have to lift up the skirts of their wives who wear these peculiar costumes so they don't step on them.[2]

As he wrote this, Hondō was gripped by an emotion approaching fear as he wondered whether someday Japanese men would have to do this for their wives. But he resigned himself to the likelihood that such practices would have to be adopted if they were a product of Western civilization and the custom observed in Europe and the United States.

After an ocean voyage of nearly a month, the ship finally docked in San Francisco. Hondō recorded his impressions of seeing a foreign land for the first time that day in a letter addressed to Oyō:

A thick fog early in the morning. The deck was soaked. They finally made the ship heave to and waited for the dawn. As the dawn broke and the fog lifted, the mountains of Karihorunia (California) appeared before us. Two mountain peaks parted to form a gateway, while the bay beyond was filled with seawater. We could see smoke rising from the steamers that came in and out of the bay. This was the fabled "Golden Gate." We had journeyed across the ocean for twenty-two days, and since this was the first landscape we had seen east of Japan, our joy was indescribable.

More than one hundred Japanese lined the deck, enjoying the picturesque view of the Golden Gate. The members of the Iwakura Mission were particularly nervous about the upcoming treaty revision negotiations, but they were confident about their prospects for success.

They had given scarcely any thought to what sort of obstacles might arise in their negotiations in this country because of the policy of suppression that the Japanese government had adopted toward the Urakami Kirishitans.

Once they made land in the United States, everything the members of the delegation experienced in the great city of San Francisco was a source of astonishment to them. For instance, Shuntarō wrote candidly in his diary and in his letters to Oyō about his experience of riding for the first time on a hotel elevator:

A boy led me into a tiny room occupied by two or three Americans. Suddenly the little room was hoisted up with a loud noise. Then it came to a stop, and at the boy's insistence, I was driven out of the room, where I stood in a daze for a few moments. It's called an "elevator," and it's a useless contraption that goes up and down the stairs.

Everything they saw and heard amazed and stupefied them. Amid their amazement and stupefaction, the members of the Japanese delegation made modest efforts to stroke their own pride by noting that America knew nothing of the Way of Confucius and Mencius and that its people were lacking in decorum.

When the group bound for Washington, D.C., left San Francisco and stopped off in Salt Lake City, they learned from a local newspaper that another group of Kirishitans had been arrested in Japan. Hondō translated the article for them.

Another group of hidden Kirishitans had been discovered in Takashima, Iōjima, Shitsu, and Kurosaki in Imari Prefecture (present-day Saga Prefecture), and sixty-seven of them had been jailed in the courthouse.

Hondō finally came to the realization that this incident, combined with the earlier imprisonments of all the Kirishitans in Urakami, was going to have a profound impact on the treaty negotiations. He reached this conclusion after reading about the public's response in the newspapers and from the reactions of the dignitaries they met in Salt Lake City. He expressed his concerns to his superiors, and some in the delegation began to fear what might lie ahead.

Those fears took tangible form when the New Year arrived and they had an audience with President Grant in Washington.

Ambassador Iwakura and his four deputy delegates, clad in traditional court dress and ceremonial robes, called on the White House, and in a state room they listened to a speech from President Grant in which he declared:

"The reason that we in the United States have been able to enjoy prosperity and happiness is because we have placed no limits on freedom of association with foreign lands, on freedom of the press, freedom of religious conscience, and freedom of worship for all our citizens and for every foreigner residing in our country."

His implied exhortation was that in order for Japan to become a modern nation, it would have to open its doors to the world and grant its citizens freedoms of the press, of thought, and of religion; it was in essence a demand that the Japanese release the Urakami Kirishitans.

Two weeks later, the delegation's conversations with the U.S. Secretary of State, Hamilton Fish, even more concretely backed the president's remarks. Fish declared that any treaty revision would have to be predicated on guarantees that Japan would grant freedom of religion to its people.

By now the delegation had gotten the message that recognition of the freedoms of religion and thought was going to be a significant issue as they attempted to achieve revisions in the unequal treaties. They had no choice but to acknowledge that the events in the little village of Urakami in Kyushu, events that they had essentially forgotten all about, were going to play a major role in the treaty revision negotiations between Japan and various foreign powers.

In addition, although the Iwakura Mission had traveled to the United States in order to negotiate for treaty revision, the Japanese government had not granted them full authority to sign any treaty drafts on their behalf.

The delegation, thrown into disarray because the United States had detected their inexperience and ineptitude, sent Itō Hirobumi, a member of their entourage, and Mori Arinori,[3] who was already living in the United States

3. Mori Arinori (1847–1889) studied in London and later became the first Japanese ambassador to the United States. He also served as ambassador to England and as Minister of Education during Itō Hirobumi's term as prime minster. Although scholars doubt rumors that he was a Christian himself, Mori argued for religious freedom in his homeland. Largely because of his pro-Western attitudes, he was assassinated by an ultranationalist on the day the Meiji Constitution was promulgated.

as chargé d'affaires, back to Japan to solicit credentials granting them full diplomatic powers.

The negotiations ran into rough waters. With no resolution to the outstanding issues, the delegation left the United States and sailed across the Atlantic Ocean, but in England, too, they encountered many who were critical of the persecution of Kirishitans in Japan.

It is no longer wise policy to prohibit the practice of the Kirishitan faith. Hondō Shuntarō gradually arrived at that conclusion. Throughout the United States and Europe, Hondō saw majestic church steeples piercing the skies. On Sundays, the bells in those steeples would ring out like undulating waves. He witnessed multitudes of people who dressed up in formal clothes and climbed into horse-drawn carriages to attend those churches. These observations persuaded Hondō of the necessity of allowing religious freedom in Japan, even if only superficially, while still rejecting the Kirishitan faith behind the scenes. His experiences abroad planted in his already pragmatic mind the belief that Japan must make these changes or face the prospect that treaty revisions and modernization would run into a dead end.

Every member of the delegation agreed with this conclusion. They sent numerous letters back to Japan, in which they began to urge the abolition of the placards proclaiming the ban on the Kirishitan faith.

As a result—

In the second month of 1873, the government agreed to the delegation's request and ordered all of the prohibition placards removed.

In Tsuwano there was a complete reversal in the treatment of the prisoners. Following the investigation by Kusumoto and Katō, the daily ration of less than six ounces of rice was increased to almost sixteen ounces, and the tortures were eliminated. After the placards were taken down, the men were granted considerably more freedom in their daily activities. The officers and police no longer watched them with piercing eyes, and at times they even tried to go out of their way to humor the prisoners.

Some officers went so far as to admit, "Well . . . you men certainly endured it all very bravely. From our standpoint, it's true that you were stubborn, but I was honestly impressed by your courage in not caving in, even though you're nothing but peasants!"

A full five years had elapsed since Sen'emon and the rest of the first group of exiles had come to Tsuwano, and forty-one of their number (among them five who apostatized) had died from hunger and cold and torture. Those who abandoned their faith, unable to bear the extreme suffering, numbered fifty-four, while sixty-eight men and women clung to their beliefs to the very end.

But the remaining sixty-eight had absolutely no way of knowing why their situation suddenly changed so dramatically. They had been utterly cut off from the outside world in this prison, their internments ranging from three to five years.

"We defeated them by our stubbornness!" Sen'emon muttered with a sly grin.

They did not know. They had no idea that they had become a great stumbling block in Japan's interactions with foreign nations. They did not know. They were not aware that their situation had been discussed by people in the United States and Europe in conversations regarding Japan's modernization. They did not know. They could not have known that even the president of the United States had warned a delegation from Japan to put an end to the persecution they were enduring. . . .

We might return to Urakami alive—

A muted hope began to rise in each of their hearts at this time. That hope was as tiny and wispy as the cirrus clouds of spring, but gradually it began to swell in their hearts. Seikichi was among the hopeful.

If I'm able to go back to Urakami— When Seikichi thought of those long-unseen hills and trees and the smell of the earth in Nakano, he also thought of Kiku. During the long years of his painful incarceration, at some point in his mind Kiku had developed into a song of comfort, a wellspring of solace, and an object of love.

These long months and years, during which he had been forsaken by everyone. Of late, he had had no word from her, but there was no way to describe what a tremendous support it had been, not only to him, but to all the prisoners, to receive through Itō the food and the bleached cotton material and the medicines that Kiku alone had sent. There was even one old woman who clasped her hands in a prayer of thanksgiving for a tiny rice cake. Kiku's gifts became a matchless testament of love to Seikichi. . . .

No matter what it takes . . . I've got to see her again. He wanted to see her, he *had* to see her. That was the most earnest desire of his heart now. The image of Kiku's almond-shaped eyes and the lively expression of her face were constantly before him.

I . . . I think I may be in love with her! Even as his face flushed, he could not help but affirm what his heart felt.

In the spring of 1873, he began to feel as though his wish might be fulfilled.

"They're saying that those who were exiled to Wakayama are returning to Urakami." Someone who heard this barely credible news from one of the officers came racing back to their cell to tell everybody.

"From Wakayama . . . ?"

"Yes!"

A shout of joy rose from all sixty-eight throats. The women covered their faces with both hands and wept aloud. The end to their very long, very painful life in prison was at last approaching. Kanzaburō asked one of the officers,

"Then will we be going home soon, too?" The officer merely shook his head, "I don't know." But it was clear from the expression on his face that he was concealing something.

In the fifth month, when young leaves flourished in the mountains of Tsuwano and fluttered in the wind as a balmy breeze blew fragrantly by, Sen'emon received a summons after breakfast one day.

"Sen'emon. It's been a long and painful time for you," the officer Chiba said consolingly to Sen'emon, who sat in a respectful posture. "The authorities out of their exceptional benevolence have notified us that all sixty-eight of you will be permitted to return to Urakami Village."

"Yes, sir." Sen'emon stared at the ground as he listened to the words, pushing back the warm emotions welling in his breast.

"Make your preparations and clean your cells so that you can leave here on the ninth."

"Yes, sir." He stood up, but Sen'emon's legs faltered because of his excitement.

The instant he returned to the cell, Sen'emon repeated the officer's words to the other sixty-seven men and women. When he finished speaking, the group maintained their silence for a few moments. Not one of them gave a cry of joy or wept from emotion. Although it was something they had anticipated, when they were notified that they would in fact be set free, they could say nothing.

A short time passed before the room rippled with sobs. The men, too, wept, their shoulders quivering.

"Listen, everyone," Sen'emon sniffled and encouraged the group, "let's kneel. We need to pray."

All sixty-eight crossed themselves and in one voice intoned the Lord's Prayer and the Hail Mary.

As they prayed, the faces and forms of relatives who had died in this prison passed through each of their minds. They would now finally be able to take back to Urakami the locks of hair they had collected from the deceased.

Even after night fell, there was no one who went right to sleep. All were in high spirits, and some even sang, but on this night no policeman or officer came to chastise them.

I'll be able to see Kiku now. Seikichi thought as he clapped his hands along with the others. The joy of being able to return to Urakami and the delight at being able to see Kiku again surged up in equal measures in his heart.

"Back in Urakami," someone muttered, "can you imagine how beautiful the mountains and the new leaves are right now? But the fields are probably a disaster."

Because they were farmers, it was only natural that they were most worried about their fields. Over the course of these many years, the neglected plots of land had most likely fallen into ruin and were buried in weeds. They would soon need to commence the labors of tilling, digging, and planting crops there.

They were freed from prison on the ninth day of the fifth month. At the time of their release, it was decided that for each person, the government office in Tsuwano would ship eighty-eight pounds of their possessions back to Urakami, with any remainder to be carried individually. It was an unimaginably generous arrangement.

Before their departure, the officers invited five of the men—Sen'emon, Tomo-hachi, Kanzaburō, Sōichi, and Seikichi—to have a drink with them. It seemed to be an attempt at an apology for the way they had been treated all this time.

"You men are samurai. Because you maintained your honor right up to the end." The officers were united in their praise for these men who had not abandoned their beliefs.

The sky was clear on the ninth. On the previous day, the sixty-eight men and women had taken the ashes of the forty-one who had died and buried them at Senninzuka—the "Graves of a Thousand"—at the pass atop Mount Kabusaka. On the ninth they set out from Tsuwano, planning to cover eighteen miles a day.

From Shimonoseki to Kokura, then by steamship from there to Ōmura . . .

Their elation expanded with each passing day. Their irrepressible joy made them want to break into dance. They could now live their Kirishitan faith without anyone pointing fingers at them. That was thrilling.

We . . . we won!

Mocked as shit-kickers, as *Kuros*, they had won out over the authorities not through uprising or rebellion but merely by the power of their faith, Sen'emon thought. By nothing other than their fragile faith . . .

EPILOGUE

TODAY, URAKAMI VILLAGE looks nothing like it did when the captives finally returned to it. The village is now a part of Nagasaki City, and hills have been leveled and trees in the groves felled to make way for residential neighborhoods.

But the Urakami they came home to was in utter disarray. In one of his letters, Father Laucaigne wrote:

Sadly, during the time of their exile, their lands had passed into the hands of others. Their homes had been torn down, or other people had moved into them. No matter which direction they turned, all was misery and deprivation. The Nagasaki Prefectural Office quickly built temporary shanties to protect them from the rain.

Almost every day, Kirishitan peasants who had been sent off to Tsuwano or to several other locations returned home on steamships. When they arrived in Nagasaki, the bell of the Nambanji at Ōura rang out loudly, celebrating their return. When they made land, they lined up and, before doing anything else, went to the Nambanji and knelt in prayer. The missionaries buttressed their prayers by playing the organ.

Once they returned to their neighborhoods, however, their lives were harsh. Without fields or homes to call their own, they suffered from hunger just as much as they had during their imprisonment. With the meager cash they received from the prefectural office, they were able to stave off starvation by buying dried potato strips in Sotome. One of them reported that the potato strips were infested with bugs and they had no pans or kettles to cook them in, so they just soaked them in water and drank the broth. "We ate them, bugs and all. Didn't have any bowls either, so I just used a chipped one I picked up somewhere."

And they labored. As soon as dawn broke they went out to the fields to work, and they did not return until sunset. Sometimes when they got back home, they would sit on the step above the dirt entryway to eat their raw potato broth and then go right to sleep. They had no changes of clothes and no futons.

Their only joy after the daily routine of toil was the opportunity to go to the church at Ōura on Sundays. The distance from Urakami to Ōura was six miles, but not one of them considered it a long walk. Ultimately, though, they began to hope that they could have their own church in Urakami. It would be many years before their dream was realized with the building of the Urakami Cathedral.[1]

On one of those difficult days, Seikichi heard a young woman call his name while he was at the Ōura Church.

"Aren't you Seikichi? I'm . . . I'm Mitsu."

He remembered her face, though she now looked much like a housewife. It was the same Mitsu who had worked alongside Kiku at the Gotōya.

In surprise he cried out, "Yes! But what are you doing here? And where is Kiku?" Ever since he returned home, he had wanted to find Kiku. But Father Laucaigne and the other missionaries, concerned perhaps at the shock it might cause him, said nothing about her, and whenever he asked someone from Magome, for some reason they would prevaricate and say something like "I don't know what happened to her after she went to Nagasaki to work."

"But you . . . I'm sure you know where Kiku is!" He said it in a loud voice, but Mitsu turned pale and lowered her eyes. "What's happened to her?"

"She died," Mitsu mumbled. "It was a snowy day two years ago. . . . She coughed up blood. Here inside the Ōura Church." Mitsu stood in front of the statue of the Blessed Mother beside the altar and quietly pointed out the spot where Kiku had died. Taking a deep breath, Seikichi lowered his eyes to the spot Mitsu had indicated. After a period of silence, he muttered in a hoarse voice, "And . . . where is her grave?"

"She was buried in Magome, where her family is from. But my husband and I were able to get some of her hair, and we secretly made a separate little grave

1. Construction on the cathedral began in 1895, but it was not completed until 1914. On August 9, 1945, the atomic bomb that was dropped on Nagasaki destroyed the structure, its epicenter being only 546 yards away. The clergymen who were inside the cathedral and the many Christians who had come to make confession in preparation for the Feast of the Assumption on the fifteenth were killed. A new cathedral was built in 1959. Blackened statuary from the original cathedral is displayed on the grounds, and portions of the original walls can be seen in the Nagasaki Peace Park.

for her. We thought we'd put it in a place you could visit if you ever came back from Tsuwano."

"Where is it?"

"In Gentio Valley—the Valley of the Gentiles."

"Gentio Valley? But Mitsu, you've become a Kirishitan, have you?"

"Yes. My husband is . . ." She lowered her eyes. "My husband is Kumazō from Nakano."

Mitsu explained to a startled Seikichi how she had met Kumazō and what had been happening in her life. She told him that Kumazō did not have the courage to return to Nakano because he couldn't bring himself to look anyone in the face but that he had confessed everything to Father Laucaigne and had declared his intention to return to the faith.

"We run a plaster shop in Teramachi," she smiled wistfully.

The following Sunday, two men and a woman—Seikichi, Kumazō, and his wife Mitsu—walked the seven and a half miles from Ōura to Fukahori-machi and, from there, climbed up Mount Shiroyama in Ōgomori-machi.

"There were some Kirishitans hiding here in Ōgomori-machi, and I think they sometimes come to Kiku's grave to pay their respects," Kumazō explained to Seikichi.

When they reached the top of the steep mountain path, the tin-colored ocean was visible directly below them. In the offing of Nagasaki Bay, the ocean glittered like a carpet of needles.

We were sent off to Tsuwano that day across this ocean. Seikichi reflected on the agony of that day, but to avoid upsetting Kumazō, he said nothing. Kumazō had stopped walking and raised his right hand.

"It's over there."

The giant camphor tree cast a broad shadow on the ground, and at its base they saw a stone cross. Kumazō had chiseled it out of a stone. Birds shrieked in the tree overhead.

"This is Kiku's grave."

"I wonder what kind of work Kiku was doing . . . there in Maruyama?" Seikichi asked the couple the question that weighed most heavily on his mind.

"We . . . we really don't know," Mitsu sidestepped the question. The three folded their hands, uttered a prayer, then swatted away the insects that swarmed around them, drawn by their sweat.

For a long, long while thereafter, Seikichi did not marry. The image of Kiku, with her beautiful almond eyes, lingered incessantly in his mind. But when he reached the age of thirty-five, a friend persisted in recommending a potential spouse for him, and he ended up marrying a woman from Togitsu. They had four children.

In the late summer of 1913, Seikichi received a letter without a name in the return address. The sender lived in Akita. The letter contained a money order. Seikichi's complexion changed dramatically as he read the letter.

For a long while, Seikichi stared at the strange letter. But when he heard his wife's footsteps, he hurriedly concealed it.

"I'm going to go buy some things in Saga," he told her. Since he was now selling farm equipment and seeds, his travels took him not only to Nagasaki but occasionally also to Saga. So his wife had no reason to suspect what he told her.

About ten days later Seikichi left Urakami and headed for Nagasaki. His family, of course, had no idea what he was actually doing.

After taking a train from Nagasaki to Moji, he crossed over to the Honshu mainland by boat, continued from there to Yamaguchi, and then boarded a Yamaguchi Line train.

Before long from the train window he saw ears of rice tinted gold from the first autumn chill, and soon the train ascended into the mountain range from which he could see the Niho River. At that time, the Yamaguchi Line did not extend as far as Tsuwano as it does now, terminating instead at Mitani.

With his face pressed against the window, Seikichi gazed at the mountains and the river as a flood of thoughts overcame him. The realization that Tsuwano was not far from here sent myriad thoughts whirling through his mind like a revolving lantern.

If I hadn't received that letter . . . I'm sure I would never have come here again, he whispered to himself.

Not once had he ever considered revisiting Tsuwano, the scene of so many painful memories, during his lifetime. But the letter had compelled him to come. Something the man who had written the letter had said drove him here.

The letter's author had included with the letter a money order to cover his round-trip fare to Tsuwano. And he had asked that Seikichi tell no one about this. Honoring that request, Seikichi had not revealed the secret to his family or to anyone else in Nakano.

The air grew chilly once the train entered the mountains. The chill reminded him of the frigid autumn air during the years he had spent confined in Tsuwano.

The train sluggishly stitched its way through the mountains, panting and coughing up black smoke, reaching Mitani near sundown.

People had gotten off the train one after another at small stations along the way before the train arrived at the terminus, so only five or six passengers remained to step out onto the tiny platform feebly illuminated by the sun on this autumn evening. Seikichi was the last to get off, and he stood on the platform gazing all around.

At the end of the platform stood a scrawny old man with a bent back, holding an umbrella. He watched as all the other passengers passed through the ticket gate and then approached Seikichi.

"Are you Seikichi? I . . . I thought you might come." Blinking his eyes, the old man held out both his hands.

Seikichi hesitated to take them. This was one of the pairs of hands that had beaten and slapped Seikichi and his comrades in Tsuwano. Instead he said, "How well you remember my name."

"Yes. Not a single day has passed that I haven't thought about you," the old man replied. His name was Itō Seizaemon.

The two stayed that night at a small inn across from the Mitani Station. They booked separate rooms, perhaps because Itō could not bear to look Seikichi squarely in the face. As a result, even after they left the station that was now shrouded in twilight, the two men scarcely exchanged anything resembling a conversation at the inn.

Weary from the journey, when Seikichi sat down under a dim light to a plate of food that the maid had brought to his room, he asked her to lay out his bedding, and after saying brief prayers, he fell into a deep sleep. The light remained on in Itō's room for quite some time, but after that light was extinguished, they both were wrapped in a profound stillness.

Early the next morning they set out for Tsuwano in two rickshaws. Although they left the inn early in the morning, it was not until around 2:00 P.M. that they reached Tsuwano as they descended through the Nosaka Pass along the San'in Road. When they looked down at the village of Tsuwano below, even though he had anticipated that this would happen, Seikichi felt a shock as powerful as though he had been whacked with a club.

Pure white autumnal clouds hovered over Mount Shiroyama. The blue-green ribbon of the Tsuwano River meandered through the village, which was cradled among the mountains. Nothing had changed over time. The village and its surrounding nature were positioned deep in the valley, peacefully, quietly, as though nothing had ever happened there, as though they had retained no memory of how brutally Seikichi and the other Urakami Kirishitans had suffered over five long years.

For an instant, tears filled Seikichi's aging eyes, then trickled down his cheeks. How appalling it had all been! How deplorable!

Ahead of him, the rickshaw carrying Itō forged ahead, its carriage creaking. Seikichi couldn't imagine how Itō felt right now, sitting beneath the rickshaw's canopy and looking down at Tsuwano below. He knew from reading Itō's letter why he had been invited here, and though in his mind he wanted as a Christian to accept Itō's apology, in his heart Seikichi still was not sure he could sincerely forgive the man.

The two rickshaws, carrying passengers whose thoughts were very different right now, finally reached Tsuwano. Weaving between houses that looked unchanged from the past, they scurried through the town, where the current of the irrigation water was audible and the leaves were at last turning yellow.

Itō's rickshaw halted. It stopped at the entrance leading to the Kōrinji Temple, where Seikichi had been incarcerated along with Sen'emon, Kanzaburō, and the others.

Seikichi knew he was not the first person from Urakami to retrace his steps up this mountain road. In the summer of 1891, Father Villion, who was serving at the Ōura Church, had come in search of the remains of the Kōrinji, taking with him Miss Iwanaga from Hiroshima as his guide. She had been exiled here from Urakami along with her father. But Seikichi was the first to ascend this path alongside the mountain stream in the company of one of his former persecutors.

A swarm of red dragonflies whizzed past their faces. The autumn sun that afternoon was gentle. Lacking the vigor of their youth, the two elderly men had to stop several times to catch their breath on the way up. When one came to a halt, the other would also pause to rest, waiting for his companion's breathing to settle down.

Anyone ignorant of their situation would have thought these men were two longtime close friends. They said nothing to each other, but having come this far, they knew that shortly they would arrive at a place where they both would have to speak.

A mountain stream flowed near the road, and as the old men silently climbed the slope listening to the sound of the current, their eyes caught glimpses of ashen gravestones that poked up here and there amid the silver pampas grass.

"Ah!" A memory slashed across Itō's breast with a pain so sharp that he felt as though he had been jabbed with a knife. He had seen these gravestones in the past every time he climbed this path upon his return from Nagasaki. They must have belonged to Buddhist priests who worked at the Kōrinji Temple.

They came to a hollow lit by the autumn sun. Here, too, the pampas grass glistened whitely, the fall flowers grew in abundance, and they heard the chirping of katydids here and there. Surprised by the footsteps of the two men, a swarm of red dragonflies flitted up from the leaves and grasses.

There was not even a trace of the former prison. The office used by the guards, the policemen, and the officers and the interrogation hut had vanished, buried under the grasses. Only the bluish black surface of the pond remained. It was the pond of torment into which Sen'emon and Kanzaburō had been thrown in the dead of winter in an attempt to force them to apostatize.

"It was here . . ." Staring at the pond, Itō announced hoarsely, "It was here that you people were confined."

"Yes." Seikichi nodded.

The two stood like stone statues for a time, saying nothing.

Suddenly Itō exclaimed, "You must hate me."

"Well, I do blame you. I realize that I've got to forget my hatred. . . . But so far, I can't."

"That's what I would expect." Itō dropped his eyes and nodded. "You were treated so cruelly. You couldn't help hating me for the rest of your life. . . . I'm aware of that."

"No matter how hard I try to forgive all of you in my head . . . , my heart . . . my heart won't let me." Seikichi's cry was almost a groan.

"I see," Itō said lifelessly. "I understand. I imagine I'll spend the rest of my life and then go to my grave carrying the spite of each one of you on my scrawny back. Seikichi, do you want to hear something funny? I . . . even someone as pathetic as me . . . I was baptized twenty years ago at a church in Akita. I don't suppose you can believe that."

"Baptized?!" Seikichi was, understandably enough, taken aback. "You were?"

"Yes. There was a priest living in Akita named Father Houissan. . . . I decided I wanted to tell him everything I had done, so I did. Seikichi. It was a time when I was so alone and in so much agony that I couldn't bear my misery. But even after I was baptized by that priest . . . I kept on committing one terrible sin after another. I lied to people . . . I made women weep. . . . And every time, Father Houissan would have to clean up the messes I had made, and he would help me through it. And then I'd commit the same sin all over again. I concluded that Lord Jezusu had given up on me, but Father Houissan said that Lord Jezusu would never, ever abandon me. . . . "

Seikichi gazed at the man sympathetically. Being a strong man, he could not understand the sorrows of a man like Itō. . . .

Then Seikichi noticed that a faint smell of alcohol drifted from Itō's mouth as he spoke. The smell signified the weakness of Itō's will. Seikichi sensed the despondency of this man who had to borrow strength from alcohol in order to beg him for forgiveness.

"There's something . . . there's something I have to say to you." Itō spoke again, keeping his eyes averted from Seikichi's. "Do you . . . do you still remember a woman named Kiku?"

"Kiku . . ." Seikichi nodded solemnly. "I remember her. But she died a long time ago."

"I'm well aware of that. I was the one who performed the inquest at her death. But do you know . . . do you know what caused her to die?"

"She had problems here, in her chest. . . . Why?"

"That's right. But the reason she had problems . . . no, what caused those problems in her chest . . ." Itō's words broke off there, and he continued to stare at the ground. His expression was exactly like that of a believer hesitating in the confessional just before he divulges to the priest the sins he has kept secret for many long years. "What caused those problems in her chest . . . Seikichi, it was me!"

Seikichi had no response.

"That woman . . . she was a saint. I'm a sinful man, but I learned through her that there can be such a thing as a saintly woman in this world. It was so that she could send you money while you were here . . . It was for you . . . for you that she sold her body. She even gave her body to me."

"For me?" The tone of Seikichi's voice took on the nature of a scream. He had come here to Tsuwano never dreaming he would be told such a thing, never imagining he would hear such a story from Itō's lips.

"She degraded her body so that she could make money to give to you. And it wasn't a small amount of money. . . . She'd give me two or three *ryo* at a time. She'd hand it to me and . . . and ask me to plead with the officers . . . that they not treat you roughly . . ." At that point, Itō's voice cracked in anguish, and he began to speak haltingly. "And I . . . and I . . ." He could say no more.

For a few moments, Seikichi said nothing, either. Then, "Are you saying . . . that you used the money yourself?"

"Yes . . ."

"How monstrous! That was . . . that was a heartless thing to do!" Torrents of anger and exasperation coursed through Seikichi's body. He clenched his fists and struggled with all his might to hold back his rage and vexation. In truth, he wanted to pound Itō with his fists, to pound him and knock him to the ground.

"Please forgive me!" Itō bowed his head and turned to face Seikichi. Seikichi glared at the bald head and the unkempt tufts of white hair around the man's temples.

Seikichi realized that the victims of this man's tortures were not just the Kirishitan men and women such as himself. He had even betrayed and brutalized Kiku, who wasn't even a Kirishitan.

"How could you do something so cruel?" Seikichi's voice shook with fury. "She wasn't a Kirishitan like the rest of us! A man who would exploit a blameless woman like her isn't even human, he's a devil!"

"You're right. I wasn't human back then. This is hard for me to say, but . . . but, Seikichi, I was envious of you. I was jealous. . . ."

"Why?"

"Because . . ." Itō hesitated. "Because . . . because back then, I loved her, too."

At those words, Seikichi could no longer control the anger he had suppressed. This filthy wretch says he loved Kiku? The words themselves sounded like a defilement of Kiku. He shouted harshly, like a father whose own daughter has been violated. "*You?!* You thought you were qualified to love her? When there was no one to help me, that woman gave me gifts of *mochi* and bleached cloth. Are you telling me you abused Kiku because you were jealous of me?!"

"I wanted her. I wanted her so very badly!" Itō crouched down in the clump of grass and began to weep.

"Forgive me! Kiku, please forgive me! It was because I witnessed your life, that's how I came to understand the meaning of the kind of love that Father Houissan often talks about. I understood how precious a woman is to a man. After he listened to my confession, Father Houissan said that you were like a saint. . . . Kiku, no matter how hard I try, I will never forget . . . I will never forget the tears you shed . . . the tears you shed when I took your body. . . ."

His shoulders trembling, Itō continued speaking, but not to Seikichi—to Kiku, who was no longer in this world. Looking at Itō's pathetic figure, Seikichi lost all desire to hurl insults at him.

"It's all right, Itō. Kiku suffered at your hands, but she was able to lead you toward a different life. That by itself proves that her life was not without meaning . . . it was not without meaning."

Seikichi, too, sniffled, and spoke the words as though to himself. A single red dragonfly lighted on his shoulder, and another landed on Itō's shoulder as he squatted on the ground. The two men remained there for a long while, like statues, not saying a word, not moving a muscle.

BETWEEN THE LINES

Author's Afterword

I WROTE *Kiku's Prayer* to try to repay some of my debt to Nagasaki, the city that is my heart's homeland.

I wasn't born in Nagasaki or raised there. But since the first time I visited the city more than a dozen years ago, my attachment to the place has only deepened and never faded.

The more I learn and study about the history of Nagasaki, the more I am filled with admiration for the depth and significance of the city's many layers. And I have come to sense that there are many more questions that must be asked in my life. I think it's fair to say that I have been writing novels, beginning with *Silence*, in an attempt to answer each one of those questions. For these several years, Nagasaki has played a central role in the maturation of my heart. It has become like a womb that has provided me with delectable nourishment.

One of the great joys of life for me as a novelist has been my encounter with a city like Nagasaki. And I have been able to savor that joy over these many years. The writing of *Kiku's Prayer* was my attempt to repay some of my debt to Nagasaki.

This first of two novels[1] is based on the persecution of the Kirishitans at the end of the Tokugawa and the beginning of the Meiji periods, known in history as the "Fourth Persecution of Urakami." As a result, there are models for many

---

1. The second novel, *The Life of Sachiko*, is also set in Nagasaki, during the years leading up to the atomic bombing of the city. It was published in Japan in 1983 but has not yet been translated into English.

of the characters that appear in the story. There are also some characters, such as Fathers Petitjean and Laucaigne, Takagi Sen'emon and Moriyama Kanzaburō, who appear under their real names.

There is also a model for Itō Seizaemon, but in my initial plan for the novel, he was not going to play such a significant role.

But as I wrote, I began to sympathize with this despicable man—and I felt not just sympathy but even a love for him. Up to the very end of the novel I couldn't bear to forsake him.

I visited Nagasaki a couple of times while I was serializing this novel.[2] As I went up and down the streets where Kiku and Mitsu walked, climbed the slopes that Itō rambled up, and stood atop the hills overlooking Urakami, I felt as though the Kirishitans of Urakami Village were shouting to me "Write! Please write about us!" Kiku's hometown of Magome no longer exhibits any traces of its earlier self, and a new, modern building has been erected on the site of the magistrate's office where Itō worked. The only place that retains its former appearance is the Ōura Catholic Church—what was then called the Ōura Nambanji—but I wonder how much the tourists who flock there realize the degree of influence that the Fourth Persecution of Urakami had on Japan's modernization.

The statue of the Blessed Mother Mary is still in the same spot in this church—the spot where Petitjean discovered the Japanese Kirishitans, and the spot where Kiku died . . .

---

2. The novel appeared as a newspaper serial in the *Asahi shimbun* from November 1, 1980, to July 1, 1981.